Desmond
Bagley

Desmond Bagley

The Golden Keel

Running Blind

CHANCELLOR PRESS

The Golden Keel first published in Great Britain
in 1963 by William Collins Sons & Co. Ltd.
Running Blind first published in Great Britain
in 1970 by William Collins Sons & Co. Ltd.

This edition first published in Great Britain in 1983 by
Chancellor Press
59 Grosvenor Street
London, W.1.

ISBN: 0 907486 35 5

Printed and Bound in Great Britain by Collins, Glasgow

Desmond Bagley

Contents

The Golden Keel

Running Blind

Desmond Bagley

The Golden Keel

BOOK ONE
The Men

1 *Walker*

My name is Peter Halloran, but everyone calls me 'Hal' excepting my wife, Jean, who always called me Peter. Women seem to dislike nicknames for their menfolk. Like a lot of others I emigrated to the 'colonies' after the war, and I travelled from England to South Africa by road, across the Sahara and through the Congo. It was a pretty rough trip, but that's another story; it's enough to say that I arrived in Cape Town in 1948 with no job and precious little money.

During my first week in Cape Town I answered several of the Sit. Vac. advertisements which appeared in the *Cape Times* and while waiting for answers I explored my environment. On this particular morning I had visited the docks and finally found myself near the yacht basin.

I was leaning over the rail looking at the boats when a voice behind me said, 'If you had your choice, which would it be?'

I turned and encountered the twinkling eyes of an elderly man, tall, with stooped shoulders and grey hair. He had a brown, weather-beaten face and gnarled hands, and I estimated his age at about sixty.

I pointed to one of the boats. 'I think I'd pick that one,' I said. 'She's big enough to be of use, but not too big for single-handed sailing.'

He seemed pleased. 'That's *Gracia*,' he said. 'I built her.'

'She looks a good boat,' I said. 'She's got nice lines.'

We talked for a while about boats. He said he had a boatyard a little way outside Cape Town towards Milnerton, and that he specialized in building the fishing boats used by the Malay fishermen. I'd noticed these already; sturdy unlovely craft with high bows and a wheelhouse stuck on top like a chicken-coop, but they looked very seaworthy. *Gracia* was only the second yacht he had built.

'There'll be a boom now the war's over,' he predicted. 'People will have money in their pockets, and they'll go in for yachting. I'd like to expand my activities in that direction.'

13

Presently he looked at his watch and nodded towards the yacht club. 'Let's go in and have a coffee,' he suggested.

I hesitated. 'I'm not a member.'

'I am,' he said. 'Be my guest.'

So we went into the club house and sat in the lounge overlooking the yacht basin and he ordered coffee. 'By the way, my name's Tom Sanford.'

'I'm Peter Halloran.'

'You're English,' he said. 'Been out here long?'

I smiled. 'Three days.'

'I've been out just a bit longer—since 1910.' He sipped his coffee and regarded me thoughtfully. 'You seem to know a bit about boats.'

'I've been around them all my life,' I said. 'My father had a boatyard on the east coast, quite close to Hull. We built fishing boats, too, until the war.'

'And then?'

'Then the yard went on to contract work for the Admiralty,' I said. 'We built harbour defence launches and things like that— we weren't geared to handle anything bigger.' I shrugged. 'Then there was an air-raid.'

'That's bad,' said Tom. 'Was everything destroyed?'

'Everything,' I said flatly. 'My people had a house next to the yard—that went, too. My parents and my elder brother were killed.'

'Christ!' said Tom gently. 'That's very bad. How old were you?'

'Seventeen,' I said. 'I went to live with an aunt in Hatfield; that's when I started to work for de Havilland—building Mosquitos. It's a wooden aeroplane and they wanted people who could work in wood. All I was doing, as far as I was concerned, was filling in time until I could join the Army.'

His interest sharpened. 'You know, that's the coming thing— the new methods developed by de Havilland. That hot-moulding process of theirs—d'you think it could be used in boat-building?'

I thought about it. 'I don't see why not—it's very strong. We did repair work at Hatfield, as well as new construction, and I saw what happens to that type of fabric when it's been hit very hard. It would be more expensive than the traditional methods, though, unless you were mass-producing.'

'I was thinking about yachts,' said Tom slowly. 'You must tell me more about it some time.' He smiled. 'What else do you know about boats?'

I grinned. 'I once thought I'd like to be a designer,' I said. 'When I was a kid – about fifteen – I designed and built my own racing dinghy.'

'Win any races?'

'My brother and I had 'em all licked,' I said. 'She was a fast boat. After the war, when I was cooling my heels waiting for my discharge, I had another go at it – designing, I mean. I designed half a dozen boats – it helped to pass the time.'

'Got the drawings with you?'

'They're somewhere at the bottom of my trunk,' I said. 'I haven't looked at them for a long time.'

'I'd like to see them,' said Tom. 'Look, laddie; how would you like to work for me? I told you I'm thinking of expanding into the yacht business, and I could use a smart young fellow.'

And that's how I started working for Tom Sanford. The following day I went to the boatyard with my drawings and showed them to Tom. On the whole he liked them, but pointed out several ways in which economies could be made in the building. 'You're a fair designer,' he said. 'But you've a lot to learn about the practical side. Never mind, we'll see about that. When can you start?'

Going to work for old Tom was one of the best things I ever did in my life.

II

A lot of things happened in the next ten years – whether I deserved them or not is another matter. It was good to work in a boatyard again. The skills I had learned from my father had not deserted me, and although I was a bit rusty to begin with, soon I was as good as any man in the yard, and maybe a bit better. Tom encouraged me to design, ruthlessly correcting my errors.

'You've got a good eye for line,' he said. 'Your boats would be sweet sailers, but they'd be damned expensive. You've got to spend more time on detail; you must cut down costs to make an economical boat.'

Four years after I joined the firm Tom made me yard foreman, and just after that, I had my first bit of luck in designing. I submitted a design to a local yachting magazine, winning second prize and fifty pounds. But better still, a local yachtsman liked the design and wanted a boat built. So Tom built it for him and I got the designer's fee which went to swell my growing bank balance.

Tom was pleased about that and asked if I could design a class boat as a standard line for the yard, so I designed a six-tonner which turned out very well. We called it the Penguin Class and Tom built and sold a dozen in the first year at £2000 each. I liked the boat so much that I asked Tom if he would build one for me, which he did, charging rock-bottom price and letting me pay it off over a couple of years.

Having a design office gave the business a fillip. The news got around and people started to come to me instead of using British and American designs. That way they could argue with their designer. Tom was pleased because most of the boats to my design were built in the yard.

In 1954 he made me yard manager, and in 1955 he offered me a partnership.

'I've got no one to leave it to,' he said bluntly. 'My wife's dead and I've got no sons. And I'm getting old.'

I said, 'You'll be building boats when you're a hundred, Tom.'

He shook his head. 'No, I'm beginning to feel it now.' He wrinkled his brow. 'I've been going over the books and I find that you're bringing more business into the firm than I am, so I'll go easy on the money for the partnership. It'll cost you five thousand pounds.'

Five thousand was ridiculously cheap for a half-share in such a flourishing business, but I hadn't got anywhere near that amount. He saw my expression and his eyes crinkled. 'I know you haven't got it – but you've been doing pretty well on the design side lately. My guess is that you've got about two thousand salted away.'

Tom, shrewd as always, was right. I had a couple of hundred over the two thousand. 'That's about it,' I said.

'All right. Throw in the two thousand and borrow another three from the bank. They'll lend it to you when they see the books. You'll be able to pay it back out of profits in under three years, especially if you carry out your plans for that racing dinghy. What about it?'

'OK, Tom,' I said. 'It's a deal.'

The racing dinghy Tom had mentioned was an idea I had got by watching the do-it-yourself developments in England. There are plenty of little lakes on the South African high-veld and I thought I could sell small boats away from the sea if I could produce them cheaply enough – and I would sell either the finished boat or a do-it-yourself building kit for the impoverished enthusiast.

We set up another woodworking shop and I designed the boat which was the first of the Falcon Class. A young fellow, Harry Marshall, was promoted to run the project and he did very well.

This wasn't Tom's cup of tea and he stayed clear of the whole affair, referring to it as 'that confounded factory of yours'. But it made us a lot of money.

It was about this time that I met Jean and we got married. My marriage to Jean is not really a part of this story and I wouldn't mention it except for what happened later. We were very happy and very much in love. The business was doing well – I had a wife and a home – what more could a man wish for?

Towards the end of 1956 Tom died quite suddenly of a heart attack. I think he must have known that his heart wasn't in good shape although he didn't mention it to anyone. He left his share in the business to his wife's sister. She knew nothing about business and less about boat-building, so we got the lawyers on to it and she agreed to sell me her share. I paid a damn' sight more than the five thousand I had paid Tom, but it was a fair sale although it gave me financier's fright and left me heavily in debt to the bank.

I was sorry that Tom had gone. He had given me a chance that fell to few young fellows and I felt grateful. The yard seemed emptier without him pottering about the slips.

The yard prospered and it seemed that my reputation as a designer was firm, because I got lots of commissions. Jean took over the management of the office, and as I was tied to the drawing board for a large proportion of my time I promoted Harry Marshall to yard manager and he handled it very capably.

Jean, being a woman, gave the office a thorough spring cleaning as soon as she was in command, and one day she unearthed an old tin box which had stayed forgotten on a remote shelf for years. She delved into it, then said suddenly, 'Why have you kept this clipping?'

'What clipping?' I asked abstractedly. I was reading a letter which could lead to an interesting commission.

'This thing about Mussolini,' she said. 'I'll read it.' She sat on the edge of the desk, the yellowed fragment of newsprint between her fingers. ' "Sixteen Italian Communists were sentenced in Milan yesterday for complicity in the disappearance of Mussolini's treasure. The treasure, which mysteriously vanished at the end of the war, consisted of a consignment of gold from the Italian State Bank and many of Mussolini's personal possessions, including the Ethiopian crown. It is believed that a large number of important State documents were with the treasure. The sixteen men all declared their innocence." '

She looked up. 'What was all that about?'

I was startled. It was a long time since I'd thought of Walker and

Coertze and the drama that had been played out in Italy. I smiled and said, 'I might have made a fortune but for that news story.'

'Tell me about it.'

'It's a long story,' I protested. 'I'll tell you some other time.'

'No,' she insisted. 'Tell me now; I'm always interested in treasure.'

So I pushed the unopened mail aside and told her about Walker and his mad scheme. It came back to me hazily in bits and pieces. Was it Donato or Alberto who had fallen – or been pushed – from the cliff? The story took a long time in the telling and the office work got badly behind that day.

III

I met Walker when I had arrived in South Africa from England just after the war. I had been lucky to get a good job with Tom but, being a stranger, I was a bit lonely, so I joined a Cape Town Sporting Club which would provide company and exercise.

Walker was a drinking member, one of those crafty people who joined the club to have somewhere to drink when the pubs were closed on Sunday. He was never in the club house during the week, but turned up every Sunday, played his one game of tennis for the sake of appearances, then spent the rest of the day in the bar.

It was in the bar that I met him, late one Sunday afternoon. The room was loud with voices raised in argument and I soon realized that I had walked into the middle of a discussion on the Tobruk surrender. The very mention of Tobruk can start an argument anywhere in South Africa because the surrender is regarded as a national disgrace. It is always agreed that the South Africans were let down but from then on it gets heated and rather vague. Sometimes the British generals are blamed and sometimes the South African garrison commander, General Klopper; and it's always good for one of those long, futile bar-room brawls in which tempers are lost but nothing is ever decided.

It wasn't of much interest to me – my army service was in Europe – so I sat quietly nursing my beer and keeping out of it. Next to me was a thin-faced young man with dissipated good looks who had a great deal to say about it, with many a thump on the counter with his clenched fist. I had seen him before but didn't know who he was. All I knew of him was by observation; he seemed to drink a lot, and even now was drinking two brandies to my one beer.

At length the argument died a natural death as the bar emptied and soon my companion and I were the last ones left. I drained my glass and was turning to leave when he said contemptuously, 'Fat lot they know about it.'

'Were you there?' I asked.

'I was,' he said grimly. 'I was in the bag with all the others. Didn't stay there long, though; I got out of the camp in Italy in '43.' He looked at my empty glass. 'Have one for the road.'

I had nothing to do just then, so I said, 'Thanks; I'll have a beer.'

He ordered a beer for me and another brandy for himself and said, 'My name's Walker. Yes, I got out when the Italian Government collapsed. I joined the partisans.'

'That must have been interesting,' I said.

He laughed shortly. 'I suppose you could call it that. Interesting and scary. Yes, I reckon you could say that me and Sergeant Coertze had a really interesting time – he was a bloke I was with most of the time.'

'An Afrikaner?' I hazarded. I was new in South Africa and didn't know much about the set-up then, but the name sounded as though it might be Afrikaans.

'That's right,' said Walker. 'A real tough boy, he was. We stuck together after getting out of the camp.'

'Was it easy – escaping from the prison camp?'

'A piece of cake,' said Walker. 'The guards co-operated with us. A couple of them even came with us as guides – Alberto Corsa and Donato Rinaldi. I liked Donato – I reckon he saved my life.'

He saw my interest and plunged into the story with gusto. When the Government fell in 1943 Italy was in a mess. The Italians were uneasy; they didn't know what was going to happen next and they were suspicious of the intentions of the Germans. It was a perfect opportunity to break camp, especially when a couple of the guards threw in with them.

Leaving the camp was easy enough, but trouble started soon after when the Germans laid on an operation to round up all the Allied prisoners who were loose in Central Italy.

'That's when I copped it,' said Walker. 'We were crossing a river at the time.'

The sudden attack had taken them by surprise. Everything had been silent except for the chuckling of the water and the muffled curses as someone slipped – then suddenly there was the sound of ripped calico as the Spandau opened up and the night was made hideous by the eerie whine of bullets as they ricocheted from exposed rocks in the river.

The two Italians turned and let go with their sub-machine-guns. Coertze, bellowing like a bull, scrabbled frantically at the pouch pocket of his battle-dress trousers and then his arm came up in an overarm throw. There was a sharp crack as the hand grenade exploded in the water near the bank. Again Coertze threw and this time the grenade burst on the bank.

Walker felt something slam his leg and he turned in a twisting fall and found himself gasping in the water. His free arm thrashed out and caught on a rock and he hung on desperately.

Coertze threw another grenade and the machine-gun stopped. The Italians had emptied their magazines and were busy reloading. Everything was quiet again.

'I reckon they thought we were Germans, too,' said Walker. 'They wouldn't expect to be fired on by escaping prisoners. It was lucky that the Italians had brought some guns along. Anyway, that bloody machine-gun stopped.'

They had stayed for a few minutes in midstream with the quick cold waters pulling at their legs, not daring to move in case there was a sudden burst from the shore. After five minutes Alberto said in a low voice, 'Signor Walker, are you all right?'

Walker pulled himself upright and to his astonishment found himself still grasping his unfired rifle. His left leg felt numb and cold. 'I'm all right,' he said.

There was a long sigh from Coertze, then he said, 'Well, come on. Let's get to the other side – but quietly.'

They reached the other side of the river and, without resting, pressed on up the mountainside. After a short time Walker's leg began to hurt and he lagged behind. Alberto was perturbed. 'You must hurry; we have to cross this mountain before dawn.'

Walker stifled a groan as he put down his left foot. 'I was hit,' he said. 'I think I was hit.'

Coertze came back down the mountain and said irritably, '*Magtig*, get a move on, will you?'

Alberto said, 'Is it bad, Signor Walker?'

'What's the matter?' asked Coertze, not understanding the Italian.

'I have a bullet in my leg,' said Walker bitterly.

'That's all we need,' said Coertze. In the darkness he bulked as a darker patch and Walker could see that he was shaking his head impatiently. 'We've got to get to that partisan camp before daylight.'

Walker conferred with Alberto, then said in English, 'Alberto says there's a place along there to the right where we can hide. He says that someone should stay with me while he goes for help.'

Coertze grunted in his throat. 'I'll go with him,' he said. 'The other Eytie can stay with you. Let's get to it.'

They moved along the mountainside and presently the ground dipped and suddenly there was a small ravine, a cleft in the mountain. There were stunted trees to give a little cover and underfoot was a dry watercourse.

Alberto stopped and said, 'You will stay here until we come for you. Keep under the trees so that no one will see you, and make as little movement as possible.'

'Thanks, Alberto,' said Walker. There were a few brief words of farewell, then Alberto and Coertze disappeared into the night. Donato made Walker comfortable and they settled down to wait out the night.

It was a bad time for Walker. His leg was hurting and it was very cold. They stayed in the ravine all the next day and as night fell Walker became delirious and Donato had trouble in keeping him quiet.

When the rescuers finally came Walker had passed out. He woke up much later and found himself in a bed in a room with white-washed walls. The sun was rising and a little girl was sitting by the bedside.

Walker stopped speaking suddenly and looked at his empty glass on the bar counter. 'Have another drink,' I said quickly.

He needed no encouraging so I ordered another couple of drinks. 'So that's how you got away,' I said.

He nodded. 'That's how it was. God, it was cold those two nights on that bloody mountain. If it hadn't been for Donato I'd have cashed in my chips.'

I said, 'So you were safe – but where were you?'

'In a partisan camp up in the hills. The *partigiani* were just getting organized then; they only really got going when the Germans began to consolidate their hold on Italy. The Jerries ran true to form – they're arrogant bastards, you know – and the Italians didn't like it. So everything was set for the partisans; they got the support of the people and they could begin to operate on a really large scale.

'They weren't all alike, of course; there was every shade of political opinion from pale blue to bright red. The Communists hated the Monarchists' guts and vice versa and so on. The crowd I dropped in on were Monarchist. That's where I met the Count.'

Count Ugo Montepescali di Todi was over fifty years old at that time, but young-looking and energetic. He was a swarthy man with an aquiline nose and a short greying beard which was split at the end and forked aggressively. He came of a line which was old during the Renaissance and he was an aristocrat to his finger-tips.

Because of this he hated Fascism – hated the pretensions of the parvenu rulers of Italy with all their corrupt ways and their money-sticky fingers. To him Mussolini always remained a mediocre journalist who had succeeded in demagoguery and had practically imprisoned his King.

Walker met the Count the first day he arrived at the hill camp. He had just woken up and seen the solemn face of the little girl. She smiled at him and silently left the room, and a few minutes later a short stocky man with a bristling beard stepped through the doorway and said in English, 'Ah, you are awake. You are quite safe now.'

Walker was conscious of saying something inane. 'But where am I?'

'Does that really matter?' the Count asked quizzically. 'You are still in Italy – but safe from the *Tedesci*. You must stay in bed until you recover your strength. You need some blood putting back – you lost a lot – so you must rest and eat and rest again.'

Walker was too weak to do more than accept this, so he lay back on the pillow. Five minutes later Coertze came in; with him was a young man with a thin face.

'I've brought the quack,' said Coertze. 'Or at least that's what he says he is – if I've got it straight. My guess is that he's only a medical student.'

The doctor – or student – examined Walker and professed satisfaction at his condition. 'You will walk within the week,' he said, and packed his little kit and left the room.

Coertze rubbed the back of his head. 'I'll have to learn this slippery *taal*,' he said. 'It looks as though we'll be here for a long time.'

'No chance of getting through to the south?' asked Walker.

'No chance at all,' said Coertze flatly. 'The Count – that's the little man with the *bokbaardjie* – says that the Germans down south are thicker on the ground than stalks in a mealie field. He reckons they're going to make a defence line south of Rome.'

Walker sighed. 'Then we're stuck here.'

Coertze grinned. 'It is not too bad. At least we'll get better food than we had in camp. The Count wants us to join his little lot – it seems he has some kind of *skietkommando* which holds quite a

22

bit of territory and he's collected men and weapons while he can. We might as well fight here as with the army – I've always fancied fighting a war my way.'

A plump woman brought in a steaming bowl of broth for Walker, and Coertze said, 'Get outside of that and you'll feel better. I'm going to scout around a bit.'

Walker ate the broth and slept, then woke and ate again. After a while a small figure came in bearing a basin and rolled bandages. It was the little girl he had seen when he had first opened his eyes. He thought she was about twelve years old.

'My father said I have to change your bandages,' she said in a clear young voice. She spoke English.

Walker propped himself up on his elbow and watched her as she came closer. She was neatly dressed and wore a white, starched apron. 'Thank you,' he said.

She bent to cut the splint loose from his leg and then she carefully loosened the bandage round the wound. He looked down at her and said, 'What is your name?'

'Francesca.'

'Is your father the doctor?' Her hands were cool and soft on his leg.

She shook her head. 'No,' she said briefly.

She bathed the wound in warm water containing some pungent antiseptic and then shook powder on to it. With great skill she began to rebandage the leg.

'You are a good nurse,' said Walker.

It was only then that she looked at him and he saw that she had cool, grey eyes. 'I've had a lot of practice,' she said, and Walker was abashed at her gaze and cursed a war which made skilled nurses out of twelve-year-olds.

She finished the bandaging and said, 'There – you must get better soon.'

'I will,' promised Walker. 'As quickly as I can. I'll do that for you.'

She looked at him with surprise. 'Not for me,' she said. 'For the war. You must get better so that you can go into the hills and kill a lot of Germans.'

She gravely collected the soiled bandages and left the room, with Walker looking after her in astonishment. Thus it was that he met Francesca, the daughter of Count Ugo Montepescali.

In a little over a week he was able to walk with the aid of a stick and to move outside the hospital hut, and Coertze showed him round the camp. Most of the men were Italians, army deserters

23

who didn't like the Germans. But there were many Allied escapees
of different nationalities.

The Count had formed the escapees into a single unit and had
put Coertze in command. They called themselves the 'Foreign
Legion'. During the next couple of years many of them were to be
killed fighting against the Germans with the partisans. At Coertze's
request, Alberto and Donato were attached to the unit to act as in-
terpreters and guides.

Coertze had a high opinion of the Count. 'That *kêrel* knows
what he's doing,' he said. 'He's recruiting from the Italian army
as fast as he can – and each man must bring his own gun.'

When the Germans decided to stand and fortified the *Winter-
stellung* based on the Sangro and Monte Cassino, the war in Italy
was deadlocked and it was then that the partisans got busy attacking the German communications. The Foreign Legion took part
in this campaign, specializing in demolition work. Coertze had been
a gold miner on the Witwatersrand before the war and he knew
how to handle dynamite. He and Harrison, a Canadian geologist,
instructed the others in the use of explosives.

They blew up road and rail bridges, dynamited mountain passes,
derailed trains and occasionally shot up the odd road convoy, always retreating as soon as heavy fire was returned. 'We must not
fight pitched battles,' said the Count. 'We must not let the Germans
pin us down. We are mosquitoes irritating the German hides – let
us hope we give them malaria.'

Walker found this a time of long stretches of relaxation punctuated by moments of fright. Discipline was easy and there was no
army spit-and-polish. He became lean and hard and would think
nothing of making a day's march of thirty miles over the mountains burdened with his weapons and a pack of dynamite and
detonators.

By the end of 1944 the Foreign Legion had thinned down considerably. Some of the men had been killed and more elected to
make a break for the south after the Allies had taken Rome. Coertze
said he would stay, so Walker stayed with him. Harrison also
stayed, together with an Englishman called Parker. The Foreign
Legion was now very small indeed.

'The Count used us as bloody pack horses,' said Walker. He
had ordered another round of drinks and the brandy was getting at him. His eyes were red-veined and he stumbled over the
odd word.

'Pack horses?' I queried.

'The unit was too small to really fight,' he explained. 'So he

24

used us to transport guns and food around his territory. That's how we got the convoy.'

'Which convoy?'

Walker was beginning to slur his words. 'It was like this. One of the Italian units had gone to carve up a German post and the job was being done in co-operation with another partisan brigade. But the Count was worried because this mob were Communists – real treacherous bastards they were. He was scared they might renege on us; they were always doing that because he was a Monarchist and they hated him worse than they did the Germans. They were looking ahead to after the war and they didn't do much fighting while they were about it. Italian politics, you see.'

I nodded.

'So he wanted Umberto – the chap in charge of our Italians – to have another couple of machine-guns, just in case, and Coertze said he'd take them.'

He fell silent, looking into his glass.

I said, 'What about this convoy?'

'Oh, what the hell,' he said. 'There's not a hope of getting it out. It'll stay there for ever, unless Coertze does something. I'll tell you. We were on our way to Umberto when we bumped into this German convoy driving along where no convoy should have been. So we clobbered it.'

They had got to the top of a hill and Coertze called a halt. 'We stay here for ten minutes, then we move on,' he said.

Alberto drank some water and then strolled down to where he could get a good view of the valley. He looked first at the valley floor where a rough, unmetalled road ran dustily, then raised his eyes to look south.

Suddenly he called Coertze. 'Look,' he said.

Coertze ran down and looked to where Alberto was pointing. In the distance, where the faraway thread of brown road shimmered in the heat, was a puff of dust. He unslung his glasses and focused rapidly.

'What the hell are they doing here?' he demanded.

'What is it?'

'German army trucks,' said Coertze. 'About six of them.' He pulled down the glasses. 'Looks as though they're trying to slip by on the side roads. We *have* made the main roads a bit unhealthy.'

Walker and Donato had come down. Coertze looked back at the machine-guns, then at Walker. 'What about it?'

Walker said, 'What about Umberto?'

25

'Oh, he's all right. It's just the Count getting a bit fretful now the war's nearly over. I think we should take this little lot – it should be easy with two machine-guns.'

Walker shrugged. 'OK with me,' he said.

Coertze said, 'Come on,' and ran back to where Parker was sitting. 'On your feet, *kêrel*,' he said. 'The war's still on. Where the hell is Harrison?'

'Coming,' called Harrison.

'Let's get this stuff down to the road on the double,' said Coertze. He looked down the hill. 'That bend ought to be a *lekker* place.'

'A what?' asked Parker plaintively. He always pulled Coertze's leg about his South Africanisms.

'Never mind that,' snapped Coertze. 'Get this stuff down to the road quick. We've got a job on.'

They loaded up the machine-guns and plunged down the hillside. Once on the road Coertze did a quick survey. 'They'll come round that bend slowly,' he said. 'Alberto, you take Donato and put your machine-gun there, where you can open up on the last two trucks. The last two, you understand. Knock 'em out fast so the others can't back out.'

He turned to Harrison and Parker. 'Put your gun over here on the other side and knock out the first truck. Then we'll have the others boxed in.'

'What do I do?' asked Walker.

'You come with me.' Coertze started to run up the road, followed by Walker. He ran almost to the bend, then left the road and climbed a small hillock where he could get a good sight of the German convoy. When Walker flopped beside him he already had the glasses focused.

'It's four trucks not six,' he said. 'There's a staff car in front and a motor-cycle combination in front of that. Looks like one of those BMW jobs with a machine-gun in the sidecar.'

He handed the glasses to Walker. 'How far from the tail of the column to that staff car?'

Walker looked at the oncoming vehicles. 'About sixty-five yards,' he estimated.

Coertze took the glasses. 'OK. You go back along the road sixty-five yards so that when the last truck is round the bend the staff car is alongside you. Never mind the motor-cycle – I'll take care of that. Go back and tell the boys not to open up until they hear loud bangs; I'll start those off. And tell them to concentrate on the trucks.'

He turned over and looked back. The machine-guns were invisible and the road was deserted. 'As nice an ambush as anyone could set,' he said. 'My *oupa* never did better against the English.' He tapped Walker on the shoulder. 'Off you go. I'll help you with the staff car as soon as I've clobbered the motor-cycle.'

Walker slipped from the hillock and ran back along the road, stopping at the machine-guns to issue Coertze's instructions. Then he found himself a convenient rock about sixty yards from the bend, behind which he crouched and checked his sub-machine-gun.

It was not long before he heard Coertze running along the road shouting, 'Four minutes. They'll be here in four minutes. Hold your fire.'

Coertze ran past him and disappeared into the verge of the road about ten yards farther on.

Walker said that four minutes in those conditions could seem like four hours. He crouched there, looking back along the silent road, hearing nothing except his own heart beating. After what seemed a long time he heard the growl of engines and the clash of gears and then the revving of the motor-cycle.

He flattened himself closer to the road and waited. A muscle twitched in his leg and his mouth was suddenly dry. The noise of the motor-cycle now blanked out all other sounds and he snapped off the safety catch.

He saw the motor-cycle pass, the goggled driver looking like a gargoyle and the trooper in the sidecar turning his head to scan the road, hands clutching the grips of the machine-gun mounted in front of him.

As in a dream he saw Coertze's hand come into view, apparently in slow motion, and toss a grenade casually into the sidecar. It lodged between the gunner's back and the coaming of the sidecar and the gunner turned in surprise. With his sudden movement the grenade disappeared into the interior of the sidecar.

Then it exploded.

The sidecar disintegrated and the gunner must have had his legs blown off. The cycle wheeled drunkenly across the road and Walker saw Coertze step out of cover, his sub-machine-gun pumping bullets into the driver. Then he had stepped out himself and his own gun was blazing at the staff car.

He had orientated himself very carefully so that he had a very good idea of where the driver would be placed. When he started firing, he did so without aiming and the windscreen shattered in the driver's face.

In the background he was conscious of the tac-a-tac of the machine-guns firing in long bursts at the trucks, but he had no time or desire to cast a glance that way. He was occupied in jumping out of the way of the staff car as it slewed towards him, a dead man's hand on the wheel.

The officer in the passenger seat was standing up, his hand clawing at the flap of his pistol holster. Coertze fired a burst at him and he suddenly collapsed and folded grotesquely over the metal rim of the broken windscreen as though he had suddenly turned into a rag doll. The pistol dropped from his hand and clattered on the ground.

With a rending jar the staff car bumped into a rock on the side of the road and came to a sudden stop, jolting the soldier in the rear who was shooting at Walker. Walker heard the bullets going over his head and pulled the trigger. A dozen bullets hit the German and slammed him back in his seat. Walker said that the range was about nine feet and he swore he heard the bullets hit, sounding like a rod hitting a soft carpet several times.

Then Coertze was shouting at him, waving him on to the trucks. He ran up the road following Coertze and saw that the first truck was stopped. He fired a burst into the cab just to be on the safe side, then took shelter, leaning against the hot radiator to reload.

By the time he had reloaded the battle was over. All the vehicles were stopped and Alberto and Donato were escorting a couple of dazed prisoners forward.

Coertze barked, 'Parker, go up and see if anyone else is coming,' then turned to look at the chaos he had planned.

The two men with the motor-cycle had been killed outright, as had the three in the staff car. Each truck had carried two men in the cab and one in the back. All the men in the cabs had been killed within twenty seconds of the machine-guns opening fire. As Harrison said, 'At twenty yards we couldn't miss – we just squirted at the first truck, then hosed down the second. It was like using a howitzer at a coconut-shy – too easy.'

Of the seventeen men in the German party there were two survivors, one of whom had a flesh wound in his arm.

Coertze said, 'Notice anything?'

Walker shook his head. He was trembling in the aftermath of danger and was in no condition to be observant.

Coertze went up to one of the prisoners and fingered the emblem on his collar. The man cringed.

'These are SS men. All of them.'

He turned and went back to the staff car. The officer was lying on his back, half in and half out of the front door, his empty eyes looking up at the sky, terrible in death. Coertze looked at him, then leaned over and pulled a leather brief-case from the front seat. It was locked.

'There's something funny here,' he said. 'Why would they come by this road?'

Harrison said, 'They might have got through, you know. If we hadn't been here they would have got through – and we were only here by chance.'

'I know,' said Coertze. 'They had a good idea and they nearly got away with it – that's what I'm worrying about. The Jerries aren't an imaginative lot, usually; they follow a routine. So why would they do something different? Unless this wasn't a routine unit.'

He looked at the trucks. 'It might be a good idea to see what's in those trucks.'

He sent Donato up the road to the north to keep watch and the rest went to investigate the trucks, excepting Alberto who was guarding the prisoners.

Harrison looked over the tailboard of the first truck. 'Not much in here,' he said.

Walker looked in and saw that the bottom of the truck was filled with boxes – small wooden boxes about eighteen inches long, a foot wide and six inches deep. He said, 'That's a hell of a small load.'

Coertze frowned and said, 'Boxes like that ring a bell with me, but I just can't place it. Let's have one of them out.'

Walker and Harrison climbed into the truck and moved aside the body of a dead German which was in the way. Harrison grasped the corner of the nearest box and lifted. 'My God!' he said. 'The damn' thing's nailed to the floor.'

Walker helped him and the box shifted. 'No, it isn't, but it must be full of lead.'

Coertze let down the tailboard. 'I think we'd better have it out and opened,' he said. His voice was suddenly croaking with excitement.

Walker and Harrison manhandled a box to the edge and tipped it over. It fell with a loud thump to the dusty road. Coertze said, 'Give me that bayonet.'

Walker took the bayonet from the scabbard of the dead German and handed it to Coertze, who began to prise the box open. Nails squealed as the top of the box came up. Coertze ripped it off and

29

said, 'I thought so.'

'What is it?' asked Harrison, mopping his brow.

'Gold,' said Coertze softly.

Everyone stood very still.

Walker was very drunk when he got to this point of his story. He was unsteady on his feet and caught the edge of the bar counter to support himself as he repeated solemnly, 'Gold.'

'For the love of Mike, what did you do with it?' I said. 'And how much of it was there?'

Walker hiccoughed gently. 'What about another drink?' he said.

I beckoned to the bar steward, then said, 'Come on; you can't leave me in suspense.'

He looked at me sideways. 'I really shouldn't tell,' he said. 'But what the hell! There's no harm in it now. It was like this . . .'

They had stood looking at each other for a long moment, then Coertze said, 'I knew I recognized those boxes. They use boxes like that on the Reef for packing the ingots for shipment.'

As soon as they had checked that all the boxes in that truck were just as heavy, there was a mad rush to the other trucks. These were disappointing at first – the second truck was full of packing cases containing documents and files.

Coertze delved into a case, tossing papers out, and said, 'What the hell's all this bumph?' He sounded disappointed.

Walker picked up a sheaf and scanned through it. 'Seems to be Italian Government documents of some sort. Maybe this is all top-secret stuff.'

The muffled voice of Harrison come from the bowels of the truck. 'Hey, you guys, look what I've found.'

He emerged with both hands full of bundles of lire notes – fine, newly printed lire notes. 'There's at least one case full of this stuff,' he said. 'Maybe more.'

The third truck had more boxes of gold, though not as much as the first, and there were several stoutly built wooden cases which were locked. They soon succumbed to a determined assault with a bayonet.

'Christ!' said Walker as he opened the first. In awe he pulled out a shimmering sparkle of jewels, a necklace of diamonds and emeralds.

'What's that worth?' Coertze asked Harrison.

Harrison shook his head dumbly. 'Gee, I wouldn't know.' He smiled faintly. 'Not my kind of stone.'

They were ransacking the boxes when Coertze pulled out a gold cigarette case. 'This one's got an inscription,' he said, and read it aloud. ' *"Caro Benito da part di Adolf – Brennero – 1940."* '

Harrison said slowly, 'Hitler had a meeting with Mussolini at the Brenner Pass in 1940. That's when Musso decided to kick in on the German side.'

'So now we know who this belongs to,' said Walker, waving his hand.

'Or used to belong to,' repeated Coertze slowly. 'But who does it belong to now?'

They looked at each other.

Coertze broke the silence. 'Come on, let's see what's in the last truck.'

The fourth truck was full of packing cases containing more papers. But there was one box holding a crown.

Harrison struggled to lift it. 'Who's the giant who wears this around the palace?' he asked nobody in particular. The crown was thickly encrusted with jewels – rubies and emeralds, but no diamonds. It was ornate and very heavy. 'No wonder they say "uneasy the head that wears a crown",' cracked Harrison.

He lowered the crown into the box. 'Well, what do we do now?'

Coertze scratched his head. 'It's quite a problem,' he admitted.

'I say we keep it,' said Harrison bluntly. 'It's ours by right of conquest.'

Now it was in the open – the secret thought that no one would admit except the extrovert Harrison. It cleared the air and made things much easier.

Coertze said, 'I suppose we must bring in the rest of the boys and vote on it.'

'That'll be no good unless it's a unanimous vote,' said Harrison almost casually.

They saw his point. If one of them held out in favour of telling the Count, then the majority vote would be useless. At last Walker said, 'It may not arise. Let's vote on it and see.'

All was quiet on the road so Donato and Parker were brought in from their sentry duty. The prisoners were herded into a truck so that Alberto could join in the discussion, and they settled down as a committee of ways and means.

Harrison needn't have worried – it *was* a unanimous vote. There was too much temptation for it to be otherwise.

'One thing's for sure,' said Harrison. 'When this stuff disappears there's going to be the biggest investigation ever, no matter who wins the war. The Italian Government will never rest until it's found, especially those papers. I'll bet they're dynamite.'

Coertze was thoughtful. 'That means we must hide the treasure *and* the trucks. *Nothing* must be found. It must be as though the whole lot vanished into thin air.'

'What are we going to do with it?' asked Parker. He looked at the stony ground and the thin soil. 'We might just bury the treasure if we took a week doing it, but we can't even begin to bury one truck, let alone four.'

Harrison snapped his fingers. 'The old lead mines,' he said. 'They're not far from here.'

Coertze's face lightened. '*Ja*,' he said. 'There's one winze that would take the lot.'

Parker said, 'What lead mines – and what's a winze, for God's sake?'

'It's a horizontal shaft driven into a mountain,' said Harrison. 'These mines have been abandoned since the turn of the century. No one goes near them any more.'

Alberto said, 'We drive all the trucks inside . . .'

'. . . and blow in the entrance,' finished Coertze with gusto.

'Why not keep some of the jewels?' suggested Walker.

'No,' said Coertze sharply. 'It's too dangerous – Harrison is right. There'll be all hell breaking loose when this stuff vanishes for good. Everything must be buried until it's safe to recover it.'

'Know any good jewel fences?' asked Harrison sardonically. 'Because if you don't, how would you get rid of the jewels?'

They decided to bury everything – the trucks, the bodies, the gold, the papers, the jewels – everything. They restowed the trucks, putting all the valuables into two trucks and all the non-valuables such as the documents into the other two. It was intended to drive the staff car into the tunnel first with the motor-cycle carried in the back, then the trucks carrying papers and bodies, and lastly the trucks with the gold and jewels.

'That way we can get out the stuff we want quite easily,' said Coertze.

The disposal of the trucks was easy enough. There was an unused track leading to the mines which diverged off the dusty road they were on. They drove up to the mine and reversed the trucks into the biggest tunnel in the right order. Coertze and Harrison prepared a charge to blow down the entrance, a simple job taking only a few minutes, then Coertze lit the fuse and ran back.

When the dust died down they saw that the tunnel mouth

was entirely blocked – making a rich mausoleum for seventeen men.

'What do we tell the Count?' asked Parker.

'We tell him we ran into a little trouble on the way,' said Coertze. 'Well, we did, didn't we?' He grinned and told them to move on.

When they got back they heard that Umberto had run into trouble and had lost a lot of men. The Communists hadn't turned up and he hadn't had enough machine-guns.

I said, 'You mean the gold's still there.'

'That's right,' said Walker, and hammered his fist on the counter. 'Let's have another drink.'

I didn't get much out of him after that. His brain was pickled in brandy and he kept wandering into irrelevancies. But he did answer one question coherently.

I asked, 'What happened to the two German prisoners?'

'Oh, them,' he said carelessly. 'They were shot while escaping. Coertze did it.'

IV

Walker was too far gone to walk home that night, so I got his address from a club steward, poured him into a taxi and forgot about him. I didn't think much of his story – it was just the maunderings of a drunk. Maybe he had found something in Italy, but I doubted if it was anything big – my imagination boggled at the idea of four truck-loads of gold and jewels.

I wasn't allowed to forget him for long because I saw him the following Sunday in the club bar gazing moodily into a brandy glass. He looked up, caught my eye and looked away hastily as though shamed. I didn't go over to speak to him; he wasn't altogether my type – I don't go for drunks much.

Later that afternoon I had just come out of the swimming pool and was enjoying a cigarette when I became aware that Walker was standing beside me. As I looked up, he said awkwardly, 'I think I owe you some money – for the taxi fare the other night.'

'Forget it,' I said shortly.

He dropped on one knee. 'I'm sorry about that. Did I cause any trouble?'

I smiled. 'Can't you remember?'

'Not a damn' thing,' he confessed. 'I didn't get into a fight or anything, did I?'

'No, we just talked.'

His eyes flickered. 'What about?'

'Your experiences in Italy. You told me a rather odd story.'

'I told you about the gold?'

I nodded. 'That's right.'

'I was drunk,' he said. 'As shickered as a coot. I shouldn't have told you about that. You haven't mentioned it to anyone, have you?'

'No, I haven't,' I said. 'You don't mean it's true?' He certainly wasn't drunk now.

'True enough,' he said heavily. 'The stuff's still up there – in a hole in the ground in Italy. I'd not like you to talk about it.'

'I won't,' I promised.

'Come and have a drink,' he suggested.

'No, thanks,' I said. 'I'm going home now.'

He seemed depressed. 'All right,' he said, and I watched him walk lethargically up to the club house.

After that, he couldn't seem to keep away from me. It was as though he had delivered a part of himself into my keeping and he had to watch me to see that I kept it safe. He acted as though we were both partners in a conspiracy, with many a nod and wink and a sudden change of subject if he thought we were being overheard.

He wasn't so bad when you got to know him, if you discounted the incipient alcoholism. He had a certain charm when he wanted to use it and he most surely set out to charm me. I don't suppose it was difficult; I was a stranger in a strange land and he was company of sorts.

He ought to have been an actor for he had the gift of mimicry. When he told me the story of the gold his mobile face altered plastically and his voice changed until I could see the bull-headed Coertze, gentle Donato and the tougher-fibred Alberto. Although Walker had normally a slight trace of a South African accent, he could drop it at will to take on the heavy gutturals of the Afrikaner or the speed and sibilance of the Italian. His Italian was rapid and fluent and he was probably one of those people who can learn a language in a matter of weeks.

I had lost most of my doubts about the truth of his story. It was too damned circumstantial. The bit about the inscription on the cigarette case impressed me a lot; I couldn't see Walker making up a thing like that. Besides, it wasn't the brandy talking all the time; he still stuck to the same story, which didn't change a fraction under many repetitions – drunk and sober.

Once I said, 'The only thing I can't figure is that big crown.'

'Alberto thought it was the royal crown of Ethiopia,' said Walker. 'It wouldn't be worn about the palace – they'd only use it for coronations.'

That sounded logical. I said, 'How do you know that the others haven't dug up the lot? There's still Harrison and Parker – and it would be dead easy for the two Italians; they're on the spot.'

Walker shook his head. 'No, there's only Coertze and me. The others were all killed.' His lips twisted. 'It seemed to be unhealthy to stick close to Coertze. I got scared in the end and beat it.'

I looked hard at him. 'Do you mean to say that Coertze murdered them?'

'Don't put words in my mouth,' said Walker sharply. 'I didn't say that. All I know is that four men were killed when they were close to Coertze.' He ticked them off on his fingers. 'Harrison was the first – that happened only three days after we buried the loot.'

He tapped a second finger. 'Next came Alberto – I saw that happen. It was as neat an accident as anyone could arrange. Then Parker. He was killed in action just like Harrison, and just like Harrison, the only person who was anywhere near him was Coertze.'

He held up three fingers and slowly straightened the fourth. 'Last was Donato. He was found near the camp with his head bashed in. They said he'd been rock-climbing, so the verdict was accidental death – but not in my book. That was enough for me, so I quit and went south.'

I thought about this for a while, then said, 'What did you mean when you said you saw Alberto killed?'

'We'd been on a raid,' said Walker. 'It went OK but the Germans moved fast and got us boxed in. We had to get out by the back door, and the back door was a cliff. Coertze was good on a mountain and he and Alberto went first, Coertze leading. He said he wanted to find the easiest way down, which was all right – he usually did that.

'He went along a ledge and out of sight, then he came back and gave Alberto the OK sign. Then he came back to tell us it was all right to start down, so Parker and I went next. We followed Alberto and when we got round the corner we saw that he was stuck.

'There were no hand holds ahead of him and he'd got himself into a position where he couldn't get back, either. Just as we got there he lost his nerve – we could see him quivering and shaking. There he was, like a fly on the side of that cliff with a hell of a long drop under him and a pack of Germans ready to drop on top of him, and he was shaking like a jelly.

'Parker shouted to Coertze and he came down. There was just room enough for him to pass us, so he said he'd go to help Alberto. He got as far as Alberto and Alberto fell off. I swear that Coertze pushed him.'

'Did you see Coertze push him?' I asked.

'No,' Walker admitted. 'I couldn't see Alberto at all once Coertze had passed us. Coertze's a big bloke and he isn't made of glass. But why did he give the OK sign to go along that ledge?'

'It could have been an honest mistake.'

Walker nodded. 'That's what I thought at the time. Coertze said afterwards that he didn't mean that Alberto should go as far as that. There *was* an easier way down just short of where Alberto got stuck. Coertze took us down there.'

He lit a cigarette. 'But when Parker was shot up the following week I started to think again.'

'How did it happen?'

Walker shrugged. 'The usual thing – you know how it is in a fight. When it was all over we found Parker had a hole in his head. Nobody saw it happen, but Coertze was nearest.' He paused. 'The hole was in the *back* of the head.'

'A German bullet?'

Walker snorted. 'Brother, we didn't have time for an autopsy; but it wouldn't have made any difference. We were using German weapons and ammo – captured stuff; and Coertze *always* used German guns; he said they were better than the British.' He brooded. 'That started me thinking seriously. It was all too pat – all these blokes being knocked off so suddenly. When Donato got his, I quit. The Foreign Legion was just about busted anyway. I waited until the Count had sent Coertze off somewhere, then I collected my gear, said goodbye and headed south to the Allied lines. I was lucky – I got through.'

'What about Coertze?'

'He stayed with the Count until the Yanks came up. I saw him in Jo'burg a couple of years ago. I was crossing the road to go into a pub when I saw Coertze going through the door. I changed my mind; I had a drink, but not in *that* pub.'

He shivered suddenly. 'I want to stay as far from Coertze as I can. There's a thousand miles between Cape Town and Johannes-

36

burg – that ought to be enough.' He stood up suddenly. 'Let's go and have a drink, for God's sake.'

So we went and had a drink – several drinks.

V

During the next few weeks I could see that Walker was on the verge of making me a proposition. He said he had some money due to him and that he would need a good friend. At last he came out with it.

'Look,' he said. 'My old man died last year and I've got two thousand pounds coming when I get it out of the lawyer's hands. I could go to Italy on two thousand pounds.'

'So you could,' I said.

He bit his lip. 'Hal, I want you to come with me.'

'For the gold?'

'That's right; for the gold. Share and share alike.'

'What about Coertze?'

'To hell with Coertze,' said Walker violently. 'I don't want to have anything to do with him.'

I thought about it. I was young and full of vinegar in those days, and this sounded just the ticket – if Walker was telling the truth. And if he wasn't telling the truth, why would he finance me to a trip to Italy? It seemed a pleasantly adventurous thing to do, but I hesitated. 'Why me?' I asked.

'I can't do it myself,' he said. 'I wouldn't trust Coertze, and you're the only other chap who knows anything about it. And I trust you, Hal, I really do.'

I made up my mind. 'All right, it's a deal. But there are conditions.'

'Trot them out.'

'This drinking of yours has to stop,' I said. 'You're all right when you're sober, but when you've got a load on you're bloody awful. Besides, you know how you spill things when you're cut.'

He rearranged his eager face into a firm expression. 'I'll do it, Hal; I won't touch a drop,' he promised.

'All right,' I said. 'When do we start?'

I can see now that we were a couple of naïve young fools. We expected to be able to lift several tons of gold from a hole in the ground without too much trouble. We had no conception of the brains and organization that would be needed – and were needed in the end.

Walker said, 'The lawyer tells me that the estate will be settled finally in about six weeks. We can leave any time after that.'

We discussed the trip often. Walker was not too much concerned with the practical difficulties of getting the gold, nor with what we were going to do with it once we had it. He was mesmerized by the millions involved.

He said once, 'Coertze estimated that there were four tons of gold. At the present price that's well over a million pounds. Then there's the lire – packing cases full of the stuff. You can get a hell of a lot of lire into a big packing case.'

'You can forget the paper money,' I said. 'Just pass one of those notes and you'll have the Italian police jumping all over you.'

'We can pass them outside Italy,' he said sulkily.

'Then you'll have to cope with Interpol.'

'All right,' he said impatiently. 'We'll forget the lire. But there's still the jewellery – rings and necklaces, diamonds and emeralds.' His eyes glowed. 'I'll bet the jewels are worth more than the gold.'

'But not as easily disposed of,' I said.

I was getting more and more worried about the sheer physical factors involved. To make it worse, Walker wouldn't tell me the position of the lead mine, so I couldn't do any active planning at all.

He was behaving like a child at the approach of Christmas, eager to open his Christmas stocking. I couldn't get him to face facts and I seriously contemplated pulling out of this mad scheme. I could see nothing ahead but a botched job with a probably lengthy spell in an Italian jail.

The night before he was to go to the lawyer's office to sign the final papers and receive his inheritance I went to see him at his hotel. He was half-drunk, lying on his bed with a bottle conveniently near.

'You promised you wouldn't drink,' I said coldly.

'Aw, Hal, this isn't drinking; not what I'm doing. It's just a little taste to celebrate.'

I said, 'You'd better cut your celebration until you've read the paper.'

'What paper?'

'This one,' I said, and took it from my pocket. 'That little bit at the bottom of the page.'

He took the paper and looked at it stupidly. 'What must I read?'

'That paragraph headed : "Italians Sentenced".'

It was only a small item, a filler for the bottom of a page.

Walker was suddenly sober. 'But they *were* innocent,' he whispered.

'That didn't prevent them from getting it in the neck,' I said brutally.

'God!' he said. 'They're still looking for it.'

'Of course they are,' I said impatiently. 'They'll keep looking until they find it.' I wondered if the Italians were more concerned about the gold or the documents.

I could see that Walker had been shocked out of his euphoric dreams of sudden wealth. He now had to face the fact that pulling gold out of an Italian hole had its dangers.

'This makes a difference,' he said slowly. 'We can't go now. We'll have to wait until this dies down.'

'Will it die down – ever?' I asked.

He looked up at me. 'I'm not going now,' he said with the firmness of fear. 'The thing's off – it's off for a long time.'

In a way I was relieved. There was a weakness in Walker that was disturbing and which had been troubling me. I had been uneasy for a long time and had been very uncertain of the wisdom of going to Italy with him. Now it was decided.

I left him abruptly in the middle of a typical action – pouring another drink.

As I walked home one thought occurred to me. The newspaper report confirmed Walker's story pretty thoroughly. That was something.

VI

It was long past lunch-time when I finished the story. My throat was dry with talking and Jean's eyes had grown big and round.

'It's like something from the Spanish Main,' she said. 'Or a Hammond Innes thriller. Is the gold still there?'

I shrugged. 'I don't know. I haven't read anything about it in the papers. For all I know it's still there – if Walker or Coertze haven't recovered it.'

'What happened to Walker?'

'He got his two thousand quid,' I said. 'Then embarked on a career of trying to drink the distilleries dry. It wasn't long before he lost his job and then he dropped from sight. Someone told me he'd gone to Durban. Anyway, I haven't seen him since.'

Jean was fascinated by the story and after that we made a game of it, figuring ways and means of removing four tons of gold from

Italy as unobtrusively as possible. Just as an academic exercise, of course. Jean had a fertile imagination and some of her ideas were very good.

Because that was the problem – the sheer physical difficulty of moving four tons of gold without anyone being aware that it was even there to be moved.

In 1959 we got clear of our indebtedness to the bank by dint of strict economy. The yard was ours now with no strings attached and we celebrated by laying the keel of a 15-tonner I had designed for Jean and myself. My old faithful *King Penguin*, one of the first of her class, was all right for coastal pottering, but we had the idea that one day we would do some ocean voyaging, and we wanted a bigger boat.

A 15-tonner is just the right size for two people to handle and big enough to live in indefinitely. The boat was to be forty feet overall, thirty feet on the waterline with eleven feet beam. She would be moderately canvased for ocean voyaging and would have a big auxiliary diesel engine. We were going to call her *Sanford* in memory of old Tom.

When she was built we would take a year's leave, sail north to spend some time in the Mediterranean, and come back by the east coast, thus making a complete circumnavigation of Africa. Jean had a mischievous glint in her eye. 'Perhaps we'll bring that gold back with us,' she said.

But two months later the blow fell.

I had designed a boat for Bill Meadows and had sent him the drawings for approval. By mishap the accommodation plans had been left out of the packet, so Jean volunteered to take them to Fish Hoek where Bill lives.

It's a nice drive to Fish Hoek along the Chapman's Peak road with views of sea and mountain, far better than anything I have since seen on the Riviera. Jean delivered the drawings and on the way back in the twilight a drunken oaf in a high-powered American car forced her off the road and she fell three hundred feet into the sea.

The bottom dropped out of my life.

It meant nothing to me that the driver of the other car got five years for manslaughter – that wouldn't bring Jean back. I let things slide at the yard and if it hadn't been for Harry Marshall the business would have gone to pot.

It was then that I tallied up my life and made a sort of mental balance sheet. I was thirty-six years old; I had a good business which I had liked but which now I didn't seem to like so much;

I had my health and strength – boat-building and sailing tend to keep one physically fit – and I had no debts. I even had money in the bank with more rolling in all the time.

On the other side of the balance sheet was the dreadful absence of Jean, which more than counter-balanced all the advantages.

I felt I couldn't stay at the yard or even in Cape Town, where memories of Jean would haunt me at every corner. I wanted to get away. I was waiting for something to happen.

I was ripe for mischief.

VII

A couple of weeks later I was in a bar on Adderley Street having a drink or three. It wasn't that I'd taken to drink, but I was certainly drinking more than I had been accustomed to. I had just started on my third brandy when I felt a touch at my elbow and a voice said, 'Hallo, I haven't seen you for a long time.'

I turned and found Walker standing next to me.

The years hadn't dealt kindly with Walker. He was thinner, his dark, good looks had gone, to be replaced by a sharpness of feature, and his hairline had receded. His clothes were unpressed and frayed at the edges, and there was an air of seediness about him which was depressing.

'Hallo,' I said. 'Where did you spring from?' He was looking at my full glass of brandy, so I said, 'Have a drink.'

'Thanks,' he said quickly. 'I'll have a double.'

That gave me a pretty firm clue as to what had happened to Walker, but I didn't mind being battened upon for a couple of drinks, so I paid for the double brandy.

He raised the glass to his lips with a hand that trembled slightly, took a long lingering gulp, then put the glass down, having knocked back three-quarters of the contents. 'You're looking prosperous,' he said.

'I'm not doing too badly.'

He said, 'I was sorry to hear of what happened to your wife.' He hurried on as he saw my look of inquiry. 'I read about it in the paper. I thought it must have been your wife – the name was the same and all that.'

I thought he had spent some time hunting me up. Old friends and acquaintances are precious to an alcoholic; they can be touched for the odd drink and the odd fiver.

'That's finished and best forgotten,' I said shortly. Unwittingly, perhaps, he had touched me on the raw – he had brought Jean back. 'What are you doing now?'

He shrugged. 'This and that.'

'You haven't picked up any gold lately?' I said cruelly. I wanted to pay him back for putting Jean in my mind.

'Do I look as though I have?' he asked bitterly. Unexpectedly, he said, 'I saw Coertze last week.'

'Here – in Cape Town?'

'Yes. He'd just come back from Italy. He's back in Jo'burg now, I expect.'

I smiled. 'Did *he* have any gold with him?'

Walker shook his head. 'He said that nothing's changed.' He suddenly gripped me by the arm. 'The gold's still there – nobody's found it. It's still there – four tons of gold in that tunnel – and all the jewels.' He had a frantic urgency about him.

'Well, why doesn't he do something about it?' I said. 'Why doesn't he go and get it out? Why don't you both go?'

'He doesn't like me,' said Walker sulkily. 'He'll hardly speak to me.' He took one of my cigarettes from the packet on the counter, and I lit it for him amusedly. 'It isn't easy to get it out of the country,' he said. 'Even Sergeant High-and-Mighty Coertze hasn't found a way.'

He grinned tightly. 'Imagine that,' he said, almost gaily. 'Even the brainy Coertze can't do it. He put the gold in a hole in the ground and he's too scared to get it out.' He began to laugh hysterically.

I took his arm. 'Take it easy.'

His laughter choked off suddenly. 'All right,' he said. 'Buy me another drink; I left my wallet at home.'

I crooked my finger at the bartender and Walker ordered another double. I was beginning to understand the reason for his degradation. For fourteen years the knowledge that a fortune in gold was lying in Italy waiting to be picked up had been eating at him like a cancer. Even when I knew him ten years earlier I was aware of the fatal weakness in him, and now one could see that the bitterness of defeat had been too much. I wondered how Coertze was standing up to the strain. At least he seemed to be doing something about it, even if only keeping an eye on the situation.

I said carefully, 'If Coertze was willing to take you, would you be prepared to go to Italy to get the stuff out?'

He was suddenly very still. 'What d'you mean?' he demanded. 'Have you been talking to Coertze?'

'I've never laid eyes on the man.'

Walker's glance shifted nervously about the bar, then he straightened. 'Well, if he . . . wanted me; if he . . . needed me – I'd be prepared to go along.' He said this with bravado but the malice showed through when he said, 'He needed me once, you know; he needed me when we buried the stuff.'

'You wouldn't be afraid of him?'

'What do you mean – afraid of him? Why should I be afraid of him? I'm afraid of nobody.'

'You seemed pretty certain he'd committed at least four murders.'

He seemed put out. 'Oh, that! That was a long time ago. And I never said he'd murdered anybody. I never said it.'

'No, you never actually said it.'

He shifted nervously on the bar stool. 'Oh, what's the use? He won't ask me to go with him. He said as much last week.'

'Oh, yes, he will,' I said softly.

Walker looked up quickly. 'Why should he?'

I said quietly, 'Because I know a way of getting that gold out of Italy and of taking it anywhere in the world, quite simply and relatively safely.'

His eyes widened. 'What is it? How can you do it?'

'I'm not going to tell you,' I said equably. 'After all, you wouldn't tell me where the gold's hidden.'

'Well, let's do it,' he said. 'I'll tell you where it is, you get it, and Bob's your uncle. Why bring Coertze into it?'

'It's a job for more than two men,' I said. 'Besides, he deserves a share – he's been keeping an eye on the gold for fourteen years, which is a damn' sight more than you've been doing.' I failed to mention that I considered Walker the weakest of reeds. 'Now, how will you get on with Coertze if this thing goes through?'

He turned sulky. 'All right, I suppose, if he lays off me. But I won't stand for any of his sarcasm.' He looked at me in wonder as though what we were talking about had just sunk in. 'You mean there's a chance we can get the stuff out – a real chance?'

I nodded and got off the bar stool. 'Now, if you'll excuse me.'

'Where are you going?' he asked quickly.

'To phone the airline office,' I said. 'I want a seat on tomorrow's Jo'burg plane. I'm going to see Coertze.

The sign I had been waiting for had arrived.

2 Coertze

Air travel is wonderful. At noon the next day I was booking into a hotel in Johannesburg, a thousand miles from Cape Town.

On the plane I had thought a lot about Coertze. I had made up my mind that if he didn't bite then the whole thing was off – I couldn't see myself relying on Walker. And I had to decide how to handle him – from Walker's account he was a pretty tough character. I didn't mind that; I could be tough myself when the occasion arose, but I didn't want to antagonize him. He would probably be as suspicious as hell, and I'd need kid gloves.

Then there was another thing – the financing of the expedition. I wanted to hang on to the boatyard as insurance in case this whole affair flopped, but I thought if I cut Harry Marshall in for a partnership in the yard, sold my house and my car and one or two other things, I might be able to raise about £25,000 – not too much for what I had in mind.

But it all depended on Coertze. I smiled when I considered where he was working. He had a job in the Central Smelting Plant which refined gold from all the mines on the Reef. More gold had probably passed through his hands in the last few years than all the Axis war-lords put together had buried throughout the world.

It must have been tantalizing for him.

I phoned the smelting plant in the afternoon. There was a pause before he came on the line. 'Coertze,' he said briefly.

I came to the point. 'My name's Halloran,' I said. 'A mutual friend – Mr Walker of Cape Town – tells me you have been experiencing difficulty in arranging for the delivery of goods from Italy. I'm in the import-export business; I thought I might be able to help you.'

A deep silence bored into my ear.

I said, 'My firm is fully equipped to do this sort of work. We never have much trouble with the Customs in cases like this.'

It was like dropping a stone into a very deep well and listening for the splash.

'Why don't you come to see me,' I said. 'I don't want to take up your time now; I'm sure you're a busy man. Come at seven this evening and we'll discuss your difficulties over dinner. I'm staying at the Regency – it's in Berea, in . . .'

'I know where it is,' said Coertze. His voice was deep and harsh with a guttural Afrikaans accent.

'Good; I'll be expecting you,' I said, and put down the phone.

I was pleased with this first contact. Coertze was suspicious and properly so – he'd have been a fool not to be. But if he came to the hotel he'd be hooked, and all I had to do would be to jerk on the line and set the hook in firmly.

I was certain he'd come; human curiosity would see to that. If he didn't come, then he wouldn't be human – or he'd be superhuman.

He came, but not at seven o'clock and I was beginning to doubt my judgement of the frailty of human nature. It was after eight when he knocked on the door, identified me, and said, 'We'll forget the dinner; I've eaten.'

'All right,' I said. 'But what about a drink?' I crossed the room and put my hand on the brandy bottle. I was pretty certain it would be brandy – most South Africans drink it.

'I'll have a Scotch,' he said unexpectedly. 'Thanks,' he added as an afterthought.

As I poured the drinks I glanced at him. He was a bulky man, broad of chest and heavy in the body. His hair was black and rather coarse and he had a shaggy look about him. I'd bet that when he stripped he'd look like a grizzly bear. His eyebrows were black and straight over eyes of a snapping electric blue. He had looked after himself better than Walker; his belly was flat and there was a sheen of health about him.

I handed him a drink and we sat down facing each other. He was tense and wary, although he tried to disguise it by over-relaxing in his chair. We were like a couple of duellists who have just engaged blades.

'I'll come to the point,' I said. 'A long time ago Walker told me a very interesting story about some gold. That was ten years ago and we were going to do something about it, but it didn't pan out. That might have been lucky because we'd have certainly made a botch of the job.'

I pointed my finger at him. 'You've been keeping an eye on it. You've probably popped across to Italy from time to time just to keep your eye on things in general. You've been racking your brains trying to think of a way of getting that gold out of Italy, but you haven't been able to do it. You're stymied.'

His face had not changed expression; he would have made a good poker player. He said, 'When did you see Walker?'

'Yesterday – in Cape Town.'

The craggy face broke into a derisive grin. 'And you flew up to Jo'burg to see me just because a *dronkie* like Walker told you a cock-and-bull story like that? Walker's a no-good hobo; I see a dozen like him in the Library Gardens every day,' he said contemptuously.

'It's not a cock-and-bull story, and I can prove it.'

Coertze just sat and looked at me like a stone gargoyle, the whisky glass almost lost in his huge fist.

I said, 'What are you doing here – in this room? If there was no story, all you had to do was to ask me what the hell I was talking about when I spoke to you on the phone. The fact that you're here proves there's something in it.'

He made a fast decision. 'All right,' he said. 'What's your proposition?'

I said, 'You still haven't figured a way of moving four tons of gold out of Italy. Is that right?'

He smiled slowly. 'Let's assume so,' he said ironically.

'I've got a foolproof way.'

He put down his glass and produced a packet of cigarettes. 'What is it?'

'I'm not going to tell you – yet.'

He grinned. 'Walker hasn't told you where the gold is, has he?'

'No, he hasn't,' I admitted. 'But he would if I put pressure on him. Walker can't stand pressure; you know that.'

'He drinks too much,' said Coertze. 'And when he drinks he talks; I'll bet that's how he came to spill his guts to you.' He lit his cigarette. 'What do you want out of it?'

'Equal shares,' I said firmly. 'A three-way split after all expenses have been paid.'

'And Walker comes with us on the job. Is that right?'

'Yes,' I said.

Coertze moved in his chair. 'Man, it's like this,' he said. 'I don't know if you've got a foolproof way of getting the gold out or if you haven't. I thought *I* had it licked a couple of times. But let's assume your way is going to work. Why should we take Walker?'

He held up his hand. 'I'm not suggesting we do him down or anything like that – although he'd think nothing of cheating us. Give him his share after it's all over, but for God's sake keep him out of Italy. He'll make a balls-up for sure.'

I thought of Harrison and Parker and the two Italians. 'You don't seem to like him.'

Coertze absently fingered a scar on his forehead. 'He's unreliable,'

46

he said. 'He almost got me killed a couple of times during the war.'

I said, 'No, we take Walker. I don't know for certain if three of us can pull it off, and with two it would be impossible. Unless you want to let someone else in?'

He smiled humourlessly. 'That's not on – not with you coming in. But Walker had better keep his big mouth shut from now on.'

'Perhaps it would be better if he stopped drinking,' I suggested.

'That's right,' Coertze agreed. 'Keep him off the pots. A few beers are all right, but keep him off the hard-tack. That'll be your job; I don't want to have anything to do with the rat.'

He blew smoke into the air, and said, 'Now let's hear your proposition. If it's good, I'll come in with you. If I don't think it'll work, I won't touch it. In that case, you and Walker can do what you damn' well like, but if you go for that gold you'll have me to reckon with. I'm a bastard when I'm crossed.'

'So am I,' I said.

We grinned at each other. I liked this man, in a way. I wouldn't trust him any more than I'd trust Walker, but I had the feeling that while Walker would stick a knife in your back, Coertze would at least shoot you down from the front.

'All right,' he said. 'Let's have it.'

'I'm not going to tell you – not here in this room.' I saw his expression and hurried on. 'It isn't that I don't trust you, it's simply that you wouldn't believe it. You have to see it – and you have to see it in Cape Town.'

He looked at me for a long moment, then said, 'All right, if that's the way you want it, I'll play along.' He paused to think. 'I've got a good job here, and I'm not going to give it up on your say-so. There's a long week-end coming up – that gives me three days off. I'll fly down to Cape Town to see what you have to show me. If it's good, the job can go hang; if it isn't, then I've still got the job.'

'I'll pay your fare,' I said.

'I can afford it,' he grunted.

'If it doesn't pan out, I'll pay your fare,' I insisted. 'I wouldn't want you to be out of pocket.'

He looked up and grinned. 'We'll get along,' he said. 'Where's that bottle?'

As I was pouring another couple of drinks, he said, 'You said you were going to Italy with Walker. What stopped you?'

I took the clipping from my pocket and passed it to him. He read

47

it and laughed. 'That must have scared Walker. I was there at the time,' he said unexpectedly.

'In Italy?'

He sipped the Scotch and nodded. 'Yes; I saved my army back-pay and my gratuity and went back in '48. As soon as I got there all hell started popping about this trial. I read about it in the papers and you never heard such a lot of bull in your life. Still, I thought I'd better lie low, so I had a *lekker* holiday with the Count.'

'With the Count?' I said in surprise.

'Sure,' he said. 'I stay with the Count every time I go to Italy. I've been there four times now.'

I said, 'How did you reckon to dispose of the gold once you got it out of Italy?'

'I've got all that planned,' he said confidently. 'They're always wanting gold in India and you get a good price. You'd be surprised at the amount of gold smuggled out of this country in small packets that ends up in India.'

He was right – India is the gold sink of the world – but I said casually, 'My idea is to go the other way – to Tangier. It's an open port with an open gold market. You should be able to sell four tons of gold there quite easily – and it's legal, too. No trouble with the police.'

He looked at me with respect. 'I hadn't thought of that. I don't know much about this international finance.'

'There's a snag,' I said. 'Tangier is closing up shop next year; it's being taken over by Morocco. Then it won't be a free port any more and the gold market will close.'

'When next year?'

'April 19,' I said. 'Nine months from now. I think we'll just about have enough time.'

He smiled. 'I never thought about selling the gold legally; I didn't think you could. I thought the governments had got all that tied up. Maybe I should have met you sooner.'

'It wouldn't have done you any good,' I said. 'I hadn't the brains then that I have now.'

He laughed and we proceeded to kill the bottle.

II

Coertze came down to Cape Town two weeks later. I met him at the airport and drove him directly to the yard, where Walker was waiting.

Walker seemed to shrink into himself when I told him that
Coertze was visiting us. In spite of his braggart boasts, I could see
he didn't relish close contact. If half of what he had said about
Coertze was true, then he had every reason to be afraid.

Come to think of it – so had I !

It must have been the first time that Coertze had been in a
boatyard and he looked about him with keen interest and asked a
lot of questions, nearly all of them sensible. At last, he said, 'Well,
what about it ?'

I took them down to the middle slip where Jimmy Murphy's
Estralita was waiting to be drawn up for an overhaul. 'That's a
sailing yacht,' I said. 'A 15-tonner. What would you say her draft
is – I mean, how deep is she in the water ?'

Coertze looked her over and then looked up at the tall mast.
'She'll need to be deep to counter-balance that lot,' he said. 'But
I don't know how much. I don't know anything about boats.'

Considering he didn't know anything about boats, it was a very
sensible answer.

'Her draft is six feet in normal trim,' I said. 'She's drawing less
now because a lot of gear has been taken out of her.'

His eyes narrowed. 'I'd have thought it would be more than
that,' he said. 'What happens when the wind blows hard on the
sails ? Won't she tip over ?'

This was going well and Coertze was on the ball. I said, 'I have
a boat like this just being built, another 15-tonner. Come and have
a look at her.'

I led the way up to the shed where *Sanford* was being built
and Coertze followed, apparently content that I was leading up to
a point. Walker tagged on behind.

I had pressed to get *Sanford* completed and she was ready for
launching as soon as the glass-fibre sheathing was applied and the
interior finished.

Coertze looked up at her. 'They look bloody big out of the
water,' he commented.

I smiled. That was the usual reaction. 'Come aboard,' I said.

He was impressed by the spaciousness he found below and commented favourably on the way things were arranged. 'Did you
design all this ?' he asked.

I nodded.

'You could live in here, all right,' he said, inspecting the galley.

'You could and you will,' I said. 'This is the boat in which
we're going to take four tons of gold out of Italy.'

He looked surprised and then he frowned. 'Where are you going to put it?'

I said, 'Sit down and I'll tell you something about sailing boats you don't know.' Coertze sat uncomfortably on the edge of the starboard settee which had no mattress as yet, and waited for me to explain myself.

'This boat displaces – weighs, that is – ten tons, and . . .'

Walker broke in. 'I thought you said she was a 15-tonner.'

'That's Thames measure – yacht measure. Her displacement is different.'

Coertze looked at Walker. 'Shut up and let the man speak.' He turned to me. 'If the boat weighs ten tons and you add another four tons, she'll be pretty near sinking, won't she? And where are you going to put it? It can't be out in the open where the cops can see it.'

I said patiently, 'I said I'd tell you something about sailing boats that you didn't know. Now, listen – about forty per cent of the weight of any sailing boat is ballast to keep her the right way up when the wind starts to press on those sails.'

I tapped the cabin sole with my foot. 'Hanging on the bottom of this boat is a bloody great piece of lead weighing precisely four tons.'

Coertze looked at me incredulously, a dawning surmise in his eyes. I said, 'Come on, I'll show you.'

We went outside and I showed them the lead ballast keel. I said, 'All this will be covered up next week because the boat will be sheathed to keep out the marine borers.'

Coertze was squatting on his heels looking at the keel. 'This is it,' he said slowly. 'This is it. The gold will be hidden under water – built in as part of a boat.' He began to laugh, and after a while Walker joined in. I began to laugh too, and the walls of the shed resounded.

Coertze sobered suddenly. 'What's the melting point of lead?' he asked abruptly.

I knew what was coming. 'Four-fifty degrees centigrade,' I said. 'We've got a little foundry at the top of the yard where we pour the keels.'

'*Ja*,' he said heavily. 'You can melt lead on a kitchen stove. But gold melts at over a thousand centigrade and we'll need more than a kitchen stove for that. I *know*; melting gold is my job. Up at the smelting plant we've got bloody big furnaces.'

I said quickly, 'I've thought of that one, too. Come up to the

50

workshop – I'll show you something else you've never seen before.'

In the workshop I opened a cupboard and said, 'This gadget
is brand new – just been invented.' I hauled out the contraption
and put it on the bench. Coertze looked at it uncomprehendingly.

There wasn't much to see; just a metal box, eighteen inches by
fifteen inches by nine inches, on the top of which was an asbestos
mat and a Heath Robinson arrangement of clamps.

I said, 'You've heard of instant coffee – this is instant heat.' I
began to get the machine ready for operation. 'It needs cooling
water at at least five pounds an inch pressure – that we get from an
ordinary tap. It works on ordinary electric current, too, so you can
set it up anywhere.'

I took the heart of the machine from a drawer. Again, it wasn't
much to look at; just a piece of black cloth, three inches by four. I
said, 'Some joker in the States discovered how to spin and weave
threads of pure graphite, and someone else discovered this application.'

I lifted the handle on top of the machine, inserted the graphite
mat, and clamped it tight. Then I took a bit of metal and gave it
to Coertze.

He turned it in his fingers and said, 'What is it?'

'Just a piece of ordinary mild steel. But if this gadget can melt
steel, it can melt gold. Right?'

He nodded and looked at the machine dubiously – it wasn't very
impressive.

I took the steel from his fingers and dropped it on to the graphite
mat, then I gave Walker and Coertze a pair of welders' goggles
each. 'Better put these on : it gets a bit bright.'

We donned the goggles and I switched on the machine. It was
a spectacular display. The graphite mat flashed instantly to a white
heat and the piece of steel glowed red, then yellow and finally
white. It seemed to slump like a bit of melting wax and in less
than fifteen seconds it had melted into a little pool. All this to
the accompaniment of a violent shower of sparks as the metal
reacted with the air.

I switched off the machine and removed my goggles. 'We won't
have all these fireworks when we melt gold; it doesn't oxidize as
easily as iron.'

Coertze was staring at the machine. 'How does it do that?'

'Something like a carbon arc,' I said. 'You can get temperatures

51

up to five thousand degrees centigrade. It's only intended to be a laboratory instrument, but I reckon we can melt two pounds of gold at a time. With three of these gadgets and a hell of a lot of spare mats we should be able to work pretty fast.'

He said doubtfully, 'If we can only pour a couple of pounds at a time, the keel is going to be so full of cracks and flaws that I'm not sure it won't break under its own weight.'

'I've thought of that one, too,' I said calmly. 'Have you ever watched anyone pour reinforced concrete?'

He frowned and then caught on, snapping his fingers.

'We make the mould and put a mesh of wires inside,' I said. 'That'll hold it together.'

I showed him a model I had made, using fuse wire and candle wax, which he examined carefully. 'You've done a hell of a lot of thinking about this,' he said at last.

'Somebody has to,' I said. 'Or that gold will stay where it is for another fourteen years.'

He didn't like that because it made him appear stupid; but there wasn't anything he could do about it. He started to say something and bit it short, his face flushing red. Then he took a deep breath and said, 'All right, you've convinced me, I'm in.'

Then *I* took a deep breath – of relief.

III

That night we had a conference.

I said, 'This is the drill. *Sanford* – my yacht – will be ready for trials next week. As soon as the trials are over you two are going to learn how to sail under my instruction. In under four months from now we sail for Tangier.'

'Christ!' said Walker. 'I don't know that I like the sound of that.'

'There's nothing to it,' I said. 'Hundreds of people are buzzing about the Atlantic these days. Hell, people have gone round the world in boats a quarter this size.'

I looked at Coertze. 'This is going to take a bit of financing. Got any money?'

'About a thousand,' he admitted.

'That gets tossed into the kitty,' I said. 'Along with my twenty-five thousand.'

'*Magtig*,' he said. 'That's a hell of a lot of money.

'We'll need every penny of it,' I said. 'We might have to buy a small boatyard in Italy if that's the only way we can cast the keel in secrecy. Besides, I'm lending it to the firm of Walker, Coertze and Halloran at one hundred per cent interest. I want fifty thousand back before the three-way split begins. You can do the same with your thousand.'

'That sounds fair enough,' agreed Coertze.

I said, 'Walker hasn't any money and once you've thrown your thousand in the kitty, neither have you. So I'm putting you both on my payroll. You've got to have your smokes and three squares a day while all this is going on.'

This bit of information perked Walker up considerably. Coertze merely nodded in confirmation. I looked hard at Walker. 'And you stay off the booze or we drop you over the side. Don't forget that.'

He nodded sullenly.

Coertze said, 'Why are we going to Tangier first?'

'We've got to make arrangements to remelt the gold into standard bars,' I said. 'I can't imagine any banker calmly taking a golden keel into stock. Anyway, that's for the future; right now I have to turn you into passable seamen – we've got to get to the Mediterranean first.'

I took *Sanford* on trials and Walker and Coertze came along for the ride and to see what they were letting themselves in for. She turned out to be everything I've ever wanted in a boat. She was fast for a deep-sea cruiser and not too tender. With a little sail adjustment she had just the right amount of helm and I could see she was going to be all right without any drastic changes.

As we went into a long reach she picked up speed and went along happily with the water burbling along the lee rail and splashing on deck. Walker, his face a little green, said, 'I thought you said a keel would hold this thing upright.' He was hanging tightly on to the side of the cockpit.

I laughed. I was happier than I had been for a long time. 'Don't worry about that. That's not much angle of heel. She won't capsize.'

Coertze didn't say anything – he was busy being sick.

The next three months were rough and tough. People forget that the Cape was the Cape of Storms before some early public relations officer changed the name to the Cape of Good Hope. When the Berg Wind blows it can be as uncomfortable at sea as anywhere in the world.

I drove Walker and Coertze unmercifully. In three months I had to turn them into capable seamen, because *Sanford* was a bit too big to sail single-handed. I hoped that the two of them would equal one able-bodied seaman. It wasn't as bad as it sounds because in those three months they put in as much sea time as the average weekend yachtsman gets in three years, and they had the dubious advantage of having a pitiless instructor.

Shore time was spent in learning the theory of sail and the elements of marlin-spike seamanship – how to knot and splice, mend a sail and make baggywrinkle. They grumbled a little at the theory, but I silenced that by asking them what they'd do if I was washed overboard in the middle of the Atlantic.

Then we went out to practise what I had taught – at first in the bay and then in the open sea, cruising coastwise around the peninsula at first, and then for longer distances well out of sight of land.

I had thought that Coertze would prove to be as tough at sea as apparently he was on land. But he was no sailor and never would be. He had a queasy stomach and couldn't stand the motion, so he turned out to be pretty useless at boat handling. But he was hero enough to be our cook on the longer voyages, a thankless job for a sea-sick man.

I would hear him swearing below when the weather was rough and a pot of hot coffee was tossed in his lap. He once told me that he now knew what poker dice felt like when they were shaken in the cup. He wouldn't have stood it for any lesser reason, but the lust for gold was strong in him.

Walker was the real surprise. Coertze and I had weaned him from his liquor over many protests, and he was now eating more and the air and exercise agreed with him. He put on weight, his thin cheeks filled out and his chest broadened. Nothing could replace the hair he had lost, but he seemed a lot more like the handsome young man I had known ten years earlier.

More surprisingly, he turned out to be a natural sailor. He liked *Sanford* and she seemed to like him. He was a good helmsman and could lay her closer to the wind than I could when we were beating to windward. At first I was hesitant to give him a free hand with *Sanford*, but as he proved himself I lost my reluctance.

At last we were ready and there was nothing more to wait for. We provisioned *Sanford* and set sail for the north on November 12, to spend Christmas at sea. Ahead of us was a waste of water with the beckoning lure of four tons of gold at the other side.

I suppose one *could* have called it a pleasure cruise!

BOOK TWO
The Gold

3 *Tangier*

Two months later we sailed into Tangier harbour, the 'Q' flag hoisted, and waited for the doctor to give us pratique and for the Customs to give us the once-over. To port of *Sanford* was the modern city with its sleek, contemporary buildings sharply outlined against the sky. To starboard was the old city – the Arab city – squat and low-roofed and hugging a hill, the skyline only broken by the up-flung spear of a minaret.

To port – Europe; to starboard – Africa.

This was nothing new to Walker and Coertze. They had sown a few wild oats in their army days, roistering in Cairo and Alexandria. On the voyage from Cape Town they had talked much about their army days – and all in Italian, too. We made it a rule to speak as much Italian as possible, and while the others were on a refresher course, I didn't lag far behind even though I had to start from scratch.

We had settled on a good cover story to veil our activities in the Mediterranean. I was a South African boat-builder on a cruise combining business with pleasure. I was thinking of expanding into the lucrative Mediterranean market and might buy a boatyard if the price and conditions were right. This story had the advantage of not departing too far from the truth and would serve if we really had to buy a yard to cast the golden keel.

Coertze was a mining man with medical trouble. His doctor had advised him to take a leisurely holiday and so he was crewing *Sanford* for me. His cover story would account for any interest he might take in derelict lead mines.

Walker, who proved to be something of an actor, was a moderately wealthy playboy. He had money but disliked work and was willing to go a long way to avoid it. He had come on this Mediterranean trip because he was bored with South Africa and wanted a change. It was to be his job to set things up in Tangier; to acquire a secluded house where we could complete the last stages of the operation.

All in all, I was quite satisfied, even though I had got a bit

55

tired of Coertze on the way north. He didn't like the way I seemed to be taking charge of things and I had to ram home very forcibly the fact that a ship can only have one skipper. He had seen the point when we ran into heavy weather off the Azores, and it galled him that the despised Walker was the better seaman.

Now we were in Tangier, he had recovered his form and was a bit more inclined to throw his weight around. I could see that I'd have to step on him again before long.

Walker looked about the yacht basin. 'Not many sailing boats here,' he commented.

That was true. There were a few ungainly-looking fishing boats and a smart ketch, probably bound for the Caribbean. But there were at least twenty big power craft, fast-looking boats, low on the water. I knew what they were.

This was the smuggling fleet. Cigarettes to Spain, cigarette-lighters to France, antibiotics to where they could make a profit (although that trade had fallen off), narcotics to everywhere. I wondered if there was much arms smuggling to Algeria.

At last the officials came and went, leaving gouges in my planking from their hob-nailed boots. I escorted them to their launch, and as soon as they had left, Walker touched my arm.

'We've got another visitor,' he said.

I turned and saw a boat being sculled across the harbour. Walker said, 'He was looking at us through glasses from that boat across there.' He pointed to one of the motor craft. 'Then he started to come here.'

I watched the approaching dinghy. A European was rowing and I couldn't see his face, but as he dextrously backed-water and swung round to the side of *Sanford* he looked up and I saw it was Metcalfe.

Metcalfe is one of that international band of scallywags of whom there are about a hundred in the world. They are soldiers of fortune and they flock to the trouble spots, ignoring the danger and going for the money. I was not really surprised to see Metcalfe in Tangier; it had been a pirates' stronghold from time immemorial and would be one of Metcalfe's natural hang-outs.

I had known him briefly in South Africa but I didn't know what he was at the time. All I knew was that he was a damned good sailor who won a lot of dinghy races at Cape Town and who came close to winning the South African dinghy championship. He bought one of my Falcons and had spent a lot of time at the yard tuning it.

I had liked him and had crewed for him a couple of times. We had had many a drink together in the yacht club bar and he spent a weekend at Kirstenbosch with Jean and myself. It was in the way of being a firmly ripening friendship between us when he had left South Africa a hop, skip and a jump ahead of the police, who wanted to nail him on a charge of I.D.B. Since then I had not seen him, but I had heard passing mentions and had occasionally seen his name in the papers, usually quoted as being in trouble in some exotic hot-spot.

Now he was climbing on to the deck of *Sanford*.

'I thought it was you,' he said. 'So I got the glasses to make sure. What are you doing here?'

'Just idly cruising,' I said. 'Combining business with pleasure. I thought I might see what the prospects in the Med. are like.'

He grinned. 'Brother, they're good. But that's not in your line, is it?'

I shook my head, and said, 'Last I heard of you, you were in Cuba.'

'I was in Havana for a bit,' he said. 'But that was no place for me. It was an *honest* revolution, or at least it was until the Commies moved in. I couldn't compete with them, so I quit.'

'What are you doing now?'

He smiled and looked at Walker. 'I'll tell you later.'

I said, 'This is Walker and this is Coertze.' There was hand-shaking all round and Metcalfe said, 'It's good to hear a South African accent again. You'd have a good country there if the police weren't so efficient.'

He turned to me. 'Where's Jean?'

'She's dead,' I said. 'She was killed in a motor smash.'

'How did it happen?'

So I told him of Chapman's Peak and the drunken driver and the three-hundred-foot fall to the sea. As I spoke his face hardened, and when I had finished, he said, 'So the bastard only got five years, and if he's a good boy he'll be out in three and a half.'

He rubbed his finger against the side of his nose. 'I liked Jean,' he said. 'What's the bludger's name? I've got friends in South Africa who can see to him when he comes out.'

'Forget it,' I said. 'That won't bring Jean back.'

He nodded, then slapped his hands together. 'Now you're all staying with me at my place; I've got room enough for an army.'

I said hesitantly, 'What about the boat?'

He smiled. 'I see you've heard stories about the Tangier dock thieves. Well, let me tell you they're all true. But that doesn't matter; I'll put one of my men on board. Nobody steals from my men – or me.'

He rowed back across the harbour and presently returned with a scar-faced Moroccan, to whom he spoke in quick and guttural Arabic. Then he said, 'That's all fixed. I'll have the word passed round the docks that you're friends of mine. Your boat's safe enough, as safe as though it lay in your own yard.'

I believed him. I could believe he had a lot of pull in a place like Tangier.

'Let's go ashore,' he said. 'I'm hungry.'

'So am I,' said Coertze.

'It'll be a relief not to do any more cooking for a while, won't it?' I said.

'Man,' said Coertze. 'I wouldn't mind if I never saw a fry-pan again.'

'That's a pity,' said Metcalfe. 'I was looking forward to you making me some *koeksusters*; I always liked South African grub.' He roared with laughter and slapped Coertze on the back.

Metcalfe had a big apartment on the Avenida de España and he gave me a room to myself while Coertze and Walker shared a room. He stayed and chatted while I unpacked my bag.

'South Africa too quiet for you?' he asked.

I went into my carefully prepared standard talk on the reasons I had left. I had no reason to trust Metcalfe more than anyone else – probably less – judging by the kind of man he was. I don't know whether he believed me or not, but he agreed that there was scope in the Mediterranean for a good boatyard.

'You may not get as many commissions to build,' he said. 'But there certainly is room for a good servicing and maintenance yard. I'd go east, towards Greece, if I were you. The yards in the islands cater mostly for the local fishermen; there's room for someone who understands yachts and yachtsmen.'

'What have you got a boat for?' I asked banteringly. 'Hiring it out for charter cruises?'

He grinned. 'Aw, you know me. I carry all sorts of cargoes; anything except narcotics.' He pulled a face. 'I'm a bad bastard, I know, but I draw the line at drugs. Anything else I'm game for.'

He laughed. 'The French in Algiers hate my guts – they tried to do me down a couple of months ago. I'd unloaded a cargo into some fishing boats and then I ran into Algiers to refuel. I was clean, see! they couldn't touch me – my papers were in order and everything.

'I let the crew go ashore for a drink and I turned in and had a zizz. Then something woke me up – I heard a thump and then a queer noise that seemed to come from *underneath* the boat. So I got up and had a look around. When I got on deck I saw a boat pulling away and there seemed to be a man in the water, swimming alongside it.'

He grinned. 'Well, I'm a careful and cautious man, so I got my snorkel and my swim-fins and went over the side to have a look-see. What do you think those French Security bastards had done to me?'

I shook my head. 'I wouldn't know.'

'They'd put a limpet mine on my stern gear. They must have reckoned that if they couldn't nail me down legally they'd do it illegally. If that thing went off it would blow the bottom out of my stern. Well, I got it off the boat and did a bit of heavy thinking. I knew they wouldn't have timed it to blow up in harbour – it wouldn't have looked nice – so I reckoned it was set to blow after I left.

'I slung it round my neck by the cord and swam across the harbour to where the police patrol boat was lying and stuck it under their stern. Let them have the trouble of buying a new boat.

'Next day we left early as planned and, as we moved out, I heard the police boat revving up. They followed us a long way while I was taking it nice and easy, cruising at about ten knots so they wouldn't lose me. They hung on to my tail for about thirty miles, waiting for the bang and laughing to themselves fit to bust, I suppose. But they didn't laugh when the bang came and blew the arse off their own boat.

'I turned and picked them up. It was all good clean fun – no one was hurt. When I'd got them out of the water I took them back to Algiers – the noble rescuer. You ought to have seen the faces of the Security boys when I pitched up. Of course, they had to go through the motions of thanking me for rescuing those lousy, shipwrecked mariners. I kept a straight face and said I thought it must have been one of the anti-submarine depth charges in the stern that had gone off. They said it couldn't have been that because police boats don't carry depth charges. And that was that.'

He chuckled. 'No, they don't like me in Algiers.'

I laughed with him. It was a good story and he had told it well.

I was in two minds about Metcalfe; he had his advantages and his disadvantages. On the one hand, he could give us a lot of help in Tangier; he knew the ropes and had contacts. On the other hand, we had to be careful he didn't get wind of what we were doing. He was a hell of a good chap and all that, but if he knew we were going to show up with four tons of gold he would hijack us without a second thought. We were his kind of meat.

Yes, we had to be very careful in our dealings with Mr Metcalfe. I made a mental note to tell the others not to let anything drop in his presence.

I said, 'What kind of boat have you got?'

'A Fairmile,' he said. 'I've re-engined it, of course.'

I knew of the Fairmiles, but I had never seen one close up. They had been built in the hundreds during the war for harbour defence. The story was that they were built by the mile and cut off as needed. They were 112 feet overall with powerful engines and could work up over twenty knots easily, but they had the reputation of being bad rollers in a cross sea. They were not armoured or anything like that, being built of wood, and when a few of them went into St Nazaire with the *Campbelltown* they got shot up very badly.

After the war you could buy a surplus Fairmile for about five thousand quid and they had become a favourite with the smugglers of Tangier. If Metcalfe had re-engined his Fairmile, he had probably gone for power to outrun the revenue cutters and his boat would be capable of at least twenty-six knots in an emergency. *Sanford* would have no chance of outrunning a boat like that if it came to the push.

'I'd like to see her some time,' I said. There was no harm in looking over a potential enemy.

'Sure,' said Metcalfe expansively. 'But not just yet. I'm going out tomorrow night.'

That was good news – with Metcalfe out of the way we might be able to go about our business undisturbed. 'When are you coming back?' I asked.

'Some time next week,' he said. 'Depending on the wind and the rain and suchlike things.'

'Such as those French Security bastards?'

'That's right,' he said carelessly. 'Let's eat.'

II

Metcalfe made us free of his flat and said we could live there in his absence – the servants would look after us. That afternoon he took me round town and introduced me to several people. Some were obviously good contacts to have, such as a ship's chandler and a boat-builder. Others were not so obviously good; there was a villainous-looking café proprietor, a Greek with no discernible occupation and a Hungarian who explained volubly that he was a 'Freedom Fighter' who had escaped from Hungary after the abortive revolution of 1956. I was particularly cynical about him.

I think that Metcalfe was unobtrusively passing the word that we were friends of his, and so immune to any of the usual tricks played on passing yachtsmen. Metcalfe was not a bad man to have around if he was your friend and you were a yachtsman. But I wasn't an ordinary yachtsman and that made Metcalfe a potential bomb.

Before we left the flat I had the chance to talk to Coertze and Walker privately. I said, 'Here's where we keep our mouths shut and stick to our cover story. We don't do a damn' thing until Metcalfe has pushed off – and we try to finish before he gets back.'

Walker said, 'Why, is he dangerous?'

'Don't you know about Metcalfe?' I explained who he was. They had both heard of him; he had made quite a splash in the South African Press – the reporters loved to write about such a colourful character.

'Oh, *that* Metcalfe,' said Walker, impressed.

Coertze said, 'He doesn't look much to me. He won't be any trouble.'

'It's not Metcalfe alone,' I said. 'He's got an organization and he's on his own territory. Let's face it; he's a professional and we're amateurs. Steer clear of Metcalfe.'

I felt like adding 'and that's an order', but I didn't. Coertze might have taken me up on it and I didn't want to force a show-down with him yet. It would come of its own accord soon enough.

So for a day and a half we were tourists in Tangier, rubber-necking our way about the town. It we hadn't had so much on our minds it might have been interesting, but as it was, it was a waste of time.

Luckily, Metcalfe was preoccupied by his own mysterious business and we saw little of him. However, I did instruct Walker to ask one crucial question before Metcalfe left.

Over breakfast, he said, 'You know – I *like* Tangier. It might be nice to stay here for a few months. Is the climate always like this?'

'Most of the time,' answered Metcalfe. 'It's a good, equable climate. There's lots of people retire here, you know.'

Walker smiled. 'Oh, I'm not thinking of retiring. I've nothing to retire from.' He was proving to be a better actor than I had expected – that touch was perfect. He said, 'No, what I thought was that I might like to buy a house here. Somewhere I could live a part of the year.'

'I should have thought the Med. would be your best bet,' said Metcalfe. 'The Riviera, or somewhere like that.'

'I don't know,' said Walker. 'This seems to be as good a place as any, and the Riviera is *so* crowded these days.' He paused as though struck by a sudden thought. 'I'd want a boat, of course. Could you design one for me? I'd have it built in England.'

'Sure I could,' I said. 'All you have to do is pay me enough.'

'Yes,' said Walker. 'You can't do without the old boat, can you?'

He was laying it on a bit too thick and I could see that Metcalfe was regarding him with amused contempt, so I said quickly, 'He's a damned good sailor. He nearly ran off with the Cape Dinghy Championship last year.'

That drew Metcalfe as I knew it would. 'Oh,' he said with more respect, and for a few minutes he and Walker talked boats. At last Walker came out with it. 'You know, what would be really perfect would be a house on the coast somewhere with its own anchorage and boat-shed. Everything self-contained, as it were.'

'Thinking of joining us?' asked Metcalfe with a grin.

'Oh, no,' said Walker, horrified. 'I wouldn't have the nerve. I've got enough money, and besides, I don't like your smelly Fairmiles with their stinking diesel oil. No, I was thinking about a *real* boat, a sailing boat.'

He turned to me. 'You know, the more I think about it the better I like it. You could design a 10-tonner for me. Something I could handle myself, and this place is a perfect jumping-off place for the Caribbean. A transatlantic crossing might be fun.'

He confided in Metcalfe. 'You know, these ocean-crossing johnnies are all very well, but most of them are broke and they have to live on their boats. Why should I do that? Think how much better it would be if I had a house here with a boat-shed at the bottom of the garden, as it were, where I could tune the boat for the trip instead of lying in that stinking harbour.'

It *was* a damned good idea if you were a wealthy playboy with a yen to do a single-handed Atlantic crossing. I gave Walker full credit for his inventive powers.

Metcalfe didn't find it unreasonable, either. He said, 'Not a bad idea if you can afford it. I tell you what; go and see Aristide, a friend of mine. He'll try to rent you a flat, he's got dozens empty, but tell him that I sent you and he'll be more reasonable.' He scribbled an address on a piece of paper and handed it to Walker.

'Oh, thanks awfully,' said Walker. 'It's really very kind of you.'

Metcalfe finished his coffee. 'I've got to go now; see you tonight before I leave.'

When he had gone Coertze, who had sat through all this with no expression at all on his face, said, 'I've been thinking about the go . . .'

I kicked his ankle and jerked my head at the Moroccan servant who had just come into the room. '*Tula*,' I said. '*Moenie hier praat nie.*' Then in English, 'Let's go out and have a look round.'

We left the flat and sat at a table of a nearby café. I said to Coertze, 'We don't know if Metcalfe's servants speak English or not, but I'm taking no chances. Now, what did you want to say?'

He said, 'I've been thinking about bringing the gold in here. How are we going to do it? You said yesterday that bullion has to be declared at Customs. We can't come in and say, "Listen, man; I've got a golden keel on my boat and I think it weighs about four tons." '

'I've been thinking about that myself,' I said. 'It looks as though we'll have to smuggle it in, recast it into standard bars, smuggle it out again a few bars at a time, then bring the bars in openly and declare them to Customs.'

'That's going to take time,' objected Coertze. 'We haven't got the time.'

I sighed. 'All right; let's take a good look at this time factor. Today is 12th January and Tangier shuts up shop as far as gold is concerned on 19th April – that's – let me see, er – ninety-seven days – say fourteen weeks.'

I began to calculate and to allocate the time. It would be a week before we left Tangier and another fortnight to get to Italy. That meant another fortnight coming back, too, and I would like a week spare in case of bad weather. That disposed of six weeks. Two weeks for making preparations and for getting the gold out, and three weeks for casting the keel – eleven weeks altogether, leaving a margin of three weeks. We were cutting it fine.

I said, 'We'll have to see what the score is when we get back here with the gold. Surely to God someone will buy it, even if it is in one lump. But we don't say anything until we've got it.'

I began to have visions of sailing back to Egypt or even India like some sort of modern Flying Dutchman condemned to sail the seas in a million pound yacht.

Walker did not go much for these planning sessions. He was content to leave that to Coertze and me. He had been sitting listening with half an ear, studying the address which Metcalfe had given him.

Suddenly he said, 'I thought old Aristide would have been an estate agent, but he's not.' He read the address from the slip of paper. ' "Aristide Theotopopoulis, Tangier Mercantile Bank, Boulevard Pasteur." Maybe we could ask him something about it.'

'Not a chance,' I said derisively. 'He's a friend of Metcalfe.' I looked at Walker. 'And another thing,' I said. 'You did very well with Metcalfe this morning, but for God's sake, don't put on that phoney Oxford accent, and less of that "thanks awfully" stuff. Metcalfe's a hard man to fool; besides, he's been to South Africa and knows the score. You'd have done better to put on a Malmesbury accent, but it's too late to change now. But tone it down a bit, will you?'

Walker grinned and said, 'OK, old chappie.'

I said, 'Now we'll go and see Aristide Theoto-whatever-it-is. It wouldn't be a bad idea if we hired a car, too. It'll help us get around and it adds to the cover. We *are* supposed to be rich tourists, you know.'

III

Aristide Theotopopoulis was a round man. His girth was roughly equal to his height, and as he sat down he creased in the middle like a half-inflated football bladder. Rolls of fat flowed over his collar from his jowls and the back of his neck. Even his hands were round – pudgy balls of fat with the glint of gold shining from deeply embedded rings.

'Ah, yes. Mr Walker; you want a house,' he said. 'I received a phone call from Mr Metcalfe this morning. I believe I have the very thing.' His English was fluent and colloquial.

'You mean you have such a house?' enquired Walker.

'Of course! Why do you suppose Mr Metcalfe sent you to me? He knows the Casa Saeta.' He paused. 'You don't mind if it's an old house?' he asked anxiously.

'Not at all,' replied Walker easily. 'I can afford any alterations provided the house suits me.' He caught my eye, then said hastily, 'But I would like to suggest that I rent it for six months with an option to buy.'

Aristide's face lengthened from a circle to an ellipse. 'Very well, if that is what you wish,' he said dubiously.

He took us up the north coast in a Cadillac with Coertze following in our hired car. The house looked like something from a Charles Addams' cartoon and I expected to see Boris Karloff peering from a window. There was no Moorish influence at all; it was the most hideous Victorian Gothic in the worst possible taste. But that didn't matter if it could give us what we wanted.

We went into the house and looked cursorily over the worm-eaten panelling and viewed the lack of sanitation. The kitchen was primitive and there was a shaggy garden at the back of the house. Beyond was the sea and we looked over a low cliff to the beach.

It was perfect. There was a boat-house big enough to take *Sanford* once we unstepped the mast, and there was a crude slip badly in need of repair. There was even a lean-to shed where we could set up our foundry.

I looked at everything, estimating how long it would take to put in order, then I took Coertze to one side while Aristide extolled the beauties of the house to Walker.

'What do you think?' I asked.

'Man, I think we should take it. There can't be another place like this in the whole of North Africa.'

'That's just what I was thinking,' I said. 'I hope we can find something like this in Italy. We can get local people to fix up the slip, and with a bit of push we should be finished in a week. We'll have to do some token work on the house, but the bulk of the money must go on essentials – there'll be time to make the house livable when we come back. I'll tip Walker off about that; he's good at thinking up wacky reasons for doing the damndest things.'

We drifted back to Walker and Aristide who were still going at it hammer and tongs, and I gave Walker an imperceptible nod. He smiled dazzlingly at Aristide, and said, 'It's no use, Mr Theotopopoulis, you can't talk me out of taking this house. I'm determined to have it at once – on a six months' rental, of course.'

Aristide, who hadn't any intention of talking anyone out of anything, was taken aback, but making a game recovery, said, 'You understand, Mr Walker, I can give no guarantees . . .' His voice tailed off, giving the impression that he was doing Walker a favour.

'That's all right, old man,' said Walker gaily. 'But I must have a six months' option on the house, too. Remember that.'

'I think that can be arranged,' said Aristide with spurious dubiety.

'Won't it be fun, living in this beautiful house?' said Walker to me. I glared at him. That was the trouble with Walker; he got wrapped up in his part too much. My glare went unnoticed because he had turned to Aristide. 'The house isn't haunted, or anything like that?' he demanded, as though he equated ghosts with dead rats in the wainscotting.

'Oh, no,' said Aristide hurriedly. 'No ghosts.'

'A pity,' said Walker negligently. 'I've always wanted to live in a haunted house.'

I saw Aristide changing his mind about the ghosts, so I spoke hastily to break up this buffoonery. I had no objection to Aristide thinking he was dealing with a fool, but no one could be as big a damn' fool as Walker was acting and I was afraid that Aristide might smell a rat.

I said, 'Well, I suggest we go back to Mr Theotopopoulis's office and settle the details. It's getting late and I have to do some work on the boat.'

To Coertze, I said, 'There's no need for you to come. We'll meet you for lunch at the restaurant we went to last night.'

I had watched his blood pressure rising at Walker's fooleries and I wanted him out of the way in case he exploded. It's damned difficult working with people, especially antagonistic types like Walker and Coertze.

We went back to Aristide's office and it all went off very well. He stung us for the house, but I had no objection to that. No one who splashed money around like Walker could be anything but an honest man.

Then Walker said something that made my blood run cold, although afterwards, on mature consideration, I conceded that he had built up his character so that he could get away with it. He said to Aristide, 'Tangier is a funny place. I hear you've got bars of gold scattered about all over the place.'

Aristide smiled genially. He had cut his pound of flesh and was willing to waste a few minutes in small talk; besides, this idiot

Walker was going to live in Tangier – he could be milked a lot more. 'Not scattered exactly,' he said. 'We keep our gold in very big safes.'

'Um,' said Walker. 'You know, it's a funny thing, but I've lived all my life in South Africa where they mine scads of gold, and I've never seen any. You can't buy gold in South Africa, you know.'

Aristide raised his eyebrows as though this was unheard of.

'I've heard you can buy gold here by the pound like buying butter over the counter. It might be fun to buy some gold. Imagine me with all my money and I've never seen a gold bar,' he said pathetically. 'I've got a lot of money, you know. Most people say I've got too much.'

Aristide. frowned. This was heresy; in his book no one could have too much money. He became very earnest. 'Mr Walker, the best thing anyone can do in these troubled times is to buy gold. It's the only safe investment. The value of gold does not fluctuate like these paper currencies.' With a flick of his fingers he stripped the pretensions from the US dollar and the pound sterling. 'Gold does not rust or waste away; it is always there, always safe and valuable. If you want to invest, I am always willing to sell gold.'

'Really?' said Walker. 'You sell it, just like that?'

Aristide smiled. 'Just like that.' His smile turned to a frown. 'But if you want to buy, you must buy now, because the open market in Tangier is closing very soon.' He shrugged. 'You say that you have never seen a bar of gold. I'll show you bars of gold – many of them.' He turned to me. 'You too, Mr Halloran, if you wish,' he said off-handedly. 'Please come this way.'

He led us down into the bowels of the building, through grilled doors and to the front of an immense vault. On the way down, two broad-shouldered bodyguards joined us. Aristide opened the vault door, which was over two feet thick, and led us inside.

There was a lot of gold in that vault. Not four tons of it, but still a lot of gold. It was stacked up neatly in piles of bars of various sizes; it was boxed in the form of coins; it was a hell of a lot of gold.

Aristide indicated a bar. 'This is a Tangier standard bar. It weighs 400 ounces troy – about twenty-seven and a half pounds avoirdupois. It is worth over five thousand pounds sterling.' He picked up a smaller bar. 'This is a more convenient size. It weighs a kilo – just over thirty-two ounces – and is worth about four hundred pounds.'

He opened a box and let coins run lovingly through his pudgy fingers. 'Here are British sovereigns – and here are American double eagles. These are French napoleons and these are Austrian ducats.' He looked at Walker with a gleam in his eye and said, 'You see what I mean when I say that gold never loses its value?'

He opened another box. 'Not all gold coins are old. These are made privately by a bank in Tangier – not mine. This is the Tangier Hercules. It contains exactly one ounce of fine gold.'

He held the coin out on the palm of his hand and let Walker take it. Walker turned it in his fingers and then passed it to me reluctantly.

It was then that this whole crazy, mad expedition ceased to be just an adventure to me. The heavy, fatty feel of that gold coin turned something in my guts and I understood what people meant when they referred to gold lust. I understood why prospectors would slave in arid, barren lands looking for gold. It is not just the value of the gold that they seek – it is gold itself. This massive, yellow metal can do something to a man; it is as much a drug as any hell-born narcotic.

My hand was trembling slightly when I handed the coin back to Aristide.

He said, tossing it, 'This costs more than bullion of course, because the cost of coining must be added. But it is in a much more convenient form.' He smiled sardonically. 'We sell a lot to political refugees and South American dictators.'

When we were back in his office, Walker said, 'You have a lot of gold down there. Where do you get it from?'

Aristide shrugged. 'I buy gold and I sell gold. I make my profit on both transactions. I buy it where I can; sell it when I can. It is not illegal in Tangier.'

'But it must come from somewhere,' persisted Walker. 'I mean, suppose one of those pirate chaps, I mean one of the smuggling fellows, came to you with half a ton of gold. Would you buy it?'

'If the price was right,' said Aristide promptly.

'Without knowing where it came from?'

A faint smile came to Aristide's eyes. 'There is nothing more anonymous than gold,' he said. 'Gold has no master; it belongs only temporarily to the man who touches it. Yes, I would buy the gold.'

'Even when the gold market closes?'

Aristide merely shrugged and smiled.

'Well, now, think of that,' said Walker fatuously. 'You must get a lot of gold coming into Tangier.'

'I will sell you gold when you want it, Mr Walker,' said Aristide,

68

seating himself behind his desk. 'Now, I assume that, since you are coming to live in Tangier, you will want to open an account.' He was suddenly all businessman.

Walker glanced at me, then said, 'Well, I don't know. I'm on this cruise with Hal here, and I'm taking care of my needs with a letter of credit that was issued in South Africa. I've already cashed in a lot of boodle at one of the other banks here – I didn't realize I would have the good fortune to meet a friendly banker.' He grinned engagingly.

'We're not going to stay here long,' he said. 'We'll be pushing off in a couple of weeks, but I'll be back; yes, I'll be back. When will we be back, Hal?'

I said, 'We're going to Spain and Italy, and then to Greece. I don't think we'll push on as far as Turkey or the Lebanon, although we might. I should say we'll be back here in three or four months.'

'You see,' said Walker. 'That's when I'll move into the house properly. Casa Saeta,' he said dreamily. 'That sounds fine.'

We took our leave of Aristide, and when we got outside, I said furiously, 'What made you do a stupid thing like that?'

'Like what?' asked Walker innocently.

'You know very well what I mean. We agreed not to mention gold.'

'We've got to say something about it some time,' he said. 'We can't sell gold to anyone without saying something about it. I just thought it was a good time to find out something about it, to test Aristide's attitude towards gold of unknown origin. I thought I worked up to it rather well.'

I had to give him credit for that. I said, 'And another thing: let's have less of the silly ass routine. You nearly gave me a fit when you started to pull Aristide's leg about the ghosts. There are more important things at stake than fooling about.'

'I know,' he said soberly. 'I realized that when we were in the vault. I had forgotten what gold felt like.'

So it had hit him too. I calmed down and said, 'OK. But don't forget it. And for God's sake don't act the fool in front of Coertze. I have enough trouble keeping the peace as it is.'

IV

When we met Coertze for lunch, I said, 'We saw a hell of a lot of gold this morning.'

He straightened. 'Where?'

Walker said, 'In a bloody big safe at Aristide's bank.'

'I thought . . .' Coertze began.

'No harm done,' I said. 'It went very smoothly. We saw a lot of ingots. There are two standard sizes readily acceptable here in Tangier. One is 400 ounces, the other is one kilogram.' Coertze frowned, and I said, 'That's nearly two and a quarter pounds.'

He grunted and drank his Scotch. I said, 'Walker and I have been discussing this and we think that Aristide will buy the gold under the counter, even after the gold market closes – but we'll probably have to approach him before that so he can make his arrangements.'

'I think we should do it now,' said Walker.

I shook my head. 'No! Aristide is a friend of Metcalfe; that's too much like asking a tiger to come to dinner. We mustn't tell him until we come back and then we'll have to take the chance.'

Walker was silent so I went on. 'The point is that it's un-likely that Aristide will relish taking a four-ton lump of gold into stock, so we'll probably have to melt the keel down into ingots, any-way. In all probability Aristide will fiddle his stock sheets somehow so that he can account for the four extra tons, but it means that he must be told before the gold market closes – which means we must be back before April 19.'

Coertze said, 'Not much time.'

I said, 'I've worked out all the probable times for each stage of the operation and we have a month in hand. But there'll be snags and we'll need all of that. But that isn't what's worrying me now – I've got other things on my mind.'

'Such as?'

'Look. When – and if – we get the gold here and we start to melt it down, we're going to have a hell of a lot of ingots lying around. I don't want to dribble them to Aristide as they're cast – that's bad policy, too much chance of an outsider catching on. I want to let him have the lot at once, get paid with a cast-iron draft on a Swiss bank and then clear out. But it does mean that we'll have a hell of a lot of ingots lying around loose in the Casa Saeta and that's bad.'

I sighed. 'Where do we keep the damn' things? Stacked up in the living-room? And how many of these goddamned ingots will there be?' I added irritably.

Walker looked at Coertze. 'You said there was about four tons, didn't you?'

'*Ja*,' said Coertze. 'But that was only an estimate.'

I said, 'You've worked with bullion since. How close is that estimate?'

He thought about it, sending his mind back fifteen years and comparing what he saw then with what he had learned since. The human mind is a marvellous machine. At last he said slowly, 'I think it is a close estimate, very close.'

'All right,' I said. 'So it's four tons. That's 9000 pounds as near as dammit. There's sixteen ounces to the pound and . . .'

'No,' said Coertze suddenly. 'Gold is measured in troy ounces. There's 14.58333 recurring ounces troy to the English pound.'

He had the figures so pat that I was certain he knew what he was talking about. After all, it was his job. I said, 'Let's not go into complications; let's call it fourteen and a half ounces to the pound. That's good enough.'

I started to calculate, making many mistakes although it should have been a simple calculation. The mathematics of yacht design don't have the same emotional impact.

At last I had it. 'As near as I can make out, in round figures we'll have about 330 bars of 400 ounces each.'

'What's that at five thousand quid a bar?' asked Walker.

I scribbled on the paper again and looked at the answer unbelievingly. It was the first time I had worked this out in terms of money. Up to this time I had been too busy to think about it, and four tons of gold seemed to be a good round figure to hold in one's mind.

I said hesitantly, 'I work it out as £1,650,000!'

Coertze nodded in satisfaction. 'That is the figure I got. And there's the jewels on top of that.'

I had my own ideas about the jewels. Aristide had been right when he said that gold is anonymous – but jewels aren't. Jewels have a personality of their own and can be traced too easily. If I had my way the jewels would stay in the tunnel. But that I had to lead up to easily.

Walker said, 'That's over half a million each.'

I said, 'Call it half a million each, net. The odd £150,000 can go to expenses. By the time this is through we'll have spent more than we've put in the kitty.'

I returned to the point at issue. 'All right, we have 330 bars of gold. What do we do with them?'

Walker said meditatively. 'There's a cellar in the house.'

'That's a start, anyway.'

He said, 'You know the fantastic thought I had in that vault? I thought it looked just like a builder's yard with a lot of bricks

71

lying all over the place. Why couldn't we build a wall in the cellar?'

I looked at Coertze and he looked at me, and we both burst out laughing.

'What's funny about that?' asked Walker plaintively.

'Nothing,' I said, still spluttering. 'It's perfect, that's all.'

Coertze said, grinning, 'I'm a fine bricklayer when the rates of pay are good.'

A voice started to bleat in my ear and I turned round. It was an itinerant lottery-ticket seller poking a sheaf of tickets at me. I waved him away, but Coertze, in a good mood for once, said tolerantly, 'No, man, let's have one. No harm in taking out insurance.'

The ticket was a hundred pesetas, so we scraped it together from the change lying on the table, and then we went back to the flat.

V

The next day we started work in earnest. I stayed with *Sanford*, getting her ready for sea by dint of much bullying of the chandler and the sailmaker. By the end of the week I was satisfied that she was ready and was able to leave for anywhere in the world.

Coertze and Walker worked up at the house, rehabilitating the boat-shed and the slip and supervising the local labour they had found through Metcalfe's kind offices. Coertze said, 'You have no trouble if you treat these wogs just the same as the Kaffirs back home.' I wasn't so sure of that, but everything seemed to go all right.

By the time Metcalfe came back from whatever nefarious enterprise he had been on, we were pretty well finished and ready to leave. I said nothing to Metcalfe about this, feeling that the less he knew, the better.

When I'd got *Sanford* ship-shape I went over to Metcalfe's Fairmile to pay my promised visit. A fair-haired young man who was flushing the decks with a hose said, 'I guess you must be Halloran. I'm Krupke, Metcalfe's side-kick.'

'Is he around?'

Krupke shook his head. 'He went off with that friend of yours – Walker. He said I was to show you around if you came aboard.'

I said, 'You're an American, aren't you?'

He grinned. 'Yep, I'm from Milwaukee. Didn't fancy going back to the States after the war, so I stayed on here. Hell, I was only a kid then, not more'n twenty, so I thought that since Uncle Sam paid my fare out here, I might as well take advantage of it.'

I thought he was probably a deserter and couldn't go back to the States, although there might have been an amnesty for deserters. I didn't know how the civil statute limitations worked in military law. I didn't say anything about that, though – renegades are touchy and sometimes unaccountably patriotic.

The wheelhouse – which Krupke called the 'deckhouse' – was well fitted. There were two echo sounders, one with a recording pen. Engine control was directly under the helmsman's hand and the windows in front were fitted with Kent screens for bad weather. There was a big marine radio transceiver – and there was radar.

I put my hand on the radar display and said, 'What range does this have?'

'It's got several ranges,' he said. 'You pick the one that's best at the time. I'll show you.'

He snapped a switch and turned a knob. After a few seconds the screen lit up and I could see a tiny plan of the harbour as the scanner revolved. Even *Sanford* was visible as one splotch among many.

'That's for close work,' said Krupke, and turned a knob with a click. 'This is maximum range – fifteen miles, but you won't see much while we're in harbour.'

The landward side of the screen was now too cluttered to be of any use, but to seaward, I saw a tiny speck. 'What's that?'

He looked at his watch. 'That must be the ferry from Gibraltar. It's ten miles away – you can see the mileage marked on the grid.'

I said, 'This gadget must be handy for making a landfall at night.'

'Sure,' he said. 'All you have to do is to match the screen profile with the chart. Doesn't matter if there's no moon or if there's a fog.'

I wished I could have a set like that on *Sanford* but it's difficult installing radar on a sailing vessel – there are too many lines to catch in the antenna. Anyway, we wouldn't have the power to run it.

I looked around the wheelhouse. 'With all this gear you can't need much of a crew, even though she is a biggish boat,' I said. 'What crew do you have?'

'Me and Metcalfe can run it ourselves,' said Krupke. 'Our trips aren't too long. But usually we have another man with us – that

73

Moroccan you've got on *Sanford*.'

I stayed aboard the Fairmile for a long time, but Metcalfe and Walker didn't show up, so after a while I went back to Metcalfe's flat. Coertze was already there, but there was no sign of the others, so we went to have dinner as a twosome.

Over dinner I said, 'We ought to be getting away soon. Everything is fixed at this end and we'd be wasting time if we stayed any longer.'

'*Ja*,' Coertze agreed. 'This isn't a pleasure trip.'

We went back to the flat and found it empty, apart from the servants. Coertze went to his room and I read desultorily from a magazine. About ten o'clock I heard someone coming in and looked up.

I was immediately boiling with fury.

Walker was drunk – blind, paralytic drunk. He was clutching on to Metcalfe and sagging at the knees, his face slack and his bleared eyes wavering unseeingly about him. Metcalfe was a little under the weather himself, but not too drunk. He gave Walker a hitch to prevent him from falling, and said cheerily, 'We went to have a night on the town, but friend Walker couldn't take it. You'd better help me dump him on his bed.'

I helped Metcalfe support Walker to his room and we laid him on his bed. Coertze, dozing in the other bed, woke up and said, 'What's happening?'

Metcalfe said, 'Your pal's got no head for liquor. He passed out on me.'

Coertze looked at Walker, then at me, his black eyebrows drawing angrily over his eyes. I made a sign for him to keep quiet.

Metcalfe stretched and said, 'Well, I think I'll turn in myself.' He looked at Walker and there was an edge of contempt to his voice. 'He'll be all right in the morning, barring a hell of a hangover. I'll tell Ismail to make him a prairie oyster for breakfast.' He turned to Coertze. 'What do you call it in Afrikaans?'

' *'n regmaker*,' Coertze growled.

Metcalfe laughed. 'That's right. A *regmaker*. That was the first word I ever learned in Afrikaans.' He went to the door. 'See you in the morning,' he said, and he was gone.

I closed the door. 'The damn' fool,' I said feelingly.

Coertze got out of bed and grabbed hold of Walker, shaking him. 'Walker,' he shouted. 'Did you tell him anything?'

Walker's head flapped sideways and he began to snore. I took Coertze's shoulder. 'Be quiet; you'll tell the whole household,' I said. 'It's no use, anyway; you won't get any sense out of him tonight. He's unconscious. Leave it till morning.'

Coertze shook off my hand and turned. He had a black anger in him. 'I told you,' he said in a suppressed voice. 'I told you he was no good. Who knows what the *dronkie* said?'

I took off Walker's shoes and covered him with a blanket. 'We'll find out tomorrow,' I said. 'And I mean *we*. Don't you go off pop at him, you'll scare the liver out of him and he'll close up tight.'

'I'll *donner* him up,' said Coertze grimly. 'That's God's truth.'

'You'll leave him alone,' I said sharply. 'We may be in enough trouble without fighting among ourselves. We need Walker.'

Coertze snorted.

I said, 'Walker has done a job here that neither of us could have done. He has a talent for acting the damn' fool in a believable manner.' I looked down at him, then said bitterly, 'It's a pity he can be a damn' fool without the acting. Anyway, we may need him again, so you leave him alone. We'll both talk to him tomorrow, together.'

Coertze grudgingly gave his assent and I went to my room.

VI

I was up early next morning, but not as early as Metcalfe, who had already gone out. I went in to see Walker and found that Coertze was up and half dressed. Walker lay on his bed, snoring. I took a glass of water and poured it over his head. I was in no mood to consider Walker's feelings.

He stirred and moaned and opened his eyes just as Coertze seized the carafe and emptied it over him. He sat spluttering, then sagged back. 'My head,' he said, and put his hands to his temples.

Coertze seized him by the front of the shirt. '*Jou goggamannetjie*, what did you say to Metcalfe?' He shook Walker violently. 'What did you tell him?'

This treatment was doing Walker's aching head no good, so I said, 'Take it easy; I'll talk to him.'

Coertze let go and I stood over Walker, waiting until he had recovered his wits. Then I said, 'You got drunk last night, you stupid fool, and of all people to get drunk with you had to pick Metcalfe.'

Walker looked up, the pain of his monumental hangover filming his eyes. I sat on the bed. 'Now, did you tell him anything about the gold?'

'No,' cried Walker. 'No, I didn't.'

I said evenly, 'Don't tell us any lies, because if we catch you out in a lie you know what we'll do to you.'

He shot a frightened glance at Coertze who was glowering in the background and closed his eyes. 'I can't remember,' he said. 'It's a blank; I can't remember.'

That was better; he was probably telling the truth now. The total blackout is a symptom of alcoholism. I thought about it for a while and came to the conclusion that even if Walker hadn't told Metcalfe about the gold he had probably blown his cover sky high. Under the influence, the character he had built up would have been irrevocably smashed and he would have reverted to his alcoholic and unpleasant self.

Metcalfe was sharp – he wouldn't have survived in his nefarious career otherwise. The change in character of Walker would be the tip-off that there was something odd about old pal Halloran and his crew. That would be enough for Metcalfe to check further. We would have to work on the assumption that Metcalfe would consider us worthy of further study.

I said, 'What's done is done,' and looked at Walker. His eyes were downcast and his fingers were nervously scrabbling at the edge of the blanket.

'Look at me,' I said, and his eyes rose slowly to meet mine. 'I think you're telling the truth,' I said coldly. 'But if I catch you in a lie it will be the worse for you. And if you take another drink on this trip I'll break your back. You think you're scared of Coertze here; but you'll have more reason to be scared of me if you take just one more drink. Understand?'

He nodded.

'I don't care how much you drink once this thing is finished. You'll probably drink yourself to death in six months, but that's got nothing to do with me. But just one more drink on this trip and you're a dead man.'

He flinched and I turned to Coertze. 'Now, leave him alone; he'll behave.'

Coertze said, 'Just let me get at him. Just once,' he pleaded.

'It's finished,' I said impatiently. 'We have to decide what to do next. Get your things packed – we're moving out.'

'What about Metcalfe?'

'I'll tell him we want to see some festival in Spain.'

'What festival?'

'How do I know which festival? There's always some goddamn festival going on in Spain; I'll pick the most convenient. We sail

76

this afternoon as soon as I can get harbour clearance.'

'I still think I could do something about Metcalfe,' said Coertze meditatively.

'Leave Metcalfe alone,' I said. 'He *may* not suspect anything at all, but if you try to beat him up then he'll *know* there's something fishy. We don't want to tangle with Metcalfe if we can avoid it. He's bigger than we are.'

We packed our bags and went to the boat, Walker very quiet and trailing in the rear. Moulay Idriss was squatting on the fore-deck smoking a *kif* cigarette. We went below and started to stow our gear.

I had just pulled out the chart which covered the Straits of Gibraltar in preparation for planning our course when Coertze came aft and said in a low voice, 'I think someone's been searching the boat.'

'What the hell!' I said. Metcalfe *had* left very early that morning – he would have had plenty of time to give *Sanford* a good going over. 'The furnaces?' I said.

We had disguised the three furnaces as well as we could. The carbon clamps had been taken off and scattered in tool boxes in the forecastle where they would look just like any other junk that accumulates over a period. The main boxes with the heavy transformers were distributed about *Sanford*, one cemented under the cabin sole, another disguised as a receiving set complete with the appropriate knobs and dials, and the third built into a marine battery in the engine space.

It is doubtful if Metcalfe would know what they were if he saw them, but the fact that they were masquerading in innocence would make him wonder a lot. It would be a certain clue that we were up to no good.

A check over the boat showed that everything was in order. Apart from the furnaces, and the spare graphite mats which lined the interior of the double coach roof, there was nothing on board to distinguish us from any other cruising yacht in these waters.

I said, 'Perhaps the Moroccan has been doing some exploring on his own account.'

Coertze swore. 'If he's been poking his nose in where it isn't wanted I'll throw him overboard.'

I went on deck. The Moroccan was still squatting on the fore-deck. I said interrogatively, 'Mr Metcalfe?'

He stretched an arm and pointed across the harbour to the Fairmile. I put the dinghy over the side and rowed across. Metcalfe hailed me as I got close. 'How's Walker?'

'Feeling sorry for himself,' I said, as Metcalfe took the painter. 'A pity it happened; he'll probably be as sick as a dog when we get under way.'

'You leaving?' said Metcalfe in surprise.

I said, 'I didn't get the chance to tell you last night. We're heading for Spain.' I gave him my prepared story, then said, 'I don't know if we'll be coming back this way. Walker will, of course, but Coertze and I might go back to South Africa by way of the east coast.' I thought that there was nothing like confusing the issue.

'I'm sorry about that,' said Metcalfe. 'I was going to ask you to design a dinghy for me while you were here.'

'Tell you what,' I said. 'I'll write to Cape Town and get the yard to send you a Falcon kit. It's on me; all you've got to do is pay for the shipping.'

'Well, thanks,' said Metcalfe. 'That's decent of you.' He seemed pleased.

'It's as much as I can do after all the hospitality we've had here,' I said.

He stuck out his hand and I took it. 'Best of luck, Hal, in all your travels. I hope your project is successful.'

I was incautious. 'What project?' I asked sharply.

'Why, the boatyard you're planning. You don't have anything else in mind, do you?'

I cursed myself and smiled weakly. 'No, of course not.' I turned to get into the dinghy, and Metcalfe said quietly, 'You're not cut out for my kind of life, Hal. Don't try it if you're thinking of it. It's tough and there's too much competition.'

As I rowed back to *Sanford* I wondered if that was a veiled warning that he was on to our scheme. Metcalfe was an honest man by his rather dim lights and wouldn't willingly cut down a friend. But he would if the friend didn't get out of his way.

At three that afternoon we cleared Tangier harbour and I set course for Gibraltar. We were on our way, but we had left too many mistakes behind us.

4 *Francesca*

When we were beating through the Straits Coertze suggested that we should head straight for Italy. I said, 'Look, we've told Metcalfe we were going to Spain, so that's where we are going.'

He thumped the cockpit coaming. 'But we haven't time.'

'We've got to make time,' I said doggedly. 'I told you there would be snags which would use up our month's grace; this is one of the snags. We're going to take a month getting to Italy instead of a fortnight, which cuts us down to two weeks in hand – but we've got to do it. Maybe we can make it up in Italy.'

He grumbled at that, saying I was unreasonably frightened of Metcalfe. I said, 'You've waited fifteen years for this opportunity – you can afford to wait another fortnight. We're going to Gibraltar, to Malaga and Barcelona; we're going to the Riviera, to Nice and to Monte Carlo; after that, Italy. We're going to watch bullfights and gamble in casinos and do everything that every other tourist does. We're going to be the most innocent people that Metcalfe ever laid eyes on.'

'But Metcalfe's back in Tangier.'

I smiled thinly. 'He's probably in Spain right now. He could have passed us any time in that Fairmile of his. He could have flown or taken the ferry to Gibraltar, dammit. I think he'll keep an eye on us if he reckons we're up to something.'

'Damn Walker,' burst out Coertze.

'Agreed,' I said. 'But that's water under the bridge.'

I was adding up the mistakes we had made. Number one was Walker's incautious statement to Aristide that he had drawn money on a letter of credit. That was a lie – a needless one, too – I had the letter of credit and Walker could have said so. Keeping control of the finances of the expedition was the only way I had of making sure that Coertze didn't get the jump on me. I still didn't know the location of the gold.

Now, Aristide would naturally make enquiries among his fellow bankers about the financial status of this rich Mr Walker. He would get the information quite easily – all bankers hang together and the hell with ethics – and he would find that Mr Walker had *not* drawn any money from any bank in Tangier. He might not be too perturbed about that, but he might ask Metcalfe about it, and

Metcalfe would find it another item to add to his list of suspicions. He would pump Aristide to find that Walker and Halloran had taken an undue interest in the flow of gold in and out of Tangier.

He would go out to the Casa Saeta and sniff around. He would find nothing there to conflict with Walker's cover story, but it would be precisely the cover story that he suspected most – Walker having blown hell out of it when he was drunk. The mention of gold would set his ears a-prick – a man like Metcalfe would react very quickly to the smell of gold – and if I were Metcalfe I would take great interest in the movements of the cruising yacht, *Sanford*.

All this was predicated on the fact that Walker had *not* told about the gold when he was drunk. If he *had*, then the balloon had really gone up.

We put into Gibraltar and spent a day rubber-necking at the Barbary apes and looking at the man-made caves. Then we sailed for Malaga and heard a damn' sight more flamenco music than we could stomach.

It was on the second day in Malaga, when Walker and I went out to the gipsy caves like good tourists, that I realized we were being watched. We were bumping into a sallow young man with a moustache everywhere we went. He sat far removed when we ate in a sidewalk café, he appeared in the yacht basin, he applauded the flamenco dancers when we went to see the gipsies.

I said nothing to the others, but it only went to confirm my estimate of Metcalfe's abilities. He would have friends in every Mediterranean port, and it wouldn't be difficult to pass the word around. A yacht's movements are not easy to disguise, and he was probably sitting in Tangier like a spider in the centre of a web, receiving phone calls from wherever we went. He would know all our movements and our expenditure to the last peseta.

The only thing to do was to act the innocent and hope that we could wear him out, string him on long enough so that he would conclude that his suspicions were unfounded, after all.

In Barcelona we went to a bullfight – the three of us. That was after I had had a little fun in trying to spot Metcalfe's man. He wasn't difficult to find if you were looking for him and turned out to be a tall, lantern-jawed cut-throat who carried out the same routine as the man in Malaga.

I was reasonably sure that if anyone was going to burgle *Sanford* it would be one of Metcalfe's friends. The word would have been passed round that we were his meat and so lesser fry would leave us alone. I hired a watchman who looked as though he would sell his grandmother for ten pesetas and we all went to the bullfight.

Before I left I was careful to set the stage. I had made a lot of phoney notes concerning the costs of setting up a boatyard in Spain, together with a lot of technical stuff I had picked up. I also left a rough itinerary of our future movements as far as Greece and a list of addresses of people to be visited. I then measured to a millimetre the position in which each paper was lying.

When we got back the watchman said that all had been quiet, so I paid him off and he went away. But the papers had been moved, so the locked cabin had been successfully burgled in spite of – or probably because of – the watchman. I wondered how much he had been paid – and I wondered if my plant had satisfied Metcalfe that we were wandering innocents.

From Barcelona we struck across the Gulf of Lions to Nice, giving Majorca a miss because time was getting short. Again I went about my business of visiting boatyards and again I spotted the watcher, but this time I made a mistake.

I told Coertze.

He boiled over. 'Why didn't you tell me before?' he demanded.

'What was the point?' I said. 'We can't do anything about it.'

'Can't we?' he said darkly, and fell into silence.

Nothing much happened in Nice. It's a pleasant place if you haven't urgent business elsewhere, but we stayed just long enough to make our cover real and then we sailed the few miles to Monte Carlo, which again is a nice town for the visiting tourist.

In Monte Carlo I stayed aboard *Sanford* in the evening while Coertze and Walker went ashore. There was not much to do in the way of maintenance beyond the usual house-keeping jobs, so I relaxed in the cockpit enjoying the quietness of the night. The others stayed out late and when they came back Walker was unusually silent.

Coertze had gone below when I said to Walker, 'What's the matter? The cat got your tongue? How did you like Monte?'

He jerked his head at the companionway. 'He clobbered someone.'

I went cold. 'Who?'

'A chap was following us all afternoon. Coertze spotted him and said that he'd deal with it. We let this bloke follow us until it got dark and then Coertze led him into an alley and beat him up.'

I got up and went below. Coertze was in the galley bathing swollen knuckles. I said, 'So you've done it at last. You must use your goddamn fists and not your brains. You're worse than Walker; at least you can say he's a sick man.'

Coertze looked at me in surprise. 'What's the matter?'

'I hear you hit someone.'

Coertze looked at his fist and grinned at me. 'He'll never bother us again – he'll be in hospital for a month.' He said this with pride, for God's sake.

'You've blown it,' I said tightly. 'I'd just about got Metcalfe to the point where he must have been convinced that we were OK. Now you've beaten up one of his men, so he knows we are on to him, and he knows we must be hiding something. You might as well have phoned him up and said, "We've got some gold coming up; come and take it from us." You're a damn' fool.'

His face darkened. 'No one can talk to me like that.' He raised his fist.

'I *am* talking to you like that,' I said. 'And if you lay one finger on me you can kiss the gold goodbye. You can't sail this or any other boat worth a damn, and Walker won't help you – he hates your guts. You hit me and you're out for good. I know you could probably break me in two and you're welcome to try, but it'll cost you a cool half-million for the pleasure.'

This showdown had been coming for a long time.

He hesitated uncertainly. 'You damned Englishman,' he said.

'Go ahead – hit me,' I said, and got ready to take his rush.

He relaxed and pointed his finger at me threateningly. 'You wait until this is over,' he said. 'Just you wait – we'll sort it out then.'

'All right, we'll sort it out then,' I said. 'But until then I'm the boss. Understand?'

His face darkened again. 'No one bosses me,' he blustered.

'Right,' I said. 'Then we start going back the way we came – Nice, Barcelona, Malaga, Gibraltar. Walker will help me sail the boat, but he won't do a damn' thing for you.' I turned away.

'Wait a minute,' said Coertze and I turned back. 'All right,' he said hoarsely. 'But wait till this is over; by God, you'll have to watch yourself then.'

'But until then I'm the boss?'

'Yes,' he said sullenly.

'And you take my orders?'

His fists tightened but he held himself in. 'Yes.'

'Then here's your first one. You don't do a damn' thing without consulting me first.' I turned to go up the companionway, got half-way up, then had a sudden thought and went below again.

I said, 'And there's another thing I want to tell you. Don't get any ideas about double-crossing me or Walker, because if you do, you'll not only have me to contend with but Metcalfe as well. I'd be glad to give Metcalfe a share if you did that. And there wouldn't be a place in the world you could hide if Metcalfe got after you.'

He stared at me sullenly and turned away. I went on deck.

Walker was sitting in the cockpit. 'Did you hear that?' I said.

He nodded. 'I'm glad you included me on your side.'

I was exasperated and shaking with strain. It was no fun tangling with a bear like Coertze – he was all reflex and no brain and he could have broken me as anyone else would break a match-stick. He was a man who had to be governed like a fractious horse.

I said, 'Dammit, I don't know why I came on this crazy trip with a *dronkie* like you and a maniac like Coertze. First you put Metcalfe on our tracks and then he clinches it.'

Walker said softly, 'I didn't mean to do it. I don't think I told Metcalfe anything.'

'I don't think so either, but you gave the game away somehow.' I stretched, easing my muscles. 'It doesn't matter; we either get the gold or we don't. That's all there is to it.'

Walker said, 'You can rely on me to help you against Coertze, if it comes to that.'

I smiled. Relying on Walker was like relying on a fractured mast in a hurricane – the hurricane being Coertze. He affected people like that; he had a blind, elemental force about him. An overpowering man, altogether.

I patted Walker on the knee. 'OK. You're my man from now on.' I let the hardness come into my voice because Walker had to be kept to heel, too. 'But keep off the booze. I meant what I said in Tangier.'

II

The next stop was Rapallo, which was first choice as our Italian base, provided we could get fixed up with a suitable place to do our work. We motored into the yacht basin and damned if I didn't see a Falcon drawn up on the hard. I knew the firm had sold a few kits in Europe but I didn't expect to see any of them.

As we had come from a foreign port there were the usual Customs and medical queries – a mere formality. Yachtsmen are very well treated in the Mediterranean. I chatted with the Customs men, discussing yachts and yachting and said that I was a boat designer and builder myself. I gave the standard talk and said that I was thinking of opening a yard in the Mediterranean, pointing to the Falcon as a sample of my work.

They were impressed at that. Anyone whose product was used six thousand miles from where it was made must obviously be someone to be reckoned with. They didn't know much about local conditions but they gave me some useful addresses.

I was well satisfied. If I had to impress people with my integrity I might as well start with the Customs. That stray Falcon came in very handy.

I went ashore, leaving Walker and Coertze aboard by instruction. There was no real need for such an order but I wanted to test my new-found ascendancy over them. Coertze had returned to his old self, more or less. His mood was equable and he cracked as few jokes as usual – the point being that he cracked jokes at all. But I had no illusions that he had forgotten anything. The Afrikaner is notorious for his long memory for wrongs.

I went up to the Yacht Club and presented my credentials. One of the most pleasant things about yachting is that you are sure of a welcome in any part of the world. There is a camaraderie among yachtsmen which is very heartening in a world which is on the point of blowing itself to hell. This international brotherhood, together with the fact that the law of the sea doesn't demand a licence to operate a small boat, makes deep-sea cruising one of the most enjoyable experiences in the world.

I chatted with the secretary of the club, who spoke very good English, and talked largely of my plans. He took me into the bar and bought me a drink and introduced me to several of the members and visiting yachtsmen. After we had chatted at some length about the voyage from South Africa I got down to finding out about the local boatyards.

On the way round the Mediterranean I had come to the conclusion that my cover story need not be a cover at all – it could be the real thing. I had become phlegmatic about the gold, especially after the antics of Walker and Coertze, and my interest in the commercial possibilities of the Mediterranean was deepening. I was nervous and uncertain as to whether the three of us could carry the main job through – the three-way pull of character was causing tensions which threatened to tear the entire fabric of the plan apart.

So I was hedging my bet and looking into the business possibilities seriously.

The lust for gold, which I had felt briefly in Aristide's vault, was still there but lying dormant. Still, it was enough to drive me on, enough to make me out-face Coertze and Walker and to try to circumvent Metcalfe.

But if I had known then that other interests were about to enter the field of battle I might have given up there and then, in the bar of the Rapallo Yacht Club.

During the afternoon I visited several boatyards. This was not all business prospecting – *Sanford* had come a long way and her bottom was foul. She needed taking out of the water and scraping, which would give her another half-knot. We had agreed that this would be the ostensible reason for pulling her out of the water, and a casual word dropped in the Yacht Club that I had found something wrong with her keel bolts would be enough excuse for making the exchange of keels. Therefore I was looking for a quiet place where we could cast our golden keel.

I was perturbed when I suddenly discovered that I could not spot Metcalfe's man. If he had pulled off his watchdogs because he thought we were innocent, then that was all right. But it seemed highly unlikely now that Coertze had given the game away. What seemed very likely was that something was being cooked up – and whatever was going to happen would certainly involve *Sanford*. I dropped my explorations and hurried back to the yacht basin.

'I wasn't followed,' I said to Coertze.

'I told you my way was best,' he said. 'They've been frightened off.'

'If you think that Metcalfe would be frightened off because a hired wharf rat was beaten up, you'd better think again,' I said. I looked hard at him. 'If you go ashore to stretch your legs can I trust you not to hammer anyone you might think is looking at you cross-eyed?'

He tried to hold my eye and then his gaze wavered. 'OK,' he said sullenly. 'I'll be careful. But you'll find out that my way is best in the end.'

'All right; you and Walker can go ashore to get a bite to eat.' I turned to Walker. 'No booze, remember. Not even wine.'

Coertze said, 'I'll see to that. We'll stick close together, won't we?' He clapped Walker on the back.

They climbed on to the dockside and I watched them go, Coertze striding out and Walker hurrying to keep pace. I wondered what

Metcalfe was up to, but finding that profitless, I went below to review our needs for the next few days. I stretched on the port settee and must have been very tired, because when I woke it was dark except for the lights of the town glimmering through the ports.

And it was a movement on deck that had wakened me!

I lay there for a moment until I heard another sound, then I rose cautiously, went to the companionway very quietly and raised my head to deck level. 'Coertze?' I called softly.

A voice said, 'Is that Signor Halloran?' The voice was very feminine.

I came up into the cockpit fast. 'Who is that?'

A dark shape moved towards me. 'Mr Halloran, I want to talk to you.' She spoke good English with but a trace of Italian accent and her voice was pleasantly low and even.

I said, 'Who are you?'

'Surely introductions would be more in order if we could see each other.' There was a hint of command in her voice as though she was accustomed to getting her own way.

'OK,' I said. 'Let's go below.'

She slipped past me and went down the companionway and I followed, switching on the main cabin lights. She turned so that I could see her, and she was something worth looking at. Her hair was raven black and swept up into smooth wings on each side of her head as though to match the winged eyebrows which were dark over cool, hazel eyes. Her cheekbones were high, giving a trace of hollow in the cheeks, but she didn't look like one of the fashionably emaciated models one sees in *Vogue*.

She was dressed in a simple woollen sheath which showed off a good figure to perfection. It might have been bought from a local department store or it might have come from a Parisian fashion house; I judged the latter – you can't be married to a woman for long without becoming aware of the price of feminine fripperies.

She carried her shoes in her hand and stood in her stockinged feet, that was a point in her favour. A hundred-pound girl in a spike heel comes down with the force of two tons, and that's hell on deck planking. She either knew something about yachts or . . .

I pointed to the shoes and said, 'You're a pretty inexperienced burglar. You ought to have those slung round your neck to leave your hands free.'

She laughed. 'I'm not a burglar, Mr Halloran, I just don't like shoes very much; and I have been on yachts before.'

I moved towards her. She was tall, almost as tall as myself. I

86

judged her to be in her late twenties or possibly, but improbably, her early thirties. Her lips were pale and she wore very little make-up. She was a very beautiful woman.

'You have the advantage of me,' I said.

'I am the Contessa di Estrenoli.'

I gestured at the settee. 'Well, sit down, Contessa.'

'Not Contessa – Madame,' she said, and sat down, pulling the dress over her knees with one hand and placing the shoes at her side. 'In our association together you will call me Madame.'

I sat down slowly on the opposite settee. Metcalfe certainly came up with some surprises. I said carefully, 'So we are going to be associated together? I couldn't think of a better person to be associated with. When do we start?'

There was frost in her voice. 'Not the kind of association you are obviously thinking of, Mr Halloran.' She went off at a tangent. 'I saw your . . . er . . . companions ashore. They didn't see me – I wanted to talk to you alone.'

'We're alone,' I said briefly.

She gathered her thoughts, then said precisely, 'Mr Halloran, you have come to Italy with Mr Coertze and Mr Walker to remove something valuable from the country. You intend to do this illicitly and illegally, therefore your whole plan depends on secrecy; you cannot – shall we say "operate" – if someone is looking over your shoulder. I intend to look over your shoulder.'

I groaned mentally. Metcalfe had the whole story. Apparently the only thing he didn't know was where the treasure was hidden. The girl was quite right when she said that it couldn't be lifted if we were under observation, so he was coming right out and asking for a cut. Walker really *must* have talked in Tangier if Metcalfe could pinpoint it as close as Rapallo.

I said, 'OK, Contessa; how much does Metcalfe want?'

She raised her winged eyebrows. 'Metcalfe?'

'Yes, Metcalfe; your boss.'

She shook her head. 'I know of no Metcalfe, whoever he is. And I am my own boss, I assure you of that.'

I think I kept my face straight. The surprises were certainly piling up. If this Estrenoli woman was mixed up with Metcalfe, then why would she deny it? If she wasn't, then who the devil was she – and how did she know of the treasure?

I said, 'Supposing I tell you to jump over the side?'

She smiled. 'Then you will never get these valuables out of Italy.'

There seemed to be a concession there, so I said, 'And if I *don't* tell you to jump over the side, then we *will* get the stuff out of the country, is that it?'

'Some of it,' she compromised. 'But without my co-operation you will spend a long time in an Italian prison.'

That was certainly something to think about when I had time. I said, 'All right; who are you, and what do you know?'

'I knew that the news was out on the waterfront to watch for the yacht *Sanford*. I knew that the yacht was owned by Mr Halloran and that Mr Coertze and Mr Walker were his companions. That was enough for me.'

'And what has the Contessa di Estrenoli got to do with waterfront rumours? What has an Italian aristocrat got to do with the jailbirds that news was intended for?'

She smiled and said, 'I have strange friends, Mr Halloran. I learn all that is interesting on the waterfront. I realize now that perhaps your Mr Metcalfe was responsible for the circulation of those instructions.'

'So you learned that a yacht and three men were coming to Rapallo, and you said to yourself, "Ah, these three men are coming to take something out of Italy illegally." ' I said with heavy irony. 'You'll have to do better than that, Contessa.'

'But you see, I know Mr Coertze and Mr Walker,' she said. 'The heavy and clumsy Mr Coertze has been to Italy quite often. I have always known about him and I always had him watched.' She smiled. 'He was like a dog at a rabbit hole who yelps because it is too small and he cannot get in. He always left Italy empty-handed.'

That did it. Coertze must have shown his hand on one of his periodic trips to Italy. But how the devil did she know Walker? He hadn't been to Italy recently – or had he?

She continued. 'So when I heard that Mr Coertze was returning with Mr Walker and the unknown Mr Halloran, then I knew that something big was going to happen. Then you were ready to take away whatever was buried, Mr Halloran.'

'So you don't know exactly what we're after?'

'I know that it is very valuable,' she said simply.

'I might be an archaeologist,' I said.

She laughed. 'No, you are not an archaeologist, Mr Halloran; you are a boat-builder.' She saw the surprise in my eyes, and added, 'I know a lot about you.'

I said, 'Let's quit fencing; how do you know about whatever it is?'

She said slowly, 'A man called Alberto Corso had been writing a letter to my father. He was killed before the letter was finished, so there was not all the information that could be desired. But there was enough for me to know that Mr Coertze must be watched.'

I snapped my fingers. 'You're the Count's little daughter. You're . . . er . . . Francesca.'

She inclined her head. 'I am the daughter of a count.'

'Not so little now,' I said. 'So the Count is after the loot.'

Her eyes widened. 'Oh, no. My father knows nothing about it. Nothing at all.'

I thought that could do with a bit of explanation and was just going to query the statement when someone jumped on deck. 'Who is that?' asked the Contessa.

'Probably the others coming back,' I said, and waited. Perhaps there were to be some more surprises before the evening was out.

Walker came down the companionway and stopped when he saw her. 'Oh,' he said. 'I hope I'm not butting in.'

I said, 'This is the Contessa di Estrenoli – Mr Walker.' I watched him to see if he recognized her, but he didn't. He looked at her as one looks at a beautiful woman and said, in Italian, 'A pleasure, signora.'

She smiled at him and said, 'Don't you know me, Mr Walker? I bandaged your leg when you were brought into the hill camp during the war.'

He looked at her closely and said incredulously, 'Francesca!'

'That's right; I'm Francesca.'

'You've changed,' he said. 'You've grown up. I mean . . . er . . .' He was confused.

She looked at him. 'Yes, we've all changed,' she said. I thought I detected a note of regret. They chatted for a few minutes and then she picked up her shoes. 'I must go,' she said.

Walker said, 'But you've only just got here.'

'No, I have an appointment in twenty minutes.' She rose and went to the companionway and I escorted her on deck.

She said, 'I can understand Coertze, and now I can understand Walker; but I cannot understand you, Mr Halloran. Why are you doing this? You are a successful man, you have made a name in an honourable profession. Why should you do this?'

I sighed and said, 'I had a reason in the beginning; maybe I still have it – I don't know. But having come this far I must go on.'

She nodded, then said, 'There is a café on the waterfront called the Three Fishes. Meet me there at nine tomorrow morning. Come alone; don't bring Coertze or Walker. I never liked Coertze, and now I don't think I like Walker any more. I would prefer not to talk to them.'

'All right,' I said. 'I'll be there.'

She jumped lightly on the jetty and swayed a little as she put her shoes on. I watched her go away, hearing the sharp click of her heels long after the darkness had swallowed her. Then I went below.

Walker said, 'Where did she come from? How did she know we were here?'

'The gaff has been blown with a loud trumpeting noise,' I said. 'She knows all – or practically all – and she's putting the screws on.'

Walker's jaw dropped. 'She knows about the gold?'

'Yes,' I said. 'But I'm not going to talk about it till Coertze comes. No point in going over it twice.'

Walker protested, but swallowed his impatience when I made it clear that I wasn't going to talk, and sat wriggling on the settee. After half an hour we heard Coertze come on board.

He was affable – full of someone else's cooking for a change, and he'd had a few drinks. 'Man,' he said, 'these Italians can cook.'

'Francesca was here,' I said.

He looked at me, startled. 'The Count's daughter?'

'Yes.'

Walker said, 'I want to know how she found us.'

'What did the stuck-up bitch want?' asked Coertze.

I raised my eyebrows at that. Apparently the dislike between these two was mutual. 'She wants a cut of the treasure,' I said bluntly.

Coertze swore. 'How the hell did she get to know about it?'

'Alberto wrote a letter before he was killed.'

Coertze and Walker exchanged looks, and after a pregnant silence, Coertze said, 'So Alberto was going to give us away, after all.'

I said, 'He *did* give you away.'

'Then why is the gold still there?' demanded Coertze.

'The letter was incomplete,' I said. 'It didn't say exactly where the gold is.'

Coertze sighed windily. 'Well, there's not too much damage done.'

I fretted at his stupidity. 'How do you suppose we're going to get it out with half of Italy watching us?' I asked. 'She's been

90

on to you all the time – she's watched you every time you've been in Italy and she's been laughing at you. And she knows there's something big under way now.'

'That bitch would laugh at me,' said Coertze viciously. 'She always treated me like dirt. I suppose the Count has been laughing like hell, too.'

I rubbed my chin thoughtfully. 'She says the Count knows nothing about it. Tell me about him.'

'The Count? Oh, he's an old no-good now. He didn't get his estates back after the war – I don't know why – and he's as poor as a church mouse. He lives in a poky flat in Milan with hardly enough room to swing a cat.'

'Who supports him?'

Coertze shrugged. 'I dunno. Maybe she does – she can afford it. She married a Roman count; I heard he was stinking rich, so I suppose she passes on some of the housekeeping money to the old boy.'

'Why don't you like her?'

'Oh, she's one of these stuck-up society bitches – I never did like that kind. We get plenty in Houghton, but they're worse here. She wouldn't give me the time of day. Not like her old man. I get on well with him.'

I thought perhaps that on one of his visits to Italy Coertze had made a pass at her and been well and truly slapped down. A pass from Coertze would be clumsy and graceless, like being propositioned by a gorilla.

I said, 'Was she around often during the times you were in Italy?'

He thought about that, and said, 'Sometimes. She turned up at least once on every trip.'

'That's all she'd need. To locate you, I mean. She seems to have a circle of pretty useful friends and apparently they're not the crowd you'd think a girl like that would mix with. She picked up Metcalfe's signals to the Mediterranean ports and interpreted them correctly, so it looks as though she has brains as well as beauty.'

Coertze snorted. 'Beauty! She's a skinny bitch.'

She *had* got under his skin. I said, 'That may be, but she's got us cold. We can't do a damn' thing while she's on our necks. To say nothing of Metcalfe, who'll be on to us next. Funny that he hasn't shown his hand in Rapallo yet.'

'I tell you he's scared off,' growled Coertze.

I let that pass. 'Anyway, we can't do any heavy thinking about it until we find out exactly what she wants. I'm seeing her to-morrow morning, so perhaps I'll be able to tell you more after that.'

'I'll come with you,' said Coertze instantly.

'She wants to see me, not you,' I said. 'That was something she specified.'

'The bloody little bitch,' exploded Coertze.

'And for God's sake, think up another word; I'm tired of that one,' I said irritably.

He glowered at me. 'You falling for her?'

I said wearily, 'I don't know the woman – I've seen her for just fif-teen minutes. I'll be better able to tell you about that tomorrow, too.'

'Did she say anything about me?' asked Walker.

'No,' I lied. There wasn't any point in having both of them irritated at her – it was likely that we'd all have to work closely together, and the less friction the better. 'But I'd better see her alone.'

Coertze growled under his breath, and I said, 'Don't worry; neither she nor I know where the gold is. We still need you – she and I and Metcalfe. We mustn't forget Metcalfe.'

III

Early next morning I went to find the Three Fishes. It was just an ordinary dockside café, the kind of dump you find on any waterfront. Having marked it, I went for a stroll round the yacht basin, looking at the sleek sailing yachts and motor craft of the European rich. A lot were big boats needing a paid crew to handle them while the owner and his guests took it easy, but some were more to my taste – small, handy sailing cruisers run by their owners who weren't afraid of a bit of work.

After a pleasant hour I began to feel hungry so I went back to the Three Fishes for a late breakfast and got there on the dot of nine. She wasn't there, so I ordered breakfast and it turned out better than I expected. I had just started to eat when she slid into the seat opposite.

'Sorry I'm late,' she said.

'That's OK.'

She was wearing slacks and sweater, the kind of clothes you see in the women's magazines but seldom in real life. The sweater suited her.

She looked at my plate and said, 'I had an early breakfast, but I think I'll have another. Do you mind if I join you?'

'It's your party.'

'The food is good here,' she said, and called a waiter, ordering in rapid Italian. I continued to eat and said nothing. It was up to her to make the first move. As I had said – it was her party.

She didn't say anything, either; but just watched me eat. When her own breakfast arrived she attacked it as though she hadn't eaten for a week. She was a healthy girl with a healthy appetite. I finished my breakfast and produced a packet of cigarettes. 'Do you mind?' I asked.

I caught her with her mouth full and she shook her head, so I lit a cigarette. At last she pushed her plate aside with a sigh and took the cigarette I offered. Do you know our *Espresso?*' she asked.

'Yes, I know it.'

She laughed. 'Oh, yes, I forgot that it must have penetrated even your Darkest Africa. It is supposed to be for after dinner, but I drink it all the time. Would you like some?'

I said that I would, so she called out to the waiter, '*Due Espressi,*' and turned back to me. 'Well, Mr Halloran, have you thought about our conversation of last night?'

I said I had thought about it.

'And so?'

'And so,' I repeated. 'Or more precisely – so what? I'll need to know a lot more about you before I start confiding in you, Contessa.'

She seemed put out. 'Don't call me Contessa,' she said pettishly. 'What do you want to know?'

I flicked ash into the ash-tray. 'For one thing, how did you intercept Metcalfe's message? It doesn't seem a likely thing for a Contessa to come across – just like that.'

'I told you I have friends,' she said coldly.

'Who are these friends?'

She sighed. 'You know that my father and I were rebels against the Fascist Government during the war?'

'You were with the partisans, I know.'

She gestured with her hand. 'All right, with the partisans, if you wish. Although do not let my friends hear you say that – the Communists have made it a dirty word. My friends were also partisans and I have never lost contact with them. You see, I was only a little girl at the time and they made me a sort of mascot of the brigade. After the war most of them went back to their work, but some of them had never known any sort of life other than killing Germans. It is a hard thing to forget, you understand?'

I said, 'You mean they'd had a taste of adventure, and liked it.'

'That is right. There was plenty of adventure even after the war. Some of them stopped killing Germans and started to kill Communists – Italian Communists. It was dreadful. But the Communists were too strong, anyway. A few turned to other adventures – some are criminals – nothing serious, you understand; some smuggling, some things worse, but nothing very terrible in most cases. Being criminals, they also know other criminals.'

I began to see how it had been worked; it was all very logical, really.

'There is a big man in Genoa, Torloni; he is a leader of criminals, a very big man in that sort of thing. He sent word to Savona, to Livorno, to Rapallo, to places as far south as Napoli, that he was interested in you and would pay for any information. He gave all your names and the name of your boat.'

That was the sort of pull Metcalfe would have. Probably this Torloni owed him a favour and was paying it off.

Francesca said, 'My friends heard the name – Coertze. It is very uncommon in Italy, and they knew I was interested in a man of that name, so I was told of this. When I also heard the name of Walker I was sure that something was happening.' She shrugged. 'And then there was this Halloran – you. I did not know about you, so I am finding out.'

'Has Torloni been told about us?'

She shook her head. 'I told my friends to see that Torloni was not told. My friends are very strong on this coast; during the war all these hills belonged to us – not to the Germans.'

I began to get the picture. Francesca had been the mascot and, besides, she was the daughter of the revered leader. She was the Lady of the Manor, the Young Mistress who could do no wrong.

It looked also as though, just by chance, Metcalfe had been stymied – temporarily, at least. But I was landed with Francesca and her gang of merry men who had the advantage of knowing just what they wanted.

I said, 'There's another thing. You said your father doesn't know anything about this. How can that be when Alberto Corso wrote him a letter?'

'I never gave it to him,' she said simply.

I looked at her quizzically. 'Is that how a daughter behaves to her father? Not only reading his correspondence, but with-holding it as well.'

'It was not like that at all,' she said sharply. 'I will tell you how it was.' She leaned her elbows on the table. 'I was very young during the war, but my father made me work, everyone had to work. It was one of my tasks to gather together the possessions of those who were killed so that useful things could be saved and anything personal could be passed on to the family.

'When Alberto was killed on the cliff I gathered his few things and I found the letter. It was addressed to my father and there were two pages, otherwise it was unfinished. I read it briefly and it seemed important, but how important it was I did not know because I was very young. I put it in my pocket to give to my father.

'But there was a German attack and we had to move. We sheltered in a farmhouse but we had to move even from there very quickly. Now, I carried my own possessions in a little tin box and that was left in the farmhouse. It was only in 1946 that I went back to the farm to thank those people – the first chance I had.

'They gave me wine and then the farmer's wife brought out the little box and asked if it was mine. I had forgotten all about it and I had forgotten what was in it.' She smiled. 'There was a doll – no, not a doll; what you call an . . . Eddy-bear?'

'A Teddy-bear.'

'That is right; a Teddy-bear – I have still got it. There were some other things and Alberto's letter was there also.'

I said, 'And you still didn't give it to your father. Why not?'

She thumped the table with a small fist. 'It is difficult for you to understand the Italy of just after the war, but I will try to explain. The Communists were very strong, especially here in the north, and they ruined my father after the war. They said he had been a collaborationist and that he had fought the Communist partisans instead of fighting the Fascists. My father, who had been fighting the Fascists all his life! They brought up false evidence and no one would listen to him.

'His estates had been confiscated by the Fascist Government and he could not get them back. How could he when Togliatti, the Vice-Premier of the Government, was the leader of the Italian Communist Party? They said, "No, this man was a collaborator, so he must be punished." But even with all their false evidence they dared not bring him to trial, but he could not get back his estates, and today he is a poor man.'

Francesca's eyes were full of tears. She wiped them with a tissue and said, 'Excuse me, but my feeling on this is strong.'

I said awkwardly, 'That's all right.'

She looked up and said, 'These Communists with their fighting against the Fascists. My father fought ten times harder than any of them. Have you heard of the 52nd Partisan Brigade?'

I shook my head.

'That was the famous Communist Brigade which captured Mussolini. The famous Garibaldi Brigade. Do you know how many men were in this so-famous Garibaldi Brigade in 1945?'

I said, 'I know very little about it.'

'Eighteen men,' she said contemptuously. 'Eighteen men called themselves the 52nd Brigade. My father commanded fifty times as many men. But when I went to Parma for the anniversary celebrations in 1949 the Garibaldi Brigade marched through the street and there were hundreds of them. All the Communist scum had crawled out of their holes now the war was over and it was safe. They marched through the streets and every man wore a red scarf about his neck and every man called himself a partisan. They even painted the statue of Garibaldi so that it had a red shirt and a red hat. So my friends and I do not call ourselves partisans, and you must not call us by that word the Communists have made a mockery of.'

She was shaking with rage. Her fists were clenched and she looked at me with eyes bright with unshed tears.

'The Communists ruined my father because they knew he was a strong man and because they knew he would oppose them in Italy. He was a liberal, he was for the middle of the road – the middle way. He who is in the middle of the road gets knocked down, but he could not understand that,' she said sombrely. 'He thought it was an honourable fight – as though the Communists have ever fought honourably.'

It was a moving story and typical of our times. I also observed that it fitted in with what Coertze had told me. I said, 'But the Communists are not nearly as strong today. Is it not possible for your father to appeal and to have his case reviewed?'

'Mud sticks, whoever throws it,' she said sadly. 'Besides, the war was a long time ago – people do not like to be reminded about those times – and people, especially officials, never like to admit their mistakes.'

She was realistic about the world and I realized that I must be realistic too. I said, 'But what has this got to do with the letter?'

'You wanted to know why I did not give the letter to my father

96

after the war; is that not so?'

'Yes.'

She smiled tightly. 'You must meet my father and then you would understand. You see, whatever you are looking for is valuable. I understood from Alberto's letter that there are papers and a lot of gold bars. Now, my father is an honourable man. He would return everything to the Government because from the Government it came. To him, it would be unthinkable to keep any of the gold for himself. It would be dishonourable.'

She looked down at the backs of her hands. 'Now, I am not an honourable woman. It hurts me to see my father so poor he has to live in a Milan slum, that he has to sell his furniture to buy food to eat. He is an old man – it is not right that he should live like that. But if I can get some money I would see that he had a happy old age. He does not need to know where the money comes from.'

I leaned back in my chair and looked at her thoughtfully. I looked at the expensive, fashion-plate clothing she was wearing, and she coloured under my scrutiny. I said softly, 'Why don't *you* send him money? I hear you made a good marriage; you ought to be able to spare a little for an old man.'

Her lips twisted in a harsh smile. 'You don't know anything about me, do you, Mr Halloran? I can assure you that I have no money and no husband, either – or no one that I would care to call my husband.' She moved her hands forward on the table. 'I sold my rings to get money to send to my father, and that was a long time ago. If it were not for my friends I would be on the streets. No, I have no money, Mr Halloran.'

There was something here I did not understand, but I didn't press it. The reason she wanted to cut in didn't matter; all that mattered was she had us over a barrel. With her connections we could not make a move in Italy without falling over an ex-partisan friend of hers. If we tried to lift the gold without coming to terms with her she would coolly step in at the right time and take the lot. She had us taped.

I said, 'You're as bad as Metcalfe.'

'That is something I wanted to ask you,' she said. 'Who is this Metcalfe?'

'He's up to the same lark that you are.'

Her command of English was not up to that. 'Lark?' she said in mystification. 'That is a bird?'

I said, 'He's one of our mutual competitors. He's after the gold, too.' I leaned over the table. 'Now, if we cut you in, we would want

97

certain guarantees.'

'I do not think you are in a position to demand guarantees,' she said coldly.

'Nevertheless, we would want them. Don't worry, this is in your interest, too. Metcalfe is the man behind Torloni and he's quite a boy. Now, we would want protection against Metcalfe and anything he could throw against us. From what you've said, Torloni carries a bit of weight, and if he hasn't got enough, Metcalfe can probably drum up some more. What I want to know is – can you give us protection against that lot?'

'I can find a hundred men, any time I want,' she said.

'What kind of men?' I asked bluntly. 'Old soldiers on pension?'

She smiled. 'Most of my war-time friends live quietly and go about their work. I would not want them to be mixed up in anything illegal or violent, although they would help if they had to. But my . . .' she hesitated for a word, '. . . my more unsavoury friends I would willingly commit to this affair. I told you they are adventurous and they are not old men – no older than you, Mr Halloran,' she ended sweetly.

'A hundred of them?'

She thought a little. 'Fifty, then,' she compromised. 'My father's hill fighters will be more than a match for those dockland gangsters.'

I had no doubt about that – if they fought man to man. But Metcalfe and Torloni could probably whip up every thug in Italy, and would do for a stake as large as this.

I said, 'I want further guarantees. How do I know we won't be double-crossed?'

'You don't,' she said meagrely.

I decided to go in for some melodramatics. 'I want you to swear that you won't double-cross us.'

She raised her hand. 'I swear that I, Francesca di Estrenoli, promise faithfully not to trick, in any way, Mr Halloran of South Africa.' She smiled at me. 'Is that good enough?'

I shook my head. 'No, it isn't enough. You said yourself that you were a dishonourable woman. No, I want you to swear on your father's name and honour.'

Pink anger spots burned on her cheeks and I thought for a moment that she was going to slap my face. I said gently, 'Do you swear?'

She dropped her eyes. 'I swear,' she said in a low voice.

'On your father's name and honour,' I persisted.

'On my father's name and on his honour,' she said, and looked up. 'Now I hope you are satisfied.' There were tears in her eyes again.

I relaxed. It wasn't much but it was the best I could do and I hoped it would hold her.

The man from behind the counter came over to the table slowly. He looked at me with dislike and said to Francesca, 'Is everything all right, Madame?'

'Yes, Giuseppi, everything is all right.' She smiled at him. 'Nothing is wrong.'

Giuseppi smiled back at her, gave me a hard look and returned to the counter. I felt a prickle at the back of my neck. I had the feeling that if Francesca had said that everything was *not* all right I would have been a candidate for a watery dockside grave before the week was out.

I cocked my thumb at the counter. 'One of your soldier friends?'

She nodded. 'He saw you had hurt me, so he came over to see what he could do.'

'I didn't mean to hurt you,' I said.

'You shouldn't have come here. You shouldn't have come to Italy. What is it to you? I can understand Coertze and Walker; they fought the Germans, they buried the gold. But I cannot understand you.'

I said gently, 'I fought the Germans, too, in Holland and Germany.'

'I'm sorry,' she said. 'I shouldn't have said that.'

'That's all right. As for the rest . . .' I shrugged. 'Somebody had to plan – Coertze and Walker couldn't do it. Walker is an alcoholic and Coertze is all beef and no subtlety. They needed someone to get behind and push.'

'But why is it you who has to push?'

'I had a reason once,' I said shortly. 'Forget it. Let's get some things straightened out. What about the split?'

'The split?'

'How do we divide the loot?'

'I hadn't thought of that – it will need some thinking about.'

'It will,' I agreed. 'Now, there's the three of us, there's you and there's fifty of your friends – fifty-four in all. If you're thinking along the lines of fifty-four equal shares you can forget about it. We won't have it.'

'I can't see how we can work this out when we don't know how much money will be involved.'

'We work it on a percentage basis,' I said impatiently. 'This is how I see it – one share each for the three of us, one share for you and one share to be divided among your friends.'

'No,' she said firmly. 'That's not fair. You have done nothing about this, at all. You are just a plunderer.'

'I thought you'd take that attitude,' I said. 'Now, listen, and listen damned carefully because I'm not going to repeat this. Coertze and Walker are entitled to a share each. They fought for the gold and they disposed of it carefully. Besides, they are the only people who know where it is. Right?'

She nodded agreement.

I smiled grimly. 'Now we come to me whom you seem to despise.' She made a sudden gesture with her hand and I waved her down. 'I'm the brains behind this. I know a way of getting the stuff out of Italy and I've arranged a sale for it. Without me this whole plan would flop, and I've invested a lot of time and money in it. Therefore I think I'm entitled to an equal share.'

I stabbed my finger at her. 'And now you come along and blackmail us. Yes, blackmail,' I said as she opened her mouth to protest. 'You've done nothing constructive towards the plan and you complain about getting an equal share. As for your friends, as far as I'm concerned, they are hired muscle to be paid for. If you don't think they're being paid enough with one-fifth between them you can supplement it out of your own share.'

'But it will be so little for them,' she said.

'Little!' I said, and was shocked into speechlessness. I recovered my breath. 'Do you know how much is involved?'

'Not exactly,' she said cautiously.

I threw discretion to the winds. 'There's over £1,500,000 in gold alone – and there's probably an equal amount in cut gem-stones. The gold alone means £300,000 for a fifth share and that's £6000 each for your friends. If you count the jewels you can double those figures.'

Her eyes widened as she mentally computed this into lire. It was an astronomical calculation and took her some time. 'So much,' she whispered.

'So much,' I said. I had just had an idea. The gems had been worrying me because they would be hot – in the criminal sense. They would need recutting and disguising and the whole thing would be risky. Now I saw the chance of doing an advantageous deal.

'Look here,' I said generously. 'I've just offered you and your friends two-fifths of the take. Supposing the jewels are worth more than two-fifths – and I reckon they are – then you can take the lot of them, leaving the disposal of the gold to the three of us. After all, gems are more portable and easily hidden.'

She fell for it. 'I know a jeweller who was with us during the war; he could do the valuation. Yes, that seems reasonable.'

It seemed reasonable to me, also, since I had been taking only the gold into my calculations all the time. Coertze, Walker and myself would still come out with half a million each.

'There's one other thing,' I said.

'What's that?'

'There's a lot of paper money in this hoard – lire, francs, dollars and so on. Nobody takes any of that – there'll be records of the numbers lodged with every bank in the world. You'll have to control your friends when it comes to that.'

'I can control them,' she said loftily. She smiled and held out her hand. 'It's a deal, then, as the Americans say.'

I looked at her hand but didn't touch it. I shook my head. 'Not yet. I still have to discuss it with Coertze and Walker. They'll take a hell of a lot of convincing – especially Coertze. What did you do to him, anyway?'

She withdrew her hand slowly and looked at me strangely. 'Almost you convince me that you are an honest man.'

I grinned at her cheerfully. 'Out of necessity, that's all. Those two are the only ones who know where the gold is.'

'Oh, yes, I had forgotten. As for Coertze, he is a boor.'

'He'd be the first to agree with you,' I said. 'But it means something different in Afrikaans.' I had a sudden thought. 'Does anyone else know what you know – about Alberto's letter and all that?'

She started to shake her head but stopped suddenly, deciding to be honest. 'Yes,' she said. 'One man, but he can be trusted – he is a true friend.'

'OK,' I said. 'I just wanted to be sure that no one else will try to pull the same stunt that you've just pulled. The whole damn' Mediterranèan seems to be getting into the act. I wouldn't tell your friends anything you don't have to – at least, not until it's all over. If they are criminals, as you say, they might get their own ideas.'

'I haven't told them anything so far, and I'm not going to tell them now.'

'Good. But you *can* tell them to watch for Torloni's men. They'll be keeping an eye on *Sanford* when they get round to finding where she is.'

'Oh, yes, Mr Halloran; I'll certainly tell them to keep a watch on your boat,' she said sweetly.

I laughed. 'I know you will. When you've got things organized drop in and see us any time – but make it quick, there's a time limit on all this.'

I got up from the table and left her. I thought she might as well pay for the breakfast since we were partners – or, as she had put it, 'in association'.

IV

She came that afternoon, accompanied by a man even bigger than Coertze, which she introduced as Piero Morese. He nodded civilly enough to me, ignored Walker and regarded Coertze watchfully.

I had had trouble with Coertze – he had taken a lot of convincing and had reiterated in a bass growl, 'I will not be cheated, I will not be cheated.'

I said wearily, 'OK. The gold is up in those hills somewhere; you know where it is. Why don't you go and get it? I'm sure you can fight Torloni and Metcalfe and the Contessa and her cut-throats single-handed; I'm sure you can bring back the gold and take it to Tangier before April 19. Why don't you just go ahead and stop bothering me?'

He had calmed down but was not altogether happy and he rumbled like a volcano which does not know whether to erupt again or not. Now he sat in the cabin looking at the Contessa with contempt and the big Italian with mistrust.

Morese had no English so the meeting came to order in Italian, which I could understand if it was not spoken too quickly. The Contessa said, 'It is all right to speak in front of Piero, he knows everything that I know.'

'I know you: you were with Umberto,' said Coertze in mashed Italian.

Morese gave a quick nod but said nothing. The Contessa said, 'Here is where we talk seriously.' She looked at me. 'Have you talked this over?'

'We have.'

'Do they accept the terms?'

'They do.'

'Very well, where is the gold?'

There was a growl from Coertze which I covered with a quick burst of laughter. 'Contessa, you'll be the death of me,' I said. 'I'll die laughing. You don't suppose we'll tell you that, do you?'

She smiled acidly. 'No – but I thought I would try it. All right, how do we go about this?'

I said, 'First of all, there's a time limit. We'll want the gold delivered to Rapallo by the 1st of March at the latest. We also want a place where we can work undisturbed with this boat; either a private boat-shed or a boatyard. That must be arranged for now.'

Her eyes narrowed. 'Why the 1st of March?'

'That is of no consequence to you, but that is the way it must be.'

Morese said, 'That does not leave us much time. The first of the month is in two weeks.'

'True,' I said. 'But that is the way it must be. The next thing is that only the five of us will go to the gold. There must be no one else. We will unseal the place where it is hidden, pack what we want into strong boxes and move it out. Then we will seal the hidden place again. After that, and only after that, will we need the help of anyone else, and even then, only for lifting and transport to the coast. There is no need to have too many people knowing what we are doing.'

'That is well thought of,' said Morese.

I said, 'Everything will be brought to the boat-shed – everything, including the jewels. We five will live together for one month while my friends and I do what we have to do. If you want the jewels valued you must bring your valuer to the jewels – not vice versa. The final share-out will be decided when the stones have been valued, but will not take place until the boat is in the water.'

'You talk as though you do not trust us,' said Morese.

'I don't,' I said bluntly. I jerked my thumb at the Contessa. 'Your friend here is blackmailing us into all this, so I don't see where the trust comes in.'

His face darkened. 'That is unworthy of you.'

I shrugged. 'Say, rather, it is unworthy of her. She started all this and those are the facts.'

The Contessa put her hand on Morese's shoulder and he subsided. Coertze barked a short laugh. '*Magtig*, but you have taken her measure.' He nodded. 'You'll have to watch her, she's a *slim meisie*.'

I turned to him. 'Now it's up to you. What will you need to get the gold?'

Coertze leaned forward. 'When I was here last year nothing had changed or been disturbed. The place is in the hills where no one goes. There is a rough road so we can take a lorry right up to the place. The nearest village is four miles away.'

'Can we work at night?'

Coertze thought about that. 'The fall of rock looks worse than it is,' he said. 'I know how to blast and I made sure of that. Two men with picks and shovels will be able to get through in four hours – longer at night, perhaps – I would say six hours at night.'

'So we will be there at least one whole night and probably longer.'

'*Ja*,' he said. 'If we work at night only, it will take two nights.'

The Contessa said, 'Italians do not walk the hills at night. It will be safe to have lights if they cannot be seen from the village.'

Coertze said, 'No lights can be seen from the village.'

'All the same, we must have a cover,' I said. 'If we have to hang around in the vicinity for at least one day then we must have a sound reason. Has anyone got any ideas?'

There was a silence and suddenly Walker spoke for the first time. 'What about a car and a caravan? The English are noted for that kind of thing – camping and so on. The Italians don't even have a word for it, they use the English word. If we camp out for a couple of nights we'll be only another English crowd as far as the peasants are concerned.'

We all thought about that and it seemed a good idea. The Contessa said, 'I can arrange for the car and the caravan and a tent.'

I started to tick off all the things we would need. 'We want lights.'

'We use the headlights of the car,' said Coertze.

'That's for outside,' I said. 'We'll need lights for inside. We'll need torches – say a dozen – and lots of torch cells.' I nodded to Morese. 'You get those. We need picks and shovels, say four of each. We'll need lorries. How many to do the job in one haul?'

'Two three-tonners,' said Coertze with certainty. 'The Germans had four, but they were carrying a lot of stuff we won't want.'

'We'll have to have those standing by with the drivers,' I said. 'Then we'll need a lot of timber to make crates. The gold will need re-boxing.'

'Why do that when it's already in boxes?' objected Coertze. 'It's just a lot of extra work.'

'Think back,' I said patiently. 'Think back to the first time you saw those boxes in the German truck. You *recognized* them as bullion boxes. We don't want any snooper doing the same on the way back.'

Walker said, 'You don't have to take the gold out, and it wouldn't need much timber. Just nail thin pieces of wood on the outside of the bullion boxes to change their shape and make them look different.'

Walker was a real idea machine when he wasn't on the drink. He said, 'There must be plenty of timber down there we can use.'

'No,' I said. 'We use new wood. I don't want anything that looks or even smells as though it's come from a hole in the ground. Besides, there might be a mark on the wood we could miss which would give the game away.'

'You don't take any chances, do you?' observed the Contessa.

'I'm not a gambler,' I said shortly. 'The timber can go up in the trucks.' I looked at Morese.

'I will get it,' he said.

'Don't forget hammers and nails,' I said. I was trying to think of everything. If we slipped up on this job it would be because of some insignificant item which nobody had thought important.

There was a low, repeated whistle from the dockside. Morese looked at the Contessa and she nodded almost imperceptibly. He got up and went on deck.

I said to Coertze, 'Is there anything else we ought to know, anything you've forgotten or left out?'

'No,' he said. 'That's all.'

Morese came back and said to the Contessa, 'He wants to talk to you.'

She rose and left the cabin and Morese followed her on deck. Through the open port I could hear a low-voiced conversation.

'I don't trust them,' said Coertze violently. 'I don't trust that bitch and I don't trust Morese. He's a bad bastard; he was a bad bastard in the war. He didn't take any prisoners – according to him they were all shot while escaping.'

'So were yours,' I said, 'when you took the gold.'

He bridled. 'That was different; they *were* escaping.'

'Very conveniently,' I said acidly. It galled me that this man, whom I had good reason to suspect of murdering at least four others, should be so mealy-mouthed.

He brooded a little, then he said, 'What's to stop them taking it all from us when we've got it out? What's to stop them shooting us and leaving us in the tunnel when they seal it up again?'

'Nothing that you'd understand,' I said. 'Just the feeling of a girl for her father and her family.' I didn't elaborate on that; I wasn't certain myself that it was a valid argument.

The Contessa and Morese came back. She said, 'Two of Torloni's men are in Rapallo. They were asking the Port Captain about you not ten minutes ago.'

I said, 'Don't tell me that the Port Captain is one of your friends.'

'No, but the Chief Customs Officer is. He recognized them immediately. One of them he had put in jail three years ago for smuggling heroin; the other he has been trying to catch for a long time. Both of them work for Torloni, he says.'

'Well, we couldn't hope to hide from them indefinitely,' I said. 'But they mustn't connect you with us – not yet, anyway – so you'll have to wait until it's dark before you leave.'

She said, 'I am having them watched.'

'That's fine, but it's not enough,' I said. 'I want to do to Metcalfe what he's been doing to us. I want Torloni watched in Genoa; I want the docks watched all along this coast for Metcalfe's boat. I want to know when he comes to Italy.' I gave her a detailed description of Metcalfe, of Krupke and the Fairmile. 'Can you do all that?'

'Of course. You will know all about this Metcalfe as soon as he sets foot in Italy.'

'Good,' I said. 'Then what about a drink?' I looked at Coertze. 'It seems you didn't scare Metcalfe off, after all.' He looked back at me with an expressionless face, and I laughed. 'Don't look so glum. Get out the bottle and cheer up.'

V

We didn't see the Contessa or Morese after that. They stayed out of sight, but next morning I found a note in the cockpit telling me to go to the Three Fishes and say that I wanted a watchman for *Sanford*.

I went, of course, and Giuseppi was more friendly than when I had last seen him. He served me personally and, as he put down the plate, I said, 'You ought to know what goes on on the water-front. Can you recommend a watchman for my boat? He must be honest.'

'Ah, yes, signor,' he said. 'I have the very man – old Luigi there. It is a pity; he was wounded during the war and since then he has been able to undertake only light work. At present he is unemployed.'

'Send him over when I have finished breakfast,' I said.

Thus it was that we got an honest watchman and old Luigi

became the go-between between the Contessa and *Sanford*. Every morning he would bring a letter in which the Contessa detailed her progress.

Torloni was being watched, but nothing seemed to be happening; his men were still in Rapallo watching *Sanford* and being watched themselves; the trucks had been arranged for and the drivers were ready; the timber was prepared and the tools had been bought; she had been offered a German caravan but she had heard of an English caravan for sale in Milan and thought it would be better – would I give her some money to buy it as she had none.

It all seemed to be working out satisfactorily.

The three of us from *Sanford* spent our time sight-seeing, much to the disgust of Torloni's spies. I spent a lot of time in the Yacht Club and it was soon noised about that I intended to settle in the Mediterranean and was looking for a suitable boatyard to buy.

On our fifth day in Rapallo the morning letter instructed me to go to the boatyard of Silvio Palmerini and to ask for a quotation for the slipping and painting of *Sanford*. 'The price will be right,' wrote the Contessa. 'Silvio is one of my – our – friends.'

Palmerini's yard was some way out of Rapallo. Palmerini was a gnarled man of about sixty who ruled his yard and his three sons with soft words and a will of iron. I said, 'You understand, Signor Palmerini, that I am a boat-builder, too. I would like to do the job myself in your yard.'

He nodded. It was only natural that a man must look after his own boat if he could; besides, it would be cheaper.

'And I would want it under cover,' I said. 'I fastened the keel in an experimental way and I may want to take it off to see if it is satisfactory.'

He nodded again. Experimental ways were risky and a man should stick to the old traditional ways of doing things. It would be foolish, indeed, if milord's keel dropped off in the middle of the Mediterranean.

I agreed that I should look a fool, and said, 'My friends and I are capable of doing the work and we shall not need extra labour. All that is required is a place where we can work undisturbed.'

He nodded a third time. He had a large shed we could use and which could be locked. No one would disturb us, not even himself – certainly no one outside his family – he would see to that. And was milord the rich Englishman who wanted to buy a boatyard? If so, then perhaps the milord would consider the boatyard Palmerini, the paragon of the Western Mediterranean.

That brought me up with a jerk. Another piece of polite blackmail was under way and I could see that I would have to buy the yard, probably at an exorbitant price – the price of silence.

I said diplomatically, 'Yes, I am thinking of buying a yard, but the wise man explores every avenue.' Dammit, I was falling into his way of speech. 'I have been to Spain and France; now I am in Italy and after Italy I am going to Greece. I must look at everything.'

He nodded vigorously, his crab-apple head bobbing up and down. Yes, the milord was indeed wise to look at everything, but in spite of that he was sure that the milord would unfailingly return to the boatyard Palmerini because it was certainly the best in the whole Mediterranean.

Pah, what did the Greeks know of fine building? All they knew were their clumsy caiques. The price would be reasonable for milord since it appeared that they had mutual friends, and such price could be spread over a period provided the proper guarantees could be given.

From this I understood the old rascal to say that he would wait until the whole job was completed and I had fluid capital, if I could prove that I would keep my word.

I went back to *Sanford* feeling satisfied that this part of the programme was going well. Even if I had to buy Palmerini's yard, it would not be a bad thing and any lengthening of the price could be written off as additional expenses.

On the ninth day of our stay in Rapallo the usual morning letter announced that all was now ready and we could start at any time. However, it was felt that, since the next day was Sunday, it would be more fitting to begin the expedition inland on Monday. That gave an elevating tone to the whole thing, I thought; another crazy aspect of a crazy adventure.

The Contessa wrote: 'Torloni's men will be discreetly taken care of, and will not connect their inability to find you with any trickery on your part. They will have no suspicions. Leave your boat in the care of Luigi and meet me at nine in the morning at the Three Fishes.'

I put a match to the letter and called Luigi below. 'They say you are an honest man, Luigi; would you take a bribe?'

He was properly horrified. 'Oh no, signor.'

'You know this boat is being watched?'

'Yes, signor. They are enemies of you and Madame.'

'Do you know what Madame and I are doing?'

He shook his head. 'No, signor. I came because Madame said

you needed my help. I did not ask questions,' he said with dignity.

I tapped on the table. 'My friends and I are going away for a few days soon, leaving the boat in your charge. What will you do if the men who are watching want to bribe you to let them search the boat?'

He drew himself up. 'I would slap the money out of their hands, signor.'

'No, you won't,' I said. 'You will say it is not enough and you will ask for more money. When you get it, you will let them search the boat.'

He looked at me uncomprehendingly. I said slowly, 'I don't mind if they search – there is nothing to be found. There is no reason why you should not make some money out of Madame's enemies.'

He laughed suddenly and slapped his thigh. 'That is good, signor; that is very good. You *want* them to search.'

'Yes,' I replied. 'But don't make it too easy for them or they will be suspicious.'

I wanted, as a last resort, to try to fool Metcalfe as I had fooled him in Barcelona, or rather, as I had hoped to fool him before Coertze put his foot in it. I wrote a letter to the Contessa telling her what I was doing, and gave it to Luigi to pass on.

'How long have you known Madame?' I asked curiously.

'Since the war, signor, when she was a little girl.'

'You would do anything for her, wouldn't you?'

'Why not?' he asked in surprise. 'She has done more for me than I can ever repay. She paid for the doctors after the war when they straightened my leg. It is not her fault they could not get it properly straight – but I would have been a cripple, otherwise.'

This was a new light on Francesca. 'Thank you, Luigi,' I said. 'Give this letter to Madame when you see her.'

I told Coertze and Walker what was happening. There was nothing else to do now but wait for Monday morning.

5 *The Tunnel*

On Monday morning I again set the stage, leaving papers where they could easily be found. On the principle of the Purloined Letter I had even worked out a costing for a refit of *Sanford* at Palmerini's boatyard, together with some estimates of the probable cost of buying the yard. If we were seen there later we would have good reason.

We left just before nine, saying goodbye to Luigi, who gave me a broad wink, and arrived at the Three Fishes on time. The Contessa and Morese were waiting and we joined them for breakfast. The Contessa wore clothing of an indefinably English cut of which I approved; she was using her brains.

I said, 'How did you get rid of Torloni's boys?'

Morese grinned. 'One of them had an accident with his car. The other, who was waiting for him at the dock, got tired of waiting and unaccountably fell into the water. He had to get a taxi to his hotel so that he could change his clothes.'

'Your friend Metcalfe arrived in Genoa last night,' said the Contessa.

'You're sure?'

'I'm certain. He went straight to Torloni and stayed with him for a long time. Then he went to a hotel.'

That settled that. I had wondered for a long time if my suspicions of Metcalfe hadn't been just a fevered bit of imagination. After all, my whole case against Metcalfe had been built up of supposition and what I knew of his character.

'You're having him watched?'

'Of course.'

Breakfast arrived and all conversation stopped until Giuseppi went back to his counter. Then I said, 'All right, friend Kobus, this is where you tell us where the gold is.'

Coertze's head came up with a jerk. 'Not on,' he said. 'I'll take you there, but I'm not telling first.'

I sighed. 'Look, these good people have laid on transport. How can they tell the trucks where to rendezvous unless we know where we're going?'

'They can telephone back here.'

'From where?'

'There'll be a phone in the village.'

'None of us is going anywhere near the village,' I said. 'Least of all one of us foreigners. And if you think I'll let one of these two go in alone, you're crazy. From now on we don't let either of them out of our sight.'

'Not very trusting, are you?' observed the Contessa.

I looked at her. 'Do you trust me?'

'Not much.'

'Then we're even.' I turned back to Coertze. 'Any telephoning the Contessa is going to do is from that telephone in the corner there – with me at her elbow.'

'Don't call me the Contessa,' she snapped.

I ignored her and concentrated on Coertze. 'So, you see, we have to know the spot. If you won't tell us, I'm sure that Walker will – but I'd rather it was you.'

He thought about it for quite a while, then he said, '*Magtig*, but you'll argue your way into heaven one day. All right, it's about forty miles north of here, between Varsi and Tassaro.' He went into detailed explanations and Morese said, 'It's right in the hills.'

I said, 'Do you think you can direct the trucks to this place?'

Francesca said, 'I will tell them to wait in Varsi. We will not need them until the second night; we can go to Varsi and direct them from there tomorrow.'

'OK,' I said. 'Let's make that phone call.'

I escorted her to the corner and stood by while she gave the instructions, making sure she slipped nothing over. A trustful lot, we were. When we got back to the table, I said, 'That does it; we can start at any time.'

We finished breakfast and got up to go. Francesca said, 'Not by the front; Torloni's men will be back by now and they can see this café. We go this way.'

She led us out by the back door into a yard where a car was standing with an Eccles touring caravan already coupled. She said, 'I stocked up with enough food for a week – it might be necessary.'

'It won't,' I said grimly. 'If we don't have the stuff out by tomorrow night we'll never get it – not with Metcalfe sniffing on our trail.'

I looked at our party and made a quick decision. 'We look English enough, all except you, Morese; you just don't fit. You travel in the caravan and keep out of sight.'

He frowned and looked at Francesca. She said, 'Get into the

caravan, Piero; do as Mr Halloran says,' and then turned to me. 'Piero takes his instructions from no one but me, Mr Halloran. I hope you remember that in future.'

I shrugged and said, 'Let's go.'

Coertze was driving because he knew the way. Walker was also in front and Francesca and I shared the back seat. No one did much talking and Coertze drove very slowly because he was unaccustomed to towing a caravan and driving on the right simultaneously.

We left Rapallo and were soon ascending into the hills – the Ligurian Apennines. It looked poor country with stony soil and not much cultivation. What agriculture there was was scattered and devoted to vines and olives, the two trees which look as though they've been tortured to death. Within the hour we were in Varsi, and soon after that, we left the main road and bounced along a secondary country road, unmetalled and with a poor surface. It had not rained for some days and the dust rose in clouds.

After a while Coertze slowed down almost to a stop as he came to a corner. 'This is where we shot up the trucks,' he said.

We turned the corner and saw a long stretch of empty road. Coertze stopped the car and Walker got out. This was the first time he had seen the place in fifteen years. He walked a little way up the road to a large rock on the right, then turned and looked back. I guessed it was by that rock that he had stood while he poured bullets into the driver of the staff car.

I thought about the sudden and dreadful slaughter that had happened on that spot and, looking up the shaggy hillside, I visualized the running prisoners being hunted and shot down. I said abruptly, 'No point in waiting here, let's get on with it.'

Coertze put the car into gear and drove forward slowly until Walker had jumped in, then he picked up speed and we were on our way again. 'Not far now,' said Walker. His voice was husky with excitement.

Less than fifteen minutes later Coertze pulled up again at the junction of another road so unused that it was almost invisible. 'The old mine is about a mile and a half up there,' he said. 'What do we do now?'

Francesca and I got out of the car and stretched our stiffened legs. I looked about and saw a stream about a hundred yards away. 'That's convenient,' I said. 'The perfect camp site. One thing is certain – none of us so much as looks sideways at that side road during the hours of daylight.'

We pulled the caravan off the road and extended the balance

legs, then we put up the tent. Francesca went into the caravan and talked to Morese. I said, 'Now, for God's sake, let's act like innocent tourists. We're mad Englishmen who prefer to live uncomfortably rather than stay at a hotel.'

It was a long day. After lunch, which Francesca made in the little galley of the caravan, we sat about and talked desultorily and waited for the sun to go down. Francesca stayed in the caravan most of the time keeping Morese company; Walker fidgeted; Coertze was apparently lost in contemplating his navel; I tried to sleep, but couldn't.

The only excitement during the afternoon was the slow approach of a farm cart. It hove into sight as a puff of dust at the end of the road and gradually, with snail-like pace, came near enough to be identified. Coertze roused himself enough to make a number of small wagers as to the time it would draw level with the camp. At last it creaked past, drawn by two oxen and looking like a refugee from a Breughel painting. A peasant trudged alongside and I mustered my worst Italian, waved and said, '*Buon giorno.*'

He gave me a sideways look, muttered something I did not catch, and went on his way. That was the only traffic on the road the whole time we were there.

At half past four I roused myself and went to the caravan to see Francesca. 'We'd better eat early,' I said. 'As soon as it's dark we'll be taking the car to the mine.'

'Everything is in cans,' she said. 'It will be easy to prepare. We will want something to eat during the night, so I got two of these big vacuum containers – I will cook the food before we go and it will keep hot all night. There are also some vacuum flasks for coffee.'

'You've been spending my money well,' I said.

She ignored that. 'I will need some water. Will you get some from the stream?'

'If you will come with me,' I said. 'You need to stretch a bit.' I had a sudden urge to talk to her, to find out what made her tick.

'All right,' she said, and opening a cupboard, produced three canvas buckets. As we walked towards the stream, I said, 'You must have been very young during the war.'

'I was. We took to the hills, my father and I, when I was ten years old.' She waved at the surrounding mountains. 'These hills.'

'Not a very pleasant life for a little girl.'

She considered that. 'It was fun at first. Everyone likes a camping holiday and this was one long holiday for me. Yes, it was fun.'

'When did it stop being fun?'

Her face was quietly sad. 'When the men started to die; when the fighting began. Then it was not fun, it became a serious thing we were doing. It was a good thing – but it was terrible.'

'And you worked in the hospital?'

'Yes. I tended Walker when he came from the prison camp. Did you know that?'

I remembered Walker's description of the grave little girl who wanted him to be better so he could kill Germans. 'He told me,' I said.

We reached the stream and I looked at it doubtfully. It looked clear enough, but I said, 'Is it all right for drinking?'

'I will boil the water; it will be all right,' she said, and knelt to dig a hole in the shallows. 'We must have a hole deep enough to take a bucket; it is easier then.'

I helped her make a hole, reflecting that this was a product of her guerrilla training. I would have tried to fill the buckets in drips and drabs. When the hole was big enough we sat on the bank waiting for the sediment to settle, and I said, 'Was Coertze ever wounded?'

'No, he was very lucky. He was never wounded beyond a scratch, although there were many times he could have been.'

I offered her a cigarette and lit it. 'So he did a lot of fighting?'

'All the men fought,' she said, and drew on the cigarette reflectively. 'But Coertze seemed to *like* fighting. He killed a lot of Germans – and Italians.'

'What Italians?' I said quickly. I was thinking of Walker's story.

'The Fascists,' she said. 'Those who stuck by Mussolini during the time of the Salo Republic. There was a civil war going on in these mountains. Did you know that?'

'No, I didn't,' I said. 'There's a lot about Italy that I don't know.'

We sat quietly for a while, then I said, 'So Coertze was a killer?'

'He was a good soldier – the kind of man we needed. He was a leader.'

I switched. 'How was Alberto killed?'

'He fell off a cliff when the Germans were chasing Umberto's section. I heard that Coertze nearly rescued him, but didn't get there in time.'

'Um,' I said. 'I heard it was something like that. How did Harrison and Parker die?'

She wrinkled her brow. 'Harrison and Parker? Oh yes, they were in what we called the Foreign Legion. They were killed in action. Not at the same time, at different times.'

'And Donato Rinaldi; how was he killed?'

'That was a funny thing. He was found dead near the camp with his head crushed. He was lying under a cliff and it was thought that he had been climbing and had fallen off.'

'Why should he climb? Was he a mountaineer or something like that?'

'I don't think so, but he was a young man and young men do foolish things like that.'

I smiled, thinking to myself; not only the very young are foolish; and tossed a pebble into the stream. 'It sounds very like the song about the "Ten Little Niggers". "And then there were Two." Why did Walker leave?'

She looked up sharply. 'Are you saying that these men should not have died? That someone from the camp killed them?'

I shrugged. 'I'm not saying anything – but it was very convenient for someone. You see, six men hid this gold and four of them came to a sudden end shortly afterwards.' I tossed another pebble into the water. 'Who profits? There are only two – Walker and Coertze. Why did Walker leave?'

'I don't know. He left suddenly. I remember he told my father that he was going to try to join the Allied armies. They were quite close at that time.'

'Was Coertze in the camp when Walker left?'

She thought for a long time, then said, 'I don't know; I can't remember.'

'Walker says he left because he was frightened of Coertze. He still is, for that matter. Our Kobus is a very frightening man, sometimes.'

Francesca said slowly, 'There was Alberto on the cliff. Coertze could have . . .'

'. . . pushed him off? Yes, he could. And Walker said that Parker was shot in the *back* of the head. By all accounts, including yours, Coertze is a natural-born killer. It all adds up.'

She said, 'I always knew that Coertze was a violent man, but . . .'

'But? Why don't you like him, Francesca?'

She threw the stub of her cigarette into the water and watched it float downstream. 'It was just one of those things that happen between a man and a woman. He was . . . too pressing.'

'When was this?'

'Three years ago. Just after I was married.'

I hesitated. I wanted to ask her about that marriage, but she suddenly stood up and said, 'We must get the water.'

As we were going back to the caravan I said, 'It looks as though I'll have to be ready to jump Coertze – he could be dangerous. You'd better tell Piero the story so that he can be prepared if anything happens.'

She stopped. 'I thought Coertze was your friend. I thought you were on his side.'

'I'm on nobody's side,' I said shortly. 'And I don't condone murder.'

We walked the rest of the way in silence.

For the rest of the afternoon until it became dark Francesca was busy cooking in the caravan. As the light faded the rest of us began to make our preparations. We put the picks and shovels in the boot of the car, together with some torches. Piero had provided a Tilley pressure lamp together with half a gallon of paraffin – that would be a lot better than torches once we got into the tunnel. He also hauled a wheelbarrow out of the caravan, and said, 'I thought we could use this for taking the rock away; we must not leave loose rock at the entrance of the tunnel.'

I was pleased about that; it was something I had forgotten.

Coertze examined the picks with a professional air, but found no fault. To me, a pick is a pick and a spade is a bloody shovel, but I suppose that even pick-and-shovelling has its more erudite technicalities. As I was helping Piero put the wheelbarrow into the boot my foot turned on a stone and I was thrown heavily against Coertze.

'Sorry,' I said.

'Don't be sorry, be more careful,' he grunted.

We got the wheelbarrow settled – although the top of the boot wouldn't close – and I said to Coertze in a low voice, 'I'd like to talk to you . . . over there.'

We wandered a short distance from the rest of the party where we were hidden in the gathering darkness. 'What is it?' asked Coertze.

I tapped the hard bulge under the breast of his jacket, and said, 'I think that's a gun.'

'It is a gun,' he said.

'Who are you thinking of shooting?'

'Anyone who gets between me and the gold.'

'Now listen carefully,' I said in a hard voice. 'You're not going to shoot anyone, because you're going to give that gun to me. If you don't, you can get the gold yourself. I didn't come to Italy to kill anybody; *I'm* not a murderer.'

Coertze said, '*Klein man,* if you want this gun you'll have to take it from me.'

'OK. You can force us all up to the mine at pistol point. But it's dark and you'll get a rock thrown at your head as soon as you turn your back – and I'd just as soon be the one who throws it. And if you get the gold out – at pistol point – what are you going to do besides sit on it? You can't get it to the coast without Francesca's men and you can't get it out of Italy without me.'

I had him cornered in the same old stalemate that had been griping him since we left South Africa. He was foxed and he knew it.

He said, 'How do we know the Contessa's partisans aren't hiding in these damned hills waiting to jump us as soon as the tunnel is opened?'

'Because they don't know where we are,' I said. 'The only instruction that the truck drivers had was to go to Varsi. Anyway, they wouldn't try to jump us; we have the Contessa as hostage.'

He hesitated, and I said, 'Now, give me the gun.'

Slowly he put his hand inside his jacket and pulled out the gun. It was too dark to see his eyes but I knew they were filled with hate. He held the gun pointed at me and I am sure he was tempted to shoot – but he relaxed and put it into my outstretched hand.

'There'll be a big reckoning between us when this is all over,' he said.

I remained silent and looked at the gun. It was a Luger, just like my own pistol which I had left in South Africa. I held it on him, and said, 'Now stand very still; I'm going to search you.'

He cursed me, but stood quietly while I tapped his pockets. Sure enough, in his jacket pocket I found a spare magazine. I took the clip from the Luger and snapped the action to see if he had a round up the spout. He had.

He said, 'Morese is sure to have a gun.'

'We'll see about that right now,' I said. 'I'll tackle him and you stand behind him ready to sock him.'

We walked back to the caravan and I called for Francesca and Piero and when they came Coertze unobtrusively stationed himself behind the big Italian. I said to Francesca, 'Has Piero got a gun?'

She looked startled. 'I don't know.' She turned to him. 'Are you carrying a gun, Piero?'

He hesitated, then nodded. I brought up the Luger and held it on him. 'All right, bring it out – slowly.'

He looked at the Luger and his brows drew down angrily, but he obeyed orders and slowly pulled a gun from a shoulder holster. I said, 'This is one time you take orders from me, Piero. Give it to Francesca.'

He passed the pistol to Francesca and I put the Luger away and took it from her. It was an army Beretta, probably a relic of his partisan days. I took the clip out, worked the action and put it in another pocket. Coertze passed two spare clips to me which he had taken from Piero's pockets.

I said to Walker, 'Are you carrying a gun?'

He shook his head.

'Come and be searched.' I was taking no chances.

Walker was bare of guns, so I said, 'Now search the car and see if anything is tucked away there.'

I turned to Francesca. 'Are you carrying anything lethal?'

She folded her arms. 'Are you going to search me, too?'

'No, I'll take your word, if you'll give it.'

She dropped her aggressive pose. 'I haven't a gun,' she said in a low voice.

I said, 'Now listen, everybody. I've taken a gun from Coertze and a gun from Morese. I hold in my hands the ammunition for those guns.' With a quick double jerk I threw the clips away into the darkness and they clattered on a rock. 'If there's going to be any fighting between us it will be with bare fists. Nobody gets killed, do you hear?'

I took the empty pistols from my pockets and gave them back to Coertze and Piero. 'You can use these as hammers to nail the crates up.'

They took them with bad grace and I said, 'We've wasted enough time with this nonsense. Is that car ready?'

'Nothing in here,' said Walker.

As the others were getting into the car, Francesca said to me, 'I'm glad you did that. I didn't know Piero had a gun.'

'I didn't know Coertze had one, either; although I should have guessed – knowing his record.'

'How did you take it from him?' she asked curiously.

'Psychology,' I said. 'He would rather have the gold than kill me. Once he gets the gold it might be a different matter.'

'You will have to be very careful,' she said.

'It's nice to know you care,' I said. 'Let's get in the car.'

II

Coertze drove slowly without lights along the overgrown road until we had turned a corner and were out of sight of the 'main' highway. I could hear the long grass swishing on the underside of the car. Once the first corner was turned he switched on the lights and picked up speed.

No one spoke. Coertze and Morese were mad at me and so was Francesca because of what I'd said. Walker was boiling with ill-suppressed excitement, but he caught the mood of the others and remained quiet. I said nothing because I had nothing to say.

It didn't take long to get to the mine and soon the headlights swept over the ruins of buildings – the shabby remnants of an industrial enterprise. There is nothing more ruinous-looking than derelict factory buildings and neglected machinery. Not that there was much left. The surrounding peasantry must have overrun the place like a swarm of locusts very soon after the mine was abandoned and carried off everything of value. What was left was worth about ten lire and would have cost a hundred thousand lire to take away.

Coertze stopped the car and we all got out. Piero said, 'What kind of mine was this?'

'A lead mine,' said Coertze. 'It was abandoned a long time ago – about 1908, I was told.'

'That was about the time they found the big deposits in Sardinia,' said Piero. 'It was easier to ship ore to the smeltery in Spezia than to rail it from here.'

'Where's your tunnel?' I asked.

Coertze pointed. 'Over there. There were four others besides the one I blocked.'

'We might as well get the car into position,' I said, so Coertze got into the driving seat and edged the car forward. The beams of light swept round and illuminated the caved-in mouth of the tunnel. It looked as though it would need a regiment of pioneers to dig that lot away and it would probably take them a month.

Coertze leaned out of the side window. 'I did a good job there,' he said with satisfaction.

I said, 'You're sure we can get through there in one night?'

'Easy,' he said.

I suppose he knew what he was about – he had been a miner.

I went to help Piero and Walker get the tools from the boot and Coertze went to the rockfall and began to examine it. From this time on he took charge and I let him – I knew nothing about the job and he did. His commands were firm-voiced and we all jumped to it with a will.

He said, 'We don't have to dig the whole lot away. I set the charges so that the fall on this side would be fairly thin – not more than ten feet.'

I said, 'Ten feet sounds like a hell of a lot.'

'It's nothing,' he said, contemptuous of my ignorance. 'It isn't as though it was solid rock – this stuff is pretty loose.' He turned and pointed. 'Behind that building you'll find some baulks of timber I sorted out three years ago. You and Morese go and get them. Walker and I will start to dig this stuff out.'

'What can I do?' asked Francesca.

'You can load up the wheelbarrow with the stuff we dig out. Then take it away and scatter it so that it looks natural. Morese is right – we don't want to leave a pile of rocks here.'

Piero and I took torches and found the timber where Coertze had indicated. I thought of Coertze coming here every three or four years, frustrated by a problem he couldn't solve. He must have planned this excavating problem many times and spent hours sorting out this timber in readiness for a job which might never have happened. No wonder he was so touchy.

It took us about an hour to transfer all the timber and by that time Coertze and Walker had penetrated three feet into the rockfall. That was good going, and I said as much. Coertze said, 'It won't be as easy as this all the way. We'll have to stop and shore the roof; that'll take time.'

The hole he was digging was not very big; about five feet high and two feet wide – just room enough for one man to go through. Coertze began to select his timbers for the shoring and Piero and I helped Francesca to distribute the spoil.

Coertze was right. The shoring of the roof took a long time but it had to be done. It would be bad if the whole thing collapsed and we had to begin all over again; besides, someone might get hurt. A moon rose, making the distribution of the spoil easier, so the car lights were switched off and Coertze was working by the light of the Tilley lamp.

He would not let anyone work at the face except himself, so Walker, Piero and I took it in turns helping him, standing behind him and passing out the loose rocks to the entrance of the passage. After another three hours we had six feet of firmly shored passage drilled through the rockfall and at this stage we broke off for something to eat.

Piero had spoken to me about taking away his gun. He said, 'I was angry when you did it. I do not like to have guns pointed at me.'

'It was empty,' I said.

'That I found out, and it was that which made me angrier.' He chuckled suddenly. 'But I think it was well done, now I have thought about it. It is best if there is no shooting.'

We were some distance from the rockfall. I said, 'Did Francesca tell you about Coertze?'

'Yes. She told me what you said. It is something I have not thought of at all. I was surprised when Donato Rinaldi was found dead that time during the war, but I did not think anyone would have killed him. We were all friends.'

Gold is a solvent which dissolves friendships, I thought, but I could not put that into my limited Italian. Instead, I said, 'From what you know of that time, do you think that Coertze could have killed these four men?'

Piero said, 'He could not have killed Harrison because I myself saw Harrison killed. He was shot by a German and I killed the man who shot him. But the others – Parker, Corso and Rinaldi – yes, I think Coertze could have killed them. He was a man who thought nothing of killing.'

'He could have killed them, but did he?' I asked.

Piero shrugged. 'Who can tell? It was a long time ago and there are no witnesses.'

That was that, and there seemed no point in pressing it, so we returned to our work.

Coertze hurried over his meal so that he could get back to the rock face. His eyes gleamed brightly in the light of the lamp; the lust for gold was strong upon him, for he was within four feet of the treasure for which he had been waiting fifteen years. Walker was as bad; he scrambled to his feet as soon as Coertze made a move and they both hurried to the rockfall.

Piero and Francesca were more placid. They had not seen the gold and mere descriptive words have not that immediacy. Francesca leisurely finished her midnight snack and then collected the dishes and took them to the car.

I said to Piero, 'That is a very strange woman.'

'Any child who was brought up in a guerrilla camp would be

different,' he said. 'She has had a difficult life.'

I said carefully, 'I understand she has had an unfortunate marriage.'

He spat. 'Estrenoli is a degenerate.'

'Then why did she marry him?'

'The ways of the *aristos* are not our ways,' he said. 'It was an arranged marriage – or so everyone thinks. But that was not really the way of it.'

'What do you mean?'

He accepted a cigarette. 'Do you know what the Communists did to her father?'

'She told me something about it.'

'It was shameful. He was a man, a true man, and they were not fit to lick his boots. And now he is but a shell, an old broken man.' He struck a match and the flame lit up his face. 'Injustice can crush the life from a man even if his body still walks the streets,' he said.

'What has this to do with Francesca's marriage?'

'The old man was against it. He knew the Estrenoli breed. But Madame was insistent on it. You see, young Estrenoli wanted her. There was no love in him, only lust – Madame is a very beautiful woman – and so he wanted her, but he could not get her. She knew what he was.'

This was confusing. 'Then why the hell did she marry him?'

'That was where Estrenoli was clever. He has an uncle in the Government and he said that perhaps they would reconsider the case of her father. But, of course, there was a price.'

'I see,' I said thoughtfully.

'So she married him. I would as soon she married an animal.'

'And he found he could not keep his promise?'

'Could not?' said Piero disgustedly. 'He had no intention of keeping it. The Estrenolis have not kept a promise in the last five hundred years.' He sighed. 'You see, she is a good daughter of the Church and when she married him, Estrenoli knew that he had her forever. And he was proud of her; oh yes, very proud. She was the most beautiful woman in Roma, and he bought her clothes and dressed her as a child will dress a doll. She was the most expensively dressed mannequin in Italy.'

'And then?'

'And then he got tired of her. He is an unnatural man and he went back to his little boys and his drugs and all the other vices of Roma. Signor Halloran, Roman society is the most corrupt in the world.'

I had heard something of that; there had been a recent case of a drowned girl which threatened to rip apart the whole shoddy mess. But it was said that the Italian Government was intent on hushing it up.

Piero said, 'At times she helped her father and her old comrades. There were many cases of hardship and she did what she could. But Estrenoli found out and said he would not have his money squandered on a lot of filthy partisans, so he did not give her any more money – not one single lire. He tried to corrupt her, to bring her down to his level, but he could not – she was incorruptible. So then he threw her out on to the street – he had what he wanted, as much as he could get, and he was finished with her.'

'So she came back to Liguria.'

'Yes. We help her when we can because of what she is and because of her father. We also try to help him, but that is difficult because he refuses to accept what he calls charity.'

'And she is still married to Estrenoli?'

'There is no divorce in Italy and she follows the Church. But before God I say the Church is wrong when this can happen.'

I said, 'And so you are helping her in this venture.'

'I think it is wrong and I think she is mistaken,' he said. 'I think many lives will be lost because of this. But I am helping her.'

'This is what is puzzling me,' I said. 'Her father is an old man; this gold cannot help him much.'

'But it is not only for her father,' said Piero. 'She says that the money is for all the men who fought with her father and were cheated by the Communists. She says it will be used to send them to hospitals when that is necessary and to educate their children. It will be a good thing if there is no killing.'

'Yes, it will,' I said reflectively. 'I do not want killing, either, Piero.'

'I know, Signor Halloran; you have already shown that. But there are others – Torloni and this Metcalfe. And there is your friend Coertze.'

'You don't trust him, do you? What about Walker?'

'Pah – a nonentity.'

'And me? Do you trust me?'

He stood and put a foot on his cigarette deliberately. 'I would trust you in another place, Signor Halloran, such as in a boat or on a mountain. But gold is not good for the character.'

He had said in different words what I had thought earlier. I was going to reply when Coertze shouted irately, 'What the hell are you doing out there? Come and get this stuff away.'

So we went on with the work.

III

We broke through at three in the morning. Coertze gave a joyous shout as his pick point disappeared unresistingly into emptiness. Within ten minutes he had broken a hole big enough to crawl through and he went into it like a terrier after a rabbit. I pushed the Tilley lamp through the hole and followed it.

I found Coertze scrambling over fallen rocks which littered the floor of the tunnel. 'Hold on,' I said. 'There's no hurry.'

He took no notice but plunged on into the darkness. There was a clang and he started to swear. 'Bring that bloody light,' he shouted.

I moved forward and the circle of light moved with me. Coertze had run full tilt into the front of a truck. He had gashed his cheek and running blood was making runnels in the dust which coated his face, giving him a maniacal look which was accentuated by the glare of his eyes.

'Here it is,' he cackled. '*Magtig*, what did I tell you? I told you I had gold here. Well, here it is, as much gold as comes out of the Reef in a month.' He looked at me in sudden wonder. '*Christus*, but I'm happy,' he said. 'I never thought I'd make it.'

I could hear the others coming through the hole and I waited for them to come up. 'Kobus Coertze is going to give us a guided tour of his treasure cave,' I said.

Walker said, chattering, 'The gold is in the first truck, this one. Most of it, that is. There's some more, though, in the second one, but most of it is in this one. The jewels are in the second one; lots and lots of necklaces and rings, diamonds and emeralds and pearls and cigarette lighters and cases, all in gold, and there's lots of money, too, lire and dollars and pounds and stuff like that, and there's lots of papers but those are in the trucks right at the back with the bodies . . .' His voice trailed off. 'With the bodies,' he repeated vacantly.

There was a bit of a silence then as we realized that this was a mausoleum as well as a treasure cave. Coertze recovered his usual gravity and took the lamp from me. He held it up and looked at the first truck. 'I should have put it up on blocks,' he observed wryly.

The tyres were rotten and sagging, as flat as I've ever seen tyres. 'You know,' said Coertze. 'When we put this lot in here, my intention was to drive these trucks out some time. I never thought it would be fifteen years.' He gave a short laugh. 'We'd have a job starting these engines now.'

Walker said impatiently, 'Well, let's get on with it.' He had apparently recovered from the scare he had given himself.

I said, 'We'd better do this methodically, truck by truck. Let's have a look in the first one.'

Coertze led the way, holding up the Tilley lamp. There was just enough room to squeeze between the truck and the side of the tunnel. I noticed the shattered windscreen where a burst of machine-gun fire had killed the driver and his mate. Everything was covered with a heavy layer of dust, most of which must have been deposited when Coertze originally blew in the front of the tunnel.

Coertze was hammering at the bolts of the tailboard with a piece of rock. 'The damn' things have seized solid,' he said. 'I'll need a hammer.'

'Piero,' I called. 'Bring a hammer.'

'I've got one,' said Francesca quietly, so close behind me that I jumped. I took it and passed it on to Coertze. With a few blows the bolt came free and he attacked the other and caught the tailboard as it dropped. 'Right,' he said, 'here we go for the gold,' and vaulted into the truck.

I handed him the lamp and then climbed up and turned to give Francesca a hand. Walker crowded past me, eager to see the gold, while Piero climbed in more sedately. We squatted on our haunches in a circle, sitting on the bullion boxes.

'Where's the one we opened?' asked Coertze. 'It must be at the back somewhere.'

Francesca gave a yelp. 'I've got a nail in my foot.'

'That's the box,' said Coertze with satisfaction.

Francesca moved and Coertze held up the lamp. The box on which Francesca had been sitting had been torn open and the cover roughly replaced. I stretched my hand and lifted the lid slowly. In the light of the lamp there was the yellow gleam of metal, the dull radiance of gold which rusts not nor doth moth corrupt – rather like the treasure laid up in heaven. This gold, however, had been laid up in hell.

Coertze sighed. 'There it is.'

I said to Francesca, 'Did you hurt your foot?'

She was staring at the gold. 'No, it's all right,' she said absently.

Piero lifted an ingot from the box. He misjudged the weight and tried to use one hand; then he got both hands to it and rested the ingot on his thigh. 'It *is* gold!' he said in wonder.

The ingot was passed round the circle and we all handled it and stroked it. I felt a sudden resurgence of the passion I had felt in Aristide's strong-room when I held the heavy gold Hercules in my fingers.

Walker had a kind of terror in his voice. 'How do we know that all these boxes have gold in them? We never looked.'

'I know,' said Coertze. 'I tested the weight of every box fifteen years ago. I made sure all right. There's about three tons of gold in this truck and another ton in the next one.'

The gold had an insidious fascination and we were reluctant to leave it. For Walker and Coertze this was the culmination of the battle which was fought on that dusty road fifteen years previously. For me, it was the end of a tale that had been told many years before in the bars of Cape Town.

I suddenly pulled myself together. It was *not* the end of the tale, and if we wanted the tale to have a happy ending there was still much to do.

'OK, let's break it up,' I said. 'There's a lot more to see and a hell of a lot to do.'

The golden spell broken, we went to the next truck and Coertze again hammered the tailboard free. The bullion boxes were hidden this time, lying on the floor of the truck with other boxes piled on top.

'That's the box with the crown in it,' said Walker excitedly.

We all climbed in, squashed at the back of the truck, and Coertze looked round. He suddenly glanced at Francesca and said, 'Open that box and take your pick.' He pointed to a stout case with a broken lock.

She opened the box and gasped. There was a shimmer of coruscating light, the pure white of diamonds, the bright green of emeralds and the dull red of rubies. She stretched forth her hand and picked out the first thing she encountered. It was a diamond and emerald necklace.

She ran it through her fingers. 'How lovely!'

There was a catch in Piero's voice. 'How much would that be worth?' he asked huskily.

'I don't know,' I said. 'Fifty thousand pounds, perhaps. That is, if the stones are real,' I ended sardonically.

Coertze said, 'Get this stuff out, then we can see what we have. I didn't have time when we put it in here.'

'That's a good idea,' I said. 'But you won't have too much time now. It'll be dawn pretty soon, and we don't want to be seen round here.'

We began to pull the boxes out. Coertze had thoughtfully left plenty of room between the trucks so it was easy enough. There were four boxes of jewellery, one filled with nothing else but wedding rings, thousands of them. I had a vague recollection that the patriotic women of Italy had given their wedding rings to the cause – and here they were.

There was the box containing the crown, a massive head-piece studded with jewels. There were eight large cases holding paper currency, neatly packeted and bound with rotting rubber bands. The lire had the original bank wrappers round each bundle. Then there were the remaining bullion boxes on the floor of the truck – another ton of gold.

Francesca went out to the car and brought in some flasks of coffee, and then we sat about examining the loot. The box from which Francesca had taken the necklace was the only one containing jewellery of any great value – but that was enough. I don't know anything about gems, but I conservatively estimated the value of that one box at well over a million pounds.

One of the other boxes was filled with various objects of value, usually in gold, such as pocket watches of bygone design, cigarette cases and lighters, gold medals and medallions, cigar cutters and all the other usual pieces of masculine jewellery. A lot of pieces were engraved, but with differing names, and I thought that this must be the masculine equivalent of the wedding rings – sacrifices to the cause.

The third box contained the wedding rings and the last one was full of gold currency. There were a lot of British sovereigns and thousands of other coins which I identified as being similar to the coins shown to me by Aristide. There were American eagles and Austrian ducats and even some Tangier Hercules. That was a very heavy box.

Francesca picked up the necklace again. 'Beautiful, isn't it?' I said.

'It's the loveliest thing I've seen,' she breathed.

I took it from her fingers. 'Turn round,' I said, and fastened it round her neck. 'This is the only opportunity you'll have of wearing it; it's a pity to waste it.'

Her shoulders straightened and the triple line of diamonds sparkled against her black sweater. Womanlike, she said, 'Oh, I wish I had a mirror.' Her fingers caressed the necklace.

Walker laughed and staggered to his feet, clutching the crown in both hands. He placed it on Coertze's head, driving the bullet head between the broad shoulders. 'King Coertze,' he cried hysterically. 'All hail.'

Coertze braced under the weight of the crown, '*Nee, man,*' he said, 'I'm a Republican.' He looked straight at me and said sardonically, 'There's the king of this expedition.'

To an outsider it would have been a mad sight. Four dishevelled and dirty men, one wearing a golden crown and with drying blood streaking his face, and a none-too-clean woman wearing a necklace worth a queen's ransom. We ourselves were oblivious to the incongruity of the scene; it had been with us too long in our imaginations.

I said, 'Let's think of the next step.'

Coertze lifted his hands and took off the crown. The fun was over; the serious work was to begin again.

'You'll have to finish off the entrance,' I said. 'The last bit isn't big enough to take the loot out.'

Coertze said, '*Ja*, but that won't take long.'

'Nevertheless, it had better be done now; it'll soon be dawn.' I jerked my thumb at the third truck. 'Anything of value back there?'

'There's nothing there but boxes of papers and dead Germans. But you can have a look if you want.'

'I will,' I said, and looked about the tunnel. 'What I suggest is that Walker and I stay here today to get this stuff sorted out and moved to the front where it'll be easier to get out. It'll save time when the trucks come; I don't want them hanging about here for a long time.'

I had thought out this move carefully. Coertze could be relied upon to keep a close watch on Piero and Francesca and would stand no nonsense from them when they went into Varsi.

But Coertze was immediately suspicious; he didn't want to leave me and Walker alone with the loot. I said, 'Dammit, you'll seal us in, and even if we did make a break the stuff we could carry in our pockets wouldn't be worth worrying about compared with the rest of the treasure. All I want to do is save time.'

After a glowering moment he accepted it, and he and Piero went to complete the entrance. I said to Walker, 'Come on, let's take a look farther back.'

He hesitated, and then said, 'No, I'm not going back there. I'm not.'

'I'll go with you,' said Francesca quietly. 'I'm not afraid of

Germans, especially dead ones.' She gave Walker a look of contempt.

I picked up the Tilley lamp and Walker said hysterically, 'Don't take the light.'

'Don't be a damn' fool,' I said. 'Take this to Coertze; it'll suit him better than a torch. You can give him a hand, too.'

As he left I switched on my torch and Francesca did the same. I hefted the hammer and said, 'OK. Let's frighten all those ghosts.'

The third truck was full of packing cases and weapons. There looked to be enough guns to start a war. I picked up a sub-machine-gun and cocked the action; it was stiff, but it worked and a round flew out of the breech. I thought that my gallant efforts at disarming Coertze and Piero were all wasted, or would have been if Coertze had remembered that all these guns were here. I wondered if the ammunition was still safe to use.

Francesca pushed some rifles aside and pulled the lid off one of the cases. It was full of files – dusty files with the *fasces* of the Fascist Government embossed on the covers. She pulled a file out and started to read, riffling the pages from time to time.

'Anything interesting?' I asked.

'It's about the invasion of Albania,' she said. 'Minutes of the meetings of the Army Staff.' She took another file and became absorbed in it. 'This is the same kind of thing, but it's the Ethiopian campaign.'

I left her to the dusty records of forgotten wars and went back to the fourth truck. It was not pretty. The tunnel was very dry and apparently there had been no rats. The bodies were mummified, the faces blackened and the skin drawn tight into ghastly grins – the rictus of death. I counted the bodies – there were fifteen in the truck, piled in higgledy-piggledy like so many sides of beef – and two in the staff car, one of which was the body of an SS officer. There was a wooden case in the back of the truck but I did not investigate it – if it contained anything of value, the dead were welcome to keep it.

I went back to the staff car because I had seen something that interested me. Lying in the back, half hidden by the motor cycle, was a Schmeisser machine pistol. I picked it up and hefted it thoughtfully in my hand. I was thinking more of Coertze than of Metcalfe and my thoughts weren't pleasant. Coertze was suspected of having killed at least three men in order to get this treasure to himself. There was still the share-out to take place and it was on the cards that he would play the same game at some stage or other. The stake involved was tremendous.

The Schmeisser machine pistol is a very natty weapon which I had seen and admired during the war. It looks exactly like an ordinary automatic pistol and can be used as such, but there is a simple shoulder rest which fits into the holster and which clips into place at the back of the hand-grip so that you can steady the gun at your shoulder.

In principle, this is very much like the old Mauser pistol, but there the resemblance ends. Magazines for the Schmeisser come in two sizes – one of eight rounds like an ordinary pistol clip – and the long magazine holding about thirty rounds. With the long magazine in place and the gun switched to rapid fire you have a very handy sub-machine-gun, most effective at close range.

I had not fired a gun since the war and the thought of something which would make up for my lack of marksmanship by its ability to squirt out bullets was very appealing. I looked round to see if there were any spare clips but I didn't see any. Machine pistols were usually issued to sergeants and junior officers, so I prepared myself for an unpleasant task.

Then minutes later I had got what I wanted. I had the holster and belt, stiff with neglect, but containing the shoulder rest, four long clips and four short clips. There was another machine pistol, but I left that. I put the gun in the holster and left it resting in a niche in the tunnel wall together with the clips of ammunition. Then I went back to Francesca.

She was still reading the files by the light of her torch. I said, 'Still reading history?'

She looked up. 'It's a pitiful record; all the arguments and quarrels in high places, neatly tabulated and set down.' She shook her head. 'It is best that these files stay here. All this should be forgotten.'

'It's worth a million dollars,' I said, 'if we could find an American university dishonest enough to buy it. Any historian would give his right arm for that lot. But you're right; we can't let it into the world outside – that would really give the game away.'

'What is it like back there?' she asked.

'Nasty.'

'I would like to see.' she said and jumped down from the truck. I remembered the little girl of the war years who hated Germans, and didn't try to stop her.

She came back within five minutes, her face pale and her eyes stony, and would not speak of it. A long time afterwards she told me that she had vomited back there in sheer horror at the sight. She thought that the bodies ought to have been given decent burial, even though they were German.

When we got back to the front of the tunnel Coertze had finished his work and the entrance was now big enough to push the cases through. I sent Walker and Francesca back to the caravan to bring up food and bedding, then I took Coertze to one side, speaking in English so that Piero wouldn't understand.

'Is there any way to this mine other than by the road we came?' I asked.

'Not unless you travel cross-country,' he replied.

I said, 'You'll stay with Piero and Francesca at the caravan until late afternoon. You'll be able to see if anyone goes up the road; if anyone does you'll have to cut across country damn' quick and warn us, because we may be making a noise here. We'll probably sleep in the afternoon, so it should be all right then.'

'That sounds fair enough,' he said.

'Piero will probably start to look for those ammunition clips I threw away,' I said. 'So you'll have to keep an eye on him. And when you go to Varsi to pick up the trucks, make sure that you all stick together and don't let them talk to anyone unless you're there.'

'*Moenie panik nie*,' he said. 'They won't slip anything over on me.'

'Good,' I said. 'I'm just going to slip out for a breath of fresh air. It'll be the last I'll get for a long time.'

I went outside and strolled about for a while. I thought that everything was going well and if it stayed that way I would be thankful. Only one thing was worrying me. By bringing Francesca and Piero with us, we had cut ourselves off from our intelligence service and we didn't know what Metcalfe and Torloni were up to. It couldn't be helped, but it was worrying all the same.

After a while Piero came from the tunnel and joined me. He looked at the sky and said, 'It will soon be dawn.'

'Yes,' I said. 'I wish Walker and Francesca would come back.' I turned to him. 'Piero, something is worrying me.'

'What is it, Signor Halloran?'

I said, 'Coertze! He still has his gun, and I think he will try to look for those ammunition clips I threw away.'

Piero laughed. 'I will watch him. He will not get out of my sight.'

And that was that. Those two would be so busy watching each other that they wouldn't have time to get up to mischief, and they would stay awake to watch the road. I rather fancied myself as a Machiavelli. I was no longer worrying too much about Francesca; I didn't think she would double-cross anyone. Piero was different; as he had said himself – gold has a bad effect on the character.

A few minutes later, Walker and Francesca came back in the car bringing food and blankets and some upholstered cushions from the caravan to use as pillows. I asked Walker discreetly, 'Any trouble?'

'Nothing,' he said.

The first faint light of morning was in the east. I said, 'Time to go in,' and Walker and I went back into the tunnel. Coertze began to seal up the entrance and I helped him from the inside. As the wall of rock grew higher I began to feel like a medieval hermit being walled up for the good of his soul. Before the last rocks were put in place Coertze said, 'Don't worry about Varsi, it will be all right.'

I said, 'I'll be expecting you tomorrow at nightfall.'

'We'll be here,' he said. 'You don't think I trust you indefinitely with all that stuff in there?'

Then the last rock sealed the entrance, but I heard him scuffling about for a long time as he endeavoured to make sure that it looked normal from the outside.

I went back into the tunnel to find Walker elbow deep in sovereigns. He was kneeling at the box, dipping his hands into it and letting the coins fall with a pleasant jingling sound. 'We might as well make a start,' I said. 'We'll get half of the stuff to the front, then have breakfast, then shift the other half. After that we'll be ready for sleep.'

The job had to be done so we might as well do it. Besides, I wanted to get Walker dead tired so that he would be heavily asleep, when I went to retrieve the Schmeisser.

The first thing we did was to clear the fallen rocks from in front of the first truck. This would be our working space when we had to disguise the bullion boxes and recrate the other stuff. We worked quickly without chatting. There was no sound except our heavy breathing, the subdued roar of the Tilley lamp and the occasional clatter of a rock.

After an hour we had a clear space and began to bring the gold to the front. Those bullion boxes were damnably heavy and needed careful handling. One of them nearly fell on Walker's foot before I evolved the method of letting them drop from the lorry on to the piled-up caravan cushions. The cushions suffered but that was better than a broken foot.

It was awkward getting them to the front of the tunnel. The

space between the lorry and the wall was too narrow for the two of us to carry a box together and the boxes were a little too heavy for one man to carry himself. I swore at Coertze for having reversed the trucks into the tunnel.

Eventually I hunted round among the trucks and found a long towing chain which we fastened round each box in turn so that we could pull it along the ground. The work went faster then.

After we had emptied all the gold from the first truck and had taken it to the front, I declared a breakfast break. Francesca had prepared a hot meal and there was plenty of coffee. As we ate we conversed desultorily.

'What will you do with your share?' I asked Walker curiously.

'Oh, I don't know,' he said. 'I haven't any real plans. I'll have a hell of a good time, I'll tell you that.'

I grimaced. The bookmakers would take a lot of it, I guessed, and the distilleries would show a sudden burst in their profits for the first year, and then Walker would probably be dead of cirrhosis of the liver and delirium tremens.

'I'll probably do a lot of travelling,' he said. 'I've always wanted to travel. What will you do?'

I leaned my head back dreamily. 'Half a million is a lot of money,' I said. 'I'd like to design lots of boats, the experimental kind that no one in their right minds would touch with a barge pole. A big cruising catamaran, for instance; there's a lot of work to be done in that field. I'd have enough money to have any design tank-tested as it should be done. I might even finance a private entry for the America's Cup – I've always wanted to design a 12-metre, and wouldn't it be a hell of a thing if my boat won?'

'You mean you'd go on *working*?' said Walker in horror.

'I like it,' I said. 'It's not work if you like it.'

And so we planned our futures, going from vision to wilder vision until I looked at my watch and said, 'Let's get cracking; the sooner we finish, the sooner we can sleep.' It was nine o'clock and I reckoned we would be through by midday.

We moved the gold from the third truck. This was a longer haul and so took more time. After that it was easy and soon there was nothing left except the boxes of paper currency. Walker looked at them and said hesitantly, 'Shouldn't we...?'

'Nothing doing,' I said sharply. 'I'd burn the lot if I was sure no one would see the smoke.'

He seemed troubled at the heresy of someone wanting to burn money and set himself to count it while I got my blankets together and prepared for sleep. As I lay down, he said suddenly, 'There's about a thousand million lire here – that's a hell of a lot of money. And there's any amount of sterling. Thousands of British fivers.'

I yawned. 'What colour are they?'

'White,' he said. 'The biggest notes I've seen.'

'You pass one of those and you're for the high jump,' I said. 'They changed the design of the fiver when they discovered that the Germans had forged God knows how many millions. Come to think of it, it's quite likely that those are of German manu-facture.'

He seemed disappointed at that, and I said, 'Get some sleep; you'll be glad of it later.'

He gathered his blankets and settled himself down. I lay awake, fighting off sleep, until I heard the slow, regular breathing of deep slumber, then I got up and softly made my way down the tunnel. I retrieved the Schmeisser and the clips and brought them back. I didn't know where to put them at first, then I found that the cushion I was using as a pillow was torn and leaking stuff-ing. I tore out some more of the stuffing and put the gun and the clips inside. It made a hard pillow, but I didn't mind that – if people were going to wave guns at me, I wanted one to wave back.

IV

Neither of us slept very well – we had too much on our minds. I lay, turning restlessly, and hearing Walker doing the same until, at last, we could stand it no longer and we abandoned the pretence of sleep. It was four in the afternoon and I reckoned that the others should be starting for Varsi just about then.

We went up to the front of the tunnel and checked everything again, then settled to wait for nightfall. It could have been night then, if my watch hadn't told us otherwise, because there was no light in the tunnel except for the bright circle cast by the lamp, which quickly faded into darkness.

Walker was nervous. Twice he asked me if I heard a noise, not from the entrance but from back in the tunnel. The bodies of the men he had killed were worrying him. I told him to go back and look at them, thinking the shock treatment might do him good, but he refused to go.

At last I heard a faint noise from the entrance. I took the ham-mer in my hand and waited – this might not be Coertze at all. A rock clattered and a voice said, 'Halloran?'

I relaxed and blew my cheeks out. It *was* Coertze.

Another rock clattered and I said, 'Is everything all right?'

'No trouble at all,' he said, furiously pulling down the screen of rocks. 'The trucks are here.'

Walker and I helped to push down the wall from the inside and Coertze shone a torch in my face. 'Man,' he said. 'But you need a clean-up, ay.'

I could imagine what I looked like. We had no water for washing and the dust lay heavily upon us. Francesca stood next to Coertze. 'Are you all right, Mr Halloran?'

'I'm OK. Where are the trucks?'

She moved, barely distinguishable in the darkness. 'They are back there.'

'There are four Italians,' said Coertze.

'Do they know what they are doing here?' I asked swiftly.

Piero loomed up. 'They know that this is secret, and therefore certainly illegal,' he said. 'But otherwise they know nothing.'

I thought about that. 'Tell two of them to go down to the caravan, strike camp, and then wait there. Tell them to keep a watch on the road and to warn us if anyone comes up. The other two must go into the hills overlooking the mine, one to the left, the other to the right. They must watch for anyone coming across country. This is the tricky part and we don't want anyone surprising us when the gold is in the open.'

Piero moved away and I heard him giving quick instructions. I said, 'The rest of us will start work inside. Bring the timber from the trucks.'

The trucks were all right, bigger than we needed. One of them was loaded with lengths of rough boxwood and there were also some crude crates that would do for putting the loose stuff in. We hauled out the wood and took it into the tunnel, together with the tools – a couple of saws, four hammers and several packets of nails – and we started to nail covers on to the bullion boxes, changing their shape and character.

With four of us it went quickly and, as we worked, we developed an assembly-line technique. Walker sawed the wood into the correct lengths, Coertze nailed on the bottoms and the tops, I put on the sides and Piero put on the ends. Francesca was busy transferring the jewels and the gold trivia from the original boxes into the crates.

Within three hours we had finished and all there was left to do was to take the boxes outside and load them into the trucks.

I rolled my blankets and took my pillow outside and thrust them behind the driving-seat of one of the trucks – that disposed of the Schmeisser very nicely.

The boxes were heavy but Coertze and Piero had the muscle to hoist them vertically into the trucks and to stow them neatly. Walker and I used the chain again to pull the boxes through the narrow entrance. Francesca produced some flasks of coffee and a pile of cut sandwiches and we ate and drank while we worked. She certainly believed in feeding the inner man.

At last we were finished. I said, 'Now we must take away from the tunnel everything we have brought here. We mustn't leave a scrap of evidence that we have been here, not a thing that can be traced back to us.'

So we all went back into the tunnel and collected everything – blankets, cushions, tools, torches, flasks, even the discarded bent nails and fragments of stuffing from the torn cushions. All this went outside to be stowed in the trucks and I stayed behind to take one last look round. I picked up a length of wood that had been forgotten and turned to leave.

Then it happened.

Coertze must have been hasty in shoring up the last bit of the entrance – he had seen the gold and his mind wasn't on his job. As I turned to leave, the piece of timber I was carrying struck the side of the entrance and dislodged a rock. There was a warning creak and I started to run – but it was too late.

I felt a heavy blow on my shoulder which drove me to my knees. There was a rumble of falling rock and then I knew no more.

V

I came round fuzzily, hearing a voice, 'Halloran, are you all right? Halloran?'

Something soft touched my cheek and then something cold and wet. I groaned and opened my eyes but everything was hazy. The back of my head throbbed and waves of pain washed forward into my eyes.

I must have passed out again, but the next time I opened my eyes things were clearer. I heard Coertze saying, 'Can you move your legs, man; can you move your legs?'

I tried. I didn't understand why I should move my legs but I tried. They seemed to move all right so, dizzily, I tried to get up. I couldn't! There was a weight on my back holding me down.

Coertze said, 'Man, now, take it easy. We'll get you out of there, ay.'

He seemed to move away and then I heard Francesca's voice. 'Halloran, you must stay quiet and not move. Can you hear me?'

'I can hear you,' I mumbled. 'What happened?' I found it difficult to speak because the right side of my face was lying on something rough and hard.

'You are pinned down by a lot of rock,' she said. 'Can you move your legs?'

'Yes, I can move my legs.'

She went away and I could hear her talking to someone. My wits were coming back and I realized that I was lying prone with a heavy weight on my back and my head turned so that my right cheek was lying on rock. My right arm was by my side and I couldn't move it; my left arm was raised, but it seemed to be wedged tight.

Francesca came back and said, 'Now, you must listen carefully. Coertze says that if your legs are free then you are only held in your middle. He is going to get you out, but it will be very slow and you mustn't move. Do you understand?'

'I understand,' I said.

'How do you feel? Is there pain?' Her voice was low and gentle.

'I feel sort of numb,' I said. 'All I feel is a lot of pressure on my back.'

'I've got some brandy. Would you like some?'

I tried to shake my head and found it impossible. 'No,' I said. 'Tell Coertze to get cracking.'

She went away and Coertze came back. 'Man,' he said. 'You're in a spot, ay. But do not worry, I've done this sort of thing before. All you have to do is keep still.'

He moved and then I heard the scrape of rock and there was a scattering of dust on my face.

It took a long time. Coertze worked slowly and carefully, removing rocks one at a time, testing each one before he took it away. Sometimes he would go away and I would hear a low-voiced conversation, but he always came back to work again with slow patience.

At last he said, 'It won't be long now.'

He suddenly started to shovel away rocks with more energy and the weight on my back eased. It was a wonderful feeling. He said, 'I'm going to pull you out now. It might hurt a bit.'

'Pull away,' I said.

He grasped my left arm and tugged. I moved. Within two

minutes I was in the open air looking at the fading stars. I tried to get up, but Francesca said, 'Lie still.'

Dawn was breaking and there was enough light to see her face as she bent over me. The winged eyebrows were drawn down in a frown as her hands pressed gently on my body testing for broken bones. 'Can you turn over?' she asked.

It hurt, but I turned on my stomach and heard the rip as she cut away my shirt. Then I heard the sudden hiss of her breath. 'Your back is lacerated badly,' she said.

I could guess how badly. Her hands were soft and gentle as they moved over my back. 'You haven't broken anything,' she said in wonderment.

I grinned. To me it felt as though my back was broken and some-one had built a fire on it, but to hear that there were no broken bones was good. She tore some cloth and began to bind the wounds and when she had finished I sat up.

Coertze held out a baulk of six-by-six. 'You were damned lucky, man. This was across your back and kept the full weight of the rock off you.'

I said, 'Thanks, Kobus.'

He coloured self-consciously and looked away. 'That's all right – Hal,' he said. It was the first time he had ever called me Hal.

He looked at the sky. 'We had better move now.' He appealed to Francesca. 'Can he move?'

I got to my feet slowly. 'Of course I can move,' I said. Fran-cesca made a sudden gesture which I ignored. 'We've got to get out of here.'

I looked at the tunnel. 'You'd better bring down the rest of that little lot and make a good job of it. Then we'll leave.'

Coertze went off towards the tunnel, and I said, 'Where's Walker?'

Piero said, 'He is sitting in a truck.'

'Send him down to the caravan, and whistle up your other two boys – they can go with him. They can all leave now for Rapallo.'

Piero nodded and went away. Francesca said, 'Hadn't you better rest a little?'

'I can rest in Rapallo. Can you drive one of those?' I nodded towards a truck.

'Of course.'

'Good. Coertze and Piero can take one; we'll take the other. I might not be able to manage the driving part, though.'

I didn't want Piero and Francesca alone, and I wanted Walker to keep a watch on the other Italians. Of course, I could have gone as passenger with Piero, but if he tried anything rough I was no match for him in my beat-up condition. Coertze could cope with him – so that left me with Francesca.

'I can manage,' she said.

There was a rumble from the tunnel as Coertze pulled in the entrance, sealing it for ever, I hoped. He came back and I said, 'You go with Piero in that truck; he'll be back in a minute. And don't tail me too close; we don't want to look like a convoy.'

He said, 'Think you'll be all right?'

'I'll be OK,' I said, and walked stiffly towards the truck in which I had left my gear. It was a painful business getting into the cab, but I managed in the end and rested gingerly in the seat, not daring to lean back. Francesca swung easily into the driving-seat and slammed the door. She looked at me and I waved my hand. 'Off we go.'

She started the engine and got off badly by grinding the gears, and we went bouncing down the road from the mine, the rising sun shining through the windscreen.

The journey back to Rapallo was no joy-ride for me. The truck was uncomfortable as only trucks can be at the best of times, and for me it was purgatory because I was unable to lean back in my seat. I was very tired, my limbs were sore and aching, and my back was raw. Altogether I was not feeling too bright.

Although Francesca had said that she could drive the truck, she was not doing too well. She was used to the syncromesh gears of a private car and had a lot of trouble in changing the gears of the truck. To take my mind off my troubles we slowed down and I taught her how to double-declutch and after that things went easier and we began to talk.

She said, 'You will need a doctor, Mr Halloran.'

'My friends call me Hal,' I said.

She glanced at me and raised her eyebrows. 'Am I a friend now?'

'You didn't kick me in the teeth when I was stuck in the tunnel,' I said. 'So you're my friend.'

She slanted her eyes at me. 'Neither did Coertze.'

'He still needs me. He can't get the gold out of Italy without me.'

'He *was* very perturbed,' she agreed. 'But I don't think he had the gold on his mind.' She paused while she negotiated a bend. 'Walker had the gold on his mind, though. He sat in a truck all the time, ready to drive away quickly. A contemptible little man.'

I was too bemused by my tiredness to take in the implications of all this. I sat watching the ribbon of road unroll and I lapsed into an almost hypnotic condition. One of the things which fleetingly passed through my mind was that I hadn't seen the cigarette case which Walker had spoken of many years previously – the cigarette case which Hitler was supposed to have presented to Mussolini at the Brenner Pass in 1940.

I thought of the cigarette case once and then it passed from my mind, not to return until it was too late to do anything about it.

6 *Metcalfe*

The next day I felt better.

Everybody had got back to Palmerini's boatyard without untoward happenstance and we had moved into the big shed that was reserved for us. The trucks had been unloaded and returned to their owners with thanks, and the caravan stayed in a corner to provide cooking and sleeping space.

But I was in no shape to do much work, so Walker and Coertze went to bring *Sanford* from the yacht basin, after I had checked on Metcalfe and Torloni. Francesca spoke to Palmerini and soon a procession of Italians slipped into the yard to make their reports. They spoke seriously to Francesca and ducked out again, obviously delighting in their return to the role of partisans.

When she had absorbed all they could tell her, Francesca came to me with a set face. 'Luigi is in hospital,' she said unhappily. 'They broke his skull.'

Poor Luigi. Torloni's men had not bothered to bribe him, after all. The harbour police were searching for the assailants but had no success; and they wanted to see me to find out what had been stolen. As far as they were concerned it was just another robbery.

Francesca had an icy coldness about her. 'We know who they were,' she said. 'They will not walk out of Rapallo on their own legs.'

'No,' I said. 'Leave them alone.' I didn't want to show my hand yet because, with any luck, Metcalfe and Torloni might have fallen for the story I had planted. And for some reason, not yet clearly defined in my mind, I didn't want Francesca openly associ-

ated with us – she would still have to live in Italy when we had
gone.

'Don't touch them,' I said. 'We'll take care of them later. What
about Metcalfe and Torloni?'

They were still in Genoa and saw each other every day. When
they found out that we had disappeared from Rapallo they had
rushed up another three men, making five in all. Metcalfe had
pulled the Fairmile from the water and Krupke was busy repaint-
ing the bottom. The Arab, Moulay Idriss, had vanished; no one
knew where he was, but he was certainly not in Rapallo.

That all seemed satisfactory – except for the reinforcement of
Torloni's men in Rapallo. I called Coertze and told him what was
happening. 'When you get to *Sanford* tell the police that I've had a
climbing accident, and that I'm indisposed. Make a hell of a fuss
about the burglary, just as though you were an honest man. Go to
the hospital, see Luigi and tell him that his hospital bill will be
paid and that he'll get something extra for damages.'

Coertze said, 'Let me *donner* those bastards. They needn't have
hit that old man.'

'Don't go near them,' I said. 'I'll let you loose later, just before
we sail.'

He grumbled but held still, and he and Walker went to see what
damage had been done to *Sanford*. After they had gone I had a
talk with Piero. 'You heard about Luigi?'

He pulled down his mouth. 'Yes, a bad business – but just like
Torloni.'

I said, 'I am thinking we might need some protection here.'

'That is taken care of,' he said. 'We are well guarded.'

'Does Francesca know about this?'

He shook his head. 'Women do not know how to do these things
– I will tell Madame when it is necessary. But this boatyard is well
guarded; I can call on ten men within fifteen minutes.'

'They'll have to be strong and tough men to fight Torloni's
gangsters.'

His face cracked into a grim smile. 'Torloni's men know nothing,'
he said contemptuously. 'The men I have called are fighting
men; men who have killed armed Germans with their bare hands.
I would feel sorry for Torloni's gang were it not for Luigi.'

I felt satisfied at that. I could imagine the sort of dock rats Torloni would have working for him; they wouldn't stand a chance
against disciplined men accustomed to military tactics.

I said, 'Remember, we want no killing.'

'There will be no killing if they do not start it first. After that . . .' He shrugged. 'I cannot be responsible for the temper of the men.'

I left him and went into the caravan to clean and oil the Schmeisser. The tunnel had been dry and the gun hadn't taken much harm. I was more dubious about the ammunition; wondering if the charges behind the bullets had suffered chemical deterioration over the past fifteen years. That was something I would find out when the shooting started.

But perhaps there would be no shooting. There was a fair chance that Metcalfe and Torloni knew nothing of our connection with the partisans – I had worked hard enough to cover it. If Torloni attacked he would get the surprise of his life, but I hoped he wouldn't – I didn't want the Italians involved too much.

Coertze and Walker brought *Sanford* to the yard in the late afternoon and Palmerini's sons got busy slipping her and unstepping the mast. Coertze said, 'We were followed by a fast launch.'

'So they know we are here?'

'*Ja*,' he said. 'But we made them uncomfortable.'

Walker said, 'We took her out, and they had to follow us because they thought we were leaving. There was a bit of a lop outside the harbour and they were sea-sick – all three of them.' He grinned. 'So was Coertze.'

'Did they do much damage to *Sanford* when they broke in?'

'Not much,' replied Coertze. 'They turned everything out of the lockers, but the police had cleaned up after the pigs.'

'The furnaces?'

'All right; those were the first things I checked.'

That was a relief. The furnaces were now the king-pins of the plan and if they had gone the whole of our labour would have been wasted. There would have been no time to replace them and still meet the deadline at Tangier. As it was, we would have to work fast.

Coertze got busy getting the furnaces out of *Sanford*. It wasn't a long job and soon he was assembling them on a bench in the corner of the shed. Piero looked at them uncomprehendingly but said nothing.

I realized it would be pointless to try to conceal our plan from him and Francesca – it just couldn't be done. And in any case, I was getting a bit tired of the shroud of suspicion with which I had cloaked myself. The Italians had played fair with us so far and we were entirely at their mercy anyway; they could take the lot any time they wanted if they felt so inclined.

I said, 'We're going to cast a new keel for *Sanford*.'

Piero said, 'Why? What is wrong with that one?'

'Nothing, except it's made of lead. I'm a particular man – I want a keel of gold.'

His face lit up in a delighted smile. 'I wondered how you were going to get the gold out of the country. I thought about it and could see no way, but you seemed so sure.'

'Well, that's how we're going to do it,' I said, and went over to Coertze. 'Look,' I said. 'I'm not going to be any good for any heavy work over the next few days. I'll assemble these gadgets – it's a sitting job – you'd better be doing something else. What about the mould?'

'I'll get started on that,' he said. 'Palmerini has plenty of moulding sand.'

I unfastened my belt and, from the hidden pocket, I took the plan of the new keel I had designed many months previously. I said, 'I had Harry make the alterations to the keelson to go with the new keel. He thought I was nuts. All you've got to do is to cast the keel to this pattern and it'll fit sweetly.'

He took the drawing and went off to see Palmerini. I started to assemble the furnaces – it wasn't a long job and I finished that night.

II

I suppose that few people have had occasion to cut up gold ingots with a hacksaw. It's a devilish job because the metal is soft and the teeth of the saw blades soon become clogged. Walker said it was like sawing through treacle.

It had to be done because we could only melt a couple of pounds of gold at a time, and it was Walker's job to cut up the ingots into handy pieces. The gold dust was a problem which I solved by sending out for a small vacuum cleaner which Walker used assiduously, sucking up every particle of gold he could find.

And when he had finished sawing for the day he would sweep round his bench and wash the dust in a pan just like an old-time prospector. Even with all those precautions I reckon we must have wasted several pounds of gold in the sawing operation.

We all gathered round to watch the first melt. Coertze dropped the small piece of gold on to the graphite mat and switched on the machine. There was an intense white flare as the mat went incandescent and the gold drooped and flowed and, within seconds, was ready for pouring into the mould.

The three furnaces worked perfectly but as they were only laboratory instruments after all, and could only take a small amount at a time, it was going to be a long job. Inside the mould we put a tangle of wires which was to hold the gold together. Coertze was dubious about the method of pouring so little at a time and several times he stopped and removed gold already poured.

'This keel will be so full of cracks I don't think it'll hold.'

So we put in more and more wires and poured the gold round them, hoping they would bind the mass together.

I was stiff and sore and to bend was an agony, so there was not much I could do to help effectively. I discussed this with Coertze, and said, 'You know, one of us had better show his face in Rapallo. Metcalfe knows we're here and it'll look odd if we all stay in this shed and never come out. He'll know we're up to something.'

'You'd better wander round town then,' said Coertze. 'You can't do much here.'

So after Francesca had rebandaged my back, I went into town and up to the Yacht Club. The secretary commiserated with me on the fact that *Sanford* had been broken into and hoped that nothing had been stolen. 'It cannot have been done by men of Rapallo,' he said. 'We are very strict about that here.'

He also looked at my battered face in mute enquiry, so I smiled and said, 'Your Italian mountains seem to be made of harder rock than those in South Africa.'

'Ah, you've been climbing?'

'Trying to,' I said. 'Allow me to buy you a drink.'

He declined, so I went into the bar and ordered a Scotch, taking it to the table by the window where I could look over the yacht basin. There was a new boat in, a large motor yacht of about a hundred tons. You see many of those in the Mediterranean – the luxury boats of the wealthy. They put to sea in the calmest of weather and the large paid crews have the life of Reilly – hardly any work and plenty of shore time. Idly I focused the club binoculars on her. Her name was *Calabria*.

When I left the club I spotted my watchers and took delight in leading them to innocent places which any tourist might have visited. If I had been fitter I would have walked their legs off, but I compromised by taking a taxi. Their staffwork was good, because I noticed a cruising car come up from nowhere and pick them up smoothly.

I went back and reported to Francesca. She said, 'Torloni has sent more men into Rapallo.'

That sounded bad. 'How many?'

'Three more – that makes eight. We think he wants enough men to follow each of you, even if you split up. Besides, they must sleep sometimes, too.'

'Where's Metcalfe?'

'Still in Genoa. His boat was put into the water this morning.'

'Thanks, Francesca, you're doing all right,' I said.

'I will be glad when this business is finished,' she said sombrely. 'I wish I had never started it.'

'Getting cold feet?'

'I do not understand what you mean by that; but I am afraid there will be much violence soon.'

'I don't like it, either,' I said candidly. 'But the thing is under way; we can't stop now. You Italians have a phrase for it – *che sera, sera.*'

She sighed. 'Yes, in a matter like this there is no turning back once you have begun.'

I left her sitting in the caravan, thinking that she was beginning to realize that this was no light-hearted adventure she had embarked upon. This was deady serious, a game for high stakes in which a few murders would not be boggled at, at least, not by the opposition – and I wasn't too sure about Coertze.

The keel seemed to be going well. Coertze and Piero were sweating over the hot furnaces, looking demoniacal in the sudden bursts of light. Coertze pushed up his goggles and said, 'How many graphite mats did we have?'

'Why?'

'They don't last long. I'm not getting more than four melts out of each, then they burn out. We might run out of mats before the job's finished.'

'I'll check on it,' I said, and went to figure with pencil and paper. After checking my calculations and recounting the stocks of mats I went back to Coertze. 'Can you squeeze five melts out of a mat?'

He grunted. 'We'll have to be careful about it, which means we'll be slower. Can we afford the time?'

'If we burn out the mats before the job's done then the time won't matter – it'll be wasted anyway. We'll have to afford the time. How many melts a day can you do at five melts to a mat?'

He thought about that. 'It'll cut us down to twelve melts an hour, no more than that.'

I went away to do some more figuring. Taking the gold at 9000 pounds, that meant 4500 melts of which Coertze had already done 500. Twelve melts an hour means 340 working hours – at twelve hours a day, twenty-eight days.

Too long – start again.

Three hundred and forty hours working at sixteen hours a day – twenty-one days. But could he work sixteen hours a day? I cursed my lacerated back which kept me from helping, but if anything happened and it got worse then I was sure the plan would be torpedoed. Somebody had to take *Sanford* out and I had an increasing distrust of Walker, who had grown silent and secretive.

I went back to Coertze, walking stiffly because my back was hurting like hell. 'You'll have to work long hours,' I said. 'Time's running out.'

'I'd work twenty-four hours a day if I could,' he said. 'But I can't, so I'll work till I drop.'

I thought maybe I'd better go at it a different way, so I stood back and watched how Coertze and Piero were going about the job. Soon I had ideas about speeding it up.

The next morning I took charge. I told Coertze to do nothing but pour gold; he must not have anything to do with loading the furnaces or cleaning mats – all he had to do was pour gold. Piero I assigned to melting the gold and to passing the furnace with the molten gold to Coertze. The furnaces were light enough to be moved about so I arranged a table so that they could be moved bodily along it.

Walker had sawn plenty of gold, so I pulled him from his bench. He had to take a furnace from Coertze, replace the mat with a new one and put a chunk of gold on it ready for melting. Myself I set to the task of cleaning the used mats ready for re-use – this I could do sitting down.

All in all, it was a simple problem in time and motion study and assembly line technique. By the end of the day we were doing sixteen melts an hour without too many burnt-out mats.

So the days went by. We started by working sixteen hours a day but we could not keep it up and gradually our daily output dropped in spite of the increase in the hourly output. Mistakes were made in increasing numbers and the percentage of burnt-out mats went up sharply. Working in those sudden bursts of heat from the furnaces was hellish; we all lost weight and our thirst was unquenchable.

When the output dropped below 150 melts a day with another

2000 to go I began to get really worried. I wanted a clear three weeks to sail to Tangier and it looked as though I was not going to get them.

Obviously something had to be done.

That evening, when we were eating supper after finishing work for the day, and before we turned exhaustedly into our berths, I said, 'Look, we're too tired. We're going to have a day off, to-morrow. We do nothing at all – we just laze about.'

I was taking a chance, gambling that the increased output by refreshed men would more than offset the loss of a day. But Coertze said bluntly, 'No, we work. We haven't the time to waste.'

Coertze was a good man if a bit bull-headed. I said, 'I've been right up to now, haven't I?'

He grudgingly assented to that.

'The output will go up if we have a rest,' I said. 'I promise you.'

He grumbled a little, but didn't press it – he was too tired to fight. The others agreed lacklustrely, and we turned in that night knowing that the next day would be a day of rest.

III

At breakfast, next morning, I asked Francesca, 'What's the enemy doing?'

'Still watching.'

'Any reinforcements?'

She shook her head. 'No, there's just the eight of them. They take it in turns.'

I said, 'We might as well give them some exercise. We'll split up and run them about town, or even outside it. They've been having it too easy lately.'

I looked at Coertze. 'But don't touch them – we're not ready to force a showdown yet, and the later it comes the better for us. We can't afford for any one of us to be put out of action now; if that happens we're sunk. It'll take all our time to cast the keel and meet the deadline as it is.'

To Walker I said, 'And you keep off the booze. You might be tempted, but don't do it. Remember what I said in Tangier?'

He nodded sullenly and looked down at his plate. He had been too quiet lately to suit me and I wondered what he was thinking.

I said to Francesca, 'I thought you were getting a jeweller to appraise the gems.'

'I will see him today,' she said. 'He will probably come tomorrow.'

'Well, when he comes, it must be in disguise or something. Once Torloni's men know that there are jewels involved there may be no holding them.'

Piero said, 'Palmerini will bring him hidden in a lorry.'

'Good enough.' I got up from the table and stretched. 'Now to confuse the issue and the enemy. We'll all leave in different directions. Piero, you and Francesca had better leave later; we don't want any connection to be made between us. Will this place be safe with us all gone?'

Francesca said, 'There'll be ten of our men in the yard all day.'

'That's fine,' I said. 'Tell them not to be too conspicuous.'

I felt fine as I walked into town. My back was healing and my face no longer looked like a battlefield. I was exhilarated at the prospect of a day off work and Coertze must have been feeling even better, I thought. He had not left Palmerini's yard since he had brought *Sanford* in, while I had had several visits to town.

I spent the morning idling, doing a little tourist shopping in the Piazza Cavour where I found a shop selling English books. Then I had a lengthy stay at a boulevard café where I leisurely read a novel over innumerable cups of coffee, something I had not had time for for many months.

Towards midday I went up to the Yacht Club for a drink. The bar seemed noisier than usual and I traced the disturbance to an argumentative and semi-drunk group at the far end of the room. Most members were pointedly ignoring the demonstration but there were raised eyebrows at the more raucous shouts. I ordered a Scotch from the steward and said. 'Why the celebration?'

He sneered towards the end of the bar. 'No celebration, signor; just idle drunkenness.'

I wondered why the secretary didn't order the men from the club and said so. The steward lifted his shoulders helplessly. 'What can one do, signor? There are some men who can break all rules – and here is one such man.'

I didn't press it; it was no affair of mine and it wasn't my business to tell the Italians how to run the club in which I was their guest. But I did take my drink into the adjoining lounge where I settled down to finish the novel.

It was an interesting book, but I never did get it finished, and I've often wondered how the hero got out of the predicament in which the author placed him. I had not read half a dozen pages when a steward came up and said, 'There is a lady to see you, signor.'

I went into the foyer and saw Francesca. 'What the devil are you doing here?' I demanded.

'Torloni is in Rapallo,' she said.

I was going to speak when the club secretary came round the corner and saw us. I said, 'You'd better come inside; it's too damn' conspicuous here.'

The secretary hurried over, saying, 'Ah, Madame, we have not had the honour of a visit from you for a long time.'

I was a member of the club – if only honorary – so I said, 'Perhaps I could bring Madame into the club as my guest?'

He looked unaccountably startled and said nervously, 'Yes, yes, of course. No, there is no need for Madame to sign the book.'

As I escorted Francesca into the lounge I wondered what was agitating the secretary, but I had other things on my mind so I let it slide. I seated Francesca and said, 'You'd better have a drink.'

'Campari,' she said, and then quickly, 'Torloni brought a lot of men with him.'

'Relax,' I said, and ordered a Campari from the lounge steward. When he had left the table I said, 'What about Metcalfe?'

'The Fairmile left Genoa; we don't know where it is.'

'And Torloni? Where is he?'

'He booked into a hotel on the Piazza Cavour an hour ago.'

That was when I had been sitting in the pavement café. I might even have seen him. I said, 'You say he brought some men with him?'

'There are eight men with him.'

That was bad; it looked as though an attack was building up. Eight plus eight made sixteen, plus Torloni himself and possibly Metcalfe, Krupke, the Moroccan and what other crew the Fairmile might have. More than twenty men!

She said, 'We had to work quickly. There was a lot of reorganizing to do – that is why I came here myself, there was no one else.'

I said, 'Just how many men have we got?'

She furrowed her brow. 'Twenty-five – possibly more later. I cannot tell yet.'

That sounded better; the odds were still in our favour. But I wondered about Torloni's massing of force. He would not need so many men to tackle three presumably unsuspecting victims, therefore he must have got wind of our partisan allies, so perhaps we wouldn't have the advantage of surprise.

The steward came with the Campari and as I paid him Francesca looked from the window over the yacht basin. When the steward had gone, she said, 'What ship is that?'

'Which one?'

She indicated the motor yacht I had noticed on my earlier visit to the club. 'Oh, that! It's just some rich man's floating brothel.'

Her voice was strained. 'What is the name?'

I hunted in my memory. 'Er – *Calabria*, I think.'

Her knuckles were clenched white as she gripped the arms of her chair. 'It is Eduardo's boat,' she said in a low voice.

'Who is Eduardo?'

'My husband.'

A light dawned on me. So that was why the secretary had been so startled. It is not very usual for a stranger to ask a lady to be his guest when the lady's husband is within easy reach and possibly in the club at that very moment. I chuckled and said, 'I'll bet he's the chap who is kicking up such a shindy in the bar.'

She said, 'I must go.'

'Why?'

'I do not wish to meet him.' She pushed her drink to one side and picked up her handbag.

I said, 'You might as well finish your drink. It's the first drink I've ever bought you. No man is worth losing a drink over, anyway.'

She relaxed and picked up the Campari. 'Eduardo is not worth anything,' she said tightly. 'All right, I will be civilized and finish my drink; then I will go.'

But we did meet him, after all. Only an Estrenoli – from what I had heard of the breed – would have paused dramatically in the doorway, veered over to our table and have addressed Francesca as he did.

'Ah, my loving wife,' he said. 'I'm surprised to find you here in civilized surroundings. I thought you drank in the gutters.'

He was a stocky man, with good looks dissipated by red-veined eyes and a slack mouth. A wispy moustache disfigured his upper lip and his face was flushed with drink. He ignored me altogether.

Francesca looked stonily ahead, her lips compressed, and did not turn to face him even when he dropped heavily into a chair by her side.

I said, 'You weren't invited to sit with us, signor.'

He swung round and gave a short laugh, looking at me with

an arrogant stare. He turned to Francesca. 'I see that even the Italian scum is not good enough for you now; you must take foreign lovers.'

I stretched out my foot and hooked it behind the rung of his chair, then pulled hard. The chair slid from under him and he tumbled on to the floor and sprawled full length. I got up and stood over him. 'I said you weren't invited to sit down.'

He looked up at me, his face suffused with anger, and slowly scrambled to his feet. Then he glared at me. 'I'll have you out of the country within twenty-four hours,' he screamed. 'Do you know who I am?'

The chance was too good to miss. 'Scum usually floats on top,' I said equably, then I hardened my voice. 'Estrenoli, go back to Rome. Liguria isn't a healthy place for you.'

'What do you mean by that?' he said uneasily. 'Are you threatening me?'

'There are fifty men within a mile of here who would fight each other for the privilege of cutting your throat,' I said. 'I'll tell you what; I'll give *you* twenty-four hours to get out of Liguria. After that I wouldn't give a busted lira for your chances.'

I turned to Francesca. 'Let's get out of here; I don't like the smell.'

She picked up her handbag and accompanied me to the door, walking proudly and leaving Estrenoli standing there impotently. I could hear a stifled buzz of comment in the lounge and there were a few titters at his discomfiture. I suppose there were many who had wanted to do the same thing but he was too powerful a man to cross. I didn't give a damn; I was boiling with rage.

The tittering was too much for Estrenoli and he caught up with us as we were crossing the foyer. I felt his hand on my shoulder and turned my head. 'Take your hand off me,' I said coldly.

He was almost incoherent in his rage. 'I don't know who you are, but the British Ambassador will hear about this.'

'The name's Halloran, and take your goddamn hand off me.'

He didn't. Instead his hand tightened and he pulled me round to face him.

That was too much.

I sank three fingers into his soft belly and he gasped and doubled up. Then I hit him with my fist as hard as I could. All the pent-up frustrations which had accumulated over the past weeks went into that blow; I was hitting Metcalfe and Torloni and all the thugs who were gathering like vultures. I must have broken Estrenoli's jaw and I certainly scraped my knuckles. He went down like a sack of meal and lay in a crumpled heap, blood welling from his mouth.

In the moment of hitting him I felt a fierce pain in my back. 'Christ, my back!' I groaned, and turned to Francesca. But she was not there.

Instead, I was face to face with Metcalfe!

'What a punch!' he said admiringly. 'That bloke's got a busted jaw for sure; I heard it go. Ever consider fighting light-heavy-weight, Hal?'

I was too astounded to say anything, then I remembered Francesca and looked about wildly. She moved into sight from behind Metcalfe.

He said, 'Wasn't this character saying something about the British Ambassador?' He looked about the foyer. Luckily it was deserted and no one had seen the fracas. Metcalfe looked at the nearest door, which was the entrance to the men's room. He grinned. 'Shall we lug the guts into the neighbour room?'

I saw his point and together we dragged Estrenoli into the lavatory and stuffed him into a cubicle. Metcalfe straightened and said, 'If this bird is on speaking terms with the British Ambassador he must be a pretty big noise. Who is he?'

I told him and Metcalfe whistled. 'When you hit 'em, you hit 'em big! Even I have heard of Estrenoli. What did you slug him for?'

'Personal reasons,' I said.

'Connected with the lady?'

'His wife.'

Metcalfe groaned. 'Brother, you do get complicated. You're in a jam, for sure – you'll be tossed out of Italy on your ear within twelve hours.' He scratched behind his ear. 'But maybe not; maybe I can fix it. Wait here and don't let anyone use this john. I'll tell your girl-friend to stick around – and I'll be back in a couple of minutes.'

I leaned against the wall and tried to think coherently about Metcalfe, but I couldn't. My back was hurting like hell and there was a dull throbbing in the hand with which I had hit Estrenoli. It looked as though I had made a mess of everything. I had repeatedly warned Coertze not to get into brawls and now I was guilty of that same thing – and mixed up with Metcalfe to boot.

Metcalfe was as good as his word and was back within two minutes. With him was a squat, blue-jowled Italian dressed in a sharp suit. Metcalfe said, 'This is a friend of mine, Guido Torloni.

Guido, this is Peter Halloran.'

Torloni looked at me in quick surprise. Metcalfe said, 'Hal's in a jam. He's broken a governmental jaw.' He took Torloni on one side and they spoke in low tones. I watched Torloni and thought that the mess was getting worse.

Metcalfe came back. 'Don't worry, Guido can fix it, he can fix anything.'

'Even Estrenoli?' I said incredulously.

Metcalfe smiled. 'Even Estrenoli. Guido is Mr Fixit himself in this part of Italy. Come, let's leave him to it.'

We went into the foyer and I did not see Francesca. Metcalfe said, 'Mrs Estrenoli is waiting outside in my car.'

We went out to the car and Francesca said, 'Is everything all right?'

'Everything is fine,' I said.

Metcalfe chuckled. 'Excepting your husband, Madame. He will be very sorry for himself when he wakes up.'

Francesca's hand was on the edge of the door. I put my hand over hers and pressed it warningly. 'I'm sorry,' I said. 'Francesca, this is Mr Metcalfe, an old friend of mine from South Africa.'

I felt her fingers tense. I said quickly. 'Mr Metcalfe's friend, Mr Torloni, is looking after your husband. I'm sure he'll be all right.'

'Oh yes,' agreed Metcalfe cheerfully. 'Your husband will be fine. He won't make trouble for anyone.' He suddenly frowned. 'How's your back, Hal? You'd better have it seen to right away. If you like I'll drive you to a doctor.'

'It doesn't matter,' I said. I didn't want to be driving anywhere with Metcalfe.

'Nonsense!' he said. 'Who is your doctor?'

It made a bit of a difference if he would take us to a doctor of *our* choice. I looked at Francesca who said, 'I know a good doctor.'

Metcalfe clapped his hands together. 'Fine. Let's get cracking.'

So he drove us through the town and Francesca pointed out a doctor's rooms. Metcalfe pulled up and said, 'You two go in; I'll wait for you here and give you a lift to Palmerini's yard.'

That was another facer. Apparently Metcalfe didn't mind us knowing that he knew our whereabouts. There was something queer in the air and I didn't like it.

As soon as we got into the doctor's waiting-room Francesca said, 'Is *that* Metcalfe? He seems a nice man.'

'He is,' I said. 'But don't get in his way or you'll get run over.' I winced as my back gave a particularly nasty throb. 'What the hell do we do now?'

'Nothing has changed,' said Francesca practically. 'We knew they would be coming. Now they are here.'

That was true. I said, 'I'm sorry I hit your husband.'

'I'm not,' she said simply. 'The only thing I'm sorry for is that you got hurt doing it. And that it might cause trouble for you.'

'It won't,' I said grimly. 'Not while he's in Torloni's hands. And that's another thing I don't understand – why should Metcalfe and Torloni be interested in getting me out of trouble? It doesn't make sense.'

The doctor was ready for us then and he looked at my back. He said that I had torn a ligament and proceeded to truss me up like a chicken. He also bound up my hand, which was a bit damaged where the knuckles had been scraped on Estrenoli's teeth. When we came out Metcalfe waved at us from the car, and called, 'I'll take you down to the yard.'

There didn't seem to be much point in refusing under the circumstances so we climbed into the car. As we were pulling away I said casually, 'How did you know we were in Palmerini's yard?'

'I knew you were cruising in these waters so I asked the Port Captain if you'd shown up yet,' said Metcalfe airily. 'He told me all about you.'

It was logical enough, and if I hadn't known better I might have believed him. He said, 'I hear you're having trouble with your keel.'

That was cutting a bit near the bone. I said, 'Yes, I tried an experimental method of fastening but it doesn't seem to be working out. I might have to take the keel off and refasten it.'

'Make a good job of it,' he said. 'It would be a pity if it dropped off when you're off-shore. You'd capsize immediately.'

This was an uncomfortable conversation; it was reasonable small boat shop-talk, but with Metcalfe you never knew. To my relief he switched to something else. 'What did you do to your face? Been in another brawl lately?'

'I fell off a mountain,' I said lightly.

He made a sucking sound with his lips in commiseration. 'You want to take more care of yourself, Hal, my boy. I wouldn't want anything to happen to you.'

This was too much. 'Why the sudden solicitude?' I asked acidly.

He turned in surprise. 'I don't like seeing my friends get bashed about, especially you. You're quite a handsome feller, you know.'

He turned to Francesca. 'Isn't he?'

'I think so,' she said.

I was surprised at that. 'I'll survive,' I said, as Metcalfe drew up at the gate of the boatyard. 'I'm getting to be an expert at it.'

Francesca and I got out of the car, and Metcalfe said, 'Not going to show me your new keel fastening, Hal?'

I grinned. 'Hell, I'm a professional designer; I never show my mistakes to anyone.' If he could play fast and loose in a hinting conversation, so could I.

He smiled. 'Very wise of you. I'll be seeing you around, I suppose?'

I stepped up to the car out of earshot of Francesca. 'What will happen to Estrenoli?'

'Nothing much. Guido will take him to a good, safe doctor and have him fixed up, then he'll dump him in Rome after throwing a hell of a scare into him. It's my guess that Estrenoli's not very brave and our Guido is a very scary character when he wants to be. There'll be no more trouble.'

I stepped back from the car, relieved. I had been afraid that Estrenoli would be dumped at the bottom of the bay in a concrete overcoat, and I didn't want anyone's life on my conscience, not even his. I said, 'Thanks. Yes, I'll be seeing you around. One can scarcely avoid it – in a town as small as this, can one?'

He put the car into gear and moved forward slowly, grinning from the side window. 'You're a good chap, Hal; don't let anybody put one over on you.'

Then he was gone and I was left wondering what the hell it was all about.

IV

The atmosphere in the shed was tense. As we walked through the yard I noticed that there were many more people about than usual; those would be Francesca's friends. When we got into the shed Piero strode up and said, 'What happened at the club?' His voice was shaking with emotion.

'Nothing happened,' I said. 'Nothing serious.' I saw a stranger in the background, a little man with bright, watchful eyes. 'Who the devil's that?'

Piero turned. 'That's Cariaceti, the jeweller – never mind him. What happened at the club? You went in and so did Madame;

then this Metcalfe and Torloni went in; then you and Madame came out with Metcalfe. What is happening?'

I said, 'Take it easy; everything is all right. We bumped into Estrenoli and he got flattened.'

'Estrenoli?' said Piero in surprise, and looked at Francesca who nodded in confirmation. 'Where is he now?' he demanded fiercely.

'Torloni's got him,' I said.

That was too much for Piero. He sat on a trestle and gazed at the floor. 'Torloni?' he said blankly. 'What would Torloni want with Estrenoli?'

'Damned if I know,' I said. 'This whole thing is one of Metcalfe's devious ploys. All I know is that I had a bust-up with Estrenoli and Metcalfe has removed him from circulation for a while – and don't ask me why.'

He looked up. 'It is said that you were very friendly with Metcalfe today.' His voice was heavy with suspicion.

'Why not? There's nothing to be gained by antagonizing him. If you want to know what happened, ask Francesca – she was there.'

'Hal is right,' said Francesca. 'His treatment of Metcalfe was correct. He was given much provocation and refused to be annoyed by it. Besides,' she said with a slight smile, 'Metcalfe would seem to be a difficult man to hate.'

'It is not difficult to hate Torloni,' growled Piero. 'And Metcalfe is his friend.'

This wasn't getting us anywhere, so I said, 'Where are Coertze and Walker?'

'In the town,' said Piero. 'We know where they are.'

'I think they had better come in,' I said. 'Things may start to move fast – we'd better decide what to do next.'

He silently got up and went outside. I walked over to the little jeweller. 'Signor Cariaceti,' I said. 'I understand that you have come here to look at some gems.'

'That is so,' he said. 'But I do not wish to remain here long.'

I went back to Francesca. 'You'd better turn Cariaceti loose among the jewels,' I said. 'There may not be much time.'

She went to talk to Cariaceti and I looked moodily at the keel, still lacking nearly two tons of weight. Things were at a low ebb and I felt pretty desperate. It would take eight more days working at high pressure to finish the keel, another day to fasten it in position and another to replace the glass-fibre cladding and to launch Sanford.

Ten days! Would Metcalfe and Torloni wait that long?

After a little while Francesca came back. 'Cariaceti is amazed,' she said. 'He is the happiest man I have ever seen.'

'I'm glad someone is happy,' I said gloomily. 'This whole thing is on the point of falling to pieces.'

She put her hand on my arm. 'Don't blame yourself,' she said. 'No one could have done more than you.'

I sat on the trestle. 'I suppose things *could* be worse,' I said. 'Walker could get stinking drunk just when we need him, Coertze could run amok like a mad bull and I could fall and break a few bones.'

She took my bandaged hand in hers. 'I have never said this to any man,' she said. 'But you are a man I could admire very much.'

I looked at her hand on mine. 'Only admire?' I asked gently.

I looked up to see her face colouring. She took her hand away quickly and turned from me. 'Sometimes you make me very annoyed, Mr Halloran.'

I stood up. 'It was "Hal" not very long ago. I told you that my friends call me Hal.'

'I am your friend,' she said slowly.

'Francesca, I would like you to be more than my friend,' I said.

She was suddenly very still and I put my hand on her waist. I said, 'I think I love you, Francesca.'

She turned quickly, laughing through tears. 'You only think so, Hal. Oh, you English are so cold and wary. I *know* that I love you.'

Something seemed to give at the pit of my stomach and the whole dark shed seemed brighter. I said, 'Yes, I love you; but I didn't know how to say it properly – I didn't know what you would say when I told you.'

'I say "bravo".'

'We'll have a good life,' I said. 'The Cape is a wonderful place – and there is the whole world besides.'

She saddened quickly. 'I don't know, Hal; I don't know. I am still a married woman; I can't marry you.'

'Italy isn't the world,' I said softly. 'In most other countries divorce is not dishonourable. The men who made the laws for divorce were wise men; they would never tie anyone to a man like Estrenoli for life.'

She shook her head. 'Here in Italy and in the eyes of my Church, divorce is a sin.'

'Then Italy and your Church are wrong. I say it; even Piero says it.'

She said slowly, 'What is going to happen to my husband?'

'I don't know,' I said. 'Metcalfe tells me that he will be taken back to Rome – under escort.'

'That is all? Torloni will not kill him?'

'I don't think so. Metcalfe said not – and I believe Metcalfe. He may be a scoundrel, but I've never caught him out in a black lie yet.'

She nodded. 'I believe him, too.' She was silent for a while, then she said, 'When I know that Eduardo is safe, then I will come with you, to South Africa or any other place. I will get a foreign divorce and I will marry you, but Eduardo must be alive and well. I could not have that thing on my conscience.'

I said, 'I will see to it. I will see Metcalfe.' I looked at the keel. 'But I must also see this thing through. I have set my hand to it and there are others to consider – Coertze, Walker, Piero, all your men – I can't stop now. It isn't just the gold, you know.'

'I know,' she said. 'You must have been hurt by someone to start a thing like this. It is not your natural way.'

I said, 'I had a wife who was killed by a drunkard like Walker.'

'I know so little of your past life,' she said in wonder. 'I have so much to learn. Your wife – you loved her very much.' It was not a question, it was a statement.

I told her a little about Jean and more about myself and for a while we talked about each other in soft voices, the way that lovers do.

V

Then Coertze came in.

He wanted to know what all the hurry was and why his rest day had been broken into. For a man who didn't want to stop work he was most averse to being interrupted in his brief pleasures.

I brought him up to date on events and he was as puzzled as any of us. 'Why should Metcalfe want to help us?' he asked.

'I don't know, and I don't intend to ask him,' I said. 'He might tell me the truth and the truth might be worse than any suspicions we may have.'

Coertze did as I had done and went to stare at the keel. I said, 'Another eight days of casting – at the least.'

'*Magtig*,' he burst out. 'No one is going to take this away from me now.' He took off his jacket. 'We'll get busy right now.'

'You'll have to do without me for an hour,' I said. 'I have an appointment.'

Coertze stared at me but did not say anything as I struggled into my jacket. Francesca helped me to put it on over the carapace of bandaging under my shirt. 'Where are you going?' she asked quietly.

'To see Metcalfe. I want to make things quite clear.'

She nodded. 'Be careful.'

On the way out I bumped into Walker who looked depressed. 'What's the matter with you?' I said. 'You look as though you've lost a shilling and found a sixpence.'

'Some bastard picked my pocket,' he said savagely.

'Lose much?'

'I lost my ci . . .' He seemed to change his mind. 'I lost my wallet.'

'I wouldn't worry about that,' I said. 'We're going to lose the gold if we aren't careful. See Coertze, he'll tell you about it.' I pushed past him, leaving him staring at me.

I went into Palmerini's office and asked if I could borrow his car. He didn't mind so I took his little Fiat and drove down to the yacht basin. I found the Fairmile quite easily and noted that it was not visible from the Yacht Club, which was why I hadn't spotted it earlier. Krupke was polishing the bright-work on the wheelhouse.

'Hi,' he said. 'Glad to see you. Metcalfe told me you were in town.'

'Is he on board? I'd like to see him.'

'Wait a minute,' said Krupke and went below. He came back almost immediately. 'He says you're to come below.'

I jumped on to the deck and followed Krupke below to the main saloon. Metcalfe was lying on a divan reading a book. 'What brings you here so soon?' he asked.

'I want to tell you something,' I said, and glanced at Krupke.

'OK, Krupke,' said Metcalfe, and Krupke went out. Metcalfe opened a cupboard and produced a bottle and two glasses. 'Drink?'

'Thanks,' I said.

He poured out two stiff ones, and said, 'Mud in your eye.' We drank, then he said, 'What's your trouble?'

'That story you told me about Torloni taking care of Estrenoli — is it true?'

'Sure. Estrenoli's with a doctor now.'

'I just wanted to make sure,' I said. 'And to make certain, you can tell Torloni from me that if Estrenoli doesn't reach Rome safe and sound then I'll kill him personally.'

Metcalfe looked at me with wide eyes. 'Wow!' he said. 'Someone's been feeding you on tiger's milk. What's your interest in the safety of Estrenoli?' He looked at me closely, then laughed and snapped his fingers. 'Of course, the Contessa has turned chicken.'

'Leave her out of it,' I said.

Metcalfe smiled slyly. 'Ah, you young folk; there's no knowing what you'll get up to next.'

'Shut up.'

He held up his hands in mock terror. 'All right, all right.' He laughed suddenly. 'You damn' near killed Estrenoli yourself. If you had hit him a fraction harder he'd have been a dead man.'

'I couldn't hit him harder.'

'I wouldn't take any bets on that,' said Metcalfe. 'He's still unconscious. The quack has wired up his jaw and he won't be able to speak for a month.' He poured out another couple of drinks. 'All right, I'll see he gets to Rome not hurt any more than he is now.'

'I'll want that in writing,' I said. 'From Estrenoli himself — through the post in a letter from Rome datemarked not later than a week today.'

Metcalfe was still. 'You're pushing it a bit hard, aren't you?' he said softly.

'That's what I want,' I said stubbornly.

He looked at me closely. 'Someone's been making a man out of you, Hal,' he said. 'All right, that's the way it'll be.' He pushed the drink across the table. 'You know,' he said musingly, almost to himself, 'I wouldn't stay long in Rapallo if I were you. I'd get that keel fixed damn' quick and I'd clear out. Torloni's a bad man to tangle with.'

'I'm not tangling with Torloni; I only saw him for the first time today.'

He nodded. 'OK. If that's the way you're going to play it, that's your business. But look, Hal; you pushed me just now and I played along because Estrenoli is no business of mine and you're by way of being a pal and maybe I don't mind being pushed in this thing. But don't try to push Torloni; he's bad, he'd eat you for breakfast.'

'I'm not pushing Torloni,' I said. 'Just as long as he doesn't push me.' I finished the drink and stood up. 'I'll see you around.'

Metcalfe grinned. 'You certainly will. As you said — it's a small town.'

He came up on deck to see me off and as I drove back to the yard I wondered greatly about Metcalfe. There had been some plain speaking – but not plain enough – and the whole mystery of Metcalfe's position was deepened. He had as much as said, 'Get clear before Torloni chops you,' and I couldn't understand his motives – after all, Torloni was *his* man.

It was beyond me.

When I got back to the boatyard work in the shed was continuing as though there had never been a break. There was a sudden glare as a chunk of gold melted and Coertze bent over the mould to pour it.

Francesca came up to me and I said, 'It's fixed; you'll hear from Eduardo within the week.'

She sighed. 'Come and have supper. You haven't eaten yet.'

'Thanks,' I said and followed her to the caravan.

7   The Golden Keel

We worked, my God, how we worked.

The memory of that week remains with me as a dark and shadowed mystery punctuated by bright flashes of colour. We melted and poured gold for sixteen hours a day, until our arms were weary and our eyes sore from the flash of the furnaces. We dropped into our berths at night, asleep before we hit the pillows, and it would seem only a matter of minutes before we were called again to that damned assembly line I had devised.

I grew to hate the sight and the feel of gold, and the smell too – it has a distinctive odour when molten – and I prayed for the time when we would be at sea again with nothing more than a gale and a lee shore to worry about. I would rather have been alone in a small boat in a West Indies hurricane than undergo another week of that torture.

But the work was done. The mass of gold in the mould grew bigger and bigger and the pile of unmelted ingots became smaller. We were doing more than 250 melts a day and I calculated that we would gain half a day on my original ten-day schedule. A twelve-hour gain was not much, but it might mean the difference between victory and defeat.

Metcalfe and Torloni were keeping oddly quiet. We were watched – or rather, the boatyard was watched – and that was all. In spite of the reinforcements that Torloni had pushed into Rapallo, and in spite of the fact that he was personally supervising operations himself, there were no overt moves against us.

I couldn't understand it.

The only cheering aspect of the whole situation was Francesca. She cooked our food and did our housekeeping, received messages and issued instructions to the intelligence service and, although in the pace of work we had little time to be together, there was always something small like a hand's touch or a smile across the room to renew my will to go on.

Five days after I had seen Metcalfe she received a letter which she burned after reading it with a frown of pain on her brow. She came to me and said, 'Eduardo is safe in Rome.'

'Metcalfe kept his promise,' I said.

A brief smile touched her lips. 'So will I.' She grew serious. 'You must see the doctor tomorrow.'

'I haven't time,' I said impatiently.

'You must make time,' she insisted. 'You will have to sail *Sanford* very soon; you must be fit.'

She brought Coertze into the argument. He said, 'She's right. We don't want to depend on Walker, do we?'

That was another worry. Walker was deteriorating rapidly. He was moody and undependable, given to violent tempers and unpredictable fits of sulking. The gold was rotting him slowly but certainly, corrupting him far more than any alcohol.

Coertze said, 'Man, go to the doctor.' He smiled sheepishly. 'It's my fault you have a bad back, anyway. I could have shored up that passage better than I did. You go, and I'll see the work doesn't suffer.'

That was the first time that Coertze admitted responsibility for anything, and I respected him for it. But he had no sympathy for my scraped knuckles, maintaining that a man should learn how to punch without damaging himself.

So the next day Francesca drove me to see the doctor. After he had hissed and tutted and examined and rebandaged my back, he expressed satisfaction at my progress and said I must see him at the same time the following week. I said I would come, but I knew that by then we would be at sea on our way to Tangier.

When we were again seated in the car Francesca said, 'Now we go to the Hotel Levante.'

'I've got to get back.'

'A drink will do you good,' she said. 'A few minutes won't hurt.'

So we went to the Hotel Levante, wandered into the lounge and ordered drinks. Francesca toyed with her glass and then said hesitantly, 'There's something else – another reason why I brought you here. I want you to meet someone.'

'Someone here? Who?'

'My father is upstairs. It is right that you see him.'

This was unexpected. 'Does he know about us?'

She shook her head. 'I told him about the gold and the jewels. He was very angry about that, and I don't know what he is going to do. I did not tell him about you and me.'

This looked as though it was going to be a difficult interview. It is not often that a prospective son-in-law has to admit that he is a gold smuggler before he asks for a hand in marriage – a hand that is already married to someone else, to make things worse.

I said, 'I would like very much to meet your father.'

We finished our drinks and went up to the old man's room. He was sitting in an arm-chair with a blanket across his knees and he looked up sharply when we appeared. He looked tired and old; his hair was white and his beard no longer bristled, as I had heard it described, but had turned wispy and soft. His eyes were those of a beaten man and had no fight in them.

'This is Mr Halloran,' said Francesca.

I walked across to him. 'I'm very glad to meet you, sir.'

Something sparked in his eyes. 'Are you?' he said ignoring my outstretched hand. He leaned back in his chair. 'So you are the thief who is stealing my country's gold.'

I felt my jaw tightening. I said evenly, 'Apparently you do not know the laws of your own country, sir.'

He raised shaggy white eyebrows. 'Oh! Perhaps you can enlighten me, Mr Halloran.'

'This treasure falls under the legal heading of abandoned property,' I said. 'According to Italian law, whoever first takes possession of it thereafter is the legal owner.'

He mused over that. 'I dare say you could be right; but, in that case, why all this secrecy?'

I smiled. 'A lot of money is involved. Already the vultures are gathering, even with the secrecy we have tried to keep.'

His eyes snapped. 'I don't think your law is good, young man. This property was not abandoned; it was taken by force of arms from the Germans. It would make a pretty court case indeed.'

'The whole value would go in legal expenses, even if we won,' I said dryly.

'You have made your point,' he said. 'But I don't like it, and I don't like my daughter being involved in it.'

'Your daughter has been involved in worse things,' I said tightly.

'What do you mean by that?' he demanded sharply.

'I mean Estrenoli.'

He sighed and leaned back in his chair, the spark that had been in him burned out and he was once more a weary old man. 'Yes, I know,' he said tiredly. 'That was a shameful thing. I ought to have forbidden it, but Francesca . . .'

'I had to do it,' she said.

'Well, you won't have to worry about him any more,' I said. 'He'll stay away from you now.'

The Count perked up. 'What happened to him?'

There was a ghost of a smile round Francesca's mouth as she said, 'Hal broke his jaw.'

'You did? You did?' The Count beckoned. 'Come here, young man; sit close to me. You really hit Estrenoli? Why?'

'I didn't like his manners.'

He chuckled. 'A lot of people don't like the Estrenoli manners, but no one has hit an Estrenoli before. Did you hurt him?'

'A friend tells me that I nearly killed him.'

'Ah, a pity,' said the Count ambiguously. 'But you will have to be careful. He is a powerful man with powerful friends in the Government. You will have to leave Italy quickly.'

'I will leave Italy, but not because of Estrenoli. I imagine he is a very frightened man now. He will be no trouble.'

The Count said, 'Any man who can get the better of an Estrenoli must have my thanks – and my deepest respect.'

Francesca came over to me and put her hand on my shoulder. 'I also am going to leave Italy,' she said. 'I am going away with Hal.'

The Count looked at her for a long time then dropped his head and stared at the bony hands crossed in his lap. 'You must do what you think best, my child,' he said in a low voice. 'Italy has given you nothing but unhappiness; perhaps to find happiness you must go to another country and live under different laws.'

He raised his head. 'You will cherish her, Mr Halloran?'

I nodded, unable to speak.

Francesca went to him, kneeling at his side, and took his hands in hers. 'We must do it, Papa; we're in love. Can you give us your blessing?'

He smiled wryly. 'How can I give my blessing to something I think is a sin, child? But I think that God is wiser than the churchmen and He will understand. So you have my blessing and you must hope that you have God's blessing too.'

She bent her head and her shoulders shook. He looked up at me. 'I was against this marriage to Estrenoli, but she did it for me. It is our law here that such a thing cannot be undone.'

Francesca dried her eyes. She said, 'Papa, we have little time and I must tell you something. Cariaceti – you remember little Cariaceti – will come to you from time to time and give you money. You must . . .'

He broke in. 'I do not want such money.'

'Papa, listen. The money is not for you. There will be a lot of money and you must take a little for yourself if you need it, but most of it must be given away. Give some to Mario Pradelli for his youngest child who was born spastic; give some to Pietro Morelli for his son whom he cannot afford to send to university. Give it to those who fought with you in the war; those who were cheated by the Communists just like you were; those who need it.'

I said, 'My share of the gold is Francesca's, to do with as she likes. That can be added, too.'

The Count thought deeply for a long time, then he said musingly, 'So something good may come out of this after all. Very well, I will take the money and do as you say.'

She said, 'Piero Morese will help you – he knows where all your old comrades are. I will not be here; I leave with Hal in a few days.'

'No,' I said. 'You stay. I will come back for you.'

'I am coming with you,' she declared.

'You're staying here. I won't have you on *Sanford*.'

The Count said, 'Obey him, Francesca. He knows what he must do, and perhaps he could not do it if you were there.'

She was rebellious, but she acquiesced reluctantly. The Count said, 'Now you must go, Francesca. I want to talk to your Hal – alone.'

'I'll wait downstairs,' she said.

The Count watched her go. 'I think you are an honourable man, Mr Halloran. So I was told by Piero Morese when he talked to me on the telephone last night. What are your exact intentions when you take my daughter from Italy?'

'I'm going to marry her,' I said. 'Just as soon as she can get a divorce.'

'You realize that she can never come back to Italy in those circumstances? You know that such a marriage would be regarded here as bigamous?'

'I know – and Francesca knows. You said yourself that she has had nothing but unhappiness in Italy.'

'That is true.' He sighed. 'Francesca's mother died when she was young, before the war. My daughter was brought up in a partisan camp in the middle of a civil war and she has seen both the heroism and degradation of men from an early age. She is not an ordinary woman because of this; some would have been made bitter by her experiences, but she is not bitter. Her heart is big enough to have compassion for all humanity – I would not like to see it broken.'

'I love Francesca,' I said. 'I will not break her heart, not wittingly.'

He said, 'I understand you are a ship designer and a shipbuilder.'

'Not ships – small boats.'

'I understand. After I talked to Piero I thought I would see what sort of man you were, so a friend kindly asked some questions for me. It seems you have a rising reputation in your profession.'

I said, 'Perhaps in South Africa; I didn't know I was known here.'

'There has been some mention of you,' he said. 'The reason I bring this up is that I am pleased that it is so. This present venture in which you are engaged I discount entirely. I do not think you will succeed – but if you do, such wealth is like the gold of fairies, it will turn to leaves in your hands. It is good to know that you do fine work in the field of your choice.'

He pulled the blanket round him. 'Now you must go; Francesca will be waiting. I cannot give you more than my good wishes, but those you have wherever you may be.'

I took his proffered hand and said impulsively, 'Why don't you leave Italy, too, and come with us?'

He smiled and shook his head. 'No, I am old and the old do not like change. I cannot leave my country now, but thank you for the thought. Goodbye, Hal, I think you will make my daughter very happy.'

I said goodbye and left the room. I didn't see the Count ever again.

II

The time arrived when, incredibly, the keel was cast.

We all stood round the mould and looked at it a little uncertainly. It seemed impossible that all our sweat and labour should have been reduced to this inert mass of dull yellow metal, a mere eight cubic feet shaped in a particular and cunning way.

I said, 'That's it. Two more days and *Sanford* will be in the water.'

Coertze looked at his watch. 'We've got time to do some more work today; we can't knock off just because the keel is finished – there's still plenty to do.'

So we got on with it. Walker began to strip the furnaces and I directed Coertze and Piero in stripping the glass-fibre cladding from *Sanford* preparatory to removing the lead keel. We were happy that night. The change of work and pace had done us good and we all felt rested.

Francesca reported that everything was quiet on the potential battle-front – Metcalfe was on the Fairmile and Torloni was in his hotel; the watch on the boatyard had not been intensified – in fact, everything was as normal as a thoroughly abnormal situation could be.

The trouble would come, if it had to come at all, when we launched *Sanford*. At the first sign of us getting away the enemy would be forced to make a move. I couldn't understand why they hadn't jumped us before.

The next day was pure joy. We worked as hard as ever and when we had finished *Sanford* was the most expensively built boat in the world. The keel bolts which Coertze had cast into the golden keel slipped smoothly into the holes in the keelson which Harry had prepared long ago in Cape Town, and as we let down the jacks *Sanford* settled comfortably and firmly on to the gold.

Coertze said, 'I can't see why you didn't use the existing holes – the ones drilled for the old keel.'

'It's the difference in weight distribution,' I said. 'Gold is half as heavy again as lead and so this keel had to be a different shape from the old one. As it is, I had to juggle with the centre of gravity. With the ballast being more concentrated I think *Sanford* will roll like a tub, but that can't be helped.'

I looked at *Sanford*. She was now worth not much short of a million and three-quarter pounds – the most expensive 15-tonner in history. I felt quite proud of her – not many yacht designers could boast of such a design.

When we had supper that night we were all very quiet and re-laxed. I said to Francesca, 'You'd better get the jewels out tonight – it may be your last chance before the fireworks start.'

She smiled. 'That will be easy; Piero has cast them into con-crete bricks – we are learning the art of disguise from you. They are outside near the new shed that Palmerini is building.'

I laughed. 'I must see this.'

'Come,' she said. 'I will show you.'

We went into the dark night and she flashed a torch on an untidy heap of bricks near the new shed. 'There they are; the valuable bricks are spotted with whitewash.'

'Not bad,' I said. 'Not bad at all.'

She leaned against me and I put my arms around her. It was not often we had time for this sort of thing, we were missing a lot that normal lovers had. After a moment she said quietly, 'When are you coming back?'

'As soon as I've sold the gold,' I said. 'I'll take the first plane out of Tangier.'

'I'll be waiting,' she said. 'Not here – I'll be in Milan with my father.'

She gave me her address which I memorized. I said, 'You won't mind leaving Italy?'

'No, not with you.'

'I asked your father to come with us, but he wouldn't.'

'Not after seventy years,' she said. 'It's too much to ask an old man.'

I said, 'I knew that, but I thought I'd make the offer.'

We talked for a long time there in the darkness, the small personal things that lovers talk about when they're alone.

Then Francesca said that she was tired and was going to bed.

'I'll stay and have another cigarette,' I said. 'It's pleasant out here.'

I watched her melt into the darkness and then I saw the gleam of light as she opened the door of the shed and slipped inside.

A voice whispered from out of the darkness, 'Halloran!'

I started. 'Who's that?' I flashed my torch about.

'Put out that damned light. It's me – Metcalfe.'

I clicked out the torch and stooped to pick up one of the concrete bricks. I couldn't see if it had spots of whitewash on it or not; if it had, then Metcalfe was going to be clobbered by a valuable brick.

A dark silhouette moved closer. 'I thought you'd never stop making love to your girl-friend,' said Metcalfe.

'What do you want, and how did you get here?'

He chuckled. 'I came in from the sea – Torloni's boys are watching the front of the yard.'

'I know,' I said.

There was surprise in his voice. 'Do you now?' I saw the flash of his teeth. 'That doesn't matter, though; it won't make any differ-ence.'

'It won't make any difference to what?'

'Hal, boy, you're in trouble,' said Metcalfe. 'Torloni's going to jump you – tonight. I tried to hold him in, but he's got completely out of hand.'

'Whose side are you on?' I demanded.

He chuckled, 'Only my own,' he said. He changed his tone. 'What are you going to do?'

I shrugged. 'What can I do except fight?'

'Be damned to that,' he said. 'You wouldn't have a chance against Torloni's cut-throats. Isn't your boat ready for launch-ing?'

'Not yet. She still needs sheathing and painting.'

'What the hell?' he said angrily. 'What do you care if you get worm in your planking now? Is the new keel on?'

I wondered how he knew about that. 'What if it is?'

'Then get the stick put back and get the boat into the water, and do it now. Get the hell out of here as fast as you can.' He thrust something into my hand. 'I had your clearance made out. I told you I was a pal of the Port Captain.'

I took the paper and said, 'Why warn us? I thought Torloni was your boy.'

He laughed gently. 'Torloni is nobody's boy but his own. He was doing me a favour but he didn't know what was in the wind. I told him I just wanted you watched. I was sorry to hear about the old watchman – that was Torloni's thugs, it wasn't my idea.'

I said, 'I thought hammering old men wasn't your style.'

'Anyway,' he said. 'Torloni knows the score now. It was that damn' fool Walker who gave it away.'

'Walker! How?'

'One of Torloni's men picked his pocket and pinched his cigar-ette case. It wasn't a bad case, either; it was made of gold and had a nice tasteful inscription on the inside – "*Caro Benito da parte di Adolf – Brennero – 1940.*" As soon as Torloni saw that he knew what was up, all right. People have been scouring Italy for that treasure ever since the war, and now Torloni thinks he has it right in his greasy fist.'

I damned Walker at length for an incompetent, crazy idiot.

Metcalfe said, 'I tried to hold Torloni, but he won't be held any longer. With what's a stake he'd as soon cut my throat as yours – that's why I'm giving you the tip-off.'

'When is he going to make his attack?'

'At three in the morning. He's going to move in with all his crowd.'

'Any guns?'

Metcalfe's voice was thoughtful. 'No, he won't use guns. He wants to do this quietly and he wants to get the gold out. That'll take some time and he doesn't want the police breathing down his neck while he's doing it. So there'll be no guns.'

That was the only good thing I'd heard since Metcalfe had surprised me. I said, 'Where are his men now?'

'As far as I know they're getting some sleep – they don't like being up all night.'

'So they're in their usual hotels – all sixteen of them.'

Metcalfe whistled. 'You seem to know as much about it as I do.'

'I've known about it all the time,' I said shortly. 'We've had them tabbed ever since they moved into Rapallo – before that, too. We had your men spotted in every port in the Mediterranean.'

He said slowly, 'I wondered about that ever since Dino was beaten up in Monte Carlo. Was that you?'

'Coertze,' I said briefly. I gripped the brick which I was still holding. I was going to clobber Metcalfe after all – he played a double game too often and he might be playing one now. I thought we had better keep him where we could watch him.

He laughed. 'Yes, of course, that's just his mark.'

I lifted the brick slowly. 'How did you cotton on to us?' I asked. 'It must have been in Tangier, but what gave the game away?'

There was no answer.

I said, 'What was it, Metcalfe?' and raised the brick.

There was silence.

'Metcalfe?' I said uncertainly, and switched on my torch. He had gone and I heard a faint splashing from the sea and the squeak of a rowlock. I ought to have known better than to think I could outwit Metcalfe; he was too wise a bird for me.

III

As I went to the shed I looked at my watch; it was ten o'clock – five hours to go before Torloni's assault. Could we replace the mast and all the standing rigging in time? I very much doubted it. If we turned on the floodlights outside the shed, then Torloni's watchers would know that something unusual was under way and he would move in immediately. If we worked in the dark it would

be hell's own job – I had never heard of a fifty-five foot mast being stepped in total darkness and I doubted if it could be done.

It looked very much as though we would have to stay and
fight.

I went in and woke Coertze. He was drowsy but he woke up
fast enough when I told him what was happening. I omitted to
mention Walker's part in the mess – I still needed Walker and I
knew that if I told Coertze about it I would have a corpse and
a murderer on my hands, and this was no time for internal dissen-
sion.

Coertze said suspiciously, 'What the hell is Metcalfe's game?'

'I don't know and I care less. The point is that he's given us
the tip-off and if we don't use it we're fools. He must have fallen
out with Torloni.'

'*Reg*,' said Coertze and swung himself out of his berth. 'Let's get
cracking.'

'Wait a minute,' I said. 'What about the mast?' I told him
my estimate of the chance of replacing the mast in the darkness.

He rubbed his chin and the bristles crackled in the silence. 'I
reckon we should take a chance and turn the lights on,' he said
at last. 'That is, after we've made our preparations for Torloni. We
know he's going to attack and whether he does it sooner or later
doesn't matter as long as we're ready for him.'

This was the man of action – the military commander – speaking.
His reasoning was good so I left him to it. He roused Piero and they
went into a huddle while Walker and I began to clear the shed
and to load up *Sanford*. Francesca heard the noise and got up
to see what was going on and was drawn into Coertze's council of
war.

Presently Piero slipped out of the shed and Coertze called me
over. 'You might as well know what's going to happen,' he said.

He had a map of Rapallo spread out, one of the give-aways
issued by the Tourist Office, and as he spoke he pointed to the
salient features on the map. It was a good plan that he described
and like all good plans it was simple.

I think that if Coertze had not been taken prisoner at Tobruk
he would have been commissioned as an officer sooner or later. He
had a natural grasp of strategy and his plan was the classic military
design of concentration to smash the enemy in detail before they
could concentrate.

He said, 'This is the holiday season and the hotels are full. Torloni couldn't get all his men into the same hotel, so they're spread
around the town – four men here, six here, three here and the

rest with Torloni himself.' As he spoke his stubby finger pointed to places on the map.

'We can call up twenty-five men and I'm keeping ten men here at the yard. There are four of Torloni's men outside the yard right now, watching us, and we're going to jump them in a few minutes – ten men should clean them up easily. That means that when we turn on the lights there'll be no one to warn Torloni about it.'

'That seems a good idea,' I said.

'That leaves us fifteen men we can use outside the yard as a mobile force. We have two men outside each hotel excepting this one, here, where we have nine. There are four of Torloni's men staying here and when they come out they'll get clobbered. That ought to be easy, too.'

'You'll have already cut his force by half,' I said.

'That's right. Now, there'll be Torloni and eight men moving in on the yard. He'll expect sixteen, but he won't get them. This may make him nervous, but I think not. He'll think that there'll only be four men and a girl here and he'll reckon he can take us easily. But we'll have fourteen men in the yard – counting us – and I'll bring in another fifteen behind him as soon as he starts anything.'

He looked up. 'How's that, ay?'

'It's great,' I said. 'But you'll have to tell the Italians to move in fast. We want to nail those bastards quick before they can start shooting. Metcalfe said they wouldn't shoot, but they might if they see they're on the losing end.'

'They'll be quick,' he promised. 'Piero's on the blower now, giving instructions. The orders are to clean up the four watchers here at eleven o'clock.' He looked at his watch. 'That's in five minutes. Let's go and see the fun.'

Francesca said, 'I don't see how anything can go wrong.'

Neither could I – but it did!

We were leaving the shed when I noticed Walker tagging on behind. He had been keeping in the background, trying to remain inconspicuous. I let the others go and caught his arm. 'You stay here,' I said. 'If you move out of this shed I swear I'll kill you.'

His face went white. 'Why?'

'So you had your wallet stolen?' I said. 'You damn' fool, why did you have to carry that cigarette case?'

He tried to bluff his way out of it. 'Wh . . . what cigarette case?'

'Don't lie to me. You know what cigarette case. Now stay here and don't move out. I don't want you underfoot – I don't want to have to keep an eye on you all the time in case you make any more damn' silly mistakes.' I took him by the shirt. 'If you don't stay in here I'll tell Coertze just why Torloni is attacking tonight – and Coertze will dismember you limb from limb.'

His lower lip started to tremble. 'Oh, don't tell Coertze,' he whispered. 'Don't tell him.'

I let him go. 'OK. But don't move out of this shed.'

I followed the others up to Palmerini's office. Coertze said, 'It's all set.'

I said to Piero, 'You'd better get Palmerini down here; we'll need his help in rigging the mast.'

'I have telephoned him,' said Piero. 'He will be coming at eleven-fifteen – after we have finished our work here.' He nodded towards the main gate.

'Fine,' I said. 'Do you think we shall see anything of what is happening?'

'A little. One of Torloni's men is not troubling to hide himself; he is under the street lamp opposite the main gate.'

We went up to the gate, moving quietly so as not to alarm the watchers. The gate was of wood, old, unpainted and warped by the sun; there were plenty of cracks through which we could see. I knelt down and through one of the cracks saw a man on the other side of the road, illuminated by the street lamp. He was standing there, idly smoking a cigarette, with one hand in his trouser-pocket. I could hear the faint click as he jingled money or keys.

Coertze whispered, 'Any time now.'

Nothing happened for a while. There was no sound to be heard except for the sudden harsh cry of an occasional seabird. Piero said in a low voice. 'Two have been taken.'

'How do you know?'

There was laughter in his voice. 'The birds – they tell me.'

I suddenly realized what had been nagging at my mind. Sea-gulls sleep at night and they don't cry.

There was a faint sound of singing which grew louder, and presently three men came down the street bellowing vociferously. They had evidently been drinking because they wavered and staggered and one of them had to be helped by the others. The man under the lamp trod on the butt of his cigarette and moved back to the wall to let them pass. One of them waved a bottle in the air and shouted, 'Have a drink, brother; have a drink on my first-born.'

Torloni's man shook his head but they pressed round him clamouring in drunken voices for him to drink. Suddenly the bottle came down sharply and I heard the thud even from across the street.

'God,' I said. 'I hope they haven't killed him.'

Piero said, 'It will be all right; they know the thickness of a man's skull.'

The drunken men were suddenly miraculously sober and came across the street at a run carrying the limp figure of Torloni's man. Simultaneously others appeared from the left and the right, also bearing unconscious bodies. A car came up the street and swerved through the gateway.

'That's four,' said Coertze with satisfaction. 'Take them into the shed.'

'No,' I said. 'Put them in that half-finished shed.' I didn't want them to get a glimpse of anything that might do us damage later. 'Tie them up and gag them; let two men watch them.'

Piero issued orders in rapid Italian and the men were carried away. We were surrounded by a group of Italians babbling of how easy it all was until Piero shouted for silence. 'Are you veterans or are you green recruits?' he bawled. 'By God, if the Count could see you now he'd have you all shot.'

There was an abashed silence at this, and Piero said, 'Keep a watch outside. Giuseppi, go to the office and stay with the telephone; if it rings, call me. You others, watch and keep quiet.'

A car hooted outside the gate and I started nervously. Piero took a quick look outside. 'It is all right; it is Palmerini. Let him in.'

Palmerini's little Fiat came through the gateway and disgorged Palmerini and his three sons in a welter of arms and legs. He came up to me and said, 'I am told you are in a hurry to get your boat ready for sea. That will be extra for the overtime, you understand.'

I grinned. Palmerini was running true to form. 'How long will it take?'

'With the lights – four hours, if you help, too.'

That would be three-fifteen – just too late. We would probably have to fight, after all. I said, 'We may be interrupted, Signor Palmerini.'

'That is all right, but any damage must be paid for,' he answered.

Evidently he knew the score, so I said, 'You will be amply recompensed. Shall we begin?'

He turned and began to berate his sons. 'What are you waiting for, you lazy oafs; didn't you hear the signor? The good God should be ashamed for giving me sons so strong in the arm but

weak in the head.' He chased them down to the shed and I began
to feel happier about everything.

As the lights sprang up at the seaward end of the shed Francesca looked at the gate and said thoughtfully, 'If I was Torloni
and I wanted to come in here quickly I would drive right through
the gate in a car.'

'You mean ram it?'

'Yes, the gate is very weak.'

Coertze said jovially, '*Reg*, we can soon stop that. We've captured one of his cars; I'll park it across the gateway behind the
gate. If he tries that trick he'll run into something heavier than
he bargains for.'

'I'll leave you to it, then,' I said. 'I've got to help Palmerini.'
I ran down to the shed and heard the car revving up behind
me.

Palmerini met me at the door of the shed. He was outraged.
'Signor, you cannot put this boat into the water. There is no paint,
no copper, nothing on the bottom. She will be destroyed in our
Mediterranean water – the worms will eat her up entirely.'

I said, 'We have no time; she must go into the water as she
is.'

His professional ethics were rubbed raw. 'I do not know whether
I should permit it,' he grumbled. 'No boat has ever left my yard
in such a condition. If anyone hears of it they will say, "Palmerini
is an old fool! Palmerini is losing his mind – he is getting senile
in his old age."'

In my impatience to get on with the job I suspected he wasn't
far off the truth. I said, 'No one will know, Signor Palmerini. I
will tell no one.'

We walked across to *Sanford*. Palmerini was still grumbling
under his breath about the iniquity of leaving a ship's bottom unprotected against the small beasts of the sea. He looked at the keel
and rapped it with his knuckles. 'And this, signor. Whoever heard
of a brass keel?'

'I told you I was experimenting,' I said.

He cocked his head on one side and his walnut face looked
at me impishly. 'Ah, signor, never has there been such a yacht as
this in the Mediterranean. Not even the famous *Argo* was like
this boat, and not even the Golden Fleece was so valuable.' He
laughed. 'I'll see if my lazy sons are getting things ready.'

He went off into the lighted area in front of the shed, cackling
like a maniac. I suppose no one could do anything in his yard
without his knowing exactly what was going on. He was a great

leg-puller, this Palmerini.

I called him back, and said, 'Signor Palmerini, if all goes well I will come back and buy your boatyard if you are willing to sell. I will give you a good price.'

He chuckled. 'Do you think I would sell my yard to a man who would send a boat out without paint on her bottom? I was teasing you, my boy, because you always look so serious.'

I smiled. 'Very well, but there is a lead keel I have no use for. I'm sure you can use it.' At the current price of lead the old keel was worth nearly fifteen hundred pounds.

He nodded judiciously. 'I can use it,' he said. 'It will just about pay for tonight's overtime.' He cackled again and went off to crack the whip over his sons.

Walker was still sullen and pale and when I began to drive him he became even more sulky, but I ignored that and drove him all the more in my efforts to get *Sanford* ready for sea. Presently we were joined by Coertze and Francesca and the work went more quickly.

Francesca said, 'I've left Piero in charge up there. He knows what to do; besides, he knows nothing about boats.'

'Neither do you,' I said.

'No, but I can learn.'

I said, 'I think you should leave now. It might get a bit danger-ous round here before long.'

'No,' she said stubbornly, 'I'm staying.'

'You're going.'

She faced me. 'And just how will you make me go?'

She had me there and she knew it. I hesitated, and she said, 'Not only am I staying, but I'm coming with you in *Sanford*.'

'We'll see about that later,' I said. 'At the moment I've no time to argue.'

We pulled *Sanford* out of the shed and one of Palmerini's sons ran the little crane alongside. He picked up the mast and hoisted it high above the boat, gently lowering it between the mast partners. I was below, making sure that the heel of the mast was correctly bedded on the butt plate. Old Palmerini came below and said, 'I'll see to the wedges. If you are in the hurry you say you are, you had better see that your engine is fit to run.'

So I went aft and had a look at the engine. When *Sanford* had been taken from the water I had checked the engine twice a week, turning her over a few revolutions to circulate the oil. Now, she started immediately, running sweetly, and I knew with satisfaction that once we were in the water we could get away at a rate of knots.

I checked the fuel tanks and the water tanks and then went on deck to help the Palmerini boys with the standing rigging. After we had been working for some time, Francesca brought us coffee. I accepted it with thanks, and she said quietly, 'It's getting late.'

I looked at my watch; it was two o'clock. 'My God!' I said. 'Only an hour before the deadline. Heard anything from Piero?'

She shook her head. 'How long will it be before we'll be finished?' she asked, looking round the deck.

'It looks worse than it is,' I said. 'I reckon we'll be nearly two hours, though.'

'Then we fight,' she said with finality.

'It looks like it.' I thought of Coertze's plan. 'It shouldn't come to much, though.'

'I'll stay with Piero,' she said. 'I'll let you know if anything happens.'

I watched her go, then went to Walker. 'Never mind the running rigging,' I said. 'We'll fix that at sea. Just reeve the halyards through the sheaves and lash them down. We haven't much time now.'

If we worked hard before, we worked harder then – but it was no use. Francesca came running down from the office. 'Hal, Hal, Piero wants you.'

I dropped everything and ran up the yard, calling for Coertze as I went. Piero was talking on the telephone when I arrived. After a minute he hung up and said, 'It's started.'

Coertze sat on the desk upon which was spread the map. 'Who was that?'

Piero laid his finger on the map. 'These men. We have two men following.'

'Not the four we're tackling straight away?' I asked.

'No, I haven't heard of them.' He crossed to the window and spoke a few words to a man outside. I looked at my watch – it was half past two.

We sat in silence and listened to the minutes tick away. The atmosphere was oppressive and reminded me of the time during the war when we expected a German attack but didn't know just when or where it was going to come.

Suddenly the telephone rang and we all started.

Piero picked it up and as he listened his lips tightened. He put the telephone down and said, 'Torloni has got more men. They are gathering in the Piazza Cavour – there are two lorry loads.'

'Where the hell did *they* come from?' I demanded.

'From Spezia; he has called in another gang.'

My brain went into top gear. Why had Torloni done that? He didn't need so many men against four of us – unless he knew of our partisan allies – and it was quite evident that he did. He was going to overrun us by force of numbers.

'How many extra men?' asked Coertze.

Piero shrugged. 'At least thirty, I was told.'

Coertze cursed. His plan was falling to pieces – the enemy was concentrating and our own forces were divided.

I said to Piero, 'Can you get in touch with your men?'

He nodded. 'One watches – the other is near a telephone.'

I looked at Coertze. 'You'd better bring them in.'

He shook his head violently. 'No, the plan is still good. We can still engage them here and attack them in the rear.'

'How many men have we got altogether?'

Coertze said, 'Twenty-five Italians and the four of us.'

'And they've got forty-three, at least. Those are bad odds.'

Francesca said to Piero, 'The men we have are those who can fight. There are others who cannot fight but who can watch. It is a pity that the fighters have to be watchers, too. Why not get some of the old men to do the watching so that you can collect the fighters together?'

Piero's hand went to the phone but stopped as Coertze abruptly said, 'No!' He leaned back in his chair. 'It's a good idea, but it's too late. We can't start changing plans now. And I want that phone free – I want to know what is happening to our mobile force.'

We waited while the leaden minutes dragged by. Coertze suddenly said, 'Where's Walker?'

'Working on the boat,' I said. 'He's of more use down there.'

Coertze snorted. 'That's God's truth. He'll be no use in a brawl.'

The telephone shrilled and Piero scooped it up in one quick movement. He listened intently, then began to give quick instructions. I looked at Coertze and said, 'Four down.'

'... and thirty-nine to go,' he finished glumly.

Piero put down the phone. 'That was the mobile force – they are going to the Piazza Cavour.'

The phone rang again under his hand and he picked it up. I said to Francesca, 'Go down to the boat and tell Walker to work like hell. You'd better stay down there, too.'

As she left the office, Piero said, 'Torloni has left the Piazza Cavour – two cars and two trucks. We had only two men there and they have already lost one truck. The other truck and the cars are coming straight here.'

Coertze thumped the table. 'Dammit, where did that other truck go?'

I said sardonically, 'I wouldn't worry about it. Things can't help but get better from now on; they can't get any worse, and we've nowhere to go but up.'

I left the office and stood in the darkness. Giuseppi said, 'What is happening, signor.'

'Torloni and his men will be here within minutes. Tell the others to be prepared.'

After a few minutes Coertze joined me. 'The telephone line's been cut,' he said.

'That tops it,' I said. 'Now we don't know what's going on at all.'

'I hope our friends outside use their brains and concentrate into one bunch; if they don't, we're sunk,' he said grimly.

Piero joined us. 'Will Palmerini's sons fight?' I asked.

'Yes, if they are attacked.'

'You'd better go down and tell the old man to lie low. I wouldn't want him to get hurt.'

Piero went away and Coertze settled down to watch. The street was empty and there was no sound. We waited a long time and nothing happened at all. I thought that perhaps Torloni was disconcerted by finding his watchmen missing – that might put him off his stroke – and if he had a roll-call and discovered a total of eight men missing it was bound to make him uneasy.

I looked at my watch – three-fifteen. If Torloni would only hold off we might get the boat launched and away and the men dispersed. I prayed he would hold off at least another half-hour.

He didn't.

Coertze suddenly said, 'Something's coming.'

I heard an engine changing gear and the noise was suddenly loud. Headlights flashed from the left, approaching rapidly, and the engine roared. I saw it was a lorry being driven fast, and when it was abreast of the yard, it swerved and made for the gate.

I blessed Francesca's intuition and shouted in Italian, 'To the gates!'

The lorry smashed into the gates and there was a loud cracking and snapping of wood, overlaid by the crash as the lorry hit the car amidships and came to a jolting halt. We didn't wait for Torloni's men to recover but piled in immediately. I scrambled over the ruined car and got on to the bonnet of the lorry, whirling round to the passenger side. The man in the passenger seat was shaking his head groggily; he had smashed it against the windscreen, unready for such a fierce impact. I hit him with my fist and he slumped down to the floor.

The driver was frantically trying to restart his stalled engine and I saw Coertze haul him out bodily and toss him away into the darkness. Then things got confused. Someone from the back of the lorry booted me on the head and I slipped from the running-board conscious of a wave of our men going in to the attack. When I had recovered my wits it was all over.

Coertze dragged me from under the lorry and said, 'Are you all right?'

I rubbed my sore head. 'I'm OK. What happened?'

'They didn't know what hit them – or they didn't know what they hit. The smash shook them up too much to be of any use; we drove them from the lorry and they ran for it.'

'How many of them were there?'

'They were jammed in the back of the lorry like sardines. I suppose they thought they could smash in the gates, drive into the yard and get out in comfort. They didn't get the chance.' He looked at the gateway. 'They won't be coming that way again.'

The gateway, from being our weakest point, had become our strongest. The tangled mess of the lorry and the car completely blocked the entrance, making it impassable.

Piero came up and said, 'We have three prisoners.'

'Tie them up and stick them with the others,' I said. One commodity which is never in short supply in a boatyard is rope. Torloni was now missing eleven men – a quarter of his force. Perhaps that would make him think twice before attacking again.

I said to Coertze, 'Are you sure they can't attack us from the sides?'

'Positive. We're blocked in with buildings on both sides. He has to make a frontal attack. But, hell, I wish I knew where that other lorry went.'

The telephone began to ring shrilly.

I said, 'I thought you said the wire had been cut.'

'Piero said it had.'

We ran to the office and Coertze grabbed the phone. He listened for a second, then said, 'It's Torloni!'

'I'll speak to him,' I said, and took the phone. I held my hand over the mouthpiece. 'I've got an idea – get old Palmerini up here.' Then I said into the phone, 'What do you want?'

'Is that Halloran?' The English was good, if strongly tinged with an American accent.

'Yes.'

'Halloran, why don't you be reasonable? You know you haven't a chance.'

I said, 'This phone call of yours is proof that we *have* a chance. You wouldn't be speaking to me if you thought you could get what you want otherwise. Now, if you have a proposition, make it; if you haven't, shut up.'

His voice was softly ugly. 'You'll be sorry you spoke to me like that. Oh, I know all about the Estrenoli woman's old soldiers, but you haven't got enough of them. Now if you cut me in for half I'll be friendly.'

'Go to hell!'

'All right,' he said. 'I'll crush you and I'll like doing it.'

'Make one more attack and the police will be here.' I might as well try to pull a bluff.

He thought that over, then said silkily, 'And how will you call them with no telephone?'

'I've made my arrangements,' I said. 'You've already run into some of them.' I rubbed it in. 'A lot of your men are mysteriously missing, aren't they?'

I could almost hear his brain click to a decision. 'You won't send for the police,' he said with finality. 'You want the police as little as I do. Halloran, I did you a favour once; I got rid of Estrenoli, didn't I? You could return the favour.'

'The favour was for Metcalfe, not me,' I said, and hung up on him. He wouldn't like that.

Coertze said, 'What did he want?'

'A half-share – or so he said.'

'I'll see him in hell first,' he said bluntly.

'Where's Palmerini?'

'Coming up. I sent Giuseppi for him.'

Just then Palmerini came into the office. I said, 'First, how's the boat getting on?'

'Give me fifteen minutes – just fifteen minutes, that's all.'

'I may not be able to,' I said. 'You've got some portable flood-lights you use for working at night. Take two men and bring them up here quickly.'

I turned to Coertze. 'We want to be able to see what's happening. They'll have to come over the wall this time, and once they're over it won't be easy for them to get back. That means the next attack will be final — make or break. Now here's what we do.'

I outlined what I wanted to do with the lights and Coertze nodded appreciatively. It took a mere five minutes to set them up and we used the Fiat and a truck to give added light by their headlamps. We placed the men and settled down to wait for the impending attack.

It wasn't long in coming. There were scraping noises from the wall and Coertze said, 'They're coming over.'

'Wait,' I breathed.

There were several thumps which could only be made by men dropping heavily to the ground. I yelled, '*Luce!*' and the lights blazed out.

It was like a frozen tableau. Several of the enemy were on our side of the wall, squinting forward at the light pouring on to them. Several others were caught lowering themselves, their heads turned to see what was happening.

What they must have seen cannot have been reassuring — a blaze of blinding light behind which was impenetrable darkness heavy with menace, while they themselves were in the open and easily spotted — not a very comfortable thought for men supposedly making a surprise attack.

They hesitated uncertainly and in that moment we hit them on both flanks simultaneously, Piero leading from the right and Coertze from the left. I stayed with a small reserve of three men, ready to jump in if either flank party had bitten off more than it could chew.

I saw upraised clubs and the flash of knives and three of Torloni's men went down in the first ten seconds. We had caught them off balance and the flank attacks quickly rolled them up into the centre and there was a confused mob of shouting, fighting men. But more of the enemy were coming over the wall fast, and I was just going to move my little group into battle when I heard more shouting.

It came from *behind* me.

'Come on,' I yelled and ran down the yard towards *Sanford*. Now we knew what had happened to that other lorry load of men. They had come in from the seaward side and Torloni was attacking us front and rear.

Sanford was besieged. A boat was drawn up on the hard and another boat full of men was just landing. There was a fight going on round Sanford with men trying to climb up on the deck

and our working party valiantly trying to drive them off. I saw
the small figure of old Palmerini; he had a rope with a block on
the end of it which he whirled round his head like a medieval ball
and chain. He whirled it once and the block caught an attacker
under the jaw and he toppled from the ladder he was climbing
and fell senseless to the ground.

Palmerini's sons were battling desperately and I saw one go
down. Then I saw Francesca wielding a boat-hook like a spear. She
drove it at a boarder and the spike penetrated his thigh. He screamed
shrilly and fell away, the boat-hook still sticking out of his leg. I
saw the look of horror on Francesca's face and then drove home
my little attack.

It was futile. We managed to relieve the beleaguered garrison
on *Sanford,* but then we were outnumbered three to one and had
to retreat up the yard. The attackers did not press us; they were
so exultant at the capture of the *Sanford* that they stayed with her
and didn't follow us. We were lucky in their stupidity.

I looked around to see what was happening at the top of the
yard. Coertze's party was closer than I had hoped – he had been
driven back, too, but he was not under attack and I wondered
why. If both enemy groups now made a concerted effort we were
lost.

I said to Francesca, 'Duck under those sacks and stay quiet –
you may get away with it.' Then I ran over to Coertze. 'What's
happening?'

He grinned and wiped some blood from his cheek. 'Our outside
boys concentrated and hit Torloni hard on the other side of the
wall, all fifteen of them. He can't retreat now – anyone who tries
to go back over the wall gets clobbered. I'm just getting my breath
back before I hit 'em again.'

I said, 'They've got *Sanford*. They came in from the sea – we're
boxed in, too.'

His chest heaved. 'All right; we'll hit 'em down there.'

I looked up the yard. 'No,' I said. 'Look, there's Torloni.'

We could see him under the wall, yelling at his men, whipping
them up for another attack. I said, 'We attack up the yard –
all of us – and we hope that the crowd at the back of us stay put
for the time we need. We're going to snatch Torloni himself.
Where's Piero?'

'I am here.'

'Good! Tell your boys to attack when I give the signal. You
stay with Coertze and me, and the three of us will make for Torloni.'

I turned to find Francesca at my elbow. 'I thought I told you to duck out of sight.'

She shook her head stubbornly. Old Palmerini was behind her, so I said, 'See that she stays here, old friend.'

He nodded and put his arm round her. I said to Coertze, 'Remember, we want Torloni – we don't stop for anything else.'

Then we attacked up the yard. The three of us, Coertze, Piero and I, made a flying wedge, evading anyone who tried to stop us. We didn't fight, we just ran. Coertze had grasped the idea and was running as though he was on a rugby field making an effort for the final try.

The goal line was Torloni and we were on to him before he properly realized what was happening. He snarled and blue steel showed in his hand.

'Spread out!' I yelled, and we separated, coming at him from three sides. The gun in his hand flamed and Coertze staggered; then Piero and I jumped him. I raised my arm and hit him hard with the edge of my hand; I felt his collar-bone break and he screamed and dropped the pistol.

With Torloni's scream a curious hush came over the yard. There was an uncertainty in his men and they looked back to see what was happening. I picked up the gun and held it to Torloni's head. 'Call off your dogs or I'll blow your brains out,' I said harshly.

I was as close to murder then as I have ever been. Torloni saw the look in my eyes and whitened. 'Stop,' he croaked.

'Louder,' ordered Piero and squeezed his shoulder.

He screamed again, then he shouted, 'Stop fighting – stop fighting. Torloni says so.'

His men were hirelings – they fought for pay and if the boss was captured they wouldn't get paid. There is not much loyalty among mercenaries. There was an uncertain shuffling and a melting away of figures into the darkness.

Coertze was sitting on the ground, his hand to his shoulder. Blood was oozing between his fingers. He took his hand away and looked at it with stupefied amazement. 'The bastard shot me,' he said blankly.

I went over to him. 'Are you all right?'

He held his shoulder again and got to his feet. 'I'm OK.' He looked at Torloni sourly. 'I've got a bone to pick with you.'

'Later,' I said. 'Let's deal with the crowd at the bottom of the yard.'

We were being reinforced rapidly by men climbing over the wall. This was our mobile force which had taken Torloni's men in the rear and had whipped them. In a compact mass we marched down the yard towards *Sanford*, Torloni being frog-marched in front.

As we came near *Sanford* I poked the pistol muzzle into Torloni's fleshy neck. 'Tell them,' I commanded.

He shouted, 'Leave the boat. Go away. Torloni says this.'

The men around *Sanford* looked at us expressionlessly and made no move. Piero squeezed Torloni's shoulder again. 'Aaah. Leave the boat, I tell you,' he yelled.

They raised their eyes to the crowd behind us, realized they were outnumbered, and slowly began to drift towards the hard where their boats were drawn up. Piero said quietly, 'These are the men from La Spezia. That man in the blue jersey is their leader, Morlaix; he is a Frenchman from Marseilles.' He looked speculatively at their boats. 'You may have trouble with him yet. He does not care if Torloni lives or dies.'

I watched Morlaix's crowd push their boats into the water. 'We'll cross that bridge when we come to it,' I said. 'We've got to get out of here. Somebody might have notified the police about this brawl – we made enough noise, and there was a gunshot. Did we have many casualties?'

'I don't know; I will find out.'

Palmerini came pushing through the crowd with Francesca at his side. 'The boat is not harmed,' he said. 'We can put her into the water at any time.'

'Thanks,' I said. I looked at Francesca and made a quick decision. 'Still want to come?'

'Yes, I'm coming.'

'OK. You won't have time to pack, though. We're leaving within the hour.'

She smiled. 'I have a small suitcase already packed. It has been ready for a week.'

Coertze was standing guard over Torloni. 'What do we do with this one?' he asked.

I said, 'We take him with us a little way. We may need him yet. Francesca, Kobus was shot; will you strap him up?'

'Oh, I didn't know,' she said. 'Where is the wound?'

'In the shoulder,' said Coertze absently. He was watching Walker on the deck of *Sanford*. 'Where was that *kêrel* when the trouble started?'

'I don't know,' I said. 'I never saw him from start to finish.'

IV

We put Sanford into the water very easily; there were plenty of willing hands. I felt better with a living, moving deck under my feet than I had for a long time. Before I went aboard for the last time I took Piero on one side.

'Tell the Count I've taken Francesca away,' I said. 'I think it's better this way – Torloni might look for revenge. You men can look after yourselves, but I wouldn't like to leave her here.'

'That is the best thing,' he said.

'If Torloni wants to start any more funny tricks you know what to do now. Don't go for his men – go for Torloni. He cracks easily under direct pressure. I'll make it clear to him that if he starts any of his nonsense he'll wind up floating in the bay. What did you find out about casualties?'

'Nothing serious,' said Piero. 'One broken arm, three stab wounds, three or four unconscious.'

'I'm glad no one was killed,' I said. 'I wouldn't have liked that. I think Francesca would like to speak to you, so I'll leave you to it.'

We shook hands warmly and I went aboard. Piero was a fine man – a good man to have beside you in a fight.

He and Francesca talked together for a while and then she came on board. She was crying a little and I put my arm about her to comfort her. It's not very pleasant to leave one's native land at the best of times, and leaving in these circumstances the unpleasantness was doubled. I sat in the cockpit with my hand on the tiller and Walker started the engine. As soon as I heard it throb I threw it into gear and we moved away slowly.

For a long time we could see the little patch of light in front of the shed speckled with waving Italians. They waved although they could not see us in the darkness and I felt sad at leaving them. 'We'll come back some time,' I said to Francesca.

'No,' she said quietly. 'We'll never be back.'

V

We pressed on into the darkness at a steady six knots, making our way due south to clear the Portovento headland. I looked up at the mast dimly outlined against the stars and wondered how long it would take to fix the running rigging. The deck was a mess, making nonsense of the term 'ship-shape', but we couldn't do anything about that until it was light. Walker was below and Coertze was on the foredeck keeping guard on Torloni. Francesca and I conversed in low tones in the cockpit, talking of when we would be able to get married.

Coertze called out suddenly, 'When are we going to get rid of this garbage? He wants to know. He thinks we're going to put him over the side and he says he can't swim.'

'We'll slip inshore close to Portovento,' I said. 'We'll put him ashore in the dinghy.'

Coertze grumbled something about it being better to get rid of Torloni there and then, and relapsed into silence. Francesca said, 'Is there something wrong with the engine? It seems to be making a strange noise.'

I listened and there was a strange noise – but it wasn't *our* engine. I throttled back and heard the puttering of an outboard motor quite close to starboard.

'Get below quickly,' I said, and called to Coertze in a low voice, 'We've got visitors.'

He came aft swiftly. I pointed to starboard and, in the faint light of the newly risen moon, we could see the white feather of a bow wave coming closer. A voice came across the water. 'Monsieur Englishman, can you hear me?'

'It's Morlaix,' I said, and raised my voice. 'Yes, I can hear you.'

'We are coming aboard,' he shouted. 'It is useless to resist.'

'You stay clear,' I called. 'Haven't you had enough?'

Coertze got up with a grunt and went forward. I pulled Torloni's gun from my pocket and cocked it.

'There are only four of you,' shouted Morlaix. 'And many more of us.'

The bow wave of his boat was suddenly much closer and I could see the boat more clearly. It was full of men. Then it was alongside and, as it came close enough to bump gunwales, Morlaix jumped to the deck of *Sanford*. He was only four feet away from me so I shot him in the leg and he gave a shout and fell overboard.

Simultaneously Coertze rose, lifting in one hand the struggling figure of Torloni. 'Take this rubbish,' he shouted and hurled Torloni at the rush of men coming on deck. Torloni wailed and the flying body bowled them over and they fell back into their boat.

I took advantage of the confusion by suddenly bearing to port and the gap between the boats widened rapidly. Their boat seemed to be out of control — I imagine that the steersman had been knocked down.

They didn't bother us again. We could hear them shouting in the distance as they fished Morlaix from the water, but they made no further attack. They had no stomach for guns.

Our wake broadened in the moonlight as we headed for the open sea. We had a deadline to meet in Tangier and time was short.

BOOK THREE
The Sea

8   *Calm and Storm*

We had fair winds at first and *Sanford* made good time. As I had
suspected, the greater concentration of weight in the keel made
her crotchety. In a following sea she rolled abominably, going
through a complete cycle in two minutes. With the wind on the
quarter, usually *Sanford*'s best point of sailing, every leeward roll
was followed by a lurch in the opposite direction and her mast
described wide arcs against the sky.

There was nothing to be done about it so it had to be suffered.
The only cure was to have the ballast spread out more and that
was the one thing we couldn't do. The violent motion affected
Coertze most of all; he wasn't a good sailor at the best of times
and the wound in his shoulder didn't help.

With the coming of dawn after that momentous and violent
night we hove-to just out of sight of land and set to work on the
running rigging. It didn't take long – Palmerini had done more
in that direction that I'd expected – and soon we were on our way
under sail. It was then that the crankiness of *Sanford* made itself
evident, and I experimented for a while to see what I could do,
but the cure was beyond me so I stopped wasting time and we
pressed on.

We soon fell into our normal watchkeeping routine, modified
by the presence of Francesca, who took over the cooking from
Coertze. During small boat voyages one sees very little of the other
members of the crew apart from the times when the watch is
changed, but Walker was keeping more to himself than ever. Sometimes I caught him watching me and he would start and roll his
eyes like a frightened horse and look away quickly. He was obviously terrified that I would tell Coertze about the cigarette case.
I had no such intention – I needed Walker to help run *Sanford*
– but I didn't tell him so. Let him sweat, I thought callously.

Coertze's shoulder was not so bad; it was a clean flesh wound and
Francesca kept it well tended. I insisted that he sleep in the quarter
berth where the motion was least violent, and this led to a general
post. I moved to the port pilot berth in the main cabin while

Francesca had the starboard pilot berth. She rigged up a sail-cloth curtain in front of it to give herself a modicum of privacy.

This meant that Walker was banished to the forecastle to sleep on the hitherto unused pipe berth. This was intended for a guest in port and not for use at sea; it was uncomfortable and right in the bows where the motion is most felt. Serve him damn' well' right, I thought uncharitably. But it meant that we saw even less of him.

We made good time for the first five days, logging over a hundred miles a day crossing the Ligurian Sea. Every day I shot the sun and contentedly admired the course line on the chart as it stretched even farther towards the Balearics. I derived great pleasure from teaching Francesca how to handle *Sanford*; she was an apt pupil and made no more than the usual beginner's mistakes.

I observed with some amusement that Coertze seemed to have lost his antipathy towards her. He was a changed man, not as prickly as before. The gold was safe under his feet and I think the fight in the boatyard had knocked some of the violence out of him. At any rate, he and Francesca got on well together at last, and had long conversations about South Africa.

Once she asked him what he was going to do with his share of the spoil. He smiled. 'I'm going to buy a *plaas*,' he said complacently.

'A what?'

'A farm,' I translated. 'All Afrikaners are farmers at heart; they even call themselves farmers – boers – at least they used to.'

I think that those first five days after leaving Italy were the best sea days of the whole voyage. We never had better days before and we certainly didn't have any afterwards.

On the evening of the fifth day the wind dropped and the next day it kept fluctuating as though it didn't know what to do next. The strength varied between force three and dead calm and we had a lot of sail work to do. That day we only logged seventy miles.

At dawn the next day there was a dead calm. The sea was slick and oily and coming in long even swells. Our tempers tended to fray during the afternoon when there was nothing to do but watch the mast making lazy circles against the sky, while the precious hours passed and we made no way towards Tangier. I got tired of hearing the squeak of the boom in the goosenecks so I put up the crutch and we lashed down the boom. Then I went below to do some figuring at the chart table.

We had slogged twenty miles, noon to noon, and at that rate

we would reach Tangier about three months too late. I checked the fuel tank and found we had fifteen gallons left – that would take us 150 miles in thirty hours at our most economical speed. It would be better than sitting still and listening to the halyards slatting against the mast, so I started the engine and we were on our way again.

I chafed at the use of fuel – it was something we might need in an emergency – but this *was* an emergency, anyway, so I might as well use it; it was six of one and half a dozen of the other. We ploughed through the still sea at a steady five knots and I laid a course to the south of the Balearics, running in close to Majorca. If for some reason we had to put into port I wanted a port to be handy, and Palma was the nearest.

All that night and all the next morning we ran under power. There was no wind nor was there any sign that there was ever going to be any wind ever again. The sky was an immaculate blue echoing the waveless sea and I felt like hell. With no wind a sailing boat is helpless, and what would we do when the fuel ran out?

I discussed it with Coertze. 'I'm inclined to put in to Palma,' I said. 'We can fill up there.'

He threw a cigarette stub over the side. 'It's a damn' waste of time. We'd be going off course, and what if they keep us waiting round there?'

I said, 'It'll be a bigger waste of time if we're left without power. This calm could go on for days.'

'I've been looking at the Mediterranean Pilot,' he said. 'It says the percentage of calms at this time of year isn't high.'

'You can't depend on that – those figures are just averages. This could go on for a week.'

He sighed. 'You're the skipper,' he said. 'Do the best you can.'

So I altered course to the north and we ran for Palma. I checked on the fuel remaining and doubted if we'd make it – but we did. We motored into the yacht harbour at Palma with the engine coughing on the last of the fuel. As we approached the mooring jetty the engine expired and we drifted the rest of the way by momentum.

It was then I looked up and saw Metcalfe.

II

We cut the Customs formalities short by saying that we weren't going ashore and that we had only come in for fuel. The Customs officer commiserated with us on the bad sailing weather and said

he would telephone for a chandler to come down and see to our
needs.

That left us free to discuss Metcalfe. He hadn't said anything
– he had just regarded us with a gentle smile on his lips and then
had turned on his heel and walked away.

Coertze said, 'He's cooking something up.'

'Nothing could be more certain,' I said bitterly. 'Will we never
get these bastards off our backs?'

'Not while we've got four tons of gold under our feet,' said
Coertze. 'It's like a bloody magnet.'

I looked forward at Walker sitting alone on the foredeck. There
was the fool who, by his loose tongue and his stupidities, had
brought the vultures down on us. Or perhaps not – men like Metcalfe and Torloni have keen noses for gold. But Walker hadn't
helped.

Francesca said, 'What do you think he will do?'

'My guess is a simple act of piracy,' I said. 'It'll appeal to his
warped sense of humour to do some Spanish Main stuff.'

I lay on my back and looked at the sky. The club burgee at
the masthead was lifting and fluttering in a light breeze. 'And look
at that,' I said. 'We've got a wind, dammit.'

'I said we shouldn't have come in here,' grumbled Coertze. 'We'd
have had the wind anyway, and Metcalfe wouldn't have spotted
us.'

I considered Metcalfe's boat and his radar – especially the radar.

'No,' I said. 'It wouldn't have made any difference. He's probably known just where to put his hand on us ever since we left
Italy.' I made a quick calculation on the basis of a 15-mile radar
range. 'He can cover 700 square miles of sea with one pass of his
radar. That Fairmile has probably been hovering hull-down on
the horizon keeping an eye on us. We'd never spot it.'

'Well, what do we do now?' asked Francesca.

'We carry on as usual,' I said. 'There's not much else we can
do. But I'm certainly not going to hand the gold to Mr Bloody
Metcalfe simply because he shows up and throws a scare into us.
We carry on and hope for the best.'

We refuelled and topped up the water tanks and were on our
way again before nightfall. The sun was setting as we passed Cabo
Figuera and I left the helm to Francesca and went below to study
the chart. I had a plan to fox Metcalfe – it probably wouldn't
work but it was worth trying.

As soon as it was properly dark I said to Francesca, 'Steer 180
degrees.'

'South?' she said in surprise.

'That's right – south' To Coertze I said, 'Do you know what that square gadget half-way up the mast is for?'

'*Nee, man*, I've never worried about it.'

'It's a radar reflector,' I said. 'A wooden boat gives a bad radar reflection so we use a special reflector for safety – it gives a nice big blip on a screen. If Metcalfe has been following us he must have got used to that blip by now – he can probably identify us sight unseen, just from the trace on the screen. So we're going to take the reflector away. He'll still get an echo but it'll be different, much fainter.'

I fastened a small spanner on a loop round my waist and clipped a lifeline on to my safety belt and began to climb the mast. The reflector was bolted on to the lower spreaders and it was an uneasy job getting it down. *Sanford* was doing her new style dot-and-carry-one, and following the old-time sailor maxim of 'one hand for yourself and one hand for the ship' it was not easy to unfasten those two bolts. The trouble was that the bolts started to turn as well as the nuts, so I was getting nowhere fast. I was up the mast for over forty-five minutes before the reflector came free.

I got down to the deck, collapsed the reflector for stowage and said to Coertze, 'Where's Walker?'

'Dossing down; it's his watch at midnight.'

'I'd forgotten. Now we change the lights.' I went below to the chart table. I had a white light at the masthead visible all round which was coupled to a Morse key for signalling. I tied the key down so that the light stayed on all the time.

Then I called up to Coertze, 'Get a lantern out of the fo'c'sle and hoist it in the rigging.'

He came below. 'What's all this for?'

I said, 'Look, we're on the wrong course for Tangier – it's wasting time but it can't be helped because anything that puts Metcalfe off his stroke is good for us. We've altered our radar trace but Metcalfe might get suspicious and come in for a look at us, anyway. So we're festooned with lights in the usual sloppy Spanish fisherman fashion. We're line fishing and he won't see otherwise – not at night. So he just may give us the go-by and push off somewhere else.'

'You're a tricky bastard,' said Coertze admiringly.

'It'll only work once,' I said. 'At dawn we'll change course for Tangier.'

III

The wind got up during the night and we handed the light weather sails so that *Sanford* developed a fair turn of speed. Not that it helped much; we weren't making an inch of ground in the direction of Tangier.

At dawn it was blowing force five and we changed course so that the wind was on the quarter and *Sanford* began to stride out, her lee rail under the bow wave showing white foam. I checked the log and saw that she was doing seven knots, which was close to her limit under sail. We were doing all right at last – on the right course for Tangier and travelling fast.

We kept a close watch on the horizon for Metcalfe but saw nothing. If he knew where we were he wasn't showing his hand. I didn't know whether to be glad or sorry about that; I would be glad if my stratagem had deceived him, but if it hadn't then I wanted to know about it.

The fresh breeze held all day and even tended to increase towards nightfall. The waves became larger and foam-crested, breaking every now and then on *Sanford*'s quarter. Every time that happened she would shudder and shake herself free to leap forward again. I estimated that the wind was now verging on force six and, as a prudent seaman, I should have been thinking of taking a reef in the mainsail, but I wanted to press on – there was not much time left, and less if we had to tangle with Metcalfe.

I turned in early, leaving Walker at the helm, and before I went to sleep I contemplated what I would do if I were Metcalfe. We had to go through the Straits of Gibraltar – the whole Mediterranean was a funnel with the Straits forming the spout. If Metcalfe took station there his radar could cover the whole channel from shore to shore.

On the other hand, the Straits were busy waters, so he'd have to zig-zag to check dubious boats visually. Then again, if he was contemplating piracy, it would be dangerous to try it where it could be spotted easily – there were some very fast naval patrol boats at Gibraltar and I didn't think that even Metcalfe would have the nerve to tackle us in daylight.

So that settled that – we would have to run through the Straits in daylight.

If – and I was getting tired of all these ifs – if he didn't nobble us before or after the Straits. I hazily remembered a case of piracy just outside Tangier in 1956 – two groups of smugglers had tangled with each other and one of the boats had been burned. Perhaps he wouldn't want to leave it as long as that; we would be close to home and we might give him the slip after all – once we were in the yacht harbour there wouldn't be a damn thing he could do. No, I didn't think he would leave it as late as that.

But before the Straits? That was a different kettle of fish and that depended on another 'if'. If we had given him the slip on leaving Majorca – if he didn't know where we were now – then we might have a chance. But if he did know where we were, then he could close in any time and put a prize crew aboard. If – yet another if – the weather would let him.

As I drifted off to sleep I blessed the steadily rising wind which added wings to *Sanford* and which would make it impossible for the Fairmile to come alongside.

IV

Coertze woke me up. 'The wind's getting stronger; I think we should change sail or something.' He had to shout above the roar of the wind and the sea.

I looked at my watch as I pulled on my oilies; it was two o'clock and I had had six hours' sleep. *Sanford* was bucking a bit and I had a lot of trouble putting my trousers on. A sudden lurch sent me across the cabin and I carommed into the berth in which Francesca slept.

'What is wrong?' she asked.

'Nothing,' I said. 'Everything is fine; go back to sleep.'

'You think I can sleep in this?'

I grinned. 'You'll soon get used to it. It's blowing up a bit, but nothing to worry about.'

I finished dressing and went into the cockpit. Coertze was right; we should do something about taking in sail. The wind was blowing at a firm force seven – what old-time sailormen referred to contemptuously as a 'yachtsman's gale' and what Admiral Beaufort temperately called a 'strong wind'.

Tattered clouds fled across the sky, making a baffling alteration of light and shade as they crossed the moon. The seas were coming up in lumps and the crests were being blown away in streaks of foam. *Sanford* was plunging her head into the seas and every time this happened she would stop with a jerk, losing speed. A reduction of sail would hold her head up and help her motion, so I said to Coertze, my voice raised in a shout, 'You're right; I'll reef her down a bit. Hold her as she is.'

I snapped a lifeline on to my safety belt and went forward along the crazily shifting deck. It took half an hour to take in two rolls round the boom of the mainsail and to take in the jib, leaving the foresail to balance her head. As soon as I had handed the jib I could feel the difference in motion; *Sanford* rode more easily and didn't ram her bows down as often.

I went back to the cockpit and asked Coertze, 'How's that?'

'Better,' he shouted. 'She seems to be going faster, though.'

'She is; she's not getting stopped.'

He looked at the piled-up seas. 'Will it get worse than this?'

'Oh, this is not so bad,' I replied. 'We're going as fast as we can, which is what we want.' I smiled, because from a small boat everything looked larger than life and twice as dangerous. However I hoped the weather wouldn't worsen; that would slow us down.

I stayed with Coertze for a time to reassure him. It was nearly time for my watch, anyway, and there was no point in going back to sleep. After some time I slipped down into the galley and made some coffee – the stove was rocking crazily in its gimbals and I had to clamp the coffee-pot, but I didn't spill a drop.

Francesca was watching me from her berth and when the coffee was ready I beckoned to her. If she came to the coffee instead of vice versa there was less chance of it spilling. We wedged ourselves in between the galley bench and the companionway, sipping the hot coffee and talking about the weather.

She smiled at me. 'You like this weather, don't you?'

'It's fine.'

'I think it's a little frightening.'

'There's nothing to be frightened of,' I said. 'Or rather, only one thing.'

'What is that?'

'The crew,' I said. 'You see, small boat design has reached the point of perfection just about, as far as seaworthiness is concerned. A boat like this can take any weather safely if she's handled right – and I'm not saying this because I designed and built her – it applies to any boat of this general type. It's the crew that fails, rather than the boat. You get tired and then you make a mistake – and you only have to make one mistake – you can't play about with the sea.'

'How long does it take before the crew gets as tired as that?'

'We're all right,' I said cheerfully. 'There are enough of us, so that we can all get our sleep, so we can last indefinitely. It's the single-handed heroes who have the trouble.'

'You're very reassuring,' she said, and got up to take another cup from the shelf. 'I'll take Coertze some coffee.'

'Don't bother; it'll only get full of salt spray, and there's nothing worse than salted coffee. He'll be coming below in a few minutes – it's my watch.'

I buttoned my oilies and tightened the scarf round my neck. 'I think I'll relieve him now; he shouldn't really be up there in this weather with that hole in his shoulder. How's it doing anyway?'

'Healing nicely,' she said.

'If he had to have a hole in him he couldn't have done better than that one,' I said. 'Six inches lower and he'd have been plugged through the heart.'

She said, 'You know, I'm changing my mind about him. He's not such a bad man.'

'A heart of gold beneath that rugged exterior?' I queried, and she nodded. I said, 'His heart is set on gold, anyway. We may have some trouble with him if we avoid Metcalfe – don't forget his history. But give the nice man some coffee when he comes below.'

I went up into the cockpit and relieved Coertze. 'There's coffee for you,' I shouted.

'Thanks, just what I need,' he answered and went below.

Sanford continued to eat up the miles and the wind continued to increase in force. Good and bad together. I still held on to the sail I had, but when Walker came to relieve me in a cloudy and watery dawn I took in another roll of the mainsail before I went below for breakfast.

Just before I descended the companionway, Walker said, 'It'll get worse.'

I looked at the sky. 'I don't think so; it rarely gets worse than this in the Mediterranean.'

He shrugged. 'I don't know about the Mediterranean, but I have a feeling it'll get worse, that's all.'

I went below feeling glum. Walker had previously shown an uncanny ability to detect changes in the weather on no visible evidence. He had displayed this weather sense before and had invariably been proved right. I hoped he was wrong this time.

He wasn't!

I couldn't take a noonday sight because of thick cloud and bad visibility. Even if I could have seen the sun I doubt if I could have held a sextant steady on that reeling deck. The log reading was 152 miles from noon to noon, *Sanford*'s best run ever.

Shortly after noon the wind speed increased greatly to force eight verging on force nine – a strong gale. We handed the mainsail altogether and set the trysail, a triangular handkerchief-sized piece of strong canvas intended for heavy weather. The foresail we also doused with difficulty – it was becoming very dangerous to work on the foredeck.

The height of the waves had increased tremendously and they would no sooner break in a white crest than the wind would tear the foam away to blow it in ragged streaks across the sea. Large patches of foam were beginning to form until the sea began to look like a giant washtub into which someone had emptied a few thousand tons of detergent.

I gave orders that no one should go on deck but the man on watch and that he should wear a safety line at all times. For myself, I got into my berth, put up the bunkboards so that I wouldn't be thrown out, and tried unsuccessfully to read a magazine. But I kept wondering if Metcalfe was out in this sea. If he was, I didn't envy him, because a power boat does not take heavy weather as kindly as a sailing yacht, and he must be going through hell.

Things got worse later in the afternoon so I decided to heave-to. We handed the trysail and lay under bare poles abeam to the seas. Then we battened down the hatches and all four of us gathered in the main cabin chatting desultorily when the noise would allow us.

It was about this time that I started to worry about sea room. As I had been unable to take a sight I didn't know our exact position – and while dead reckoning and log readings were all very well in their way, I was beginning to become perturbed. For we were now in the throat of the funnel between Almeria in Spain and Morocco. I knew we were safe enough from being wrecked on the mainland, but just about here was a fly-speck of an island called Alboran which could be the ruin of us if we ran into it in this weather.

I studied the Mediterranean Pilot. I had been right when I said that this sort of weather was not common in the Mediterranean, but that was cold comfort. Evidently the Clerk of the Weather hadn't read the Mediterranean Pilot – the old boy was certainly piling it on.

At five o'clock I went on deck for a last look round before nightfall. Coertze helped me take away the batten boards from the companion entrance and I climbed into the cockpit. I was knee-deep in swirling water despite the three two-inch drains I had built into it; and as I stood there, gripping a stanchion, another boiling wave swept across the deck and filled the cockpit.

I made a mental note to fit more cockpit drains, then looked at the sea. The sight was tremendous; this was a whole gale and the waves were high, with threatening overhanging crests. As I stood there one of the crests broke over the deck and *Sanford* shuddered violently. The poor girl was taking a hell of a beating and I thought I had better do something about it. It would mean at least one man in the cockpit getting soaked and miserable and frightened and I knew that man must be me – I wouldn't trust anyone else with what I was about to do.

I went back below. 'We'll have to run before the wind,' I said. 'Walker, fetch that coil of 4-inch nylon rope from the fo'c'sle. Kobus, get into your oilskins and come with me.'

Coertze and I went back into the cockpit and I unlashed the tiller. I shouted, 'When we run her downwind we'll have to slow her down. We'll run a bight of rope astern and the drag will help.'

Walker came up into the cockpit with the rope and he made one end fast to the port stern bitts. I brought *Sanford* downwind and Coertze began to pay the rope over the stern. Nylon, like hemp and unlike manila, floats, and the loop of rope acted like a brake on *Sanford*'s wild rush.

Too much speed is the danger when you're running before a gale; if you go too fast then the boat is apt to trip just like a man who trips over his own feet when running. When that happens the boat is likely to capsize fore-and-aft – the bows dig into the sea, the stern comes up and the boat somersaults. It happened to *Tzu Hang* in the Pacific and it happened to Erling Tamb's *Sandefjord* in the Atlantic when he lost a man. I didn't want it to happen to me.

Steering a boat in those conditions was a bit hair-raising. The stern had to be kept dead in line with the overtaking wave and, if you got it right, then the stern rose smoothly and the wave passed underneath. If you were a fraction out then there was a thud and the wave would break astern; you would be drenched with water, the tiller would nearly be wrenched from your grasp and you would wonder how much more of that treatment the rudder would take.

Coertze had paid out all the nylon, a full forty fathoms, and *Sanford* began to behave a little better. The rope seemed to smooth the waters astern and the waves did not break as easily. I thought we were still going a little too fast so I told Walker to bring up some more rope. With another two lengths of twenty-fathom three-inch nylon also streamed astern I reckoned we had cut *Sanford*'s speed down to three knots.

There was one thing more I could do. I beckoned to Coertze

and put my mouth close to his ear. 'Go below and get the spare can of diesel oil from the fo'c'sle. Give it to Francesca and tell her to put half a pint at a time into the lavatory, then flush it. About once every two or three minutes will do.'

He nodded and went below. The four-gallon jerrycan we kept as a spare would now come in really useful. I had often heard of pouring oil on troubled waters – now we would see if there was anything in it.

Walker was busy wrapping sailcloth around the ropes streamed astern where they rubbed on the taffrail. It wouldn't take much of this violent movement to chafe them right through, and if a rope parted at the same moment that I had to cope with one of those particularly nasty waves which came along from time to time then it might be the end of us.

I looked at my watch. It was half past six and it looked as though I would have a nasty and frightening night ahead of me. But I was already getting the hang of keeping *Sanford* stern on to the seas and it seemed as though all I would need would be concentration and a hell of a lot of stamina.

Coertze came back and shouted, 'The oil's going in.'

I looked over the side. It didn't seem to be making much difference, though it was hard to tell. But anything that *could* make a difference I was willing to try, so I let Francesca carry on.

The waves were big. I estimated they were averaging nearly forty feet from trough to crest and *Sanford* was behaving like a roller-coaster car. When we were in a trough the waves looked frighteningly high, towering above us with threatening crests. Then her bows would sink as a wave took her astern until it seemed as if she was vertical and going to dive straight to the bottom of the sea. The wave would lift her to the crest and then we could see the storm-tattered sea around us, with spume being driven from the waves horizontally until it was difficult to distinguish between sea and air. And back we would go into a trough with *Sanford*'s bows pointing to the skies and the monstrous waves again threatening.

Sometimes, about four times in an hour, there was a freak wave which must have been caused by one wave catching up with another, thus doubling it. These freaks I estimated at sixty feet high – higher than *Sanford*'s mast! – and I would have to concentrate like hell so that we wouldn't be pooped.

Once – just once – we were pooped, and it was then that Walker went overboard. We were engulfed in water as a vast wave broke over the stern and I heard his despairing shout and saw his white

200

face and staring eyes as he was washed out of the cockpit and over the side.

Coertze's reaction was fast. He lunged for Walker – but missed. I shouted, 'Safety line – pull him in.'

He brushed water out of his eyes and yelled, 'Wasn't wearing one.'

'The damned fool,' I thought. I think it was a thought – I might even have yelled it. Coertze gave a great shout and pointed aft and I turned and could see a dark shape rolling in the boiling waters astern and I saw white hands clutching the nylon rope. They say a drowning man will clutch at a straw – Walker was lucky – he had grabbed at something more substantial, one of the drag ropes.

Coertze was hauling the rope in fast. It couldn't have been easy with the drag of Walker in the water pulling on his injured shoulder, but he was hauling just as fast as though the rope was free. He pulled Walker right under the stern and then belayed the rope.

He shouted to me, 'I'm going over the counter – you'll have to sit on my legs.'

I nodded and he started to crawl over the counter stern to where Walker was still tightly gripping the rope. He slithered aft and I got up from my seat and hoisted myself out of the cockpit until I could sit on his legs. In the violent motion of the storm it was only my weight that kept Coertze from being hurtled bodily into the sea.

Coertze grasped the rope and heaved, his shoulders writhing with the effort. He was lifting the dead weight of Walker five feet – the distance from the taffrail to the surface of the water. I hoped to God that Walker could hold on. If he let go then, not only would he be lost himself but the sudden release of tension would throw Coertze off balance and he would not have a hope of saving himself.

Walker's hand appeared above the taffrail and Coertze took a grip on the cuff of his coat. Then I looked aft and yelled, 'Hang on, for God's sake!'

One of those damnable freak seas was bearing on us, a terrifying monster coming up astern with the speed of an express train. *Sanford*'s bows sank sickeningly and Coertze gave Walker another heave, and grasped him by the scruff of the neck, pulling him on to the counter.

Then the wave was upon us and away as fast as it had come. Walker tumbled into the bottom of the cockpit, unconscious or dead, I couldn't tell which, and Coertze fell on top of him, his chest heaving with the strain of his exertions. He lay there for a few minutes, then bent down to loosen Walker's iron grip on the rope.

As he prised the fingers away, I said, 'Take him below – and you'd better stay there yourself for a while.'

A great light had just dawned on me but I had no time to think about it just then – I had to get that bight of rope back over the stern while still keeping a grasp of the tiller and watching the next sea coming up.

It was nearly an hour before Coertze came back – a lonely and frightening hour during which I was too busy to think coherently about what I had seen. The storm seemed to be building up even more strongly and I began to have second thoughts about what I had told Francesca about the seaworthiness of small boats.

When he climbed into the cockpit he took over Walker's job of looking after the stern ropes, giving me a grin as he settled down. 'Walker's OK,' he bawled. 'Francesca's looking after him. I pumped the water out of him – the bilges must be nearly full.' He laughed and the volume of his great laughter seemed to overpower the noise of the gale.

I looked at him in wonder.

V

A Mediterranean gale can't last; there is not the power of a huge ocean to draw upon and a great wind soon dies. At four the next morning the storm had abated enough for me to hand over the tiller to Coertze and go below. When I sat on the settee my hands were shaking with the sudden release of tension and I felt inexpressibly weary.

Francesca said, 'You must be hungry; I'll get you something to eat.'

I shook my head. 'No, I'm too tired to eat – I'm going to sleep.' She helped me take off my oilies, and I said, 'How's Walker?'

'He's all right; he's asleep in the quarter berth.'

I nodded slowly – Coertze had put Walker into his own berth. That fitted in, too.

I said, 'Wake me in two hours – don't let me sleep any longer. I don't want to leave Coertze alone too long,' and I fell on to my berth and was instantly asleep. The last thing I remembered was a fleeting vision of Coertze hauling Walker over the stern by the scruff of the neck.

Francesca woke me at six-thirty with a cup of coffee which I drank gratefully. 'Do you want something to eat?' she asked.

I listened to the wind and analysed the motion of *Sanford*. 'Make breakfast for all of us,' I said. 'We'll heave to and have a rest for a bit. I think the time has come for a talk with Coertze, anyway.'

I went back into the cockpit and surveyed the situation. The wind was still strong but not nearly as strong as it had been, and Coertze had hauled in the two twenty-fathom ropes and had coiled them neatly. I said, 'We'll heave to now; it's time you had some sleep.'

He nodded briefly and we began to haul in the bight of rope. Then we lashed the tiller and watched *Sanford* take position broadside on to the seas – it was safe now that the wind had dropped. When we went below Francesca was in the galley making breakfast. She had put a damp cloth on the cabin table to stop things sliding about and Coertze and I sat down.

He started to butter a piece of bread while I wondered how to go about what I was going to say. It was a difficult question I was going to broach and Kobus had such a thorny character that I didn't know how he would take it. I said, 'You know, I never really thanked you properly for pulling me out of the mine – you know, when the roof caved in.'

He munched on the bread and said, with his mouth full, '*Nee, man*, it was my own fault, I told you that before. I should have shored the last bit properly.'

'Walker owes you his thanks, too. You saved his life last night.'

He snorted. 'Who cares what he thinks.'

I said carefully, getting ready to duck. 'Why did you do it, anyway? It would have been worth at least a quarter of a million *not* to pull him out.'

Coertze stared at me, affronted. His face reddened with anger. 'Man, do you think I'm a bloody murderer?'

I had thought so at one time but didn't say so. 'And you didn't kill Parker or Alberto Corso or Donato Rinaldi?'

His face purpled. 'Who said I did?'

I cocked my thumb at the quarter berth where Walker was still asleep. 'He did.'

I thought he would burst. His jaws worked and he was literally speechless, unable to say a damn' thing. I said, 'According to friend Walker, you led Alberto into a trap on a cliff and then

203

pushed him off; you beat in the head of Donato; you shot Parker in the back of the head when you were both in action against the Germans.'

'The lying little bastard,' ground out Coertze. He started to get up. 'I'll ram those lies down his bloody throat.'

I held up my hand. 'Hold on – don't go off half-cocked. Let's sort it out first! I'd like to get your story of what happened at that time. You see, what happened last night has led me to reconsider a lot of things. I wondered why you should have saved Walker if you're the man he says you are. I'd like to get at the truth for once.'

He sat down slowly and looked at the table. At last he said, 'Alberto's death was an accident; I tried to save him, but I couldn't.'

'I believe you – after last night.'

'Donato I know nothing about. I remember thinking that there was something queer about it, though. I mean, why should Donato go climbing for fun? He had enough of that the way the Count sent us all over the hills.'

'And Parker?'

'I couldn't have killed Parker even if I'd wanted to,' he said flatly.

'Why not?'

Slowly he said, 'We were with Umberto doing one of the usual ambushes. Umberto split the force in two – one group on one side of the valley, the other group on the other side. Parker and Walker were with the other group. The ambush was a flop, anyway, and the two parties went back to camp separately. It was only when I got back to camp that I heard that Parker had been killed.'

He rubbed his chin. 'Did you say that Walker told you that Parker had been shot in the back of the head?'

'Yes.'

He looked at his hands spread out on the table. 'Walker could have done it, you know. It would be just like him.'

'I know,' I said. 'You told me once that Walker had got you into trouble a couple of times during the war. When exactly did that happen? Before you buried the gold or afterwards?'

He frowned in thought, casting his mind back to faraway days. He said, 'I remember once when Walker pulled some men away from a ditch when he shouldn't have. He was acting as a messenger for Umberto and said he'd misunderstood the instruction. I was leading a few chaps at the time and this left my flank wide open.' His eyes darkened. 'A couple of the boys copped it because of that and I nearly got a bayonet in my rump.' His face twisted in thought.

'It was *after* we buried the gold.'

'Are you sure?'

'I'm certain. We only joined Umberto's crowd after we'd buried the gold.'

I said softly, 'Maybe he could shoot Parker in the back of the head. Maybe he could beat in the back of Donato's head with a rock and fake a climbing accident. But maybe he was too scared of *you* to come at you front or rear – you're a bit of an awesome bastard at times, you know. Maybe he tried to arrange that the Germans should knock you off.'

Coertze's hands clenched on the table. I said, 'He's always been afraid of you – he still is.'

'*Magtig*, but he has reason to be,' he burst out. 'Donato got us out of the camp. Donato stayed with him on the hillside while the Germans were searching.' He looked at me with pain in his eyes. 'What kind of a man is it who can do such a thing?'

'A man like Walker,' I said. 'I think we ought to talk to him. I'm getting eager to know what he's arranged for me and Francesca.'

Coertze's lips tightened. '*Ja*, I think we wake him up now out of that *lekker slaap*.'

He stood up just as Francesca came in loaded with bowls. She saw Coertze's face and paused uncertainly. 'What's the matter?'

I took the bowls from her and put them in the fiddles. 'We're just going to have a talk with Walker,' I said. 'You'd better come along.'

But Walker was already awake and I could see from his expression that he knew what was coming. He swung himself from the berth and tried to get away from Coertze, who lunged at him.

'Hold on,' I said, and grabbed Coertze's arm. 'I said we're going to talk to him.'

The muscles bunched in Coertze's arm and then relaxed and I let go. I said to Walker, 'Coertze thinks you're a liar – what do you say?'

His eyes shifted and he gave Coertze a scared glance, then he looked away. 'I didn't say he killed anybody. I didn't say that.'

'No, you didn't,' I agreed. 'But you damn' well implied it.'

Coertze growled under his breath but said nothing, apparently content to let me handle it for the moment. I said, 'What about Parker? You said that Coertze was near him when he was shot – Coertze said he wasn't. What about it?'

'I didn't say that either,' he said sulkily.

'You *are* a damned liar,' I said forcibly. 'You said it to me. I've got a good memory even if you haven't. I warned you in Tangier what would happen if you ever lied to me, so you'd better watch it. Now I want the truth – was Coertze near Parker when he was killed?'

He was silent for a long time. 'Well, was he?' I demanded.

He broke. 'No, he wasn't,' he cried shrilly. 'I made that up. He wasn't there; he was on the other side of the valley.'

'Then who killed Parker?'

'It was the Germans,' he cried frantically. 'It was the Germans – I told you it was the Germans.'

I suppose it was too much to expect him to confess to murder. He would never say outright that he had killed Parker and Donato Rinaldi – but his face gave him away. I had no intention of sparing him anything, so I said to Coertze, 'He was responsible for Torloni's attack.'

Coertze grunted in surprise. 'How?'

I told him about the cigarette case, then said to Walker, 'Coertze saved your life last night, but I wish to God he'd let you drown. Now I'm going to leave him down here alone with you and he can do what he likes.'

Walker caught my arm. 'Don't leave me,' he implored. 'Don't let him get at me.' What he had always feared was now about to happen – there was no one between him and Coertze. He had blackened Coertze in my eyes so that he would have an ally to fight his battles, but now I was on Coertze's side. He feared physical violence – his killings had been done from ambush – and Coertze was the apotheosis of violence.

'Please,' he whimpered, 'don't leave.' He looked at Francesca with a passionate plea in his eyes. She turned aside without speaking and went up the companionway into the cockpit. I shook off his hand and followed her, closing the cabin hatch.

'Coertze will kill him,' she said in a low voice.

'Hasn't he the right?' I demanded. 'I don't believe in private execution as a rule, but this is one time I'm willing to make an exception.'

'I'm not thinking of Walker,' she said. 'It will be bad for Coertze. No one can kill a man like that and be the same after. It will be bad for his . . . nis spirit.'

I said, 'Coertze will do what he has to do.'

We lapsed into silence, just looking at the lumpy sea, and I began to think of the boat and what we had to do next.

The cabin hatch opened and Coertze came into the cockpit.

There was a baffled expression on his face and he said in a hoarse voice, 'I was going to kill the little bastard. I was going to hit him — I did hit him once. But you can't hit anyone who won't fight back. You can't, can you?'

I grinned and Francesca laughed joyously. Coertze looked at us and his face broke into a slow smile. 'But what are we going to do with him?' he asked.

'We'll drop him at Tangier and let him shift for himself,' I said. 'We'll give him the biggest scare any man's ever had.'

We were sitting grinning at each other like a couple of happy fools when Francesca said sharply, 'Look!'

I followed the line of her outstretched arm. 'Oh, no!' I groaned. Coertze looked and cursed.

Coming towards us through the tossing seas and wallowing atrociously was the Fairmile.

9 *Sanford*

I looked at it bitterly. I had been certain that Metcalfe must have lost us in the storm — he had the luck of the devil. He hadn't found us by radar either, because the storm had made a clean sweep of the Fairmile's upperworks — his radar antenna was gone, as also was the radio mast and the short derrick. It could only have been by sheer luck that he had stumbled upon us.

I said to Coertze, 'Get below and start the engine. Francesca, you go below, too, and stay there.'

I looked across at the Fairmile. It was about a mile away and closing at about eight knots — a little over five minutes to make what futile preparations we could. I had no illusions about Metcalfe. Torloni had been bad enough but all he knew was force — Metcalfe used his brains.

The seas were bad. When the wind had blown it exerted a discipline on the sea and the waves were regular and uniform. With the wind gone the sea was chaotic; ugly pyramidical lumps of water would heave up and disappear and *Sanford* pitched and rolled alarmingly.

The Fairmile was in no better shape, either. She staggered and wallowed as unexpected waves hit her and I could imagine the tumult inside that hull. She was an old boat, being war surplus, and her hull must have deteriorated over the years despite the care

Metcalfe had lavished on her. Then there was the fact that when she was built her life expectancy was about five years, and war-time materials weren't noted for their excessive quality.

I had the sudden idea that she couldn't move any faster, and that Metcalfe was driving her as fast as he dared in those heavy seas. Her engines were fine for twenty-six knots in calm water but if she was driven at much more than eight knots now she would be in danger of falling apart. Metcalfe might risk a lot for the gold, but he wouldn't risk that.

As I heard the engine start I opened the throttle wide and turned *Sanford* away from the Fairmile. We had a biggish engine and I could still get seven knots out of *Sanford*, even punching against these seas. Our five minutes' grace was now stretched to an hour, and maybe in that hour I'd get another bright idea.

Coertze came up and I handed the tiller over to him, and went below. I didn't bother to tell him what to do – it was obvious. I opened the locker under my berth and took out the Schmeisser machine pistol and all the magazines. Francesca looked at me from the settee. 'Must you do that?' she asked.

'I'll not shoot unless I have to,' I said. 'Not unless they start shooting first.' I looked around. 'Where's Walker?'

'He locked himself in the fo'c'sle. He's frightened of Coertze.'

'Good. I don't want him underfoot now,' I said, and went back to the cockpit.

Coertze looked incredulously at the machine pistol. 'Where the hell did you get that?'

'From the tunnel,' I said. 'I hope it works – this ammo is damned old.'

I put one of the long magazines into the butt and clipped the shoulder rest into place. I said, 'You'd better get your Luger; I'll take the helm.'

He smiled sourly. 'What's the use? You threw all the bullets away.'

'Damn! Wait a minute, though; there's Torloni's gun. It's in the chart table drawer.'

He went below and I looked back at the Fairmile. As I thought, Metcalfe didn't increase his speed when we turned away. Not that it mattered – he had the legs of us by about a knot and I could see that he was perceptibly closer.

Coertze came back with the pistol stuck in his trouser waistband. He said, 'How long before he catches up?'

'Less than an hour,' I said. I touched the Schmeisser. 'We don't shoot unless he does – and we don't shoot to kill.'

'Will he shoot to kill?'

'I don't know,' I said. 'He might.'

Coertze grunted and pulled out the gun and began to examine the action.

We fell into silence; there was nothing much to talk about, anyway. I ruminated on the firing of a sub-machine-gun. It had been a long time since I had fired one and I began to go over the training points that had been drilled into me by a red-faced sergeant. The big thing was that the recoil lifted the muzzle and if you didn't consciously hold it down most of your fire would be wasted in the air. I tried to think of other things I had learned but I couldn't think of anything else so that fragment of information would have to do.

After a while I said to Coertze, 'I could do with some coffee.'

'That's not a bad idea,' he said, and went below. An Afrikaner will never refuse the offer of coffee; their livers are tanned with it. In five minutes he was back with two steaming mugs, and said, 'Francesca wants to come up.'

I looked back at the Fairmile. 'No,' I said briefly.

We drank the coffee, spilling half of it as *Sanford* shuddered to a particularly heavy sea, and when we had finished the Fairmile was within a quarter of a mile and I could see Metcalfe quite clearly standing outside the wheelhouse.

I said, 'I wonder how he's going to go about it. He can't board us in this sea, there's too much danger of ramming us. How would you go about it, Kobus?'

'I'd lay off and knock us off with a rifle,' he grunted. 'Just like at a shooting gallery. Then when the sea goes down he can board us without a fight.'

That seemed reasonable but it wouldn't be as easy as in a shooting gallery – metal ducks don't shoot back. I handed the tiller to Coertze. 'We may have to do a bit of fancy manoeuvring,' I said. 'But you'll handle her well enough without sail. When I tell you to do something, you do it damn' quick.' I picked up the Schmeisser and held it on my knee. 'How many rounds are there in that pistol?'

'Not enough,' he said. 'Five.'

At last the Fairmile was only a hundred yards away on the starboard quarter and Metcalfe came out of the wheelhouse carrying a Tannoy loud-hailer. His voice boomed across the water. 'What are you running away for? Don't you want a tow?'

I cupped my hands around my mouth. 'Are you claiming salvage?' I asked sardonically.

He laughed. 'Did the storm do any damage?'

'None at all,' I shouted. 'We can get to port ourselves.' If he wanted to play the innocent I was prepared to go along with him. I had nothing to lose.

The Fairmile was throttled back to keep pace with us. Metcalfe fiddled with the amplification of the loud-hailer and it whistled eerily. 'Hal,' he shouted, 'I want your boat – and your cargo.'

There it was – out in the open as bluntly as that.

The loud-hailer boomed, 'If you act peaceable about it I'll accept half, if you don't I'll take the lot, anyway.'

'Torloni made the same offer and look what happened to him.'

'He was at a disadvantage,' called Metcalfe. 'He couldn't use guns – I can.'

Krupke moved into sight – carrying a rifle. He climbed on top of the deck saloon and lay down just behind the wheelhouse. I said to Coertze, 'It looks as though you called that one.'

It was bad, but not as bad as all that. Krupke had been in the army; he was accustomed to firing from a steady position even though his target might move. I didn't think he could fire at all accurately from a bouncing platform like the Fairmile.

I saw the Fairmile edging in closer and said to Coertze, 'Keep the distance.'

Metcalfe shouted, 'What about it?'

'Go to hell!'

He nodded to Krupke, who fired immediately. I didn't see where the bullet went – I don't think it hit us at all. He fired again and this time he hit something forward. It must have been metal because I heard a 'spaaang' as the bullet ricocheted away.

Coertze dug me in the ribs. 'Don't look back so that Metcalfe notices you, but I think we're in for some more heavy weather.'

I changed position on the seat so that I could look astern from the corner of my eye. The horizon was black with a vicious squall – and it was coming our way. I hoped to God it would hurry.

I said, 'We'll have to play for time now.'

Krupke fired and there was a slam astern. I looked over the side and saw a hole punched into the side of the counter. His aim was getting better.

I shouted, 'Tell Krupke not to hole us below the waterline. We might sink and you wouldn't like that.'

That held him for a while. I saw him talking to Krupke, making gestures with his hand to indicate a higher elevation. I called urgently for Francesca to come on deck. Those nickel-jacketed bullets would go through *Sanford*'s thin planking as though it was tissue paper. She came up just as Krupke fired his next shot. It went high and didn't hit anything.

As soon as Metcalfe saw her he held up his hand and Krupke stopped firing. 'Hal, be reasonable,' he called. 'You've got a woman aboard.'

I looked at Francesca and she shook her head. I shouted, 'You're doing the shooting.'

'I don't want to hurt anybody,' pleaded Metcalfe.

'Then go away.'

He shrugged and said something to Krupke, who fired again. The bullet hit the gooseneck with a clang. I grinned mirthlessly at Metcalfe's curious morality – according to him it would be my fault if anyone was killed.

I looked astern. The squall was appreciably nearer and coming up fast. It was the last dying kick of the storm and wouldn't last long – just long enough to give Metcalfe the slip, I hoped. I didn't think that Metcalfe had seen it yet; he was too busy with us.

Krupke fired again. There was a thud forward and I knew the bullet must have gone through the main cabin. I had brought Francesca up just in time.

I was beginning to worry about Krupke. In spite of the difficulties of aiming, his shooting was getting better, and even if it didn't, then sooner or later he would get in a lucky shot. I wondered how much ammunition he had.

'Metcalfe,' I called.

He held up his hand but not soon enough to prevent Krupke pulling the trigger. The cockpit coaming disintegrated into matchwood just by my elbow. We all ducked into the cockpit and I looked incredulously at the back of my hand – a two-inch splinter of mahogany was sticking in it.

I pulled it out and shouted, 'Hey, hold it! That was a bit too close.'

'What do you want?'

I noticed that the Fairmile was crowding us again so I told Coertze to pull out.

'Well?' Metcalfe's voice was impatient.

'I want to make a deal,' I shouted.

'You know my terms.'

'How do we know we can trust you?'

Metcalfe was uncompromising. 'You don't.'

I pretended to confer with Coertze. 'How's that squall coming up?'

'If you keep stringing him along we might make it.'

I turned to the Fairmile. 'I'll make a counter-proposition. We'll give you a third – Walker won't be needing his share.'

Metcalfe laughed. 'Oh, you've found him out at last, have you?'

'What about it?'

'Nothing doing – half or all of it. Make your choice; you're in no position to bargain.'

I turned to Coertze. 'What do you think, Kobus?'

He rubbed his chin. 'I'll go along with anything you say.'

'Francesca?'

She sighed. 'Do you think this other storm coming up will help?'

'It's not a storm, but it'll help. I think we can lose Metcalfe if we can hold him off for another ten minutes.'

'Can we?'

'I think so, but it might be dangerous.'

Her lips tightened. 'Then fight him.'

I looked across at Metcalfe. He was standing by the door of the wheelhouse looking at Krupke who was pointing astern.

He had seen the squall!

I shouted. 'We've been having a conference and the general consensus of opinion is that you can still go to hell.'

He jerked his hand irritably and Krupke fired again – another miss.

I said to Coertze, 'We'll give him another two shots. Immediately after the second, starboard your helm as though you are going to ram him, but for God's sake don't ram him. Get as close as you can and come back on course parallel to him. Understand?'

As he nodded there was another shot from Krupke. That one hit *Sanford* just under the cockpit – Krupke was getting too good.

Metcalfe couldn't know that we had a machine-gun. *Sanford* had been searched many times and machine-guns – even small ones – aren't to be picked up on every street corner in Italy. There was the chance we would give him a fright. I said to Francesca, 'When we start to turn get down in the bottom of the cockpit.'

Krupke fired again, missed, and Coertze swung the tiller over. It caught Metcalfe by surprise – this was like a rabbit attacking a weasel. We had something like twenty seconds to complete the manoeuvre and it worked. By the time he had recovered enough to shout to the helmsman and for the helmsman to respond, we were alongside.

Krupke fired again when he saw us coming but the bullet went wild. I saw him aim at me and looked right into the muzzle of his gun. Then I cut loose with the Schmeisser.

I had only time to fire two bursts. The first one was for Krupke — I must get him before he got me. Two or three rounds broke the saloon windows of the Fairmile and I let the recoil lift the gun. Bullets smashed into the edge of the decking and I saw Krupke reel back with both hands clasped to his face and heard a thin scream.

Then I switched to the wheelhouse and hosed it. Glass flew but I was too late to catch Metcalfe who was already out of sight. The Schmeisser jammed on a defective round and I yelled at Coertze, 'Let's get out of here,' and swung the helm over again.

'Where to?' he asked.

'Back to where we came from — into the squall.'

I looked back at the Fairmile. Metcalfe was on top of the deck saloon bending over Krupke and the Fairmile was still continuing on her original course. But her bows were swinging from side to side as though there was nobody at the helm. 'This might just work,' I said.

But after two or three minutes she started to turn and was soon plunging after us. I looked ahead and prayed we could get into the squall in time. I had never before prayed for dirty weather.

II

It was nip and tuck but we made it. The first gusts hit us when the Fairmile was barely two hundred yards behind, and ten seconds later she was invisible, lost in spearing rain and sea spume.

I throttled back the engine until it was merely ticking over; it would be suicide to try to butt our way through this. It was an angry bit of weather, all right, but it didn't have the sustained ferocity of the earlier storm and I knew it would be over in half an hour or so.

In that short time we had to lose Metcalfe.

I left the tiller to Coertze and stumbled forward to the mast and hoisted the trysail. That would give us leeway and we could pick a course of sorts. I chose to beat windward; that was the last thing Metcalfe would expect me to do in heavy weather, and I hoped that when the squall had blown out he would be searching to leeward.

Sanford didn't like it. She bucked and pitched more than ever and I cursed the crankiness caused by the golden keel, the cause of all our troubles. I said to Francesca, 'You and Kobus had better go below; there's no point in all of us getting soaked to the skin.'

I wondered what Metcalfe was doing. If he had any sense he would have the Fairmile lying head to wind with her engines turning just enough to keep position. But he wanted the gold and had guts enough to try anything weird as long as the boat didn't show signs of falling apart under him. He had shown his seamanship by coming through the big storm undamaged – this squall wouldn't hurt him.

Just then *Sanford* lurched violently and I thought for a moment that she was falling apart under *me*. There was a curious feel to the helm which I couldn't analyse – it was like nothing I had felt on a boat before. She lurched again and seemed to sideslip in the water and she swayed alarmingly even when she hadn't been pushed. I leaned on the helm tentatively and she came round with a rush.

Hastily I pulled the other way and she came back fast, overshooting. It was like riding a horse with a loose saddle and I couldn't understand it.

I had a sudden and dreadful thought and looked over the side. It was difficult to make out in the swirl of water but her boot-topping seemed to be much higher out of the water than it should have been, and I knew what had happened.

It was her keel – that goddamned golden keel.

Coertze had warned us about it. He had said that it would be full of flaws and cracks and that it would be structurally weak. *Sanford* had taken a hell of a hammering in the last couple of days and this last squall was the straw that broke the camel's back – or broke the ship's keel.

I looked over the side again, trying to estimate how much higher she was in the water. As near as I could judge three parts of the keel were gone. *Sanford* had lost three tons of ballast and she was in danger of capsizing at any moment.

I hammered on the cabin hatch and yelled at the top of my voice. Coertze popped his head out. 'What's wrong?' he shouted.

'Get on deck fast – Francesca, too. The bloody keel's gone. We're going to capsize.'

He looked at me blankly. 'What the hell do you mean?' His face flushed red as the meaning sank in. 'You mean the gold's gone?' he said incredulously.

'For Christ's sake, don't just stand there gaping,' I shouted. 'Get the hell up here – and get Francesca out of there. I don't know if I can hold her much longer.'

He whitened and his head vanished. Francesca came scrambling out of the cabin with Coertze on her heels. *Sanford* was behaving like a crazy thing and I shouted to Coertze, 'Get that bloody sail down quick or she'll be over.'

He lunged forward along the deck and wasted no time in unfastening the fall of the halyard from the cleat – instead he pulled the knife from his belt and cut it with one clean slice. As soon as the sail came down *Sanford* began to behave a little better, but not much. She slithered about on the surface of the water and it was by luck, not judgement, that I managed to keep her upright, because I had never had that experience before – few people have.

Coertze came back and I yelled, 'It's the mast that'll have us over if we're not careful.'

He looked up at the mast towering overhead and gave a quick nod. I wondered if he remembered what he had said the first time I questioned him about yachts in Cape Town. He had looked up at the mast of *Estralita* and said, 'She'll need to be deep to counterbalance that lot.'

The keel, our counter-balance, had gone and the fifty-five-foot mast was the key to *Sanford*'s survival.

I pointed to the hatchet clipped to the side of the cockpit. 'Cut the shrouds,' I shouted.

He seized the hatchet and went forward again and swung at the after starboard shroud. It bounced off the stainless steel wire and I cursed myself for having built *Sanford* so stoutly. He swung again and again and finally the wire parted.

He went on to the forward shroud and I said, 'Francesca, I'll have to help him or it may be too late. Can you take the helm?'

'What must I do?'

'I think I've got the hang of it,' I said. 'She's very tender and you mustn't move the tiller violently. She swings very easily so you must be very gentle in your movements – otherwise it's the same as before.'

I couldn't stay with her long before I had to leave the cockpit and release both the backstay runners so that the stays hung loose. The mast had no support from aft.

I went forward to the bows, clinging on for dear life, and crouched in the bow pulpit, using the marline-spike of my knife on the rigging screw of the forestay. The spike was not designed for the job and kept slipping out of the holes of the body, but I managed to loosen the screws appreciably in spite of being drenched every time *Sanford* dipped her bows. When I looked up I saw a definite curve in the stay to leeward which meant that it was slack.

I looked round and saw Coertze attacking the port shrouds before I bent to loosen the fore topmast stay. When I looked up again the mast was whipping like a fishing rod – but still the damn' thing wouldn't break.

It was only when I tripped over the fore hatch that I remembered Walker. I hammered on the hatch and shouted, 'Walker, come out; we're sinking.' But I heard nothing from below.

Damning his minuscule soul to hell, I went aft and clattered down the companionway and into the main cabin. I staggered forward, unable to keep my balance in *Sanford*'s new and uneasy motion and tried the door to the fo'c'sle. It was locked from the inside. I hammered on it with my fist, and shouted, 'Walker, come out, we're going to capsize.'

I heard a faint sound and shouted again. Then he called, 'I'm not coming out.'

'Don't be a damned fool,' I yelled. 'We're liable to sink at any minute.'

'It's a trick to get me out. I know Coertze's waiting for me.'

'You bloody idiot,' I screamed and hammered on the door again, but it was no use; he refused to answer so I left him there.

As I turned to go, *Sanford* groaned in every timber and I made a mad dash for the companionway, getting into the cockpit just in time to see the mast go. It cracked and split ten feet above the deck and toppled into the raging sea, still tethered by the back and fore stays.

I took the tiller from Francesca and tentatively moved it. *Sanford*'s motion was not much better – she still slid about unpredictably – but I felt easier with the top hamper gone. I kicked at a cockpit locker and shouted to Francesca, 'Life jackets – get them out.'

The solving of one problem led directly to another – the mast in the water was still held fore and aft and it banged rhythmically into *Sanford*'s side. Much of that treatment and she would be stove in and we would go down like a stone. Coertze was in the bows and I could see the glint of the hatchet as he raised it for another blow at the forestay. He was very much alive to the danger inherent in the mast.

I struggled into a life jacket while Francesca took the helm, then I grabbed the boat-hook from the coach roof and leaned over the side to prod the mast away when it swung in again for another battering charge. Coertze came aft and started to cut away the backstays; it was easier to cut them on the deck and within five minutes he had done it, and the mast drifted away and was lost to sight amid the sea spray.

Coertze dropped heavily into the cockpit, his face streaming with salt water, and Francesca gave him a life jacket. We fastened our safety lines and, on a sudden impulse, I battened down the main hatch – if Walker wanted to come out he could still use the fore hatch. I wanted to seal *Sanford* – if she capsized and filled with water she would sink within seconds.

Those last moments of the squall were pretty grim. If we could last them out we might stand a chance. *Sanford* would never sail again, but it might be possible to move her slowly by a judicious use of her engine. For the first time I hoped I had not misled Metcalfe and that he would be standing by.

But the squall had not done with us. A violent gust of wind coincided with a freak sea and *Sanford* tilted alarmingly. Desperately I worked the tiller, but it was too late and she heeled more and more until the deck was at an angle of forty-five degrees.

I yelled, 'Hang on, she's going,' and in that moment *Sanford* lurched right over and I was thrown into the sea.

I spluttered and swallowed salt water before the buoyancy of the jacket brought me to the surface, lying on my back. Frantically I looked round for Francesca and was relieved when her head bobbed up close by. I grabbed her safety line and pulled until we floated side by side. 'Back to the boat,' I spluttered.

We hauled on the safety lines and drew ourselves back to *Sanford*. She was lying on her starboard side, heaving sluggishly over the waves, and we painfully crawled up the vertical deck until we could grasp the stanchions of the port safety rail. I looked back over the rail and on to the new and oddly shaped upper deck – the port side of *Sanford*.

I helped Francesca over the rail and then I saw Coertze clinging to what was left of the keel – he had evidently jumped the other way. He was clutching a tangle of broken wires – the wires that were supposed to hold the keel together and which had failed in their purpose. I slid down the side and gave him a hand, and soon the three of us were uneasily huddled on the unprotected hull, wondering what the hell to do next.

That last flailing gust of wind had been the squall's final crack of the whip and the wind dropped within minutes to leave the hulk of *Sanford* tossing on an uneasy sea. I looked around hopefully for Metcalfe but the Fairmile wasn't in sight, although she could still come out of the dirty weather left in the wake of the squall.

I was looking contemplatively at the dinghy which was still lashed down to the coach roof when Coertze said, 'There's still a lot of gold down there, you know.' He was staring back at the keel.

'To hell with the gold,' I said. 'Let's get this dinghy free.'

We cut the lashings and let the dinghy fall into the sea – after I had taken the precaution of tying a line to it. It floated upside down, but that didn't worry me – the buoyancy chambers would keep it afloat in any position. I went down the deck and into the sea and managed to right it. Then I took the baler which was still clipped in place and began to bale out.

I had just finished when Francesca shouted, 'Metcalfe! Metcalfe's coming.'

By the time I got back on top of the hull the Fairmile was quite close, still plugging away at the eight knots which Metcalfe favoured for heavy seas. We weren't trying to get away this time, so it was not long before she was within hailing distance.

Metcalfe was outside the wheelhouse. He bellowed, 'Can you take a line?'

Coertze waved and the Fairmile edged in closer and Metcalfe lifted a coil of rope and began to swing it. His first throw was short, but Coertze caught the second and slid down the deck to make the line fast to the stump of the mast. I cut two lengths of line and tied them in loops round the rope Metcalfe had thrown. I said, 'We'll go over in the dinghy, pulling ourselves along the line. For God's sake, don't let go of these loops or we might be swept away.'

We got into the dinghy and pulled ourselves across to the Fairmile. It wasn't a particularly difficult job but we were cold and wet and tired and it would have been easy to make a mistake. Metcalfe helped Francesca on board and Coertze went next. As I started to climb he threw me a line and said curtly, 'Make the dinghy fast; I might need it.'

So I made fast and climbed on deck. Metcalfe stepped up to me, his face contorted with rage. He grabbed me by the shoulders with both hands and yelled, 'You damn' fool – I told you to make certain of that keel. I told you back in Rapallo.'

He began to shake me and I was too tired to resist. My head lolled back and forward like the head of a sawdust doll and when he let me go I just sat down on the deck.

He swung round to Coertze. 'How much is left?' he demanded. 'About a quarter.'

He looked at the hulk of *Sanford*, a strained expression in his eyes. 'I'm not going to lose that,' he said. 'I'm not going to lose a ton of gold.'

He called to the wheelhouse and the Moroccan, Moulay Idriss, came on deck. Metcalfe gave quick instructions in Arabic and then dropped into the dinghy and pulled himself across to *Sanford*. The Arab attached a heavy cable to the line and when Metcalfe got to the hulk he began to pull it across.

Francesca and I were not taking much interest in this. We were exhausted and more preoccupied in being alive and together than with what happened to the gold. Coertze, however, was alive to the situation and was helping the Arab make the cable fast.

Metcalfe came back and said to Coertze, 'You were right, there's about a ton left. I don't know how that wreck will behave when it's towed, but we'll try.'

As the Fairmile turned and the cable tautened, a watery sun shone out over the heaving sea and I looked back at *Sanford* as she moved sluggishly to the pull. The cockpit was half under water but the fore hatch was still free, and I said, 'My God! Walker's still in there!'

Coertze said, '*Magtig*, I'd forgotten him.'

He must have been knocked unconscious when *Sanford* capsized – otherwise we would have heard him. Francesca was staring back at *Sanford*. 'Look!' she exclaimed. 'There – in the cockpit.'

The main hatch was being forced open from the inside and I could see Walker's head as he tried to struggle out against the rush of water pouring into the boat. His hands grasped for the cockpit coaming – but it wasn't there – Krupke had shot it away. Then Walker disappeared as the force of the water pushed him back into the cabin.

If he had come out by the fore hatch he would have been safe, but even in death he had to make one of his inevitable mistakes. The main hatch was open, water was pouring into the hull and *Sanford* was sinking.

Metcalfe was in a rage. 'The damn' fool,' he cried. 'I thought you'd got rid of him. He's taking the bloody gold with him.'

Sanford was getting low in the water and as she did so, the water poured into her faster. Metcalfe stared at her in despair, his voice filled with fury. 'The stupid, bloody idiot,' he yelled. 'He's bitched things from the start.'

It wouldn't be long now – *Sanford* was going fast. The towing cable tightened as she sank lower in the water and the Fairmile went down by the stern as the pull on the cable became greater. *Sanford* gave a lurch as compressed air in the fo'c'sle blew out the forehatch and she began to settle faster as more water poured in through this new opening in her hull.

The downward drag on the stern of the Fairmile was becoming

dangerous and Metcalfe took a hatchet from a clip and stood by the cable. He looked back at *Sanford*, his face twitching with indecision, then he brought the hatchet down on the cable with a great swing. It parted with a twang, the loose end snaked away across the sea and the Fairmile bobbed up her stern.

Sanford lurched again and turned over. As she went down and out of sight amid swirling waters a vagrant sunbeam touched her keel and we saw the glint of imperishable gold. Then there was nothing but the sea.

III

Metcalfe's anger was great but, like the squall, soon subsided and he became his usual saturnine self, taking the loss with a philosophical air. 'A pity,' he said. 'But there it is. It's gone and there isn't anything we can do about it now.'

We were sitting in the saloon of the Fairmile, on our way to Malaga where Metcalfe was going to drop us. He had given us dry clothing and food and we were all feeling better.

I said, 'What will you do now?'

He shrugged. 'Tangier is just about played out now the Moroccans are taking over. I think I'll pop down to the Congo – things seem to be blowing up down there.'

Metcalfe and a few others like him would be 'popping down to the Congo', I thought. Carrion crows flocking together – but he wasn't as bad as some. I said, 'I think you've got a few things to explain.'

He grinned. 'What do you want to know?'

'Well, the thing that's been niggling me is how you got on to us in the first place. What led you to suspect that we were after the gold?'

'Suspect, old boy? I didn't suspect, I *knew*.'

'How the devil did you know?'

'It was when I got Walker drunk. He spilled the whole story about the gold, the keel – everything.'

'Well, I'm damned.' I thought of all the precautions I'd taken to put Metcalfe off the scent; I thought of all the times I'd beaten my brains out to think up new twists of evasion. All wasted – he wasn't fooled at all!

'I thought you'd get rid of him,' Metcalfe said. 'He was a dead loss all the way through. I thought you'd put him over the side or something like that.'

I looked at Coertze, who grinned at me. I said, 'He was probably a murderer, too.'

'Wouldn't be surprised,' agreed Metcalfe airily. 'He was a slimy little rat.'

That reminded me – I had probably killed a man too. 'Where's Krupke?' I asked. 'I haven't seen him around.'

Metcalfe snickered. 'He's groaning in his bunk – he got a faceful of splinters.'

I held out the back of my hand. 'Well, he did the same to me.'

'Yes,' said Metcalfe soberly. 'But Krupke is probably going to lose an eye.'

'Serve him damn' well right,' I said viciously. 'He won't be too keen to look down rifle sights again.'

I hadn't lost sight of the fact that Metcalfe and his crew of ruffians had been doing their damndest to kill us not many hours before. But there wasn't any advantage in quarrelling with Metcalfe about it – we were on his boat and he was going to put us ashore safely. Irritating him wasn't exactly the best policy just then.

He said, 'That machine-gun of yours was some surprise. You nearly plugged me.' He pointed to a battered loud-hailer on the sideboard. 'You shot that goddamn thing right out of my hand.'

Francesca said, 'Why were you so solicitous about my husband? Why did you take the trouble?'

'Oh, I felt real bad when I saw Hal slug him,' said Metcalfe seriously. 'I knew who he was, you see, and I knew he could make a stink. I didn't want anything like that. I wanted Hal to get on with casting the keel and get out of Italy. I couldn't afford to have the police rooting round.'

'That's why you tried to hold Torloni, too,' I said.

He rubbed his chin. 'That was *my* mistake,' he admitted. 'I thought I could use Torloni without him knowing it. But he's a bad bastard and when he got hold of that cigarette case the whole thing blew up in my face. I just wanted Torloni to keep an eye on you, but that damn' fool, Walker, had to go and give the game away. There was no holding Torloni then.'

'So you warned us.'

He spread his hands. 'What else could I do for a pal?'

'Pal nothing. You wanted the gold out.'

He grinned. 'Well, what the hell; you got away, didn't you?'

I had bitter thoughts of Metcalfe as the puppet master; he had manipulated all of us and we had danced to his tune. Not quite – one of his puppets had broken a string; if Walker had defeated us, he had also defeated Metcalfe.

I said, 'If you hadn't been so obvious about Torloni the keel wouldn't have broken. We had to cast it in a bloody hurry when he started putting the pressure on.'

'Yes,' said Metcalfe. 'And all those damned partisans didn't help, either.' He stood up. 'Well, I've still got to run this boat.' He hesitated, then put his hand in his pocket and pulled out a cigarette case. 'You might like this as a souvenir – Torloni mislaid it. There's something interesting inside.' He tossed it on the table and left the saloon.

I looked at Francesca and Coertze, then slowly put out my hand and picked it up. It had the heavy, familiar feel of gold, but I felt no sudden twist to my guts as I had when Walker had put the gold Hercules into my hand. I was sick of the sight of gold.

I opened the case and found a letter inside, folded in two. It was addressed to me, care of the yacht *Sanford*, Tangier Harbour, and had been opened. I started to read it and began to laugh uncontrollably.

Francesca and Coertze looked at me in astonishment. I tried to control my laughter but it kept bursting out hysterically. 'We've . . we've won . . . won a sweep . . . a lottery,' I gasped, and passed the letter to Francesca, who also started to laugh.

Coertze said blankly, 'What lottery?'

I said, 'Don't you remember? You insisted on buying a lottery ticket in Tangier – you said it was for insurance. It won!'

He started to smile. 'How much?'

'Six hundred thousand pesetas.'

'What's that in money?'

I wiped my eyes. 'A little over six thousand pounds. It won't cover expenses – what I've spent on this jaunt – but it'll help.'

Coertze looked sheepish. 'How much did you spend?'

I began to figure it out. I had lost *Sanford* – she had been worth about £12,000. I had covered all our expenses for nearly a year, and they had been high because we were supposed to be wealthy tourists; there had been the exorbitant rental of the Casa Saeta in Tangier; there was the outfitting and provisioning of the boat.

I said, 'It must run to about seventeen or eighteen thousand.'

His eyes twinkled and he put his hand to his fob pocket. 'Will these help?' he asked, and rolled four large diamonds on to the table.

'Well, I'm damned,' I said. 'Where did you get those?'

'They seemed to stick to my fingers in the tunnel.' He chuckled. 'Just like that machine pistol stuck to yours.'

Francesca started to giggle and put her hands to her breast. She produced a little wash-leather bag which was slung on a cord round her neck and emptied it. Two more diamonds joined those on the table and there were also four emeralds.

I looked at both of them and said, 'You damned thieves; you ought to be ashamed of yourselves. The jewels were supposed to stay in Italy.'

I grinned and produced my five diamonds and we all sat there laughing like maniacs.

IV

Later, when we had put the gems away safe from the prying eyes of Metcalfe, we went on deck and watched the hills of Spain emerge mistily from over the horizon. I put my arm round Francesca and said wryly, 'Well, I've still got a half-share in a boatyard in Cape Town. Will you mind being a boat-builder's wife?'

She squeezed my hand. 'I think I'll like South Africa.'

I took the cigarette case from my pocket and opened it with one hand. The inscription was there and I read it for the first time – 'Caro Benito da parte di Adolf – Brennero – 1940.'

I said, 'This is a pretty dangerous thing to have around. Some other Torloni might see it.'

She shivered and said, 'Get rid of it, Hal; please throw it away.'

So I tossed it over the side and there was just one glint of gold in the green water and then it was gone for ever.

Desmond
Bagley

Running
Blind

Chapter One

I

To be encumbered with a corpse is to be in a difficult position, especially when the corpse is without benefit of death certificate. True, any doctor, even one just hatched from medical school, would have been able to diagnose the cause of death. The man had died of heart failure or what the medical boys pompously call cardiac arrest.

The proximate cause of his pumper having stopped pumping was that someone had slid a sharp sliver of steel between his ribs just far enough to penetrate the great muscle of the heart and to cause a serious and irreversible leakage of blood so that it stopped beating. Cardiac arrest, as I said.

I wasn't too anxious to find a doctor because the knife was mine and the hilt had been in my hand when the point pricked out his life. I stood on the open road with the body at my feet and I was scared, so scared that my bowels loosened and the nausea rose in my throat to choke me. I don't know which is the worse – to kill someone you know or to kill a stranger. This particular body had been a stranger – in fact, he still was – I had never seen him before in my life.

And this was the way it happened.

Less than two hours previously the airliner had slid beneath the clouds and I saw the familiar, grim landscape of Southern Iceland. The aircraft lost height over the Reykjanes Peninsula and landed dead on time at Keflavik International Airport, where it was raining, a thin drizzle weeping from an iron grey sky.

I was unarmed, if you except the *sgian dubh*. Customs officers don't like guns so I didn't carry a pistol, and Slade said it wasn't necessary. The *sgian dubh* – the black knife of the Highlander – is a much underrated weapon if, these days, it is ever regarded as a weapon at all. One sees it in the stocking tops of sober Scotsmen when they are in the glory of national dress and it is just another piece of masculine costume jewellery.

Mine was more functional. It had been given to me by my grandfather who had it of his grandfather, so that made it at least a hundred and fifty years old. Like any good piece of killing equipment it had no unnecessary trimmings – even the apparent decorations had a function. The ebony haft was ribbed on one side in the classic Celtic basket-weave pattern to give a good grip when drawing, but smooth on the other side so it would draw clear without catching; the blade was less than four inches long, but long enough to reach a vital organ; even the gaudy cairngorm stone set in the pommel had its use – it balanced the knife so that it made a superlative throwing weapon.

It lived in a flat sheath in my left stocking top. Where else would you expect to keep a *sgian dubh*? The obvious way is often the best because most people don't see the obvious. The Customs officer didn't even look, not into my luggage and certainly not into the more intimate realms of my person. I had been in and out of the country so often that I am tolerably well known, and the fact I speak the language was a help – there are only 20,000 people who speak Icelandic and the Icelanders have a comical air of pleased surprise when they encounter a foreigner who has taken the trouble to learn it.

'Will you be fishing again, Mr Stewart?' asked the Customs officer.

I nodded. 'Yes, I hope to kill a few of your salmon. I've had my gear sterilized – here's the certificate.' The Icelanders are trying to keep out the salmon disease which has attacked the fish in British rivers.

He took the certificate and waved me through the barrier. 'The best of luck,' he said.

I smiled at him and passed through into the concourse and went into the coffee shop in accordance with the instructions Slade had given me. I ordered coffee and presently someone sat next to me and laid down a copy of the *New York Times*. 'Gee!' he said. 'It's colder here than in the States.'

'It's even colder in Birmingham,' I said solemnly, and then, the silly business of the passwords over, we got down to business.

'It's wrapped in the newspaper,' he said.

He was a short, balding man with the worried look of the ulcered executive. I tapped the newspaper. 'What is it?' I asked.

'I don't know. You know where to take it?'

'Akureyri,' I said. 'But why me? Why can't you take it?'

'Not me,' he said defiantly. 'I take the next flight out to the States.' He seemed relieved at that simple fact.

'Let's be normal,' I said. 'I'll buy you a coffee.' I caught the eye of a waitress.

'Thanks,' he said, and laid down a key-ring. 'There's a car in the parking lot outside – the registration number is written alongside the mast-head of *The Times* there.'

'Most obliging of you,' I said. 'I was going to take a taxi.'

'I don't do things to be obliging,' he said shortly. 'I do things because I'm told to do them, just like you – and right now I'm doing the telling and you're doing the doing. You don't drive along the main road to Reykjavik; you go by way of Krysuvik and Kleifavatn.'

I was sipping coffee when he said that and I spluttered. When I came to the surface and got my breath back I said, 'Why the hell should I do that? It's double the distance and along lousy roads.'

'I don't know,' he said. 'I'm just the guy who passes the word. But it was a last-minute instruction so maybe someone's got wind that maybe someone else is laying for you somewhere on the main road. I wouldn't know.'

'You don't know much, do you?' I said acidly, and tapped the newspaper. 'You don't know what's in here; you don't know why I should waste the afternoon in driving around the Reykjanes Peninsula. If I asked you the time of day I doubt if you'd tell me.'

He gave me a sly, sideways grin. 'I bet one thing,' he said. 'I bet I know more than you do.'

'That wouldn't be too difficult,' I said grumpily. It was all of a piece with everything Slade did; he worked on the 'need to know' principle and what you didn't know wouldn't hurt him.

He finished his coffee. 'That's it, buster – except for one thing. When you get to Reykjavik leave the car parked outside the Hotel Saga and just walk away from it. It'll be taken care of.'

He got up without another word and walked away, seemingly in a hurry to get away from me. All during our brief conversation he had seemed jittery, which worried me because it didn't square with Slade's description of the job. 'It'll be simple,' Slade had said. 'You're just a messenger boy.' The twist of his lips had added the implied sneer that it was all I was good for.

I stood and jammed the newspaper under my arm. The concealed package was moderately heavy but not obtrusive. I picked up my gear and went outside to look for the car; it proved to be a Ford Cortina, and minutes later I was on my way out of Keflavik and going south – away from Reykjavik. I wished I knew the idiot who said, 'The longest way round is the shortest way there.'

When I found a quiet piece of road I pulled on to the shoulder and picked up the newspaper from the seat where I had tossed it. The package was as Slade had described it – small and heavier than one would have expected. It was covered in brown hessian, neatly stitched up, and looked completely anonymous. Careful tapping seemed to indicate that under the hessian was a metal box, and there were no rattles when it was shaken.

I regarded it thoughtfully but that didn't give me any clue, so I wrapped it in the newspaper again, dropped it on the back seat, and drove on. It had stopped raining and driving conditions weren't too bad – for Iceland. The average Icelandic road makes an English farm track look like a super-highway. Where there are roads that is. In the interior, which Icelanders know as the *Obyggdir,* there are no roads and in winter the *Obyggdir* is pretty near as inaccessible as the moon unless you're the hearty explorer type. It looks very much like the moon, too; Neil Armstrong practised his moon-walk there.

I drove on and, at Krysuvik, I turned inland, past the distant vapour-covered slopes where super-heated steam boils from the guts of the earth. Not far short of the lake of Kleifavatn I saw a car ahead, pulled off the road, and a man waving the universally recognized distress signal of the stranded motorist.

We were both damned fools; I because I stopped and he because he was alone. He spoke to me in bad Danish and then in good Swedish, both of which I understand. It turned out, quite naturally, that there was something wrong with his car and he couldn't get it to move.

I got out of the Cortina. 'Lindholm,' he said in the formal Swedish manner, and stuck out his hand which I pumped up and down once in the way which protocol dictates.

'I'm Stewart,' I said, and walked over to his Volkswagen and peered at the exposed rear engine.

I don't think he wanted to kill me at first or he would have used the gun straight away. As it was he took a swipe at me with a very professionally designed lead-loaded cosh. I think it was when he got behind me that I realized I was being a flaming idiot – that's a result of being out of practice. I turned my head and saw his upraised arm and dodged sideways. If the cosh had connected with my skull it would have jarred my brains loose; instead it hit my shoulder and my whole arm went numb.

I gave him the boot in the shin, raking down from knee to ankle, and he yelped and hopped back, which gave me time to put the car between us, and groped for the *sgian dubh* as I went. Fortunately it's a left-handed weapon which was just as well because my right arm wasn't going to be of use.

He came for me again but when he saw the knife he hesitated, his lips curling away from his teeth. He dropped the cosh and dipped his hand beneath his jacket and it was my turn to hesitate. But his cosh was *too* well designed; it had a leather wrist loop and the dangling weapon impeded his draw and I jumped him just as the pistol came out.

I didn't stab him. He swung around and ran straight into the blade. There was a gush of blood over my hand and he sagged against me with a ludicrous look of surprise on his face. Then he went down at my feet and the knife came free and blood pulsed from his chest into the lava dust.

So there I was on a lonely road in Southern Iceland with a newly-created corpse at my feet and a bloody knife in my hand, the taste of raw bile in my throat and a frozen brain. From the time I had got out of the Cortina to the moment of death had been less than two minutes.

I don't think I consciously thought of what I did next; I think that rigorous training took over. I jumped for the Cortina and ran it forward a little so that it covered the body. Lonely though the road might be that didn't mean a car couldn't pass at any time and a body in plain sight would take a hell of a lot of explaining away.

Then I took the *New York Times* which, its other virtues apart, contains more newsprint than practically any other newspaper in the world, and used it to line the boot of the car. That done, I reversed again, picked up the body and dumped it into the boot and slammed the lid down quickly. Lindholm – if that was his name – was now out of sight if not out of mind.

He had bled like a cow in a Moslem slaughterhouse and there was a great pool of blood by the side of the road. My jacket and trousers were also liberally bedaubed. I couldn't do much about my clothing right then but I covered the blood pool with handfuls of lava dust. I closed the engine compartment of the Volkswagen, got behind the wheel and switched on. Lindholm had not only been an attempted murderer – he had also been a liar because the engine caught immediately. I reversed the car over the bloody bit of ground and left it there. It was too much to hope that the blood wouldn't be noticed when the car was taken away but I had to do what I could.

I got back into the Cortina after one last look at the scene of the crime and drove away, and it was then I began to think consciously. First I thought of Slade and damned his soul to hell and then I began to get ideas. I checked the petrol gauge and settled down for a long drive, hoping that the car was in good trim. To stop and be found with a blood-smeared jacket would cause the asking of pointed questions. I had another outfit in my suitcase but all at once there were too many cars about and I prefered to change discreetly.

Most of Iceland is volcanic and the south-west is particularly so with bleak vistas of lava fields, ash cones and shield volcanoes, some of them extinct, some not. In my travels I had once come across a gas vent which now seemed an ideal place for the last repose of Lindholm, and it was there I was heading.

It was a two-hour drive and, towards the end, I had to leave the road and take to the open country, bouncing across a waste of volcanic ash and scoria which did the Cortina no good. The last time I had been that way I had driven my Land-Rover which is made for that sort of country.

The place was exactly as I remembered it. There was an extinct crater with a riven side so that one could drive right into the caldera and in the middle was a rocky pustule with a hole in it through which the hot volcanic gases had driven in some long-gone eruption. The only sign that any other human being had been there since the creation of the world was the mark of tyre tracks driving up towards the lip of the crater. The Icelanders have their own peculiar form of motor sport; they drive into a crater and try to get out the hard way. I've never known anyone break his neck at this hazardous game but it's not for want of trying.

I drove the car as near to the gas vent as I could and then went forward on foot until I could look into the impenetrable darkness of the hole. I dropped a stone into it and there was a receding clatter which went on for a long time. Verne's hero who went to the centre of the earth might have had an easier time if he had picked this hole instead of Snaefellsjökull.

Before I popped Lindholm into his final resting-place I searched him. It was a messy business because the blood was still sticky and it was lucky I had not yet changed my suit. He had a Swedish passport made out in the name of Axel Lindholm, but that didn't mean a thing – passports are easy to come by. There were a few more bits and pieces but nothing of importance, and all I retained were the cosh and the pistol, a Smith & Wesson .38.

Then I carried him up to the vent and dropped him into it. There were a few soggy thumps and then silence – a silence I hoped would be eternal. I went back to the car and changed into a clean suit and pulled the stained clothing inside out so that the blood would not touch the inside of my suitcase. The cosh, the pistol and Slade's damned package I also tossed into the suitcase before I closed it, and then I set off on the wearisome way to Reykjavik.

I was very tired.

II

It was late evening when I pulled up in front of the Hotel Saga, although it was still light with the brightness of the northern summer. My eyes were sore because I had been driving right into the western sun and I stayed in the car for a moment to rest them. If I had stayed in the car two minutes more the next fateful thing would not have happened, but I didn't; I got out and was just extracting the suitcase when a tall man came out of the hotel, paused, and hailed me. 'Alan Stewart!'

I looked up and cursed under my breath because the man in the uniform of an Icelandair pilot was the last man I wanted to see – Bjarni Ragnarsson. 'Hello, Bjarni,' I said.

We shook hands. 'Elin didn't tell me you were coming.'

'She didn't know,' I said. 'It was a last-minute decision; I didn't even have time to telephone.'

He looked at my suitcase resting on the pavement. 'You're not staying at the Saga!' he said in surprise.

It was a snap judgement and I had to make it fast. 'No,' I said. 'I'll be going to the apartment.' I didn't want to bring Elin into this but now her brother knew I was in Reykjavik he would be sure to tell her and I didn't want her to be hurt in that way. Elin was very special.

I saw Bjarni looking at the car. 'I'll leave it here,' I said lightly. 'It's just a delivery job for a friend. I'll take a taxi to the apartment.'

He accepted that, and said, 'Staying long?'

'For the rest of the summer, as usual,' I said easily.

'We must go fishing,' he said.

I agreed. 'Have you become a father yet?'

'Another month,' he said glumly. 'I'm dreading it.'

I laughed. 'I should think that's Kristin's worry; you aren't even in the country half the time. No nappy-changing for you.'

We spent another few minutes in the usual idle-small-talk of old friends just met and then he glanced at his watch. 'I have a flight to Greenland,' he said. 'I must go. I'll ring you in a couple of days.'

'Do that.' I watched him go and then captured a taxi which had just dropped a fare at the hotel and told the driver where to go. Outside the building I paid him off and then stood uncertainly on the pavement wondering whether I was doing the right thing.

Elin Ragnarsdottir was someone very special.

She was a schoolteacher but, like many other Icelanders of her type, she held down two jobs. There are certain factors about Iceland – the smallness of population, the size of the country and its situation in high northern latitudes – which result in a social system which outsiders are apt to find weird. But since the system is designed to suit Icelanders they don't give a damn what outsiders think, which is just as it should be.

One result of this social system is that all the schools close down for four months in the summer and a lot of them are used as hotels. The teachers thus have a lot of spare time and many of them have quite a different summer occupation. When I first met her three years earlier, Elin had been a courier for *Ferdaskrifstofaa Nordri,* a travel agency in Reykjavik, and had shown visitors around the country.

A couple of seasons before, I had persuaded her to become my personal courier on a full-time summer basis. I had been afraid that her brother, Bjarni, might have thought that a touch irregular and put in an objection, but he didn't – presumably he thought his sister to be grown-up enough to handle her own affairs. She was an undemanding person and it was an easy relationship, but obviously it couldn't go on like that forever and I intended to do something about it, but I doubted if this was the appropriate time – it takes someone with a stronger stomach than mine to propose marriage on the same day one has dropped a body down a hole.

I went up to the apartment and, although I had a key, I didn't use it; instead I knocked on the door. Elin opened it and looked at me with an expression of surprise changing to delight, and something in me jumped at the sight of her trim figure and corn-coloured hair. 'Alan!' she said. 'Why didn't you tell me you were coming?'

'A quick decision,' I said, and held up the cased fishing-rod. 'I've got a new one.'

Her lips curved down in mock glumness. 'That makes six,' she said severely, and held the door wide. 'Oh, come in, darling!'

I went in, dropped the suitcase and the rod, and took her in my arms. She held me closely and said, with her head against my chest, 'You didn't write, and I thought . . .'

'You thought I wasn't coming.' The reason I hadn't written was because of something Slade had said, but I couldn't tell her that. I said, 'I've been very busy, Elin.'

She drew back her head and looked at me intently. 'Yes, your face is drawn; you look tired.'

I smiled. 'But I feel hungry.'

She kissed me. 'I'll prepare something.' She broke away. 'Don't worry about unpacking your bag; I'll do it after supper.'

I thought of the bloody suit. 'Not to worry,' I said. 'I can do it.' I picked up the suitcase and the rod and took them into my room. I called it my room because it was the place where my gear was stored. Actually, the whole apartment was mine because, although it was in Elin's name, I paid the rent. Spending one-third of every year in Iceland, it was convenient to have a *pied-à-terre*.

I put the rod with the others and laid down the suitcase, wondering what to do with the suit. Until that moment I had never had any secrets I wanted to keep from Elin – with the one important exception – and there wasn't a lockable cupboard or drawer in the place. I opened the wardrobe and surveyed the line of suits and jackets, each on its hanger and neatly encased in its zippered plastic bag. It would be very risky to let the suit take its place in that line; Elin was meticulous in the care of my clothes and would be certain to find it.

In the end I emptied the suitcase of everything but the suit and the weapons, locked it, and heaved it on top of the wardrobe where it usually lived when not in use. It was unlikely that Elin would pull it down and even then it was locked, although that was not usual.

I took off my shirt and examined it closely and discovered a spot of blood on the front so I took it into the bathroom and cleaned it under the cold tap. Then I scrubbed my face in cold water and felt better for it. By the time Elin called that supper was ready I was cleaned up and already in the living-room looking through the window.

I was about to turn away when my attention was caught by a flicker of movement. On the other side of the street there was an alley between two buildings and it had seemed that someone had moved quickly out of sight when I twitched the curtains. I stared across the street but saw nothing more, but when Elin called again I was thoughtful as I turned to her.

Over supper I said, 'How's the Land-Rover?'

'I didn't know when you were coming but I had a complete overhaul done last week. It's ready for anything.'

Icelandic roads being what they are, Land-Rovers are as thick as fleas on a dog. The Icelanders prefer the short wheelbase Land-Rover, but ours was the long wheelbase job, fitted out as a camping van. When we travelled we were self-contained and could, and did, spend many weeks away from civilization, only being driven into a town by running out of food. There were worse ways of spending a summer than to be alone for weeks on end with Elin Ragnarsdottir.

In other summers we had left as soon as I arrived in Reykjavik, but this time it had to be different because of Slade's package, and I wondered how I was to get to Akureyri alone without arousing her suspicions. Slade had said the job was going to be easy but the late Mr Lindholm made all the difference and I didn't want Elin involved in any part of it. Still, all I had to do was to deliver the package and the job would be over and the summer would be like all the other summers. It didn't seem too difficult.

I was mulling this over when Elin said, 'You really do look tired. You must have been overworking.'

I managed a smile. 'An exhausting winter. There was too much snow on the hills – I lost a lot of stock.' Suddenly I remembered. 'You wanted to see what the glen was like; I brought you some photographs.'

I went and got the photographs and we pored over them. I pointed out Bheinn Fhada and Sgurr Dearg, but Elin was more interested in the river and the trees. 'All those trees,' she said luxuriously. 'Scotland must be beautiful.' That was an expected reaction from an Icelander; the island is virtually treeless. 'Are there salmon in your river?'

'Just trout,' I said. 'I come to Iceland for salmon.'

She picked up another photograph – a wide landscape. 'What on here is yours?'

I looked at it and grinned. 'All you can see.'

'Oh!' She was silent for a while, then said a little shyly, 'I've never really thought about it, Alan; but you must be rich.'

'I'm no Croesus,' I said. 'But I get by. Three thousand acres of heather isn't very productive, but sheep on the hills and forestry in the glen bring in the bread, and Americans who come to shoot the deer put butter on the bread.' I stroked her arm. 'You'll have to come to Scotland.'

'I'd like that,' she said simply.

I put it to her fast. 'I have to see a man in Akureyri tomorrow – it's a favour I'm doing for a friend. That means I'll have to fly. Why don't you take up the Land-Rover and meet me there? Or would it be too much for you to drive all that way?'

She laughed at me. 'I can drive the Land-Rover better than you.' She began to calculate. 'It's 450 kilometres; I wouldn't want to do that in one day so I'd stop somewhere near Hvamm-stangi. I could be in Akureyri at mid-morning the next day.'

'No need to break your neck,' I said casually. I was relieved; I could fly to Akureyri, get rid of the package before Elin got there and all would be well. There was no need to involve her at all. I said, 'I'll probably stay at the Hotel Varborg. You can telephone me there.'

But when we went to bed I found I was strung up with unrelieved tensions and I could do nothing for her. While holding Elin in the darkness, Lindholm's face hovered ghost-like in my inner vision and again I tasted the nausea in my throat. I choked a little, and said, 'I'm sorry.'

'It doesn't matter, darling,' she said quietly. 'You're tired. Just go to sleep.'

But I couldn't. I lay on my back and reviewed the whole of an unpleasant day. I went over every word that had been said by my uncommunicative contact at Keflavik airport, the man whom Slade had said would pass me the package. '*Don't take the main road to Reykjavik*,' he said to me. '*Go by Krysuvik.*'

So I had gone by Krysuvik and come within an ace of being killed. Chance or design? Would the same thing have happened had I gone by the main road? Had I been set up as a patsy deliberately?

The man at the airport had been Slade's man, or at least he had the password that Slade had arranged. But supposing he wasn't Slade's man and still had the password – it wasn't too hard to think up ways and means of that coming about. Then why had he set me up for Lindholm? Certainly not for the package – he already had the package! Scratch that one and start again.

Supposing he *had* been Slade's man and had still set me up for Lindholm – that made less sense. And, again, it couldn't have been for the package; he needn't have given it to me in the first place. It all boiled down to the fact that the man at the airport and Lindholm had nothing to do with each other.

But Lindholm had definitely been waiting for me. He had even made sure of my name before attacking. So how in hell did he know I'd be on the Krysuvik road? That was one I couldn't answer.

Presently, when I was sure Elin was sound asleep, I got out of bed quietly and went into the kitchen, not bothering to turn on a light. I opened the refrigerator and poured myself a glass of milk, then wandered into the living-room and sat by the window. The short northern night was almost over but it was still dark enough to see the sudden glow from across the street as the watching man drew on a cigarette.

He worried me because I was no longer certain Elin was safe.

III

We were both up early, Elin because she wanted to make a quick start for Akureyri, and I because I wanted to get at the Land-Rover before Elin did. I had some things to stow in the Land-Rover that I didn't want Elin to know about; Lindholm's gun, for instance. I taped it securely to one of the main chassis girders and well out of sight. His cosh I put in my pocket. It had occurred to me that if things did not go well I might be in need of weaponry in Akureyri.

I didn't have to go out of the front door to get at the Land-Rover because the garage was at the back, and so the watcher in the alley got no sight of me. But I saw him because the next thing I did was to take a pair of field-glasses one flight up to a landing where there was a window overlooking the street.

He was a tall, lean man with a neat moustache and he looked cold. If he had been there all night without a break he would be not only frozen to the marrow but starving. I made sure I would know him again if I saw him and lowered the glasses just as someone came downstairs from an upstairs flat. It was a middle-aged grey-haired woman who looked at me and then at the glasses and gave a meaningful sniff.

I grinned. It was the first time I had been suspected of voyeurism.

I enjoyed breakfast all the more because of my hungry friend across the street. 'You're looking more cheerful,' said Elin.

'It's your cooking,' I said.

She looked at the herring, the cheese, the bread and the eggs. 'What cooking? Anyone can boil an egg.'

'Not like you,' I assured her.

But I *was* more cheerful. The dark thoughts of the night had gone and in spite of all the unanswered questions the death of Lindholm no longer oppressed me. He had tried to kill me and failed, and had suffered the penalty for failure. The fact that I had killed him didn't weigh too heavily upon my conscience. My only lingering worry was for Elin.

I said, 'There's a flight for Akureyri from Reykjavik City Airport at eleven.'

'You'll have lunch there,' said Elin. 'Spare a thought for me bouncing about down in Kaldidalur.' She swallowed hot coffee hastily. 'I'd like to leave as soon as possible.'

I waved at the laden table. 'I'll clean up here.'

She got ready to leave, then picked up the binoculars. 'I thought these were in the Land-Rover.'

'I was just checking them,' I said. 'They seemed a bit out of focus last time I used them. They're all right, though.'

'Then I'll take them,' she said.

I went with her down to the garage and kissed her goodbye. She looked at me closely, and said, 'Everything *is* all right, isn't it, Alan?'

'Of course; why do you ask?'

'I don't really know. I'm just being feminine, I suppose. See you in Akureyri.'

I waved her off and watched as she drove away. Nobody seemed to bother; no heads popped around corners and no one followed in hot pursuit. I went back into the flat and checked on the watcher in the alley. He wasn't to be seen, so I made a dash for the upstairs landing from where I could get a better view and I breathed easier when I saw him leaning against the wall, beating his hands against his arms.

It would seem that he was not aware that Elin had left or, if he was, he didn't care. It lifted a considerable load off my mind.

I washed the breakfast crockery and then went to my room where I took a camera bag and emptied it of its contents. Then I took the hessian-covered steel box and found that it fitted neatly into the leather bag. From now on it was not going to leave my person until I handed it over in Akureyri.

At ten o'clock I rang for a taxi and left for the airport, a move which resulted in some action. I looked back along the street and saw a car draw up near the alley into which my watcher jumped. The car followed the taxi all the way to the airport, keeping a discreet distance.

On arrival I went to the reservation counter. 'I have a reservation on the flight to Akureyri. My name is Stewart.'

The receptionist checked a list. 'Oh, yes; Mr Stewart.' She looked at the clock. 'But you're early.'

'I'll have a coffee,' I said. 'It passes the time.'

She gave me the ticket and I paid for it, then she said, 'Your luggage is weighed over there.'

I touched the camera case. 'This is all I have. I travel light.'

She laughed. 'So I see, Mr Stewart. And may I compliment you on how you speak our language.'

'Thank you.' I turned and saw a recognized face lurking close by – my watcher was still watching. I ignored him and headed for the coffee-counter where I bought a newspaper and settled down to wait.

My man had a hurried conversation at the reservation counter, bought a ticket, and then came my way and both of us ignored each other completely. He ordered a late breakfast and ate ravenously, his eyes flicking in my direction infrequently. Presently I had a stroke of luck; the announcement loudspeaker cleared its throat and said in Icelandic, 'Mr Buchner is wanted on the telephone.' When it repeated this in fluent German my man looked up, got to his feet, and went to answer the call.

At least I could now put a name to him, and whether the name was accurate or not was really immaterial.

He could see me from the telephone-box and spoke facing outwards as though he expected me to make a break for it. I disappointed him by languidly ordering another coffee and becoming immersed in a newspaper account of how many salmon Bing Crosby had caught on his latest visit to Iceland.

In airport waiting lounges time seems to stretch interminably and it was a couple of eons before the flight to Akureyri was announced. Herr Buchner was close behind me in the queue and in the stroll across the apron towards the aircraft, and he chose a seat on the aisle just behind me.

We took off and flew across Iceland, over the cold glaciers of Langjökull and Hofsjökull, and soon enough we were circling over Eyjafjördur preparatory to landing at Akureyri, a city of fully ten thousand souls, the metropolis of Northern Iceland. The aircraft lurched to a halt and I undid my seat-belt, hearing the answering click as Buchner, behind me, did the same.

The attack, when it came, was made with smoothness and efficiency. I left the airport building and was walking towards the taxi rank when suddenly they were all about me – four of them. One stood in front of me and grabbed my right hand, pumping it up and down while babbling in a loud voice about how good it was to see me again and the enormous pleasure it would give him to show me the marvels of Akureyri.

The man on my left crowded hard and pinned my left arm. He put his mouth close to my ear, and said in Swedish, 'Don't make trouble, Herr Stewartsen; or you will be dead.' I could believe him because the man behind me had a gun in my back.

I heard a snip and turned my head just as the man on my right cut through the shoulder-strap of the camera case with a small pair of shears. I felt the strap snake loose and then he was gone and the camera case with him, while the man behind me took his place with one arm thrown carelessly over my shoulder and the other digging the gun into my ribs.

I could see Buchner standing by a taxi about ten yards away. He looked at me with a blank face and then turned and bent to get into the car. It drove away and I saw the white smudge of his face as he looked through the back window.

They kept up the act for two minutes more to give the man with the camera time to get clear, and the man on my left said, again in Swedish, 'Herr Stewartsen: we're going to let you go now, but I wouldn't do anything foolish if I were you.'

They released me and each took a step away, their faces hard and their eyes watchful. There were no guns in sight but that didn't mean a damn thing. Not that I intended to start anything; the camera case was gone and the odds were too great anyway. As though someone had given a signal they all turned and walked away, each in a different direction, and left me standing there. There were quite a few people around but not one of the good people of Akureyri had any idea that anything untoward had just happened in their line of sight.

I felt ruffled so I straightened my jacket and then took a taxi to the Hotel Vardborg. There wasn't anything else to do.

IV

Elin had been right; I was in time to lunch at the Vardborg. I had just stuck my fork into the mutton when Herr Buchner walked in, looked around and spotted me, and headed in my direction. He stood on the other side of the table, twitched his moustache, and said, 'Mr Stewart?'

I leaned back. 'Well, if it isn't Herr Buchner! What can I do for you?'

'My name is Graham,' he said coldly. 'And I'd like to talk to you.'

'You were Buchner this morning,' I said. 'But if I had a name like that I'd want to change it, too.' I waved him towards a chair. 'Be my guest – I can recommend the soup.'

He sat down stiffly. 'I'm not in the mood for acting straight man to your comedian,' he said, extracting his wallet from his pocket. 'My credentials.' He pushed a scrap of paper across the table.

I unfolded it to find the left half of a 100-kronur banknote. When I matched it against the other half from my own wallet the two halves fitted perfectly. I looked up at him. 'Well, Mr Graham; that seems to be in order. What can I do for you?'

'You can give me the package,' he said. 'That's all I want.'

I shook my head regretfully. 'You know better than that.'

He frowned. 'What do you mean?'

'I mean that I can't give you the package because I haven't got it.'

His moustache twitched again and his eyes turned cold. 'Let's have no games, Stewart. The package.' He held out his hand.

'Damn it!' I said. 'You were there – you know what happened.'

'I don't know what you're talking about. I was where?'

'Outside Akureyri Airport. You were taking a taxi.'

His eyes flickered. 'Was I?' he said colourlessly. 'Go on!'

'They grabbed me before I knew what was happening, and they got clean away with the package. It was in my camera case.'

His voice cracked. 'You mean you haven't got it!'

I said sardonically, 'If you were supposed to be my bodyguard you did a bloody awful job. Slade isn't going to like it.'

'By God, he's not!' said Graham with feeling. A tic pulsed under his right eye. 'So it was in the camera case.'

'Where else would it be? It was the only luggage I carried. You ought to know that – you were standing right behind me with your big ears flapping when I checked in at Reykjavik airport.'

He gave me a look of dislike. 'You think you're clever, don't you?' He leaned forward. 'There's going to be a Godawful row about this. You'd better stay available, Stewart; you'd better be easy to find when I come back.'

I shrugged. 'Where would I go? Besides, I have the Scottish sense of thrift, and my room here is paid for.'

'You take this damned coolly.'

'What do you expect me to do? Burst into tears?' I laughed in his face. 'Grow up, Graham.'

His face tightened but he said nothing; instead he stood up and walked away. I put in fifteen minutes of deep thought while polishing off the mutton and at the end of that time I came to a decision, and the decision was that I could do with a drink, so I went to find one.

As I walked through the hotel foyer I saw Buchner-Graham hard at work in a telephone-box. Although it wasn't particularly warm he was sweating.

V

I came out of a dreamless sleep because someone was shaking me and hissing, 'Stewart, wake up!' I opened my eyes and found Graham leaning over me.

I blinked at him. 'Funny! I was under the impression I locked my door.'

He grinned humourlessly. 'You did. Wake up – you're going to be interviewed. You'd better have your wits sharpened.'

'What time is it?'

'Five a.m.'

I smiled. 'Gestapo technique, eh! Oh, well: I suppose I'll feel better when I've shaved.'

Graham seemed nervous. 'You'd better hurry. He'll be here in five minutes.'

'Who will?'

'You'll see.'

I ran hot water into the basin and began to lather my face. 'What *was* your function on this particular exercise, Graham? As a bodyguard you're a dead loss, so it can't have been that.'

'You'd better stop thinking about me and start to think about yourself,' he said. 'You have a lot of explaining to do.'

'True,' I said, and put down the brush and picked up the razor. The act of scraping one's face with a sliver of sharp metal always seems futile and a little depressing; I would have been happier in one of the hairier ages – counter-espionage agent by appointment to Her Majesty Queen Victoria would have been the ideal ticket.

I must have been more nervous that I thought because I shaved myself down to the blood on the first pass. Then someone knocked perfunctorily on the door and Slade came into the room. He kicked the door shut with his foot and glowered at me with a scowl on his jowly face, his hands thrust deep into his overcoat pockets. Without an overture he said briefly, 'What's the story, Stewart?'

There's nothing more calculated to put a man off his stroke than having to embark on complicated explanations with a face full of drying lather. I turned back to the mirror and continued to shave – in silence.

Slade made one of those unspellable noises – an explosive outrush of air expelled through mouth and nose. He sat on the bed and the springs creaked in protest at the excessive weight. 'It had better be good,' he said. 'I dislike being hauled out of bed and flown to the frozen north.'

I continued to shave, thinking that whatever could bring Slade from London to Akureyri must be important. After the last tricky bit around the Adam's apple, I said, 'The package must have been more important than you told me.' I turned on the cold tap and rinsed the soap from my face.

'. . . that bloody package,' he said.

'I'm sorry,' I apologized. 'I didn't hear that. I had water in my ears.'

He contained himself with difficulty. 'Where's the package?' he asked with synthetic patience.

'As of this moment I couldn't tell you.' I dried my face vigorously. 'It was taken from me at midday yesterday by four unknown males – but you know that already from Graham.'

His voice rose. 'And you let them take it – just like that!'

'There wasn't much I could do about it at the time,' I said equably. 'I had a gun in my kidneys.' I nodded towards Graham. 'What was he supposed to be doing about it – if it isn't a rude answer?'

Slade folded his hands together across his stomach. 'We thought they'd tagged Graham – that's why we brought you in. We thought they'd tackle Graham and give you a free run to the goal line.'

I didn't think much of that one. If they – whoever they were – had tagged Graham, then it wasn't at all standard procedure for him to draw attention to me by lurking outside my flat. But I let it go because Slade always had been a slippery customer and I wanted to keep something in reserve.

Instead, I said, 'They didn't tackle Graham – they tackled me. But perhaps they don't know the rules of rugby football; it's not a game they go for in Sweden.' I gave myself a last dab behind the ears and dropped the towel. 'Or in Russia,' I added as an afterthought.

Slade looked up. 'And what makes you think of Russians?'

I grinned at him. 'I always think of Russians,' I said drily. 'Like the Frenchman who always thought of sex.' I leaned over him and picked up my cigarettes. 'Besides, they called me Stewartsen.'

'So?'

'So they knew who I was – not who I am now, but what I was once. There's a distinction.'

Slade shifted his eyes to Graham and said curtly, 'Wait outside.'

Graham looked hurt but obediently went to the door. When he'd closed it I said, 'Oh, goody; now the children are out of the room we can have a grown-up conversation. And where, for Christ's sake, did you get that one? I told you I wouldn't stand for trainees on the operation.'

'What makes you think he's a trainee?'

'Come, now; he's still wet behind the ears.'

'He's a good man,' said Slade, and shifted restlessly on the bed. He was silent for a while, then he said, 'Well, you've really cocked this one up, haven't you? Just a simple matter of carrying a small parcel from A to B and you fall down on it. I knew you were past it but, by God, I didn't think you were so decrepit.' He wagged his finger. 'And they called you Stewartsen! You know what that means?'

'Kennikin,' I said, not relishing the thought. 'Is he here – in Iceland?'

Slade hunched his shoulders. 'Not that I know of.' He looked at me sideways. 'When you were contacted in Reykjavik what were you told?'

I shrugged. 'Not much. There was a car provided which I had to drive to Reykjavik by way of Krysuvik and leave parked outside the Saga. I did all that.'

Slade grunted in his throat. 'Run into any trouble?'

'Was I supposed to?' I asked blandly.

He shook his head irritably. 'We had word that something might happen. It seemed best to re-route you.' He stood up with a dissatisfied look on his face and went to the door. 'Graham!'

I said, 'I'm sorry about all this, Slade; I really am.'

'Being sorry butters no bloody parsnips. We'll just have to see what we can salvage from this mess. Hell, I brought you in because the Department is short-handed – and now we have a whole country to seal off because of your stupidity.' He turned to Graham. 'Put a call through to the Department in London; I'll take it downstairs. And talk to Captain Lee at the airport; I want that plane to be ready to take off at five minutes' notice. We may have to move fast.'

I coughed delicately. 'Me, too?'

Slade looked at me malevolently. 'You! You've caused enough of a shambles on this operation.'

'Well, what do I do?'

'You can go to hell for all I care,' he said. 'Go back to Reykjavik

247

and shack up with your girl-friend for the rest of the summer.' He turned and bumped into Graham. 'What the hell are you waiting for?' he snarled and Graham fled.

Slade paused at the door and said without turning, 'But you'd better watch out for Kennikin because I'll not lift a finger to stop him. By God, I hope he *does* nail you!'

The door slammed and I sat on the bed and brooded. I knew that if ever I met Kennikin again I would be meeting death.

Chapter Two

I

Elin rang up as I was finishing breakfast. From the static and the slight fading I could tell she was using the radio-telephone in the Land-Rover. Most vehicles travelling long distances in Iceland are fitted with radio-telephones, a safety measure called for by the difficult nature of the terrain. That's the standard explanation, but not the whole truth. The fact is that Icelanders *like* telephoning and constitute one of the gabbiest nations on earth, coming just after the United States and Canada in the number of calls per head.

She asked if I had slept well and I assured her I had, then I said, 'When will you get here?'

'About eleven-thirty.'

'I'll meet you at the camp site,' I said.

That gave me two hours which I spent in walking around Akureyri like a tourist, ducking in and out of shops, unexpectedly retracing my steps and, in general, acting the fool. But when I joined Elin at the camp site I was absolutely sure that I didn't have a tail. It seemed as though Slade had been telling the truth when he said he had no further use for me.

I opened the door of the Land-Rover, and said, 'Move over; I'll drive.'

Elin looked at me in surprise. 'Aren't we staying?'

'We'll drive a little out of town and then have lunch. There's something I want to talk to you about.'

I drove along the north road by the coast, moving fast and keeping a close check behind. As it became clear that no one was following I began to relax, although not so much as to take the worry from Elin's eyes. She could see I was preoccupied and tactfully kept silent, but at last she said, 'There's something wrong, isn't there?'

'You're so damn right,' I said. 'That's what I want to discuss.'

Back in Scotland Slade had warned me about involving Elin in the operation; he had also invoked the Official Secrets Act with its penalties for blabbermouths. But if my future life with Elin was going to mean anything at all I had to tell her the truth and to hell with Slade and to hell with the Official Secrets Act.

I slowed down and left the road to bump over turf, and stopped overlooking the sea. The land fell away in a rumble of boulders to the grey water and in the distance the island of Grimsey loomed hazily through the mist. Apart from the scrap of land there wasn't a damned thing between us and the North Pole. This was the Arctic Ocean.

I said, 'What do you know about me, Elin?'

'That's a strange question. You're Alan Stewart – whom I like very much.'

'Is that all?'

She shrugged. 'What else do I need to know?'

I smiled. 'No curiosity, Elin?'

'Oh, I have my curiosity but I keep it under control. If you want me to know anything, you'll tell me,' she said tranquilly, then hesitated. 'I do know one thing about you.'

'What's that?'

She turned to face me. 'I know that you have been hurt, and it happened not long before we met. That is why I keep my questions to myself – I don't want to bring the hurt back.'

'You're very perceptive,' I said. 'I didn't think it showed. Would it surprise you to know I was once a British agent – a spy?'

She regarded me curiously. 'A spy,' she said slowly, as though rolling the word about her mouth to taste it. 'Yes, it surprises me very much. It is not a very honourable occupation – you are not the type.'

'So someone else told me recently,' I said sardonically. 'Nevertheless, it is true.'

She was silent for a while, then she said, 'You *were* a spy. Alan, what you were in the past doesn't matter. I know you as you are now.'

'Sometimes the past catches up with you,' I said. 'It did with me. There's a man called Slade . . .' I stopped, wondering if I was doing the right thing.

'Yes?' she prompted me.

'He came to see me in Scotland. I'll tell you about that – about Slade in Scotland.'

II

The shooting was bad that day. Something had disturbed the deer during the night because they had left the valley where my calculations had placed them and had drifted up the steep slopes of Bheinn Fhada. I could see them through the telescopic sight – pale grey-brown shapes grazing among the heather. The way the wind was blowing the only chance I had of getting near them was by sprouting wings and so, since it was the last day of the season, the deer were safe from Stewart for the rest of the summer.

At three in the afternoon I packed up and went home and was scrambling down Sgurr Mor when I saw the car parked outside the cottage and the minuscule figure of a man pacing up and down. The cottage is hard to get to – the rough track from the clachan discourages casual tourists – and so anyone who arrives usually wants to see me very much. The reverse doesn't always apply; I'm of a retiring nature and I don't encourage visitors.

So I was very careful as I approached and stopped under cover of the rocks by the burn. I unslung the rifle, checked it again to make sure it was unloaded, and set it to my shoulder. Through the telescopic sight the man sprang plainly into view. He had his back to me but when he turned I saw it was Slade.

I centred the cross hairs on his large pallid face and gently squeezed the trigger, and the hammer snapped home with a harmless click. I wondered if I would have done the same had there been a bullet up the spout. The world would be a better place without men like Slade. But to load was too deliberate an act, so I put up the gun and walked towards the cottage. I should have loaded the gun.

As I approached he turned and waved. 'Good afternoon,' he called, as coolly as though he were a regular and welcome guest.

I stepped up to him. 'How did you find me?'

He shrugged. 'It wasn't too hard. You know my methods.'

I knew them and I didn't like them. I said, 'Quit playing Sherlock. What do you want?'

He waved towards the door of the cottage. 'Aren't you going to invite me inside?'

'Knowing you, I'll bet you've searched the place already.'

He held up his hands in mock horror. 'On my word of honour, I haven't.'

I nearly laughed in his face because the man had no honour. I turned from him and pushed open the door and he followed me inside, clicking his tongue deprecatingly. 'Not locked? You're very trusting.'

'There's nothing here worth stealing,' I said indifferently.

'Just your life,' he said, and looked at me sharply.

I let that statement lie and put up the rifle on its rack. Slade looked about him curiously. 'Primitive – but comfortable,' he remarked. 'But I don't see why you don't live in the big house.'

'It happens to be none of your business.'

'Perhaps,' he said, and sat down. 'So you hid yourself in Scotland and didn't expect to be found. Protective coloration, eh? A Stewart hiding among a lot of Stewarts. You've caused us some little difficulty.'

'Who said I was hiding? I am a Scot, you know.'

He smiled fatly. 'Of a sort. Just by your paternal grandfather. It's not long since you were a Swede – and before that you were Finnish. You were Stewartsen then, of course.'

'Have you travelled five hundred miles just to talk of old times?' I asked tiredly.

'You're looking very fit,' he said.

'I can't say the same for you; you're out of condition and running to fat,' I said cruelly.

He chuckled. 'The fleshpots, dear boy; the fleshpots – all those lunches at the expense of Her Majesty's Government.' He waved a pudgy hand. 'But let's get down to it, Alan.'

'To you I'm Mr Stewart,' I said deliberately.

'Oh, you don't like me,' he said in a hurt voice. 'But no matter – it makes no difference in the end. I . . . we . . . want you to do a job for us. Nothing too difficult, you understand.'

'You must be out of your mind,' I said.

'I know how you must feel, but . . .'

'You don't know a damn thing,' I said sharply. 'If you expect me to work for you after what happened then you're crazier than I thought.'

I was wrong, of course; Slade knew perfectly well how I felt – it was his business to know men and to use them like tools. I waited for him to put on the pressure and, sure enough, it came, but in his usual oblique manner.

'So let's talk of old times,' he said. 'You must remember Kennikin.'

I remembered – I'd have to have total amnesia to forget Kennikin. A vision of his face swam before me as I had last seen him; eyes like grey pebbles set above high Slavic cheekbones, and the scar ran from his right temple to the corner of his mouth standing out lividly against the suddenly pale skin. He had been angry enough to kill me at that moment.

'What about Kennikin?' I said slowly.

'Just that I hear he's been looking for you, too. You made a fool of him and he didn't like it. He wants to have you . . .' Slade paused as though groping for a thought. 'What's that delicate phrase our American colleagues of the CIA use? Oh, yes – Kennikin wants to have you "terminated with extreme prejudice". Although I daresay the KGB don't employ that exact wording.'

A damned nice term for a bullet in the back of the head one dark night. 'So?' I said.

'He's still looking for you,' Slade pointed out.

'Why?' I asked. 'I'm no longer with the Department.'

'Ah, but Kennikin doesn't know that.' Slade examined his fingernails. 'We've kept the information from him – quite successfully, I believe. It seemed useful to do so.'

I saw what was coming but I wanted to make Slade come right out with it, to commit himself in plain language – something he abhorred. 'But he doesn't know where I am.'

'Quite right, dear boy – but what if someone should tell him?'

I leaned forward and looked closely at Slade. 'And who would tell him?'

'I would,' he said blandly. 'If I thought it necessary. I'd have to do it tactfully and through a third party, of course; but it could be arranged.'

So there it was – the threat of betrayal. Nothing new for Slade; he made a life's work out of corruption and betrayal. Not that I was one to throw stones; it had been my work too, once. But the difference between us was that Slade liked his work.

I let him waffle on, driving home the point unnecessarily. 'Kennikin runs a very efficient *Mordgruppe*, as we know to our cost, don't we? Several members of the Department have been . . . er . . . terminated by Kennikin's men.'

'Why don't you just say murdered?'

He frowned and his piggy eyes sank deeper into the rolls of fat that larded his face. 'You always were blunt, Stewart; perhaps too blunt for your own good. I haven't forgotten the time you tried to get me in trouble with Taggart. I remember you mentioned that word then.'

'I'll mention it again,' I said. 'You murdered Jimmy Birkby.'

'Did I?' Slade asked softly. 'Who put the gelignite in his car? Who carefully connected the wire from the detonator to the ignition system? You did!' He cut me off with a chopping motion of his hand. 'And it was only that which got you to Kennikin, only that induced Kennikin to trust you enough so that we could break him. You did very well, Stewart – all things considered.'

'Yes, you used me,' I said.

'And I'll use you again,' he said brutally. 'Or would you rather be thrown to Kennikin?' He laughed suddenly. 'You know, I don't think Kennikin gives a damn if you're with the Department or not. He wants you for your own sweet self.'

I stared at him. 'And what do you mean by that?'

'Didn't you know that Kennikin is impotent now?' Slade said in surprise. 'I know you intended to kill him with that last shot, but the light was bad and you thought you'd merely wounded him. Indeed you had, but not merely – you castrated the poor man.' His hands, which were folded across his belly, shook with his sniggers. 'To put it crudely – or bluntly, if you like, dear boy – you shot his balls off. Can you imagine what he'll do to you if – and when – he catches up with you?'

I felt cold and there was a yawning emptiness in the pit of my stomach. 'There's only one way of opting out of the world and that's by dying,' said Slade with phoney philosophy. 'You tried your way and it doesn't work.'

He was right; I shouldn't have expected otherwise. 'What it comes to is this,' I said. 'You want me to do a job. If I don't do it, you'll tip off the opposition and the opposition will knock me off – and your hands will be theoretically clean.'

'Very succinctly put,' said Slade. 'You always did write good, clear reports.' He sounded like a schoolmaster complimenting a boy on a good essay.

'What's the job?'

'Now you're being sensible,' he said approvingly. He produced a sheet of paper and consulted it. 'We know you are in the habit of taking an annual holiday in Iceland.' He looked up. 'Still sticking to your northern heritage, I see. You couldn't very well go back to Sweden – and Finland would be even more risky. Too close to the Russian border for comfort.' He spread his hands. 'But who goes to Iceland?'

253

'So the job is in Iceland?'

'Indeed it is.' He tapped the paper with his fingernail. 'You take long holidays – three and four months at a time. What it is to have a private income – the Department did very well by you.'

'The Department gave me nothing that wasn't mine,' I said shortly.

He ignored that. 'I note you've been doing very well for yourself in Iceland. All the comforts down to a love-nest. A young lady, I believe, is . . .'

'We'll leave her out of it.'

'Just the point I'm making, dear boy. It would be most unwise if she became involved. It could be most dangerous for her, don't you think? I wouldn't tell her anything about it.' His voice was kindly.

Slade had certainly done his homework. If he knew about Elin then he must have tapped me a long time before. All the time I thought I was in cover I'd been under a microscope.

'Come to the job.'

'You will collect a package at Keflavik International Airport.' He sketched dimensions with his hands. 'About eight inches by four inches by two inches. You will deliver it to a man in Akureyri – you know where that is?'

'I know,' I said, and waited for him to continue, but he didn't. 'That's all?' I asked.

'That's all; I'm sure you will be able to accomplish it quite easily.'

I stared at him incredulously. 'Have you gone through all this rigmarole of blackmail just to give me a messenger boy's job?'

'I wish you wouldn't use such crude language,' he said peevishly. 'It's a job suitable for one who is out of practice, such as yourself. It's important enough and you were to hand, so we're using you.'

'This is something that's blown up quite quickly, isn't it?' I hazarded. 'You're forced to use me.'

Slade waggled his hand. 'We're a bit stretched for manpower, that's all. Don't get delusions of grandeur – in using you I'm scraping the bottom of the barrel.'

Slade could be blunt enough when it suited his purpose. I shrugged, and said, 'Who is the man in Akureyri?'

'He'll make himself known.' Slade took a slip of paper from his wallet and tore it jaggedly across. One piece he passed to me and it proved to be half of a 100-kronur banknote. 'He'll have the other half. Old ways are best, don't you think? Effective and uncomplicated.'

I looked at the ruined Icelandic currency in my hand and said ironically, 'I don't suppose I'll be paid for this enterprise?'

'Of course you will, dear boy. Her Majesty's Government is never niggardly when it comes to valuable services rendered. Shall we say two hundred pounds?'

'Send it to Oxfam, you bastard.'

He shook his head deprecatingly. 'Such language – but I shall do as you say. You may depend on it.'

I studied Slade and he looked back at me with eyes as candid as those of a baby. I didn't like the smell of this operation – it sounded too damned phoney. It occurred to me that perhaps he was setting up a training exercise with me as the guinea pig. The Department frequently ran games of that sort to train the new boys, but all the participants usually knew the score. If Slade was ringing me into a training scheme without telling me I'd strangle the sadistic bastard.

To test him, I said, 'Slade, if you're using me as the football in a training game it could be dangerous. You could lose some of your budding spies that way.'

He looked shocked. 'Oh, I wouldn't do that to you.'

'All right; what do I do if someone tries to take the package?'

'Stop him,' he said succinctly.

'At any cost?'

He smiled. 'You mean – should you kill? Do it any way you want. Just deliver the package to Akureyri.' His paunch shook with amusement. 'Killer Stewart!' he mocked gently. 'Well, well!'

I nodded. 'I just wanted to know. I'd hate to make your man-power problems more difficult. After Akureyri – what happens then?'

'Then you may go on your way rejoicing. Complete your holi-day. Enjoy the company of your lady friend. Feel free as air.'

'Until the next time you drop by.'

'That is a highly unlikely eventuality,' said Slade decisively. 'The world has passed you by. Things are not the same in the Department as they were – techniques are different – many changes you would not understand. You would be quite useless, Stewart, in any real work; but the job is simple and you're just a messenger boy.' He looked around the room a little disdainfully. 'No, you may come back here and rusticate peacefully.'

'And Kennikin?'

'Ah, I make no promises there. He may find you – he may not; but if he does it will not be because of my doing, I assure you.'

'That's not good enough,' I said. 'You'll tell him I haven't been a member of the Department for four years?'

'I may,' he said carelessly. 'I may.' He stood and buttoned his coat. 'Of course, whether he would believe it is one thing, and whether it would make any difference is yet another. He has his own, strictly unprofessional, reasons for wanting to find you, and I'm inclined to think that he'll want to operate on you with a sharp knife rather than to ask you to share his bottle of Calvados.'

He picked up his hat and moved over to the door. 'You will receive further instructions about picking up the package before you leave. It's been nice to see you again, Mr Stewart.'

'I wish I could say the same,' I said, and he laughed jollily.

I walked with him to his car and pointed to the rocks from where I had watched him waiting outside the cottage. 'I had you in rifle sights from up there. I even squeezed the trigger. Unfortunately the rifle wasn't loaded.'

He looked at me, his face full of confidence. 'If it had been loaded you wouldn't have pulled the trigger. You're a civilized man, Stewart; too civilized. I sometimes wonder how you lasted so long in the Department – you were always a little too soft-centred for the big jobs. If it had been my decision you'd have been out long before you decided to . . . er . . . retire.'

I looked into his pale cold eyes and knew that if it *had* been his decision I would never have been allowed to retire. He said, 'I trust you remember the terms of the Official Secrets Act.' Then he smiled. 'But of course, you remember.'

I said, 'Where are you in the hierarchy now, Slade?'

'Quite close to the top, as a matter of fact,' he said cheerfully. 'Right next to Taggart. I *do* make the decisions now. I get to have lunch with the Prime Minister from time to time.' He gave a self-satisfied laugh and got into the car. He rolled down the window, and said, 'There's just one thing. That package – don't open it, dear boy. Remember what curiosity did to the cat.'

He drove away, bumping down the track, and when he had disappeared the glen seemed cleaner. I looked up at Sgurr Mor and at Sgurr Dearg beyond and felt depressed. In less than twenty minutes my world had been smashed to pieces and I wondered how the hell I was going to pick up the bits.

And when I woke up the next morning after a broken night I knew there was only one thing to do; to obey Slade, carry out his orders and deliver the damned package to Akureyri and hope to God I could get clear without further entanglement.

III

My mouth was dry with talking and smoking. I pitched the cigarette butt from the window and it lay on a stone sending a lonely smoke signal to the North Pole. 'That's it,' I said. 'I was blackmailed into it.'

Elin shifted in her seat. 'I'm glad you've told me. I was wondering why you had to fly to Akureyri so suddenly.' She leaned forward and stretched. 'But now you've delivered this mysterious package you have nothing more to worry about.'

'That's it,' I said. 'I didn't deliver it.' I told her about the four men at Akureyri Airport and she went pale. 'Slade flew here from London. He was annoyed.'

'He was *here* – in Iceland?'

I nodded. 'He said that I'm out of it, anyway; but I'm not, you know. Elin, I want you to stay clear of me – you might get hurt.'

She regarded me intently. 'I don't think you've told me everything.'

'I haven't,' I said. 'And I'm not going to. You're better out of this mess.'

'I think you'd better complete your story,' she said.

I bit my lip. 'Have you anywhere to stay – out of sight, I mean?'

She shrugged. 'There's the apartment in Reykjavik.'

'That's compromised,' I said. 'Slade knows about it and one of his men has it tagged.'

'I could visit my father,' she said.

'Yes, you could.' I had met Ragnar Thorsson once only; he was a tough old farmer who lived in the wilds of Strandasysla. Elin would be safe enough there. I said, 'If I tell you the full story will you go and stay with him until I send for you?'

'I give no guarantees,' she said uncompromisingly.

'Christ!' I said. 'If I get out of this you're going to make me one hell of a wife. I don't know if I'll be able to stand it.'

She jerked her head. 'What did you say?'

'In a left-handed way I was asking you to marry me.'

Things immediately got confused and it was a few minutes before we got ourselves untangled. Elin, pink-faced and tousle-haired, grinned at me impishly. 'Now tell!'

I sighed and opened the door. 'I'll not only tell you, but I'll show you.'

I went to the back of the Land-Rover and took the flat metal box from the girder to which I had taped it. I held it out to Elin on the palm of my hand. 'That's what the trouble is all about,' I said. 'You brought it up from Reykjavik yourself.'

She poked at it tentatively with her forefinger. 'So those men didn't take it.'

I said, 'What they got was a metal box which originally contained genuine Scottish fudge from Oban – full of cotton wadding and hand sewn up in the original hessian.'

IV

'What about some beer?' asked Elin.

I grimaced. The Icelandic brew is a prohibition beer, tasteless stuff bearing the same relationship to alcohol as candyfloss bears to sugar. Elin laughed. 'It's all right; Bjarni brought back a case of Carlsberg on his last flight from Greenland.'

That was better; the Danes really know about beer. I watched Elin open the cans and pour out the Carlsberg. 'I want you to go to stay with your father,' I said.

'I'll think about it.' She handed me a glass. 'I want to know why you still have the package.'

'It was a phoney deal,' I said. 'The whole operation stank to high heaven. Slade said Graham had been tagged by the opposition so he brought me in at the last minute. But Graham wasn't attacked – I was.' I didn't tell Elin about Lindholm; I didn't know how much strain I could put upon her. 'Doesn't that seem odd?'

She considered it. 'Yes, it is strange.'

'And Graham was watching our apartment which is funny behaviour for a man who knows he may be under observation by the enemy. I don't think Graham had been tagged at all; I think Slade has been telling a pack of lies.'

Elin seemed intent on the bubbles glistening on the side of her glass. 'Talking of the enemy – who is the enemy?'

'I think it's my old pals of the KGB,' I said. 'Russian Intelligence. I could be wrong, but I don't think so.'

I could see by her set face that she didn't like the sound of that, so I switched back to Slade and Graham. 'Another thing – Graham saw me being tackled at Akureyri Airport and he didn't do a bloody thing to help me. He could at least have followed the man who ran off with the camera case, but he didn't do a damned thing. What do you make of that?'

'I don't know.'

'Neither do I,' I admitted. 'That's why the whole thing smells rotten. Consider Slade – he is told by Graham that I've fallen down on the job so he flies from London. And what does he do? He gives me a slap on the wrist and tells me I've been a naughty boy. And that's too bloody uncharacteristic coming from Slade.'

Elin said, 'You don't trust Slade.' It was a statement.

I pointed over the sea towards Grimsey. 'I trust Slade as far as I can throw that island. He's cooked up a complicated deal and I'd like to find out where I fit in before the chopper falls because it might be designed to fall right on my neck.'

'And what about the package?'

'That's the ace.' I lifted the metal box. 'Slade thinks the opposition have it, but as long as they haven't there's no great harm done. The opposition think they have it, assuming they haven't opened it yet.'

'Is that a fair assumption?'

'I think so. Agents are not encouraged to pry too much. The quartet who took the package from me will have orders to take it to the boss unopened, I think.'

Elin looked at the box. 'I wonder what's in it?'

I looked at it myself, and it looked right back at me and said nothing. 'Maybe I'd better get out the can-opener,' I said. 'But not just yet. Perhaps it might be better not to know.'

Elin made a sound of exasperation. 'Why must you men make everything complicated? So what are you going to do?'

'I'm going to lie low,' I said mendaciously. 'While I do some heavy thinking. Maybe I'll post the damned thing to *poste restante*, Akureyri, and telegraph Slade telling him where to pick it up.'

I hoped Elin would swallow that because I was going to do something quite different and infinitely more dangerous. Somebody was soon going to find out he'd been sold a pup; he was going to scream loudly and I wanted to be around to find out who was screaming. But I didn't want to have Elin around when that happened.

'Lie low,' repeated Elin thoughtfully. She turned to me. 'What about Asbyrgi for tonight?'

'Asbyrgi!' I laughed and drained my glass. 'Why not?'

V

In that dim and faraway time when the gods were young and Odin rode the arctic wastelands, he was out one day when his horse, Sleipnir, stumbled and planted a hoof in Northern Iceland. The place where the hoof hit the ground is now known as Asbyrgi. So runs the legend but my geologist friends tell it a little differently.

Asbyrgi is a hoof-shaped rock formation about two miles across. Within it the trees, sheltered from the killing wind, grow quite strongly for Iceland, some of them attaining a height of nearly twenty feet. It is a green and fertile place nestling between the towering rock walls which surround it. There is nothing to draw one there but the legend and the unaccustomed sight of growing trees, but although it is a tourist attraction they don't stay the night. More to the point, it is quite off the main road.

We pushed through the narrow entrance to Asbyrgi and along the track made by the wheels of visiting cars until we were well inside at a place where the rock walls drew together and the trees were thick, and there we made camp. It was our custom to sleep on the ground when the climate allowed so I erected the awning which fitted on to the side of the Land-Rover, and brought out the air mattresses and sleeping bags while Elin began to prepare supper.

Perhaps we were sybaritic about our camping because we certainly didn't rough it. I took out the folding chairs and the table and set them up and Elin put down a bottle of Scotch and two glasses and joined me in a drink before she broiled the steak. Beef is a luxury I insist upon in Iceland; one can get awfully tired of mutton.

It was quiet and peaceful and we sat and enjoyed the evening, savouring the peaty taste of the whisky and talking desultorily of the things furthest from our minds. I think we both needed a respite from the nagging problem of Slade and his damned package, and the act of setting out our camp was a return to happier days which we both eagerly grasped.

Elin got up to cook supper and I poured another drink and wondered how I was to get rid of her. If she wouldn't go voluntarily then perhaps the best way would be to decamp early in the morning leaving her a couple of cans of food and a water bottle. With those and the sleeping bag she would be all right for a day or two until someone came into Asbyrgi and gave her a lift into civilization. She would be mad as a hornet but she would still be alive.

Because lying low wasn't good enough. I had to become visible — set myself up like a tin duck at a shooting gallery so that someone would have a crack at me. I didn't want Elin around when the action started.

Elin brought the supper and we started to eat. She said, 'Alan, why did you leave the . . . the Department?'

I hesitated with my fork in the air. 'I had a difference of opinion,' I said shortly.

'With Slade?'

I laid down the fork gently. 'It was about Slade — yes. I don't want to talk about it, Elin.'

She brooded for a while, then said, 'It might be better if you talked about it. You don't want to keep things locked up.'

I laughed silently. 'That's funny,' I said. 'Telling that to an agent of the Department. Haven't you heard of the Official Secrets Act?'

'What's that?'

'If the Department found I'd talked out of turn I'd be slung into jail for the rest of my life.'

'Oh, that!' she said disparagingly. 'That doesn't count — not with me.'

'Try telling that to Sir David Taggart,' I said. 'I've told you more than enough already.'

'Then why not get it all out? You know I won't tell anyone.'

I looked down at my plate. 'Not of your own free will. I wouldn't want anyone to hurt you, Elin.'

'Who would hurt me?' she asked.

'Slade would, for one. Then there's a character called Kennikin who may be around, but I hope not.'

Elin said slowly, 'If I ever marry anyone it will be a man who has no secrets. This is not good, Alan.'

'So you think that a trouble shared is a trouble halved. I don't think the Department would go along with you on that. The powers that be don't think confession is good for the soul, and Catholic priests and psychiatrists are looked upon with deep suspicion. But since you're so persistent I'll tell you some of it — not enough to be dangerous.'

I cut into the steak again. 'I was on an operation in Sweden. I was in a counter-espionage group trying to penetrate the KGB *apparat* in Scandinavia. Slade was master-minding the operation.

I'll tell you one thing about Slade; he's very clever – devious and tricky, and he likes a ploy that wins coming and going.'

I found I had lost my appetite and pushed the plate away. 'A man called V. V. Kennikin was bossing the opposition, and I got pretty close to him. As far as he was concerned I was a Swedish Finn called Stewartsen, a fellow traveller who was willing to be used. Did you know I was born in Finland?'

Elin shook her head. 'You didn't tell me.'

I shrugged. 'I suppose I've tried to close off that part of my life. Anyway, after a lot of work and a lot of fright I was inside and accepted by Kennikin, not that he trusted me, but he used me on minor jobs and I was able to gather a lot of information which was duly passed on to Slade. But it was all trivial stuff. I was close to Kennikin, but not close enough.'

Elin said, 'It sounds awful. I'm not surprised you were frightened.'

'I was scared to death most of the time; double agents usually are.' I paused, trying to think of the simplest way to explain a complicated situation. I said deliberately, 'The time came when I had to kill a man. Slade warned me that my cover was in danger of being blown. He said the man responsible had not reported to Kennikin and the best thing to do was to eliminate him. So I did it with a bomb.' I swallowed. 'I never even saw the man I killed – I just put a bomb in a car.'

There was horror in Elin's eyes. I said harshly, 'We weren't playing patty-cake out there.'

'But someone you didn't know – that you had never seen!'

'It's better that way,' I said. 'Ask any bomber pilot. But that's not the point. The point is that I had trusted Slade and it turned out that the man I killed was a British agent – one of my own side.'

Elin was looking at me as though I had just crawled out from under a stone. I said, 'I contacted Slade and asked what the hell was going on. He said the man was a freelance agent whom neither side trusted – the trade is lousy with them. He recommended that I tell Kennikin what I'd done, so I did and my stock went up with Kennikin. Apparently he had been aware of a leak in his organization and there was enough evidence around to point to the man I had killed. So I became one of his blue-eyed boys – we got really chummy – and that was his mistake because we managed to wreck his network completely.'

Elin let out her breath. 'Is that all?'

'By Christ, it's not all!' I said violently. I reached for the whisky bottle and found my hand was trembling. 'When it was all over I went back to England. I was congratulated on doing a good job. The Scandinavian branch was in a state of euphoria and I was a minor hero, for God's sake! Then I discovered that the man I had killed was no more of a freelance agent than I was. His name – if it matters – was Birkby, and he had been a member of the Department, just as I was.'

I slopped whisky into the glass. 'Slade had been playing chess with us. Neither Birkby nor I were deep enough in Kennikin's outfit to suit him so he sacrificed a pawn to put another in a better position. But he had broken the rules as far as I was concerned – it was as though a chess player had knocked off one of his own pieces to checkmate the king, and that's not in the rules.'

Elin said in a shaking voice, 'Are there any rules in your dirty world?'

'Quite right,' I said. 'There aren't any rules. But I thought there were. I tried to raise a stink.' I knocked back the undiluted whisky and felt it burn my throat. 'Nobody would listen, of course – the job had been successful and was now being forgotten and the time had come to go on to bigger and better things. Slade had pulled it off and no one wanted to delve too deeply into how he'd done it.' I laughed humourlessly. 'In fact, he'd gone up a notch in the Department and any muck-raking would be tactless – a reflection on the superior who had promoted him. I was a nuisance and nuisances are unwanted and to be got rid of.'

'So they got rid of you,' she said flatly.

'If Slade had his way I'd have been got rid of the hard way – permanently. In fact, he told me so not long ago. But he wasn't too high in the organization in those days and he didn't carry enough weight.' I looked into the bottom of the glass. 'What happened was that I had a nervous breakdown.'

I raised my eyes to Elin. 'Some of it was genuine – I'd say about fifty-fifty. I'd been living on my nerves for a long time and this was the last straw. Anyway, the Department runs a hospital with tame psychiatrists for cases like mine. Right now there's a file stashed away somewhere full of stuff that would make Freud blush. If I step out of line there'll be a psychiatrist ready to give evidence that I suffer everything from enuresis to paranoic delusions of grandeur. Who would disbelieve evidence coming from an eminent medical man?'

Elin was outraged. 'But that's unethical! You're as sane as I am.'

'There are no rules – remember?' I poured out another drink, more gently this time. 'So I was allowed to retire. I was no use

263

to the Department anyway; I had become that anomaly, the well-known secret service agent. I crept away to a Scottish glen to lick my wounds. I thought I was safe until Slade showed up.'

'And blackmailed you with Kennikin. Would he tell Kennikin where you are?'

'I wouldn't put it past him, on his past record. And it's quite true that Kennikin has a score to settle. The word is that he's no good to the girls any more, and he blames me for it. I'd just as soon he doesn't know where to find me.'

I thought of the last encounter in the dimness of the Swedish forest. I knew I hadn't killed him; I knew it as soon as I had squeezed the trigger. There is a curious prescience in the gunman which tells him if he has hit the mark at which he aims, and I knew the bullet had gone low and that I had only wounded him. The nature of the wound was something else, and I could expect no mercy from Kennikin if he caught up with me.

Elin looked away from me and across the little glade which was quiet and still in the fading light apart from the sleepy chirrup of birds bedding down for the night. She shivered and put her arms about her body, 'You come from another world – a world I don't know.'

'It's a world I'm trying to protect you from.'

'Was Birkby married?'

'I don't know,' I said. 'One thing did occur to me. If Slade had thought that Birkby had a better chance of getting next to Kennikin, then he'd have told him to kill me, and for the same reason. Sometimes I think it would have been better that way.'

'No, Alan!' Elin leaned forward and took my hand in hers. 'Never think that.'

'Don't worry; I'm not suicidally minded,' I said. 'Anyway, you now know why I don't like Slade and why I distrust him – and why I'm suspicious of this particular operation.'

Elin looked at me closely, still holding my hand. 'Alan, apart from Birkby, have you killed anyone else?'

'I have,' I said deliberately.

Her face seemed to close tight and her hand slipped from mine. She nodded slowly. 'I have a lot to think about, Alan. I'd like to take a walk.' She rose. 'Alone – if you don't mind.'

I watched her walk into the trees and then picked up the bottle hefting it in my hand and wondering if I wanted another drink. I looked at the level of liquid and discovered that four of my un-measured slugs had nearly half-emptied the bottle. I put it down again – I have never believed in drowning my problems and this was no time to start.

I knew what was wrong with Elin. It's a shock for a woman to realize that the man accepted into her bed is a certified killer, no matter in how laudable a cause. And I had no illusions that the cause for which I had worked was particularly commendable – not to Elin. What would a peaceful Icelander know about the murkier depths of the unceasing undercover war between the nations?

I collected the dirty dishes and began to wash them, wondering what she would do. All I had going for me were the summers we had spent together and the hope that those days and nights of happiness would weigh in the balance of her mind. I hoped that what she knew of me as a man, a lover and a human being would count for more than my past.

I finished cleaning up and lit a cigarette. Light was slowly ebbing from the sky towards the long twilight of summer in northern lands. It would never really get dark – it was too close to Midsummer Day – and the sun would not be absent for long.

I saw Elin coming back, her white shirt glimmering among the trees. As she approached the Land-Rover she looked up at the sky. 'It's getting late.'

'Yes.'

She stooped, unzipped the sleeping bags, and then zipped them together to make one large bag. As she turned her head towards me her lips curved in a half-smile. 'Come to bed, Alan,' she said, and I knew that nothing was lost and everything was going to be all right.

Later that night I had an idea. I unzipped my side of the bag and rolled out, trying not to disturb Elin. She said sleepily, 'What are you doing?'

'I don't like Slade's mysterious box being in the open. I'm going to hide it.'

'Where?'

'Somewhere under the chassis.'

'Can't it wait until morning?'

I pulled on a sweater. 'I might as well do it now. I can't sleep – I've been thinking too much.'

Elin yawned. 'Can I help – hold a torch or something?'

'Go back to sleep.' I took the metal box, a roll of insulating tape and a torch, and went over to the Land-Rover. On the theory that

I might want to get at the box quickly I taped it inside the rear bumper. I had just finished when a random sweep of my hand inside the bumper gave me pause, because my fingers encountered something that shifted stickily.

I nearly twisted my head off in an attempt to see what it was. Squinting in the light of the torch I saw another metal box, but much smaller and painted green, the same colour as the Land-Rover but definitely not standard equipment as provided by the Rover Company. Gently I grasped it and pulled it away. One side of the small cube was magnetized so it would hold on a metal surface and, as I held it in my hand, I knew that someone was being very clever.

It was a radio bug of the type known as a 'bumper-bleeper' and, at that moment, it would be sending out a steady scream, shouting, '*Here I am! Here I am!*' Anyone with a radio direction finder tuned to the correct frequency would know exactly where to find the Land-Rover any time he cared to switch on.

I rolled away and got to my feet, still holding the bug, and for a moment was tempted to smash it. How long it had been on the Land-Rover I didn't know – probably ever since Reykjavik. And who else could have bugged it but Slade or his man, Graham? Not content with warning me to keep Elin out of it, he had coppered his bet by making it easy to check on her. Or was it me he wanted to find?

I was about to drop it and grind it under my heel when I paused. That wouldn't be too clever – there were other, and better, ways of using it. Slade knew I was bugged, I knew I was bugged, but Slade didn't know that I knew, and that fact might yet be turned to account. I bent down and leaned under the Land-Rover to replace the bug. It attached itself to the bumper with a slight click.

And at that moment something happened. I don't know what it was because it was so imperceptible – just a fractional altering of the quality of the night silence – and if the finding of the bug had not made me preternaturally alert I might have missed it. I held my breath and listened intently and heard it again – the faraway metallic grunt of a gear change. Then there was nothing more, but that was enough.

Chapter Three

I

I leaned over Elin and shook her. 'Wake up!' I said quietly.

'What's the matter?' she asked, still half-asleep.

'Keep quiet! Get dressed quickly.'

'But what...?'

'Don't argue – just get dressed.' I turned and stared into the trees, dimly visible in the half light. Nothing moved, nor could I hear anything – the quiet of the night was unbroken. The narrow entrance to Asbyrgi lay just under a mile away and I thought it likely that the vehicle would stop there. That would be a natural precaution – the stopper in the neck of the bottle.

It was likely that further investigation of Asbyrgi would be made on foot in a known direction given by radio direction finder and a known distance as given by a signal strength meter. Having a radio bug on a vehicle is as good as illuminating it with a searchlight.

Elin said quietly, 'I'm ready.'

I turned to her. 'We're about to have visitors,' I said in a low voice. 'In fifteen minutes – maybe less. I want you to hide.' I pointed. 'Over there would be best; find the closest cover you can among the trees and lie down – and don't come out until you hear me calling you.'

'But...'

'Don't argue – just do it,' I said harshly. I had never spoken to her before in that tone of voice and she blinked at me in surprise, but she turned quickly and ran into the trees.

I dived under the Land-Rover and groped for Lindholm's pistol which I had taped there in Reykjavik, but it had gone and all that was left was a sticky strand of insulation tape to show where it had been. The roads in Iceland are rough enough to shake anything loose and I was bloody lucky not to have lost the most important thing – the metal box.

So all I had was the knife – the *sgian dubh*. I stooped and picked it up from where it was lying next to the sleeping bag and tucked it into the waistband of my trousers. Then I withdrew into the trees by the side of the glade and settled down to wait.

It was a long time, nearer to half an hour, before anything happened. He came like a ghost, a dark shape moving quietly up the track and not making a sound. It was too dark to see his face but there was just enough light to let me see what he carried. The shape and the way he held it was unmistakable – there are ways of holding tools, and a man carries a rifle in a different way from he carries a stick. This was no stick.

I froze as he paused on the edge of the glade. He was quite still and, if I hadn't known he was there, it would have been easy for the eye to pass over that dark patch by the trees without recognizing it for what it was – a man with a gun. I was worried about the gun; it was either a rifle or a shotgun, and that was the sign of a professional. Pistols are too inaccurate for the serious business of killing – ask any soldier – and are liable to jam at the wrong moment. The professional prefers something more deadly.

If I was going to jump him I'd have to get behind him, which meant letting him pass me, but that would mean laying myself wide open for his friend – if he had a friend behind him. So I waited to see if the friend would turn up or if he was alone. I wondered briefly if he knew what would happen if he fired that gun in Asbyrgi; if he didn't then he'd be a very surprised gunman when he pulled the trigger.

There was a flicker of movement and he was suddenly gone, and I cursed silently. Then a twig cracked and I knew he was in the trees on the other side of the glade. This was a professional all right – a really careful boy. Never come from the direction in which you are expected, even if you don't think you'll be expected. Play it safe. He was in the trees and circling the glade to come in from the other side.

I also began to circle, but in the opposite direction. This was tricky because sooner or later we'd come face to face. I plucked the *sgian dubh* from my waist and held it loosely – puny protection against a rifle but it was all I had. Every step I took I tested carefully to make sure there was no twig underfoot, and it was slow and sweaty work.

I paused beneath a scrawny birch tree and peered into the semi-darkness. Nothing moved but I heard the faint click as of one stone knocking against another. I remained motionless, holding my breath, and then I saw him coming towards me, a dark moving shadow not ten yards away. I tightened my hold on the knife and waited for him.

Suddenly the silence was broken by the rustle of bushes and something white arose at his feet. It could only be one thing – he had walked right on to Elin where she had crouched in hiding. He was startled, retreated a step, and raised the rifle. I yelled, 'Get down, Elin!' as he pulled the trigger and a flash of light split the darkness.

It sounded as though a war had broken out, as though an infantry company had let off a rather ragged volley of rifle fire. The noise of the shot bounced from the cliffs of Asbyrgi, repeating from rock face to rock face in a diminishing series of multiple echoes which died away slowly in the far distance. That unexpected result of pulling the trigger unnerved him momentarily and he checked in surprise.

I threw the knife and there was the soft thud as it hit him. He gave a bubbling cry and dropped the rifle to claw at his chest. Then his knees buckled and he fell to the ground, thrashing and writhing among the bushes.

I ignored him and ran to where I had seen Elin, pulling the flashlight from my pocket as I went. She was sitting on the ground, her hair to her shoulders and her eyes wide with shock. 'Are you all right?'

She withdrew her hand and her fingers were covered in blood. 'He shot me,' she said dully.

I knelt beside her and looked at her shoulder. The bullet had grazed her, tearing the pad of muscle on top of the shoulder. It would be painful later, but it was not serious. 'We'd better put a dressing on that,' I said.

'He shot me!' Her voice was stronger and there was something like wonder in her tone.

'I doubt if he'll shoot anyone again,' I said, and turned the light on him. He was lying quite still with his head turned away.

'Is he dead?' asked Elin, her eyes on the haft of the knife which protruded from his chest.

'I don't know. Hold the light.' I took his wrist and felt the quick beat of the pulse. 'He's alive,' I said. 'He might even survive.' I pulled his head around so that I could see his face. It was Graham – and that was something of a surprise. I mentally apologized for accusing him of having been wet behind the ears; the way he had approached our camp had been all professional.

Elin said, 'There's a first-aid box in the Land-Rover.'

'Carry on,' I said. 'I'll bring him over.' I stooped and picked up Graham in my arms and followed Elin. She spread out the sleeping bag and I laid him down. Then she brought out the first-aid box and sank to her knees.

'No,' I said. 'You first. Take off your shirt.' I cleaned the wound on her shoulder, dusted it with penicillin powder, and bound a pad over it. 'You'll have trouble in raising your arm above your shoulder for the next week,' I said. 'Otherwise it's not too bad.'

She seemed mesmerized by the amber light reflected from the jewelled pommel of the knife in Graham's chest. 'That knife – do you always carry it?'

'Always,' I said. 'We have to get it out of here.' It had hit Graham in the centre of the chest just below the sternum and it had an upwards inclination. The whole of the blade was buried in him and God knows what it had sliced through.

I cut away his shirt, and said, 'Get an absorbent pad ready,' and then I put my hand on the hilt and pulled. The serrated back edge admitted air into the wound and made extraction easy and the knife came away cleanly. I half-expected a gush of arterial blood which would have been the end of Graham, but there was just a steady trickle which ran down his stomach and collected in his navel.

Elin put the pad on the wound and strapped it down with tape while I took his pulse again. It was a little weaker than it had been.

'Do you know who he is?' asked Elin, sitting back on her heels.

'Yes,' I said matter-of-factly. 'He said his name is Graham. He's a member of the Department working with Slade.' I picked up the *sgian dubh* and began to clean it. 'Right now I'd like to know if he came alone or if he has any pals around here. We're sitting ducks.'

I got up and walked back into the trees and hunted about for Graham's rifle. I found it and took it back to the Land-Rover; it was a Remington pump action carbine chambered for .30/06 ammunition – a good gun for a murderer. The barrel not too long to get in the way, the fire rapid – five aimed shots in five seconds – and a weight and velocity of slug enough to stop a man dead in his tracks. I operated the action and caught the round that jumped out. It was the ordinary soft-nosed hunting type, designed to spread on impact. Elin had been lucky.

She was bending over Graham wiping his brow. 'He's coming round.'

Graham's eyes flickered and opened and he saw me standing over him with the carbine in my hands. He tried to get up but a spasm of pain hit him and the sweat started out on his brow. 'You're not in a position to do much,' I said. 'You have a hole in your gut.'

He sagged back and moistened his lips. 'Slade said . . .' He fought for breath '. . . said you weren't dangerous.'

'Did he, now? He was wrong, wasn't he?' I held up the carbine. 'If you'd come empty-handed without this you wouldn't be lying where you are now. What was supposed to be the idea?'

'Slade wanted the package,' he whispered.

'So? But the opposition have it. The Russians – I suppose they *are* Russians?'

Graham nodded weakly. 'But they didn't get it. That's why Slade sent me in here. He said you were playing a double game. He said you weren't straight.'

I frowned. 'Now, that's interesting,' I said, and sat on my heels next to him with the carbine across my knees. 'Tell me this, Graham – who told Slade the Russians hadn't got it? I didn't tell them, that's for sure. I suppose the Russkies obligingly told him they'd been fooled.'

A look of puzzlement came over his face. 'I don't know how he knew. He just told me to come and get it.'

I lifted the carbine. 'And he gave you this. I suppose I was to be liquidated.' I glanced at Elin, and then back at Graham. 'And what about Elin here? What was to happen to her?'

Graham closed his eyes. 'I didn't know she was here.'

'Maybe not,' I said. 'But Slade did. How the hell do you think that Land-Rover got here?' Graham's eyelids flickered. 'You know damned well you'd have to kill any witnesses.'

A trickle of blood crept from the corner of his mouth. 'You lousy bastard!' I said. 'If I thought you knew what you were doing I'd kill you now. So Slade told you I'd reneged and you took his word for it – you took the gun he gave you and followed his orders. Ever hear of a man called Birkby?'

Graham opened his eyes. 'No.'

'Before your time,' I said. 'It just happens that Slade has played that trick before. But never mind that now. Did you come alone?'

Graham closed his mouth tightly and a stubborn look came over his face. 'Don't be a hero,' I advised. 'I can get it out of you easily enough. How would you like me to stomp on your belly right now?' I heard Elin gasp, but ignored her. 'You have a bad gut wound, and you're liable to die unless we can get you to a hospital. And I can't do that if someone is going to take a crack at us as we leave Asbyrgi. I'm not going to put Elin into risk just for the sake of your hide.'

He looked beyond me to Elin, and then nodded. 'Slade,' he said. 'He's here . . . about a mile . . .'

'At the entrance to Asbyrgi?'

'Yes,' he said, and closed his eyes again. I took his pulse and found it very much fainter. I turned to Elin. 'Start to load; leave enough room for Graham to lie in the back on top of the sleeping bags.' I stood up and checked the load in the carbine.

'What are you going to do?'

'Maybe I can get close enough to Slade to talk to him,' I said. 'To tell him his boy is badly hurt. Maybe I won't – in that case I'll talk to him with this.' I held up the carbine.

She whitened. 'You'll kill him?'

'Christ, I don't know!' I said exasperatedly. 'All I know is that apparently he doesn't mind if I'm killed – and you, too. He's sitting at the entrance to Asbyrgi like a bloody cork in a bottle and this is the only corkscrew I've got.'

Graham moaned a little and opened his eyes. I bent down. 'How are you feeling?'

'Bad.' The trickle of blood at the corner of his mouth had increased to a rivulet which ran down his neck. 'It's funny,' he whispered. 'How *did* Slade know?'

I said, 'What's in the package?'

'Don't . . . know.'

'Who is bossing the Department these days?'

His breath wheezed. 'Ta . . . Taggart.'

If anyone could pull Slade off my back it would be Taggart. I said, 'All right; I'll go and see Slade. We'll have you out of here in no time.'

'Slade said . . .' Graham paused and began again. He seemed to have difficulty in swallowing and he coughed a little, bringing bright red bubbles foaming to his lips. 'Slade said . . .'

The coughing increased and there was a sudden gush of red arterial blood from his mouth and his head fell sideways. I put my hand to his wrist and knew that Graham would never tell me what more Slade had said because he was dead. I closed his staring eyes, and stood up. 'I'd better talk to Slade.'

'He's dead!' said Elin in a shocked whisper.

Graham was dead – a pawn suddenly swept from the board. He had died because he followed orders blindly, just as I had done in Sweden; he had died because he didn't really understand what he was doing. Slade had told him to do something and he had tried and failed and come to his death. I didn't really understand what I was doing, either, so I'd better not fail in anything I attempted.

Elin was crying. The big tears welled from her eyes and trickled down her cheeks. She didn't sob but just stood there crying silently and looking down at the body of Graham. I said harshly, 'Don't cry for him – he was going to kill you. You heard him.'

When she spoke it was without a tremor, but still the tears came. 'I'm not crying for Graham,' she said desolately. 'I'm crying for you. Someone must.'

II

We struck camp quickly and loaded everything into the Land-Rover, and everything included the body of Graham. 'We can't leave him here,' I said. 'Someone will be sure to stumble across him soon – certainly within the week. To quote the Bard, we lug the guts into the neighbour room.'

A wan smile crossed Elin's face as she caught the allusion. 'Where?'

'Dettifoss,' I said. 'Or maybe Selfoss.' To go over a couple of waterfalls, one the most powerful in Europe, would batter the body beyond recognition and, with luck, disguise the fact that Graham had been stabbed. He would be a lone tourist who had had an accident.

So we put the body in the back of the Land-Rover, I picked up the Remington carbine, and said, 'Give me half an hour, then come along as fast as you can.'

'I can't move fast if I have to be quiet,' she objected.

'Quietness won't matter – just belt towards the entrance as fast as you can, and use the headlights. Then slow down a bit so I can hop aboard.'

'And then?'

'Then we head for Dettifoss – but not by the main road. We keep on the track to the west of the river.'

'What are you going to do about Slade? You're going to kill him, aren't you?'

'He might kill me first,' I said. 'Let's have no illusions about Slade.'

'No more killing, Alan,' she said. 'Please – no more killing.'

'It might not be up to me. If he shoots at me then I'll shoot back.'

'All right,' she said quietly.

So I left her and headed towards the entrance to Asbyrgi, padding softly along the track and hoping that Slade wouldn't come looking for Graham. I didn't think it likely. Although he must have heard the shot he would have been expecting it, and then it would have taken Graham a half-hour to return after searching for the package. My guess was that Slade wouldn't be expecting Graham for another hour.

I made good time but slowed as I approached the entrance. Slade had not bothered to hide his car; it was parked in full sight and was clearly visible because the short northern night was nearly over and the sky was light. He knew what he was doing because it was impossible to get close to the car without being seen, so I settled behind a rock and waited for Elin. I had no relish for walking across that open ground only to stop a bullet.

Presently I heard her coming. The noise was quite loud as she changed gear and I saw a hint of movement from inside the parked car. I nestled my cheek against the stock of the carbine and aimed. Graham had been professional enough to put a spot of luminous paint on the foresight but it was not necessary in the pre-dawn light.

I settled the sight on the driving side and, as the noise behind me built up to a crescendo, I slapped three bullets in as many seconds through the windscreen which must have been made of laminated glass because it went totally opaque. Slade took off in a wide sweep and I saw that the only thing that had saved him was that the car had right-hand drive, English style, and I had shot holes in the wrong side of the windscreen.

But he wasn't waiting for me to correct the error and bucked away down the track as fast as he could go. The Land-Rover came up behind me and I jumped for it. 'Get going!' I yelled. 'Make it fast.'

Ahead, Slade's car skidded around a corner in a four-wheel drift, kicking up a cloud of dust. He was heading for the main road, but when we arrived at the corner Elin turned the other way as I had instructed her. It would have been useless chasing Slade – a Land-Rover isn't built for that and he had the advantage.

We turned south on to the track which parallels the *Jökulsá á Fjöllum,* the big river that takes the melt water north from Vatnajökull, and the roughness of the ground dictated a reduction in speed. Elin said, 'Did you talk to Slade?'

'I couldn't get near him.'

'I'm glad you didn't kill him.'

'It wasn't for want of trying,' I said. 'If he had a left-hand drive car he'd be dead by now.'

'And would that make you feel any better?' she asked cuttingly.

I looked at her. 'Elin,' I said. 'The man's dangerous. Either he's gone off his nut – which I think is unlikely – or . . .'

'Or what?'

'I don't know,' I said despondently. 'It's too damned complicated and I don't know enough. But I do know that Slade wants me dead. There's something I know – or something he thinks I know – that's dangerous for him; dangerous enough for him to want to kill me. Under the circumstances I don't want you around – you could get in the line of fire. You *did* get in the line of fire this morning.'

She slowed because of a deep rut. 'You can't survive alone,' she said. 'You need help.'

I needed more than help; I needed a new set of brains to work out this convoluted problem. But this wasn't the time to do it because Elin's shoulder was giving her hell. 'Pull up,' I said. 'I'll do the driving.'

We travelled south for an hour and a half and Elin said, 'There's Dettifoss.'

I looked out over the rocky landscape towards the cloud of spray in the distance which hung over the deep gorge which the *Jökulsá á Fjöllum* has cut deep into the rock. 'We'll carry on to Selfoss,' I decided. 'Two waterfalls are better than one. Besides, there are usually campers at Dettifoss.'

We went past Dettifoss and, three kilometres farther on, I pulled off the road. 'This is as close to Selfoss as we can get.'

I got out. 'I'll go towards the river and see if anyone's around,' I said. 'It's bad form to be seen humping bodies around. Wait here and don't talk to any strange men.'

I checked to see if the body was still decently shrouded by the blanket with which we had covered it, and then headed towards the river. It was still very early in the morning and there was no one about so I went back and opened the rear door of the vehicle and climbed inside.

I stripped the blanket away from Graham's body and searched his clothing. His wallet contained some Icelandic currency and a sheaf of Deutschmarks, together with a German motoring club card identifying him as Dieter Buchner, as also did his German passport. There was a photograph of him with his arms around a pretty girl and a fascia board of a shop behind them was in German. The Department was always thorough about that kind of thing.

The only other item of interest was a packet of rifle ammunition which had been broken open. I put that on one side, pulled out the body and replaced the wallet in the pocket, and then carried him in a fireman's lift towards the river with Elin close on my heels.

I got to the lip of the gorge and put down the body while I studied the siuation. The gorge at this point was curved and the river had undercut the rock face so that it was a straight drop right into the water. I pushed the body over the edge and watched it fall in a tumble of arms and legs until it splashed into the grey, swirling water. Buoyed by air trapped in the jacket it floated out until it was caught in the quick midstream current. We watched it go downstream until it disappeared over the edge of Selfoss to drop into the roaring cauldron below.

Elin looked at me sadly. 'And what now?'

'Now I go south,' I said, and walked away quickly towards the Land-Rover. When Elin caught up with me I was bashing hell out of the radio-bug with a big stone.

'Why south?' she asked breathlessly.

'I want to get to Keflavik and back to London. There's a man I want to talk to – Sir David Taggart.'

'We go by way of Myvatn?'

I shook my head, and gave the radio-bug one last clout, sure now that it would tell no more tales. 'I'm keeping off the main roads – they're too dangerous. I go by way of the *Odádahraun* and by Askja – into the desert. But you're not coming.'

'We'll see,' she said, and tossed the car key in her hand.

III

God has not yet finished making Iceland.

In the last 500 years one-third of all the lava extruded from the guts of the earth to the face of the planet has surfaced in Iceland and, of 200 known volcanoes, thirty are still very much active. Iceland suffers from a bad case of geological acne.

For the last thousand years a major eruption has been recorded, on average, every five years. Askja – the ash volcano – last blew its top in 1961. Measurable quantities of volcanic ash settled on the roofs of Leningrad, 1500 miles away. That didn't trouble the Russians overmuch but the effect was more serious nearer home. The country to the north and east of Askja was scorched and poisoned by deep deposits of ash and, nearer to Askja, the lava flows overran the land, overlaying desolation with desolation. Askja dominates north-east Iceland and has created the most awesome landscape in the world.

It was into this wilderness, the *Odádahraun,* as remote and blasted as the surface of the moon, that we went. The name, loosely translated, means 'Murderers' Country', and was the last foothold of the outlaws of olden times, the shunned of men against whom all hands were raised.

There are tracks in the *Odádahraun* – sometimes. The tracks are made by those who venture into the interior; most of them scientists – geologists and hydrographers – few travel for pleasure in that part of the *Obyggdir*. Each vehicle defines the track a little more, but when the winter snows come the tracks are obliterated – by water, by snow avalanche, by rock slip. Those going into the interior in the early summer, as we were, are in a very real sense trail blazers, sometimes finding the track anew and deepening it a fraction, very often not finding it and making another.

It was not bad during the first morning. The track was reasonable and not too bone-jolting and paralleled the *Jökulsá á Fjöllum* which ran grey-green with melt water to the Arctic Ocean. By midday we were opposite Mödrudalur which lay on the other side of the river, and Elin broke into that mournfully plaintive song which describes the plight of the Icelander in winter : 'Short are the mornings in the mountains of Mödrudal. There it is mid-morning at daybreak.' I suppose it fitted her mood; I know mine wasn't very much better.

I had dropped all thoughts of giving Elin the slip. Slade knew that she had been in Asbyrgi – the bug planted on the Land-Rover would have told him that – and it would be very dangerous for her to appear unprotected in any of the coastal towns. Slade had been a party to attempted murder and she was a witness, and I knew he would take extreme measures to silence her. As dangerous as my position was she was as safe with me as anywhere, so I was stuck with her.

At three in the afternoon we stopped at the rescue hut under the rising bulk of the great shield volcano called Herdubreid or 'Broad Shoulders'. We were both tired and hungry, and Elin said, 'Can't we stop here for the day?'

I looked across at the hut. 'No,' I said. 'Someone might be expecting us to do just that. We'll push on a little farther towards Askja. But there's no reason why we can't eat here.'

Elin prepared a meal and we ate in the open, sitting outside the hut. Halfway through the meal I was in mid-bite of a herring sandwich when an idea struck me like a bolt of lightning. I looked up at the radio mast next to the hut and then at the whip antenna on the Land-Rover. 'Elin, we can raise Reykjavik from here, can't we? I mean we can talk to anyone in Reykjavik who has a telephone.'

Elin looked up. 'Of course. We contact Gufunes Radio and they connect us into the telephone system.'

I said dreamily, 'Isn't it fortunate that the transatlantic cables run through Iceland? If we can be plugged into the telephone system there's nothing to prevent a further patching so as to put a call through to London.' I stabbed my finger at the Land-Rover with its radio antenna waving gently in the breeze. 'Right from there.'

'I've never heard of it being done,' said Elin doubtfully.

I finished the sandwich. 'I see no reason why it can't be done. After all, President Nixon spoke to Neil Armstrong when he was on the moon. The ingredients are there – all we have to do is put them together. Do you know anyone in the telephone department?'

'I know Svein Haraldsson,' she said thoughtfully.

I would have taken a bet that she would know someone in the telephone department; everybody in Iceland knows somebody. I scribbled a number on a scrap of paper and gave it to her. 'That's the London number. I want Sir David Taggart in person.'

'What if this . . . Taggart . . . won't accept the call?'

I grinned. 'I have a feeling that Sir David will accept any call coming from Iceland right now.'

Elin looked up at the radio mast. 'The big set in the hut will give us more power.'

I shook my head. 'Don't use it – Slade might be monitoring the telephone bands. He can listen to what I have to say to Taggart but he mustn't know where it's coming from. A call from the Land-Rover could be coming from anywhere.'

Elin walked over to the Land-Rover, switched on that set and tried to raise Gufunes. The only result was a crackle of static through which a few lonely souls wailed like damned spirits, too drowned by noise to be understandable. 'There must be storms in the western mountains,' she said. 'Should I try Akureyri?' That was the nearest of the four radio-telephone stations.

'No,' I said. 'If Slade is monitoring at all he'll be concentrating on Akureyri. Try Seydisfjördur.'

Contacting Seydisfjördur in eastern Iceland was much easier and Elin was soon patched into the landline network to Reykjavik and spoke to her telephone friend, Svein. There was a fair amount of incredulous argument but she got her way. 'There's a delay of an hour,' she said.

'Good enough. Ask Seydisfjördur to contact us when the call comes through.' I looked at my watch. In an hour it would be 3.45 p.m. British Standard Time – a good hour to catch Taggart.

We packed up and we pushed south towards the distant ice blink of Vatnajökull. I left the receiver switched on but turned it low and there was a subdued babble from the speaker.

Elin said, 'What good will it do to speak to this man Taggart?'

'He's Slade's boss,' I said. 'He can get Slade off my back.'

'But will he?' she asked. 'You were supposed to hand over the package and you didn't. You disobeyed orders. Will Taggart like that?'

'I don't think Taggart knows what's going on here. I don't think he knows that Slade tried to kill me – and you. I think Slade is working on his own, and he's out on a limb. I could be wrong, of course, but that's one of the things I want to get from Taggart.'

'And if you are wrong? If Taggart instructs you to give the package to Slade? Will you do it?'

I hesitated. 'I don't know.'

Elin said, 'Perhaps Graham was right. Perhaps Slade really thought you'd defected – you must admit he would have every right to think so. Would he then . . .?'

'Send a man with a gun? He would.'

'Then I think you've been stupid, Alan; very, very stupid. I think you've allowed your hatred of Slade to cloud your judgement, and I think you're in very great trouble.'

I was beginning to think so myself. I said, 'I'll find that out when I talk to Taggart. If he backs Slade . . .' If Taggart backed Slade then I was Johnny-in-the-middle in danger of being squeezed between the Department and the opposition. The Department doesn't like its plans being messed around, and the wrath of Taggart would be mighty.

And yet there were things that didn't fit – the pointlessness of the whole exercise in the first place. Slade's lack of any real animosity when I apparently boobed, the ambivalence of Graham's role. And there was something else which prickled at the back of my mind but which I could not bring to the surface. Something which Slade had done or had not done, or had said or had not said – something which had rung a warning bell deep in my unconscious.

I braked and brought the Land-Rover to a halt, and Elin looked at me in surprise. I said, 'I'd better know what cards I hold before I talk to Taggart. Dig out the can-opener – I'm going to open the package.'

'Is that wise? You said yourself that it might be better not to know.'

'You may be right. But if you play stud poker without looking at your hole card you'll probably lose. I think I'd better know what it is that everyone wants so much.'

I got out and went to the rear bumper where I stripped the tape from the metal box and pulled it loose. When I got back behind the wheel Elin already had the can-opener – I think she was really as curious as I was.

The box was made of ordinary shiny metal of the type used for cans, but it was now flecked with a few rust spots due to its exposure. A soldered seam ran along four edges so I presumed that face to be the top. I tapped and pressed experimentally and found that the top flexed a little more under pressure than any of the other five sides, so it was probably safe to stab the blade of the can-opener into it.

I took a deep breath and jabbed the metal blade into one corner and heard the hiss of air as the metal was penetrated. That indicated that the contents had been vacuum-packed and I hoped I wasn't going to end up with a couple of pounds of pipe tobacco. The belated thought came to me that it could have been booby-trapped; there are detonators that operate on air pressure and that sudden equalization could have made the bloody thing blow up in my face.

But it hadn't, so I took another deep breath and began to lever the can-opener. Luckily it was one of the old-fashioned type that didn't need a rim to operate against; it made a jagged, sharp-edged cut – a really messy job – but it opened up the box inside two minutes.

I took off the top and looked inside and saw a piece of brown, shiny plastic with a somewhat electrical look about it – you can see bits of it in any radio repair shop. I tipped the contents of the box into the palm of my hand and looked at the gadget speculatively and somewhat hopelessly.

The piece of brown plastic was the base plate for an electronic circuit, a very complex one. I recognized resistors and transistors but most of it was incomprehensible. It had been a long time since I had studied radio and the technological avalanche of advances had long since passed me by. In my day a component was a component, but the micro-circuitry boys are now putting an entire and complicated circuit with dozens of components on to a chip of silicon you'd need a microscope to see.

'What is it?' asked Elin with sublime faith that I would know the answer.

'I'm damned if I know,' I admitted. I looked closer and tried to trace some of the circuits but it was impossible. Part of it was of modular construction with plates of printed circuits set on edge, each plate bristled with dozens of components; elsewhere it was of more conventional design, and set in the middle was a curious metal shape for which there was no accounting – not by me, anyway.

The only thing that made sense were the two ordinary screw terminals at the end of the base plate with a small engraved brass plate screwed over them. One terminal was marked '+' and the other '−', and above was engraved, '110 v. 60 ~'. I said, 'That's an American voltage and frequency. In England we use 240 volts and 50 cycles. Let's assume that's the input end.'

'So whatever it is it's American.'

'Possibly American,' I said cautiously. There was no power pack and the two terminals were not connected so presumably it would do what it was supposed to do when a 110 volt, 60 cycle current was applied across those terminals. But what it would do I had no idea at all.

Whatever kind of a whatsit it was, it was an advanced whatsit. The electronic whiz-kids have gone so far and fast that this dohickey, small enough to fit in the palm of my hand, could very well be an advanced computer capable of proving that $e = mc^2$ or alternatively, disproving it.

It could also have been something that a whiz-kid might have jack-legged together to cool his coffee, but I didn't think so. It didn't have the jack-leg look about it; it was coolly professional, highly sophisticated and had the air of coming off a very long production line – a production line in a building without windows and guarded by hard-faced men with guns.

I said thoughtfully, 'Is Lee Nordlinger still at the base at Keflavik?'

'Yes,' said Elin. 'I saw him two weeks ago.'

I poked at the gadget. 'He's the only man in Iceland who might have the faintest idea of what this is.'

'Are you going to show it to him?'

'I don't know,' I said slowly. 'He might recognize it as a piece of missing US government property and, since he's a commander in the US Navy, he might think he has to take action. After all, I'm not supposed to have it, and there'd be a lot of questions.'

I put the gadget back into its box, laid the lid on top and taped it into place. 'I don't think this had better go underneath again now that I've opened it.'

'Listen!' said Elin. 'That's our number.'

I reached up and twisted the volume control and the voice became louder. 'Seydisfjördur calling seven, zero, five; Seydisfjördur calling seven, zero, five.'

I unhooked the handset. 'Seven, zero, five answering Seydisfjördur.'

'Seydisfjördur calling seven, zero, five; your call to London has come through. I am connecting.'

'Thank you, Seydisfjördur.'

The characteristics of the noise coming through the speaker changed suddenly and a very faraway voice said, 'David Taggart here. Is that you, Slade?'

I said, 'I'm speaking on an open line – a very open line. Be careful.'

There was a pause, then Taggart said, 'I understand. Who is speaking? This is a very bad line.'

He was right, it was a bad line. His voice advanced and receded in volume and was mauled by an occasional burst of static. I said, 'This is Stewart here.'

An indescribable noise erupted from the speaker. It could have been static but more likely it was Taggart having an apoplexy. 'What the hell do you think you're doing?' he roared.

I looked at Elin and winced. From the sound of that it appeared that Taggart was not on my side, but it remained to be found if he backed Slade. He was going full blast. 'I talked to Slade this morning. He said you . . . er . . . tried to terminate his contract.' Another useful euphemism. 'And what's happened to Philips?'

'Who the hell is Philips?' I interjected.

'Oh! You might know him better as Buchner – or Graham.'

'His contract I did terminate,' I said.

'For Christ's sake!' yelled Taggart. 'Have you gone out of your mind?'

'I got in first just before he tried to terminate my contract,' I said. 'The competition is awful here in Iceland. Slade sent him.'

'Slade tells it differently.'

'I'll bet he does,' I said. 'Either he's gone off his rocker or he's joined a competing firm. I came across some of their representatives over here, too.'

'Impossible!' said Taggart flatly.

'The competing representatives?'

'No – Slade. It's unthinkable.'

'How can it be unthinkable when I'm thinking it?' I said reasonably.

'He's been with us so long. You know the good work he's done.'

'Maclean,' I said. 'Burgess, Kim Philby, Blake, the Krogers, Lonsdale – all good men and true. What's wrong with adding Slade?'

Taggart's voice got an edge to it. 'This is an open line – watch your language. Stewart, you don't know the score. Slade says you still have the merchandise – is that true?'

'Yes,' I admitted.

Taggart breathed hard. 'Then you must go back to Akureyri. I'll fix it so that Slade finds you there. Let him have it.'

'The only thing I'll let Slade have is a final dismissal notice,' I said. 'The same thing I gave Graham – or whatever his name was.'

'You mean you're not going to obey orders?' said Taggart dangerously.

'Not so far as Slade is concerned,' I said. 'When Slade sent Graham my fiancée happened to be in the way.'

There was a long pause before Taggart said in a more conciliatory tone, 'Did anything ...? Is she ...?'

'She's got a hole in her,' I said baldly, and not giving a damn if it was an open line. 'Keep Slade away from me, Taggart.'

He had been called Sir David for so long that he didn't relish the unadorned sound of his own name, and it took some time for him to swallow it. At last he said, in a subdued voice, 'So you won't accept Slade?'

'I wouldn't accept Slade with a packet of Little Noddy's Rice Crispies. I don't trust him.'

'Who would you accept?'

That I had to think about. It had been a long time since I had been with the Department and I didn't know what the turnover had been. Taggart said, 'Would you accept Case?'

Case was a good man; I knew him and trusted him as far as I'd trust anyone in the Department. 'I'll accept Jack Case.'

'Where will you meet him? And when?'

I figured out the logic of time and distance. 'At Geysir – five p.m. the day after tomorrow.'

Taggart was silent and all I heard were the waves of static beating against my eardrum. Then he said, 'Can't be done – I still have to get him back here. Make it twenty-four hours later.' He slipped in a fast one. 'Where are you now?'

I grinned at Elin. 'Iceland.'

Even the distortion could not disguise the rasp in Taggart's voice; he sounded like a concrete-mixer. 'Stewart, I hope you know that you're well on your way to ruining a most important operation. When you meet Case you take your orders from him and you'll do precisely as he says. Understand?'

'He'd better not have Slade with him,' I said. 'Or all bets are off. Are you putting your dog on a leash, Taggart?'

'All right,' said Taggart reluctantly. 'I'll pull him back to London. But you're wrong about him, Stewart. Look what he did to Kennikin in Sweden.'

It happened so suddenly that I gasped. The irritant that had been festering at the back of my mind came to the surface and it was like a bomb going off. 'I want some information,' I said quickly. 'I might need it if I'm to do this job properly.'

'All right; what is it?' said Taggart impatiently.

'What have you got on file about Kennikin's drinking habits?'

'What the hell!' he roared. 'Are you trying to be funny?'

'I need the information,' I repeated patiently. I had Taggart by the short hairs and he knew it. I had the electronic gadget and he didn't know where I was. I was bargaining from strength and I didn't think he'd hold back apparently irrelevant information just to antagonize me. But he tried.

'It'll take time,' he said. 'Ring me back.'

'Now *you're* being funny,' I said. 'You have so many computers around you that electrons shoot out of your ears. All you have to do is to push a button and you'll have the answer in two minutes. Push it!'

'All right,' he said in an annoyed voice. 'Hold on.' He had every right to be annoyed – the boss isn't usually spoken to in that way.

I could imagine what was going on. The fast, computer-controlled retrieval of microfilm combined with the wonders of closed circuit television would put the answer on to the screen on his desk in much less than two minutes providing the right coding was dialled. Every known member of the opposition was listed in that microfilm together with every known fact about him, so that his life was spread out like a butterfly pinned in a glass case. Apparent irrelevancies about a man could come in awfully useful if known at the right time or in the right place.

Presently Taggart said in a dim voice, 'I've got it.' The static was much worse and he was very far away. 'What do you want to know?'

'Speak up – I can hardly hear you. I want to know about his drinking habits.'

Taggart's voice came through stronger, but not much. 'Kennikin seems to be a bit of a puritan. He doesn't drink and, since his last encounter with you, he doesn't go out with women.' His voice was sardonic. 'Apparently you ruined him for the only pleasure in his life. You'd better watch . . .' The rest of the sentence was washed out in noise.

'What was that?' I shouted.

Taggart's voice came through the crashing static like a thin ghost. '. . . best of . . . knowledge . . . Kenni . . . Iceland . . . he's . . .'

And that was all I got, but it was enough. I tried unavailingly to restore the connection but nothing could be done. Elin pointed to the sky in the west which was black with cloud. 'The storm is moving east; you won't get anything more until it's over.'

I put the handset back in its clip. 'That bastard, Slade!' I said. 'I was right.'

'What do you mean?' asked Elin.

I looked at the clouds which were beginning to boil over Dyngjufjöll. 'I'd like to get off this track,' I said. 'We have twenty-four hours to waste and I'd rather do it right here. Let's get up into Askja before that storm really breaks.'

Chapter Four

I

The great caldera of Askja is beautiful – but not in a storm. The wind lashed the waters of the crater lake far below and someone, possibly old Odin, pulled the plug out of the sky so that the rain fell in sheets and wind-driven curtains. It was impossible to get down to the lake until the water-slippery ash had dried out so I pulled off the track and we stayed right there, just inside the crater wall.

Some people I know get jumpy even at the thought of being inside the crater of what is, after all, a live volcano; but Askja had said his piece very loudly in 1961 and would probably be quiet for a while apart from a few minor exuberancies. Statistically speaking, we were fairly safe. I put up the top of the Land-Rover so as to get headroom, and presently there were lamb chops under the grill and eggs spluttering in the pan, and we were dry, warm and comfortable.

While Elin fried the eggs I checked the fuel situation. The tank held sixteen gallons and we carried another eighteen gallons in four jerrycans, enough for over 600 miles on good roads. But we weren't on good roads and, in the *Obyggdir*, we'd be lucky to get even ten miles from a gallon. The gradients and the general roughness meant a lot of low gear work and that swallows fuel greedily, and the nearest filling station was a long way south. Still, I reckoned we'd have enough to get to Geysir.

Miraculously, Elin produced two bottles of Carlsberg from the refrigerator, and I filled a glass gratefully. I watched her as she spooned melted fat over the eggs and thought she looked pale and withdrawn. 'How's the shoulder?'

'Stiff and tender,' she said.

It would be. I said, 'I'll put another dressing on it after supper.' I drank from the glass and felt the sharp tingle of cold beer. 'I wish I could have kept you out of this, Elin.'

She turned her head and offered me a brief smile. 'But you haven't.' With a dextrous twist of a spatula she lifted an egg on to a plate. 'I can't say I'm enjoying it much, though.'

'Entertainment isn't the object,' I said.

She put the plate down before me. 'Why did you ask about Kennikin's drinking habits? It seems pointless.'

'That goes back a long way,' I said. 'As a very young man Kennikin fought in Spain on the Republican side, and when that war was lost he lived in France for a while, stirring things up for Léon Blum's Popular Front, but I think even then he was an undercover man. Anyway, it was there he picked up a taste for Calvados – the Normandy applejack. Got any salt?'

Elin passed the salt cellar. 'I think maybe he had a drinking problem at one time and decided to cut it out because, as far as the Department is aware, he's a non-drinker. You heard Taggart on that.'

Elin began to cut into a loaf of bread. 'I don't see the point of all this,' she complained.

'I'm coming to it. Like a lot of men with an alcohol problem he can keep off the stuff for months at a time, but when the going becomes tough and the pressures build up then he goes on a toot. And, by God, there are enough tensions in our line of work. But the point is that he's a secret drinker; I only found out when I got next to him in Sweden. I visited him unexpectedly and found him cut to the eyeballs on Calvados – it's the only stuff he inhales. He was drunk enough to talk about it, too. Anyway, I poured him into bed and tactfully made my exit, and he never referred to the incident again when I was with him.'

I accepted a piece of bread and dabbed at the yolk of an egg. 'When an agent goes back to the Department after a job he is de-briefed thoroughly and by experts. That happened to me when I got back from Sweden, but because I was raising a stink about what had happened to Jimmy Birkby maybe the de-briefing wasn't as thorough as it should have been, and the fact that Kennikin drinks never got put on record. It still isn't on record, as I've just found out.'

'I still don't see the point,' said Elin helplessly.

'I'm just about to make it,' I said. 'When Slade came to see me in Scotland he told me of the way I had wounded Kennikin, and made the crack that Kennikin would rather operate on me with a sharp knife than offer to split a bottle of Calvados. How in the hell would Slade know about the Calvados? He's never been within a hundred miles of Kennikin and the fact isn't on file in the Department. It's been niggling at me for a long time, but the penny only dropped this afternoon.'

Elin sighed. 'It's a very small point.'

'Have you ever witnessed a murder trial? The point which can hang a man can be very small. But add this to it – the Russians took a package which they presumably discovered to be a fake. You'd expect them to come after the real thing, wouldn't you? But who did come after it, and with blood in his eyes? None other than friend Slade.'

'You're trying to make out a case that Slade is a Russian agent,' said Elin. 'But it won't work. Who was really responsible for the destruction of Kennikin's network in Sweden?'

'Slade master-minded it,' I said. 'He pointed me in the right direction and pulled the trigger.'

Elin shrugged. 'Well, then? Would a Russian agent do that to his own side?'

'Slade's a big boy now,' I said. 'Right next to Taggart in a very important area of British Intelligence. He even lunches with the Prime Minister – he told me so. How important would it be to the Russians to get a man into that position?'

Elin looked at me as though I'd gone crazy. I said quietly, 'Whoever planned this has a mind like a pretzel, but it's all of a piece. Slade is in a top slot in British Intelligence – but how did he get there? Answer – by wrecking the Russian organization in Sweden. Which is more important to the Russians? To retain their

Swedish network – which could be replaced if necessary? Or to put Slade where he is now?'

I tapped the table with the handle of my knife. 'You can see the same twisted thinking throughout. Slade put me next to Kennikin by sacrificing Birkby; the Russkies put Slade next to Taggart by sacrificing Kennikin and his outfit.'

'But this is silly!' burst out Elin. 'Why would Slade have to go to all that trouble with Birkby and you when the Russians would be co-operating with him anyway?'

'Because it had to look good,' I said. 'The operation would be examined by men with very hard eyes and there had to be real blood, not tomato ketchup – no fakery at all. The blood was provided by poor Birkby – and Kennikin added some to it.' A sudden thought struck me. 'I wonder if Kennikin knew what was going on? I'll bet his organization was blasted from under him – the poor bastard wouldn't know his masters were selling him out just to bring Slade up a notch.' I rubbed my chin. 'I wonder if he's still ignorant of that?'

'This is all theory,' said Elin. 'Things don't happen that way.'

'Don't they? My God, you only have to read the *published* accounts of some of the spy trials to realize that bloody funny things happen. Do you know why Blake got a sentence of forty-two years in jail?'

She shook her head. 'I didn't read about it.'

'You won't find it in print, but the rumour around the Department was that forty-two was the number of our agents who came to a sticky end because he'd betrayed them. I wouldn't know the truth of it because he was in a different outfit – but think of what Slade could do!'

'So you can't trust anyone,' said Elin. 'What a life to lead!'

'It's not as bad as that. I trust Taggart to a point – and I trust Jack Case, the man I'm meeting at Geysir. But Slade is different; he's become careless and made two mistakes – one about the Calvados, and the other in coming after the package himself.'

Elin laughed derisively. 'And the only reason you trust Taggart and Case is because they've made no mistakes, as you call them?'

'Let me put it this way,' I said. 'I've killed Graham, a British Intelligence agent, and so I'm in a hot spot. The only way I can get out of it is to prove that Slade is a Russian agent. If I can do that I'll be a bloody hero and the record will be wiped clean. And it helps a lot that I hate Slade's guts.'

'But what if you're wrong?'

I put as much finality into my voice as I could. 'I'm not wrong,' I said, and hoped it was true. 'We've had a long hard day, Elin; but we can rest tomorrow. Let me put a dressing on your shoulder.'

As I smoothed down the last piece of surgical tape, she said, 'What did you make of what Taggart said just before the storm came?'

I didn't like to think of that. 'I think,' I said carefully, 'that he was telling me that Kennikin is in Iceland.'

II

Tired though I was after a hard day's driving I slept badly. The wind howled from the west across the crater of Askja, buffeting the Land-Rover until it rocked on its springs, and the heavy rain drummed against the side. Once I heard a clatter as though something metallic had moved and I got up to investigate only to find nothing of consequence and got drenched to the skin for my pains. At last I fell into a heavy sleep, shot through with bad dreams.

Still, I felt better in the morning when I got up and looked out. The sun was shining and the lake was a deep blue reflecting the cloudless sky, and in the clear, rain-washed air the far side of the crater seemed a mere kilometre away instead of the ten kilometres it really was. I put water to boil for coffee and when it was ready I leaned over and dug Elin gently in the ribs.

'Umph!' she said indistinctly, and snuggled deeper in the sleeping bag. I prodded her again and one blue eye opened and looked at me malignantly through tumbled blonde hair. 'Stop it!'

'Coffee,' I said, and waved the cup under her nose.

She came to life and clutched the cup with both hands. I took my coffee and a jug of hot water and went outside where I laid my shaving kit on the bonnet and began to whisk up a lather. After shaving, I thought, it would be nice to go down to the lake and clean up. I was beginning to feel grubby – the *Odádahraun* is a dusty place – and the thought of clean water was good.

I finished scraping my face and, as I rinsed the lather away, I ran through in my mind the things I had to do, the most important of which was to contact Taggart as soon as it was a reasonable hour to find him in his office. I wanted to give him the detailed case against Slade.

Elin came up with the coffee pot. 'More?'

'Thanks,' I said, holding out my cup. 'We'll have a lazy day.' I nodded towards the lake at the bottom of the crater. 'Fancy a swim?'

She pulled a face and moved her wounded shoulder. 'I can't do the crawl, but perhaps I can paddle with one arm.' She looked up at the sky, and said, 'It's a lovely day.'

I watched her face change. 'What's the matter?'

'The radio antenna,' she said. 'It's not there.'

I whirled around. 'Damn!' That was very bad. I climbed up and looked at the damage. It was easy to see what had happened. The rough ground in Central Iceland is enough to shake anything loose that isn't welded down; nuts you couldn't shift with a wrench somehow loosen themselves and wind off the bolts; split-pins jump out, even rivets pop. A whip antenna with its swaying motion is particularly vulnerable; I know one geologist who lost three in a month. The question here was when did we lose it?

It was certainly after I had spoken to Taggart, so it might have gone during the mad dash for Askja when we raced the storm. But I remembered the metallic clatter I had heard during the night; the antenna might have been swept away by the strong wind. I said, 'It may be around here – quite close. Let's look.'

But we didn't get that far because I heard a familiar sound – the drone of a small aircraft. 'Get down!' I said quickly. 'Keep still and don't look up.'

We dropped flat next to the Land-Rover as the light plane came over the edge of the crater wall flying low. As it cleared the edge it dipped down into the crater to our left. I said, 'Whatever you do, don't lift your head. Nothing stands out so much as a white face.'

The plane flew low over the lake and then turned, spiralling out in a search pattern to survey the interior of the crater. It looked to me like a four-seater Cessna from the brief glimpse I got of it. The Land-Rover was parked in a jumble of big rocks, split into blocks of ice and water, and maybe it wouldn't show up too well from the air providing there was no movement around it.

Elin said quietly, 'Do you think it's someone looking for us?'

'We'll have to assume so,' I said. 'It could be a charter plane full of tourists looking at the *Obyggdir* from the air, but it's a bit early in the day for that – tourists aren't awake much before nine o'clock.'

This was a development I hadn't thought of. Damn it, Slade was right; I *was* out of practice. Tracks in the *Obyggdir* are few and it would be no great effort to keep them under surveillance from the air and to direct ground transport by radio. The fact that my Land-Rover was the long wheelbase type would make identification easier – there weren't many of those about.

The plane finished quartering the crater and climbed again, heading north-west. I watched it go but made no move. Elin said, 'Do you think we were seen?'

'I don't know that, either. Stop asking unanswerable questions – and don't move because it may come back for another sweep.'

I gave it five minutes and used the time to figure out what to do next. There would be no refreshing swim in the lake, that was certain. Askja was as secluded a place as anywhere in Iceland but it had one fatal flaw – the track into the crater was a spur from the main track – a dead end – and if anyone blocked the way out of the crater there'd be no getting past, not with the Land-Rover. And I didn't have any illusions about the practicability of going anywhere on foot – you can get very dead that way in the *Obyggdir*.

'We're getting out of here fast,' I said. 'I want to be on the main track where we have some choice of action. Let's move!'

'Breakfast?'

'Breakfast can wait.'

'And the radio antenna?'

I paused, indecisive and exasperated. We *needed* that antenna – I had to talk to Taggart – but if we had been spotted from the air then a car full of guns could be speeding towards Askja, and I didn't know how much time we had in hand. The antenna could be close by but, on the other hand, it might have dropped off somewhere up the track and miles away.

I made the decision. 'The hell with it! Let's go.'

There was no packing to do beyond collecting the coffee cups and my shaving kit and within two minutes we were climbing the narrow track on the way out of Askja. It was ten kilometres to the main track and when we got there I was sweating for fear of what I might find, but nothing was stirring. I turned right and we headed south.

An hour later I pulled up where the track forked. On the left ran the *Jökulsá á Fjöllum*, now near its source and no longer the mighty force it displayed at Dettifoss. I said, 'We'll have breakfast here.'

'Why here particularly?'

I pointed to the fork ahead. 'We have a three-way choice – we can go back or take either of those tracks. If that plane is going to come back and spot us I'd just as soon he did it here. He can't stay up there forever so we wait him out before we move on and leave him to figure which way we went.'

While Elin was fixing breakfast I took the rifle and unloaded it and looked down the bore. This was no way to treat a good gun; not to clean it after shooting. Fortunately, modern powder is no longer violently corrosive and a day's wait before cleaning no longer such a heinous offence. Besides, I had neither gun oil nor solvent and engine oil would have to do.

I checked the ammunition after cleaning the rifle. Graham had loaded from a packet of twenty-five; he had shot one and I had popped off three at Slade – twenty-one rounds left. I set the sights of the rifle at a hundred yards. I didn't think that if things came to the crunch I'd be shooting at much over that range. Only film heroes can take a strange gun and unknown ammunition and drop the baddy at 500 yards.

I put the rifle where I could get at it easily and caught a disapproving glance from Elin. 'Well, what do you expect me to do?' I said defensively. 'Start throwing rocks?'

'I didn't say anything,' she said.

'No, you didn't,' I agreed. 'I'm going down to the river to clean up. Give me a shout when you're ready.'

But first I climbed a small knoll from where I could get a good view of the surrounding country. Nothing moved for as far as I could see, and in Iceland you usually see a hell of a long way. Satisfied, I went down to the river which was the milky grey-green colour of melt water and shockingly cold, but after the first painful gasp it wasn't too bad. Refreshed, I went back to tuck into breakfast.

Elin was looking at the map. 'Which way are you going?'

'I want to get between Hofsjökull and Vatnajökull,' I said. 'So we take the left fork.'

'It's a one-way track,' said Elin and passed me the map.

True enough. Printed in ominous red alongside the dashed line which denoted the track was the stern injunction : *Adeins faert til austurs* – eastward travel only. We wanted to go west.

I frowned. Most people think that because Greenland is covered with ice and is wrongly named then so is Iceland, and there's not much ice about the place. They're dead wrong. Thirty-six icefields glaciate one-eighth of the country and one of them alone – Vatnajökull – is as big as all the glaciated areas in Scandinavia and the Alps put together.

The cold wastes of Vatnajökull lay just to the south of us and the track to the west was squeezed right up against it by the rearing bulk of Trölladyngja – the Dome of Trolls – a vast shield volcano. I had never been that way before but I had a good idea why the track was one way only. It would cling to the sides of cliffs and be full of hair-pin blind bends – quite hairy enough to negotiate without the unnerving possibility of running into someone head on.

I sighed and examined other possibilities. The track to the right would take us north, the opposite direction to which I wanted to go. More damaging, to get back again would triple the mileage. The geography of Iceland has its own ruthless logic about what is and what is not permitted and the choice of routes is restricted.

I said, 'We'll take our chances going the short way and hope to God we don't meet anyone. It's still early in the season and the chances are good.' I grinned at Elin. 'I don't think there'll be any police around to issue a traffic ticket.'

'And there'll be no ambulance to pick us up from the bottom of a cliff,' she said.

'I'm a careful driver; it may never happen.'

Elin went down to the river and I walked to the top of the knoll again. Everything was quiet. The track stretched back towards Askja and there was no tell-tale cloud of dust to indicate a pursuing vehicle, nor any mysterious aircraft buzzing about the sky. I wondered if I was letting my imagination get the better of me. Perhaps I was running away from nothing.

The guilty flee where no man pursueth. I was as guilty as hell! I had withheld the package from Slade on nothing more than intuition – a hunch Taggart found difficult to believe. And I had killed Graham! As far as the Department was concerned I would already have been judged, found guilty and sentenced, and I wondered what would be the attitude of Jack Case when I saw him at Geysir.

I saw Elin returning to the Land-Rover so I took one last look around and went down to her. Her hair was damp and her cheeks glowed pink as she scrubbed her face with a towel. I waited until she emerged, then said, 'You're in this as much as I am now, so you've got a vote. What do you think I should do?'

She lowered the towel and looked at me thoughtfully. 'I should do exactly what you are doing. You've made the plan. Meet this man at Geysir and give him that . . . that whatever-it-is.'

I nodded. 'And what if someone should try to stop us?'

She hesitated. 'If it is Slade, then give him the gadget. If it is Kennikin . . .' She stopped and shook her head slowly.

I saw her reasoning. I might be able to hand over to Slade and get away unscathed; but Kennikin would not be satisfied with

293

that – he'd want my blood. I said, 'Supposing it is Kennikin – what would you expect me to do?'

She drooped. 'I think you would want to fight him – to use that rifle. You would want to kill him.' Her voice was desolate.

I took her by the arm. 'Elin, I don't kill people indiscriminately. I'm not a psychopath. I promise there will be no killing unless it is in self-defence; unless my life is in danger – or yours.'

'I'm sorry, Alan,' she said. 'But a situation like this is so alien to me. I've never had to face anything like it.'

I waved towards the knoll. 'I was doing a bit of thinking up there. It occurred to me that perhaps my assessment of everything has been wrong – that I've misjudged people and events.'

'No!' she said definitely. 'You've made a strong case against Slade.'

'And yet you would want me to give him the gadget?'

'What is it to me?' she cried. 'Or to you? Let him have it when the time comes – let us go back to living our own lives.'

'I'd like to do that very much,' I said. 'If people would let me.' I looked up at the sun which was already high. 'Come on; let's be on our way.'

As we drove towards the fork I glanced at Elin's set face and sighed. I could quite understand her attitude, which was that of any other Icelander. Long gone are the days when the Vikings were the scourge of Europe, and the Icelanders have lived in isolation for so many years that the affairs of the rest of the world must seem remote and alien.

Their only battle had been to regain their political independence from Denmark and that was achieved by peaceful negotiation. True, they are not so isolated that their economy is separated from world trade – far from it – but trade is trade and war, whether open or covert, is something for other crazy people and not for sober, sensible Icelanders.

They are so confident that no one can envy their country enough to seize it that they have no armed forces. After all, if the Icelanders with their thousand years of experience behind them still find it most difficult to scratch a living out of the country then who else in his right mind would want it?

A peaceful people with no first-hand knowledge of war. It was hardly surprising that Elin found the shenanigans in which I was involved distasteful and dirty. I didn't feel too clean myself.

III

The track was bad.

It was bad right from where we had stopped and it got steadily worse after we had left the river and began to climb under Vatna-jökull. I crunched down into a low gear and went into four-wheel drive as the track snaked its way up the cliffs, doubling back on itself so often that I had a zany idea I might drive into my own rear. It was wide enough only for one vehicle and I crept around each corner hoping to God that no one was coming the other way.

Once there was a slide of rubble sideways and I felt the Land-Rover slip with rear wheels spinning towards the edge of a sheer drop. I poured on the juice and hoped for the best. The front wheels held their grip and hauled us to safety. Soon after that I stopped on a reasonably straight bit, and when I took my hands from the wheel they were wet with sweat.

I wiped them dry. 'This is bloody tricky.'

'Shall I drive for a while?' asked Elin.

I shook my head. 'Not with your bad shoulder. Besides, it's not the driving – it's the expectation of meeting someone around every corner.' I looked over the edge of the cliff. 'One of us would have to reverse out and that's a flat impossibility.' That was the best that could happen; the worst didn't bear thinking about. No wonder this track was one way only.

'I could walk ahead,' Elin said. 'I can check around the corners and guide you.'

'That would take all day,' I objected. 'And we've a long way to go.'

She jerked her thumb downwards. 'Better than going down there. Besides, we're not moving at much more than a walking pace as it is. I can stand on the front bumper while we go on the straight runs and jump off at the corners.'

It was an idea that had its points but I didn't like it much. 'It won't do your shoulder much good.'

'I can use the other arm,' she said impatiently, and opened the door to get out.

At one time in England there was a law to the effect that every mechanically propelled vehicle on the public highway must be preceded by a man on foot bearing a red flag to warn the unwary citizenry of the juggernaut bearing down upon them. I had never expected to be put in the same position, but that's progress.

Elin would ride the bumper until we approached a corner and jump off as I slowed down. Slowing down was no trick at all, even going downhill; all I had to do was to take my foot off the accelerator. I had dropped into the lowest gear possible which, on a Land-Rover is something wondrous. That final drive ratio of about 40 : 1 gives a lot of traction and a lot of engine braking. Driven flat out when cranked as low as that the old girl would make all of nine miles an hour when delivering ninety-five horsepower – and a hell of a lot of traction was just what I needed on that Icelandic roller-coaster. But it was hell on fuel consumption.

So Elin would guide me around a corner and then ride the bumper to the next one. It sounds as though it might have been a slow job but curiously enough we seemed to make better time. We went on in this dot-and-carry-one manner for quite a long way and then Elin held up her hand and pointed, not down the track but away in the air to the right. As she started to hurry back I twisted my neck to see what she had seen.

A helicopter was coming over Trölladyngja like a grasshopper, the sun making a spinning disc of its rotor and striking reflections from the greenhouse which designers put on choppers for their own weird reasons. I've flown by helicopter on many occasions and on a sunny day you feel like a ripening tomato under glass.

But I wasn't thinking about that right then because Elin had came up on the wrong side of the Land-Rover. 'Get to the other side,' I shouted. 'Get under cover.' I dived out of the door on the other side where the cliff face was.

She joined me. 'Trouble?'

'Could be.' I held open the door and grabbed the carbine. 'We've seen no vehicles so far, but two aircraft have been interested in us. That seems unnatural.'

I peered around the rear end of the Land-Rover, keeping the gun out of sight. The helicopter was still heading towards us and losing height. When it was quite close the nose came up and it bobbed and curtsied in the air as it came to a hovering stop about a hundred yards away. Then it came down like a lift until it was level with us.

I sweated and gripped the carbine. Sitting on a ledge we were like ducks in a shooting gallery, and all that was between us and any bullets was the Land-Rover. It's a stoutly built vehicle but at that moment I wished it was an armoured car. The chopper ducked and swayed and regarded us interestedly, but I could see no human movement beyond the reflections echoed from the glass of the cockpit.

Then the fuselage began to rotate slowly until it was turned broadside on, and I let out my breath in a long sigh. Painted in large letters along the side was the single word – NAVY – and I relaxed, put down the carbine and went into the open. If there was one place where Kennikin would not be it was inside a US Navy Sikorsky LH-34 chopper.

I waved, and said to Elin, 'It's all right; you can come out.'

She joined me and we looked at the helicopter. A door in the side slid open and a crewman appeared wearing a white bone-dome helmet. He leaned out, holding on with one hand and made a whirling motion with the other and then put his fist to the side of his face. He did this two or three times before I tumbled to what he was doing.

'He want us to use the telephone,' I said. 'A pity we can't.' I climbed on top of the Land-Rover and pointed as eloquently as I could to where the whip antenna had been. The crewman caught on fast; he waved and drew himself back inside and the door closed. Within a few seconds the helicopter reared up and gained height, the fuselage turning until it was pointing south-west, and then away it went until it disappeared into the distance with a fading roar.

I looked at Elin. 'What do you suppose that was about?'

'It seemed they want to talk to you. Perhaps the helicopter will land farther down the track.'

'It certainly couldn't land here,' I said. 'Maybe you're right. I could do with a trip back to Keflavik in comfort.' I looked into the thin air into which the chopper had vanished. 'But nobody told me the Americans were in on this.'

Elin gave me a sidelong look. 'In on what?'

'I don't know, damn it! I wish to hell I did.' I retrieved the carbine. 'Let's get on with it.'

So on we went along that bastard of a track, round and round, up and down, but mostly up, until we had climbed right to the edge of Vatnajökull, next to the ice. The track could only go one way from there and that was away, so it turned at right-angles to the ice field and from then on the direction was mostly down. There was one more particularly nasty bit where we had to climb an outlying ridge of Trölladyngja but from then on the track improved and I called Elin aboard again.

I looked back the way we had come and was thankful for one

thing; it had been a bright, sunny day. If there had been mist or much rain it would have been impossible. I checked the map and found we were through the one-way section for which I was heartily thankful.

Elin looked tired. She had done a lot of walking over rough ground and a lot of jumping up and down, and her face was drawn. I checked the time, and said, 'We'll feel better after we've eaten, and hot coffee would go down well. We'll stop here a while.'

And that was a mistake.

I discovered it was a mistake two and a half hours later. We had rested for an hour and eaten, and then continued for an hour and a half until we came to a river which was brimming full. I pulled up at the water's edge where the track disappeared into the river, and got out to look at the problem.

I estimated the depth and looked at the dry stones in the banks. 'It's rising, damn it! If we hadn't stopped we could have crossed an hour ago. Now, I'm not so sure.'

Vatnajökull is well named the 'Water Glacier'. It dominates the river system of Eastern and Southern Iceland – a great reservoir of frozen water which, in slowly melting, covers the land with a network of rivers. I had been thankful it had been a sunny day, but now I was not so sure because sunny days mean full rivers. The best time to cross a glacier is at dawn when it is low. During the day, especially on a clear, sunny day, the melt water increases and the flow grows to a peak in the late afternoon. This particular river had not yet reached its peak but it was still too damned deep to cross.

Elin consulted the map. 'Where are you making for? Today, I mean.'

'I wanted to get to the main Sprengisandur route. That's more or less a permanent track; once we're on it getting to Geysir should be easy.'

She measured the distance. 'Sixty kilometres,' she said, and paused.

I saw her lips moving. 'What's the matter?'

She looked up, 'I was counting,' she said. 'Sixteen rivers to cross in that sixty kilometres before we hit the Sprengisandur track.'

'For Christ's sake!' I said. Normally in my travels in Iceland I had never been in a particular hurry to get anywhere. I had never counted the rivers and if an unfordable one had barred my path it was no great hardship to camp for a few hours until the level dropped. But the times were a-changing.

Elin said, 'We'll have to camp here.'

I looked at the river and knew I had to make up my mind quickly. 'I think we'll try to get over,' I said.

Elin looked at me blankly. 'But why? You won't be able to cross the others until tomorrow.'

I tossed a pebble into the water. If it made ripples I didn't see them because they were obliterated by the swift flowing current. I said, ' "By the pricking of my thumbs, something evil this way comes." ' I swung around and pointed back along the track. 'And I think it will come from that direction. If we have to stop I'd rather it was on the other side of this river.'

Elin looked doubtfully at the fast rip in the middle. 'It will be dangerous.'

'It might be more dangerous to stay here.' I had an uneasy feeling which, maybe, was no more than the automatic revulsion against being caught in a position from which it was impossible to run. It was the reason I had left Askja, and it was the reason I wanted to cross this river. Perhaps it was just my tactical sense sharpening up after lying dormant for so long. I said, 'And it'll be more dangerous to cross in fifteen minutes, so let's move it.'

I checked whether, in fact, the place where the track crossed the river was the most practicable. This turned out to be a waste of time but it had to be done. Anywhere upstream or downstream was impossible for various reasons, either deep water or high banks – so I concentrated on the ford and hoped the footing was sound.

Dropping again into the lowest gear possible I drove slowly into the river. The quick water swirled against the wheels and built up into waves which slapped against the side of the cab. Right in midstream the water was deep and any moment I expected to find it flowing under the door. More ominously the force of the water was so great that for one hair-raising second I felt the vehicle shift sideways and there was a curiously lifting lurch preparatory to being swept downstream.

I rammed my foot down and headed for shallower water and the opposite bank. The front wheels bit into the bed of the river but the back of the Land-Rover actually lifted and floated so that we got to the other side broadside on and climbed out awkwardly over a moss-crusted hummock of lava, streaming water like a shaggy dog just come from a swim.

I headed for the track and we bucked and lurched over the lava, and when we were finally on reasonably level ground I switched off the engine and looked at Elin. 'I don't think we'll cross any more rivers today. That one was enough. Thank God for four-wheel drive.'

She was pale. 'That was an unjustifiable risk,' she said. 'We could have been swept downsteam.'

'But we weren't,' I said, and switched on the engine again. 'How far to the next river? We'll camp there and cross at dawn.'

She consulted the map. 'About two kilometres.'

So we pushed on and presently came to river number two which was also swollen with sun-melted water from Vatnajökull. I turned the vehicle and headed towards a jumble of rocks behind which I parked, out of sight of both the river and the track – again on good tactical principles.

I was annoyed. It was still not very late and there were several hours of daylight which we could have used for mileage if it hadn't been for those damned rivers. But there was nothing for it but to wait until the next day when the flow would drop. I said, 'You look tired; you've had a hard day.'

Elin nodded dispiritedly and got out of the cab. I noticed her favouring her right arm, and said, 'How is the shoulder?'

She grimaced. 'Stiff.'

'I'd better take a look at it.'

I put up the collapsible top of the Land-Rover and set water to boil, and Elin sat on a bunk and tried to take off her sweater. She couldn't do it because she couldn't raise her right arm. I helped her take it off but, gentle though I was, she gasped in pain. Reasonably enough, she wasn't wearing a brassiere under the sweater because the shoulder strap would have cut right into the wound.

I took off the pad and looked at her shoulder. The wound was angry and inflamed but there was no sign of any pus which would indicate infection. I said, 'I told you that you'd begin to feel it. A graze like this can hurt like the devil, so don't be too stiff-upper-lipped about it – I know how it feels.'

She crossed her arms across her breasts. 'Has it ever happened to you?'

'I was grazed across the ribs once,' I said, as I poured warm water into a cup.

'So that's how you got that scar.'

'Yours is worse because it's across the trapezius muscle and you keep pulling it. You really should have your arm in a sling – I'll see what I can find.' I washed the wound and put on a new medical dressing from the first-aid box, then helped her put on the sweater. 'Where's your scarf – the new woollen one?'

She pointed. 'In that drawer.'

'Then that's your sling.' I took out the scarf and fitted it to her arm so as to immobilize the shoulder as much as possible. 'Now, you just sit there and watch me cook supper.'

I thought this was an appropriate time to open the goody box – the small collection of luxuries we kept for special occasions. We both needed cheering up and there's nothing like a first-class meal under the belt to lift the spirits. I don't know if Mr Fortnum and Mr Mason are aware of the joy they bring to sojourners in far-flung lands, but after the oyster soup, the whole roast quails and the pears pickled in cognac I felt almost impelled to write them a letter of appreciation.

The colour came back to Elin's cheeks as she ate. I insisted that she didn't use her right hand and she didn't have to – the dark, tender flesh fell away from the quail at the touch of a fork and she managed all right. I made coffee and we accompanied it with brandy which I carried for medicinal purposes.

As she sipped her coffee she sighed. 'Just like old times, Alan.'

'Yes,' I said lazily. I was feeling much better myself. 'But you'd better sleep. We make an early start tomorrow.' I calculated it would be light enough to move at three a.m. when the rivers would be at their lowest. I leaned over and took the binoculars.

'Where are you going?' she asked.

'Just to have a look around. You go to bed.'

Her eyes flickered sleepily. 'I *am* tired,' she admitted.

That wasn't surprising. We'd been on the run for a long time, and bouncing about in the *Obyggdir* wasn't helping – we'd managed to fall into every pothole on the track. I said, 'Get your head down – I won't be long.'

I hung the lanyard of the binoculars around my neck, opened the back door and dropped to the ground. I was about to walk away when I turned back on impulse, reached into the cab and picked up the carbine. I don't think Elin saw me do that.

First I inspected the river we had to cross. It was flowing well but exposed wet stone showed that the level was dropping. By dawn· crossing would be easy, and we should be able to get across all the other rivers that lay between us and Sprengisandur before the increased flow made it impossible.

I slung the carbine over my shoulder and walked back along the track towards the river we had crossed which lay a little over a mile away. I approached cautiously but everything was peaceful. The river flowed and chuckled and there was nothing in sight to cause alarm. I checked the distant view with the binoculars, then sat down with my back against a mossy boulder, lit a cigarette and started to think.

I was worried about Elin's shoulder; not that there was anything particularly alarming about its condition, but a doctor would do a better job than I could, and this bouncing about the wilderness wasn't helping. It might be difficult explaining to a doctor how Elin had come by an unmistakable gunshot wound, but accidents do happen and I thought I could get away with it by talking fast.

I stayed there for a couple of hours, smoking and thinking and looking at the river, and at the end of that time I had come up with nothing new despite my brain beating. The added factor of the American helicopter was a piece of the jigsaw that wouldn't fit anywhere. I looked at my watch and found it was after nine o'clock, so I buried all the cigarette stubs, picked up the carbine and prepared to go back.

As I stood up I saw something that made me tense – a plume of dust in the far distance across the river. I laid down the carbine and lifted the glasses and saw the little dot of a vehicle at the head of that feather of dust like a high-flying jet at the head of a contrail. I looked around – there was no cover near the river but about two hundred yards back a spasm of long gone energy had heaved up the lava into a ridge which I could hide behind. I ran for it.

The vehicle proved to be a Willys jeep – as good for this country in its way as my Land-Rover. It slowed as it came to the river, nosed forward and came to a stop at the water's edge. The night was quiet and I heard the click of the door handle as a man got out and walked forward to look at the water. He turned and said something to the driver and, although I could not hear the words, I knew he was speaking neither Icelandic nor English.

He spoke Russian.

The driver got out, looked at the water and shook his head. Presently there were four of them standing there, and they seemed to be having an argument. Another jeep came up behind and more men got out to study the problem until there were eight in all – two jeeps full. One of them, the one who made the decisive gestures and who seemed to be the boss, I thought I recognized.

I lifted the glasses and his face sprang into full view in the dimming light. Elin had been wrong; crossing the river had *not* been an unjustifiable risk, and the justification lay in the face I now saw. The scar was still there, running from the end of the right eyebrow to the corner of the mouth, and the eyes were still grey and hard as stones. The only change in him was that his close-cropped hair was no longer black but a grizzled grey and his face was puffier with incipient wattles forming on his neck.

Kennikin and I were both four years older but I think I may have worn better than he had.

Chapter Five

I

I put my hand out to the carbine and then paused. The light was bad and getting worse, the gun was strange and it hadn't the barrel to reach out and knock a man down at a distance. I estimated the range at a shade under three hundred yards and I knew that if I hit anyone at that range and in that light it would be by chance and not by intention.

If I had my own gun I could have dropped Kennikin as easily as dropping a deer. I have put a soft-nosed bullet into a deer and it has run for half a mile before dropping dead, and that with an exit wound big enough to put your fist in. A man can't do that – his nervous system is too delicate and can't stand the shock.

But I hadn't my own rifle, and there was no percentage in opening fire at random. That would only tell Kennikin I was close, and it might be better if he didn't know. So I let my fingers relax from the carbine and concentrated on watching what was going to happen next.

The arguing had stopped with Kennikin's arrival, and I knew why, having worked with him. He had no time for futile blathering; he would accept your facts – and God help you if you were wrong – and then he would make the decisions. He was busily engaged in making one now.

I smiled as I saw someone point out the tracks of the Land-Rover entering the water and then indicate the other bank of the river. There were no tracks where we had left the water because we had been swept sideways a little, and that must have been puzzling to anyone who hadn't seen it happen.

The man waved downstream eloquently but Kennikin shook his head. He wasn't buying that one. Instead he said something, snapping his fingers impatiently, and someone else rushed up with a map. He studied it and then pointed off to the right and four of the men got into a jeep, reversed up the track, and then took off across country in a bumpy ride.

That made me wrinkle my brows until I remembered there was a small group of lakes over in that direction called Gaesavötn. If Kennikin expected me to be camping at Gaesavötn he'd draw a blank, but it showed how thorough and careful he was.

The crew from the other jeep got busy erecting a camp just off the track, putting up tents rather inexpertly. One of them went to Kennikin with a vacuum flask and poured out a cup of steaming hot coffee which he offered obsequiously. Kennikin took it and sipped it while still standing at the water's edge looking across the impassable river. He seemed to be staring right into my eyes.

I lowered the glasses and withdrew slowly and cautiously, being careful to make no sound. I climbed down from the lava ridge and then slung the carbine and headed back to the Land-Rover at a fast clip, and checked to make sure there were no tyre tracks to show where we had left the track. I didn't think Kennikin would have a man swim the river – he could lose a lot of men that way – but it was best to make sure we weren't stumbled over too easily.

Elin was asleep. She lay on her left side, buried in her sleeping bag, and I was thankful that she always slept quietly and with no blowing or snoring. I let her sleep; there was no reason to disturb her and ruin her night. We weren't going anywhere, and neither was Kennikin. I switched on my pocket torch, shading it with my hand to avoid waking her, and rummaged in a drawer until I found the housewife, from which I took a reel of black thread.

I went back to the track and stretched a line of thread right across it about a foot from the ground, anchoring each end by lumps of loose lava. If Kennikin came through during the night I wanted to know it, no matter how stealthily he went about it. I didn't want to cross the river in the morning only to run into him on the other side.

Then I went down to the river and looked at it. The water level was still dropping and it might have been barely feasible to cross there and then had the light been better. But I wouldn't risk it without using headlights and I couldn't do that because they'd certainly show in the sky. Kennikin's mob wasn't all that far away.

I dropped into my berth fully clothed. I didn't expect to sleep under the circumstances but nevertheless I set the alarm on my wrist-watch for two a.m. And that was the last thing I remember until it buzzed like a demented mosquito and woke me up.

II

We were ready to move at two-fifteen. As soon as the alarm buzzed I woke Elin, ruthlessly disregarding her sleepy protests. As soon as she knew how close Kennikin was she moved fast. I said, 'Get dressed quickly. I'm going to have a look around.'

The black thread was still in place which meant that no vehicle had gone through. Any jeep moving at night would *have* to stick to the track; it was flatly impossible to cross the lava beds in the darkness. True, someone on foot might have gone through, but I discounted that.

The water in the river was nice and low and it would be easy to cross. As I went back I looked in the sky towards the east; already the short northern night was nearly over and I was determined to cross the river at the earliest opportunity and get as far ahead of Kennikin as I could.

Elin had different ideas. 'Why not stay here and let him get ahead? Just let him go past. He'd have to go a long way before he discovered he's chasing nothing.'

'No,' I said. 'We know he has two jeeps, but we don't know if he has more. It could happen that, if we let him get ahead, we could be the meat in a sandwich and that might be uncomfortable. We cross now.'

Starting an engine quietly is not easy. I stuffed blankets around the generator in an attempt to muffle that unmistakable rasp, the engine caught and purred sweetly, and I took the blankets away. And I was very light-footed on the accelerator as we drove towards the river. We got across easily, although making more noise than I cared for, and away we went towards the next river.

I told Elin to keep a sharp eye to the rear while I concentrated on moving as fast as possible compatible with quietness. In the next four kilometres we crossed two more rivers and then there was a long stretch where the track swung north temporarily, and I opened up. We were now far enough away from Kennikin to make speed more important than silence.

Sixteen rivers in sixty kilometres, Elin had said. Not counting the time spent in crossing rivers we were now averaging a bone-jarring twenty-five kilometres an hour – too fast for comfort in this country – and I estimated we would get to the main Sprengis-andur track in about four hours. It actually took six hours because some of the rivers were bastards.

In reaching the Sprengisandur track we had crossed the watershed and all the rivers from now on would be flowing south and west instead of north and east. We hit the track at eight-thirty, and I said. 'Breakfast. Climb in the back and get something ready.'

'You're not stopping?'

'Christ, no! Kennikin will have been on the move for hours. There's no way of knowing how close he is and I've no urgent inclination to find out the hard way. Bread and cheese and beer will do fine.'

So we ate on the move and stopped only once, at ten o'clock, to fill up the tank from the last full jerrycan. While we were doing that up popped our friend of the previous day, the US Navy helicopter. It came from the north this time, not very low, and floated over us without appearing to pay us much attention.

I watched it fly south, and Elin said, 'I'm puzzled about that.'

'So am I,' I said.

'Not in the same way that I am,' she said. 'American military aircraft don't usually overfly the country.' She was frowning.

'Now you come to mention it, that *is* odd.' There's a certain amount of tension in Iceland about the continuing American military presence in Keflavik. A lot of Icelanders take the view that it's an imposition and who can blame them? The American authorities are quite aware of this tension and try to minimize it, and the American Navy in Iceland tries to remain as inconspicuous as possible. Flaunting military aircraft in Icelandic skies was certainly out of character.

I shrugged and dismissed the problem, concentrating on getting the last drop out of the jerrycan, and then we carried on with not a sign of anything on our tail. We were now on the last lap, running down the straight, if rough, track between the River Thjòrsá and the ridge of Búdarháls with the main road only seventy kilometres ahead, inasmuch as any roads in Iceland can be so described.

But even a lousy Icelandic road would be perfection when compared with the tracks of the *Obyggdir*, especially when we ran into trouble with mud. This is one of the problems of June when the frozen earth of winter melts into a gelatinous car trap. Because we were in a Land-Rover it didn't stop us but it slowed us down considerably, and the only consolation I had was that Kennikin would be equally hampered when he hit the stuff.

At eleven o'clock the worst happened – a tyre blew. It was a front tyre and I fought the wheel as we jolted to a stop. 'Let's make this fast,' I said, and grabbed the wheel brace.

If we had to have a puncture it wasn't a bad place to have it.

The footing was level enough to take the jack without slipping and there was no mud at that point. I jacked up the front of the Land-Rover and got busy on the wheel with the brace. Because of Elin's shoulder she wasn't of much use in this kind of job, so I said, 'What about making coffee — we could do with something hot.'

I took the wheel off, rolled it away and replaced it with the spare. The whole operation took a little under ten minutes, time we couldn't afford — not there and then. Once we were farther south we could lose ourselves on a more-or-less complex road network, but these wilderness tracks were too restricted for my liking.

I tightened the last wheel nut and then looked to see what had caused a blowout and to put the wheel back into its rack. What I saw made my blood run cold. I fingered the jagged hole in the thick tyre and looked up at the Búdarháls ridge which dominated the track.

There was only one thing that could make a hole like that — a bullet. And somewhere up on the ridge, hidden in some crevice, was a sniper — and even then I was probably in his sights.

III

How in hell did Kennikin get ahead of me? That was my first bitter thought. But idle thoughts were no use and action was necessary.

I heaved up the wheel with its ruined tyre on to the bonnet and screwed it down securely. While I rotated the wheel brace I glanced covertly at the ridge. There was a lot of open ground before the ridge heaved itself into the air — at least two hundred yards — and the closest a sniper could have been was possibly four hundred yards and probably more.

Any man who could put a bullet into a tyre at over four hundred yards — a quarter mile — was a hell of a good shot. So good that he could put a bullet into me any time he liked — so why the devil hadn't he? I was in plain view, a perfect target, and yet no bullets had come my way. I tightened down the last nut and turned my back to the ridge, and felt a prickling feeling between my shoulder blades — that was where the bullet would hit me if it came.

I jumped to the ground and put away the brace and jack, concentrating on doing the natural thing. The palms of my hands were slippery with sweat. I went to the back of the Land-Rover and looked in at the open door. 'How's the coffee coming?'

'Just ready,' said Elin.

I climbed in and sat down. Sitting in that confined space gave a comforting illusion of protection, but that's all it was – an illusion. For the second time I wished the Land-Rover had been an armoured car. From where I was sitting I could inspect the slopes of the ridge without being too obvious about it and I made the most of the opportunity.

Nothing moved among those red and grey rocks. Nobody stood up and waved or cheered. If anyone was still up there he was keeping as quiet as a mouse which, of course, was the correct thing to do. If you pump a bullet at someone you'd better scrunch yourself up small in case he starts shooting back.

But was anybody still up there? I rather thought there was. Who in his right mind would shoot a hole in the tyre of a car and then just walk away? So he was still up there, waiting and watching. But if he was still there why hadn't he nailed me? It didn't make much sense – unless he was just supposed to be immobilizing me.

I stared unseeingly at Elin who was topping up a jar with sugar. If that was so, then Kennikin had men coming in from both sides. It wouldn't be too hard to arrange if he knew where I was – radio communication is a wonderful thing. That character up on the ridge would have been instructed to stop me so that Kennikin could catch up; and that meant he wanted me alive.

I wondered what would happen if I got into the driving seat and took off again. The odds were that another bullet would rip open another tyre. I didn't take the trouble to find out – there was a limit to the number of spare tyres I carried, and the limit had already been reached.

Hoping that my chain of reasoning was not too shaky I began to make arrangements to get out from under that gun. I took Lindholm's cosh from under the mattress where I had concealed it and put it into my pocket, then I said, 'Let's go and . . .' My voice came out as a hoarse croak and I cleared my throat. 'Let's have coffee outside.'

Elin looked up in surprise. 'I thought we were in a hurry.'

'We've been making good time,' I said. 'I reckon we're far enough ahead to earn a break. I'll take the coffee pot and the sugar; you bring the cups.' I would have dearly loved to have taken the carbine but that would have been too obvious; an unsuspecting man doesn't drink his coffee fully armed.

I jumped out of the door and Elin handed out the coffee pot and the sugar jar which I set on the rear bumper before helping her down. Her right arm was still in the sling but she could carry the cups and spoons in her left hand. I picked up the coffee pot and waved it in the general direction of the ridge. 'Let's go over there at the foot of the rocks.' I made off in that direction without giving her time to argue.

We trudged over the open ground towards the ridge. I had the coffee pot in one hand and the sugar in the other, the picture of innocence. I also had the *sgian dubh* tucked into my left stocking and a cosh in my pocket, but these didn't show. As we got nearer the ridge a miniature cliff reared up and I thought our friend up on top might be getting worried. Any moment from now he would be losing sight of us, and he might just lean forward a little to keep us in view.

I turned as though to speak to Elin and then turned back quickly, glancing upwards as I did so. There was no one to be seen but I was rewarded by the glint of something – a reflection that flickered into nothing. It might have been the sun reflecting off a surface of glassy lava, but I didn't think so. Lava doesn't jump around when left to its own devices – not after it has cooled off, that is.

I marked the spot and went on, not looking up again, and we came to the base of the cliff which was about twenty feet high. There was a straggly growth of birch; gnarled trees all of a foot high. In Iceland bonsai grow naturally and I'm surprised the Icelanders don't work up an export trade to Japan. I found a clear space, set down the coffee pot and the sugar jar, then sat down and pulled up my trouser leg to extract the knife.

Elin came up. 'What are you doing?'

I said, 'Now don't jump out of your pants, but there's a character on the ridge behind us who just shot a hole in that tyre.'

Elin stared at me wordlessly. I said, 'He can't see us here, but I don't think he's worried very much about that. All he wants to do is to stop us until Kennikin arrives – and he's doing it very well. As long as he can see the Land-Rover he knows we aren't far away.' I tucked the knife into the waistband of my trousers – it's designed for a fast draw only when wearing a kilt.

Elin sank to her knees. 'You're sure?'

'I'm positive. You don't get a natural puncture like that in the side wall of a new tyre.' I stood up and looked along the ridge. 'I'm going to winkle out that bastard; I think I know where he is.' I pointed to a crevice at the end of the cliff, a four-foot high crack in the rock. 'I want you to get in there and wait. Don't move until you hear me call – and make bloody sure it's me.'

She was a realist. I looked at her set face and said deliberately, 'In that case, if nothing else happens, you stay where you are until dark, then make a break for the Land-Rover and get the hell out of here. On the other hand, if Kennikin pitches up, try to keep out of his way – and do that by keeping out of sight.' I shrugged. 'But I'll try to get back.'

'Do you have to go at all?'

I sighed. 'We're stuck here, Elin. As long as that joker can keep the Land-Rover covered we're stuck. What do you want me to do? Wait here until Kennikin arrives and then just give myself up?'

'But you're not armed?'

I patted the hilt of the knife. 'I'll make out. Now, just do as I say.' I escorted her to the cleft and saw her inside. It can't have been very comfortable; it was a foot and a half wide by four feet high and so she had to crouch. But there are worse things than being uncomfortable.

Then I contemplated what I had to do. The ridge was seamed by gullies cut by water into the soft rock and they offered a feasible way of climbing without being seen. What I wanted to do was to get above the place where I had seen the sudden glint. In warfare – and this was war – he who holds the high ground has the advantage.

I set out, moving to the left and sticking close in to the rocks. There was a gully twenty yards along which I rejected because I knew it petered out not far up the ridge. The next one was better because it went nearly to the top, so I went into it and began to climb.

Back in the days when I was being trained I went to mountain school and my instructor said something very wise. 'Never follow a watercourse or a stream, either uphill or downhill,' he said. The reasoning was good. Water will take the quickest way down any hill and the quickest way is usually the steepest. Normally one sticks to the bare hillside and steers clear of ravines. Abnormally, on the other hand, one scrambles up a damned steep, slippery, water-worn crack in the rock or one gets one's head blown off.

The sides of the ravine at the bottom of the ridge were about ten feet high, so there was no danger of being seen. But higher up the ravine was shallower and towards the end it was only about two feet deep and I was snaking upwards on my belly. When I had gone as far as I could I reckoned I was higher than the sniper, so I cautiously pushed my head around a pitted chunk of lava and assessed the situation.

Far below me on the track, and looking conspicuously isolated, was the Land-Rover. About two hundred feet to the right and a hundred feet below was the place where I thought the sniper was hiding. I couldn't see him because of the boulders which jutted through the sandy skin of the ridge. That suited me; if I couldn't see him then he couldn't see me, and that screen of boulders was just what I needed to get up close.

But I didn't rush at it. It was in my mind that there might be more than one man. Hell, there could be a dozen scattered along the top of the ridge for all I knew! I just stayed very still and got back my breath, and did a careful survey of every damned rock within sight.

Nothing moved, so I wormed my way out of cover of the ravine and headed towards the boulders, still on my belly. I got there and rested again, listening carefully. All I heard was the faraway murmur of the river in the distance. I moved again, going upwards and around the clump of boulders, and now I was holding the cosh.

I pushed my head around a rock and saw them, fifty feet below in a hollow in the hillside. One was lying down with a rifle pushed before him, the barrel resting on a folded jacket; the other sat farther back tinkering with a walkie-talkie. He had an unlighted cigarette in his mouth.

I withdrew my head and considered. One man I might have tackled – two together were going to be tricky, especially without a gun. I moved carefully and found a better place from which to observe and where I would be less conspicuous – two rocks came almost together but not quite, and I had a peephole an inch across.

The man with the rifle was very still and very patient. I could imagine that he was an experienced hunter and had spent many hours on hillsides like this waiting for his quarry to move within range. The other man was more fidgety; he eased his buttocks on the rock on which he was sitting, he scratched, he slapped at an insect which settled on his leg, and he fiddled with the walkie-talkie.

At the bottom of the ridge I saw something moving and held my breath. The man with the rifle saw it, too, and I could see the slight tautening of his muscles as he tensed. It was Elin. She came out of cover from under the cliff and walked towards the Land-Rover.

I cursed to myself and wondered what the hell she thought she was doing. The man with the rifle settled the butt firmly into his shoulder and took aim, following her all the way with his eye glued to the telescopic sight. If he pulled that trigger I would take my chances and jump the bastard there and then.

Elin got to the Land-Rover and climbed inside. Within a minute she came out again and began to walk back towards the cliff. Half-way there she called out and tossed something into the air. I was too far away to see what it was but I thought it was a packet of cigarettes. The joker with the rifle would be sure of what it was because he was equipped with one of the biggest telescopic sights I had ever seen.

Elin vanished from sight below and I let out my breath. She had deliberately play-acted to convince these gunmen that I was still there below, even if out of sight. And it worked, too. The rifleman visibly relaxed and turned over and said something to the other man. I couldn't hear what was said because he spoke in low tones, but the fidget laughed loudly.

He was having trouble with the walkie-talkie. He extended the antenna, clicked switches and turned knobs, and then tossed it aside on to the moss. He spoke to the rifleman and pointed upwards, and the rifleman nodded. Then he stood up and turned to climb towards me.

I noted the direction he was taking, then turned my head to find a place to ambush him. There was a boulder just behind me about three feet high, so I pulled away from my peephole and dropped behind it in a crouch and took a firm hold of the cosh. I could hear him coming because he wasn't making any attempt to move quietly. His boots crunched on the ground and once there was a flow of gravel as he slipped and I heard a muttered curse. Then there was a change in the light as his shadow fell across me, and I rose up behind him and hit him.

There's quite a bit of nonsense talked about hitting men on the head. From some accounts – film and TV script writers – it's practically as safe as an anaesthetic used in the operating theatre; all that happens is a brief spell of unconsciousness followed by a headache not worse than a good hangover. A pity it isn't so because if it were the hospital anaesthetists would be able to dispense with the elaborate equipment with which they are now lumbered in favour of the time-honoured blunt instrument.

Unconsciousness is achieved by imparting a sharp acceleration to the skull bone so that it collides with the contents – the brain. This results in varying degrees of brain damage ranging from slight concussion to death, and there is always lasting damage, however slight. The blow must be quite heavy and, since men vary, a blow that will make one man merely dizzy will kill another. The trouble is that until you've administered the blow you don't know what you've done.

I wasn't in any mood for messing about so I hit this character hard. His knees buckled under him and he collapsed, and I caught him before he hit the ground. I eased him down and turned him so that he lay on his back. A mangled cigar sagged sideways from his mouth, half bitten through, and blood trickled from the cigar butt to show he had bitten his tongue. He was still breathing.

I patted his pockets and came upon the familiar hard shape, and drew forth an automatic pistol – a Smith & Wesson .38, the twin to the one I had taken from Lindholm. I checked the magazine to see if it was full and then worked the action to put a bullet into the breech.

The collapsed figure at my feet wasn't going to be much use to anybody even if he did wake up, so I didn't have to worry about him. All I had to do now was to take care of Daniel Boone – the man with the rifle. I returned to my peephole to see what he was doing.

He was doing precisely what he had been doing ever since I had seen him – contemplating the Land-Rover with inexhaustible patience. I stood up and walked into the hollow, gun first. I didn't worry overmuch about keeping quiet; speed was more important than quietness and I reckoned he might be more alarmed if I pussy-footed around than if I crunched up behind him.

He didn't even turn his head. All he did was to say in a flat Western drawl, 'You forgotten something, Joe?'

I caught my jaw before it sagged too far. A Russian I expected; an American I didn't. But this was no time to worry about nation-alities – a man who throws bullets at you is automatically a bastard, and whether he's a Russian bastard or an American bastard makes little difference. I just said curtly, 'Turn around, but leave the rifle where it is or you'll have a hole in you.'

He went very still, but the only part of him that he turned was his head. He had china-blue eyes in a tanned, narrow face and he looked ideal for type-casting as Pop's eldest son in a TV horse opera. He also looked dangerous. 'I'll be goddamned!' he said softly.

'You certainly will be if you don't take your hands off that rifle,' I said. 'Spread your arms out as though you were being crucified.'

He looked at the pistol in my hand and reluctantly extended his arms. A man prone in that position finds it difficult to get up quickly. 'Where's Joe?' he asked.

'He's gone beddy-byes.' I walked over to him and put the muzzle of the pistol to the nape of his neck and I felt him shudder. That didn't mean much; it didn't mean he was afraid – I shudder in-voluntarily when Elin kisses me on the nape of the neck. 'Just keep quiet,' I advised, and picked up the rifle.

I didn't have time to examine it closely then but I did afterwards, and it was certainly some weapon. It had a mixed ancestry and probably had started life as a Browning, but a good gunsmith had put in a lot of time in reworking it, giving it such refinements as a sculptured stock with a hole in it to put your thumb, and other fancy items. It was a bit like the man said, 'I have my grandfather's axe — my father replaced the blade and I gave it a new haft.'

What it had ended up as was the complete long-range assassin's kit. It was bolt action because it was a gun for a man who picks his target and who can shoot well enough not to want to send a second bullet after the first in too much of a hurry. It was chambered for a .375 magnum load, a heavy 300 grain bullet with a big charge behind it – high velocity, low trajectory. This rifle in good hands could reach out half a mile and snuff out a man's life if the light was good and the air still.

To help the aforesaid good hands was a fantastic telescopic sight – a variable-pokered monster with a top magnification of 30. To use it when fully racked out would need a man with no nerves – and thus no tremble – or a solid bench rest. The scope was equipped with its own range-finding system, a multiple mounting of graduated dots on the vertical cross hair for various ranges, and was sighted in at five hundred yards.

It was a hell of a lot of gun.

I straightened and rested the muzzle of the rifle lightly against my friend's spine. 'That's your gun you can feel,' I said. 'You don't need me to tell you what would happen if I pulled the trigger.'

His head was turned sideways and I saw a light film of sweat coating the tan. He didn't need to let his imagination work because he was a good craftsman and knew his tools enough to *know* what would happen – over 5000 foot-pounds of energy would blast him clean in two.

I said, 'Where's Kennikin?'

'Who?'

'Don't be childish,' I said. 'I'll ask you again – where's Kennikin?'

'I don't know any Kennikin,' he said in a muffled voice. He found difficulty in speaking because the side of his face was pressed against the ground.

'Think again.'

'I tell you I don't know him. All I was doing was following orders.'

'Yes,' I said. 'You took a shot at me.'

'No,' he said quickly. 'At your tyre. You're still alive, aren't you? I could have knocked you off any time.'

I looked down the slope at the Land-Rover. That was true; it would be like a Bisley champion shooting tin ducks at a fairground. 'So you were instructed to stop me. Then what?'

'Then nothing.'

I increased the pressure on his spine slightly. 'You can do better than that.'

'I was to wait until someone showed up and then quit and go home.'

'And who was the someone?'

'I don't know – I wasn't told.'

That sounded crazy; it was even improbable enough to be true. I said, 'What's your name?'

'John Smith.'

I smiled and said, 'All right, Johnny; start crawling – backwards and slowly. And if I see more than half an inch of daylight between your belly and the ground I'll let you have it.'

He wriggled back slowly and painfully away from the edge and down into the hollow, and then I stopped him. Much as I would have liked to carry on the interrogation I had to put an end to it because time was wasting. I said, 'Now, Johnny; I don't want you to make any sudden moves because I'm a very nervous man, so just keep quite still.'

I came up on his blind side, lifted the butt of the rifle and brought it down on the back of his head. It was no way to treat such a good gun but it was the only thing I had handy. The gun butt was considerably harder than the cosh and I regretfully decided I had fractured his skull. Anyway, he wouldn't be causing me any more trouble.

I walked over to pick up the jacket he had been using as a gun rest. It was heavy and I expected to find a pistol in the pocket, but the weight was caused by an unbroken box of rounds for the rifle. Next to the jacket was an open box. Both were unlabelled.

I checked the rifle. The magazine was designed to hold five rounds and contained four, there was one in the breech ready to pop off, and there were nineteen rounds in the opened box. Mr Smith was a professional; he had filled the magazine, jacked one into the breech, and then taken out the magazine and stuffed another round into it so he would have six rounds in hand instead of five. Not that he needed them – he had bust the tyre on a moving vehicle at over four hundred yards with just one shot.

He was a professional all right, but his name wasn't Smith because he carried an American passport in the name of Wendell George Fleet. He also carried a pass that would get him into the more remote corners of Keflavik Naval Base, the parts which the public are discouraged from visiting. He didn't carry a pistol; a rifleman as good as he usually despises handguns.

I put the boxes of ammunition into my pocket where they weighed heavy, and I stuck Joe's automatic pistol into the waistband of my trousers, unloading it first so I didn't do a Kennikin on myself. Safety catches are not all that reliable and a lot of men have ruined themselves for their wives by acting like a character in a TV drama.

I went to see how Joe was doing and found that he was still asleep and that his name wasn't even Joe according to his passport. It turned out he was Patrick Aloysius McCarthy. I regarded him speculatively; he looked more Italian than Irish to me. Probably all the names were phoney, just as Buchner who wasn't Graham turned out to be Philips.

McCarthy carried two spare magazines for the Smith & Wesson, both of them full, which I confiscated. I seemed to be building up quite an armoury on this expedition – from a little knife to a high-powered rifle in one week wasn't doing too bad. Next up the scale ought to be a burp gun or possibly a fully-fledged machine-gun. I wondered how long it would take me to graduate to something really lethal, such as an Atlas ICBM.

McCarthy had been going somewhere when I thumped him. He had been trying to contact someone by radio, but the walkie-talkie had been on the blink so he'd decided to walk, and that put whoever it was not very far away. I stared up towards the top of the ridge and decided to take a look over the next rise. It was a climb of perhaps two hundred yards and when I poked my head carefully over the top I caught my breath in surprise.

The yellow US Navy helicopter was parked about four hundred yards away and two crewmen and a civilian sat in front of it, talking casually. I lifted Fleet's rifle and looked at them through the big scope at maximum magnification. The crewmen were unimportant but I thought I might know the civilian. I didn't, but I memorized his face for future reference.

For a moment I was tempted to tickle them up with the rifle but I shelved the idea. It would be better to depart quietly and without fuss. I didn't want that chopper with me the rest of the way, so I withdrew and went back down the hill. I had been away quite a while and Elin would be becoming even more worried, if that were possible.

From where I was I had a good view along the track so I looked to see if Kennikin was yet in sight. He was! Through the scope I saw a minute black dot in the far distance crawling along the track, and I estimated that the jeep was about three miles away. There was a lot of mud along there and I didn't think he'd be making much more than ten miles an hour, so that put him about fifteen minutes behind.

I went down the hillside fast.

Elin was squashed into the crack in the rock but she came out when I called. She ran over and grabbed me as though she wanted to check whether I was all in one piece and she was laughing and crying at the same time. I disentangled myself from her arms. 'Kennikin's not far behind; let's move.'

I set out towards the Land-Rover at a dead run, holding Elin's arm, but she dragged free. 'The coffee pot!'

'The hell with it!' Women are funny creatures; this was not a time to be thinking of domestic economy. I grabbed her arm again and dragged her along.

Thirty seconds later I had the engine going and we were bouncing along the track too fast for either safety or comfort while I decided which potholes it would be safe to put the front wheels into. Decisions, decisions, nothing but bloody decisions – and if I decided wrongly we'd have a broken half-axle or be stuck in the mud and the jig would be up.

We bounced like hell all the way to the Tungnaá River and the traffic got thicker – one car passed us going the other way, the first we had seen since being in the *Obyggdir*. That was bad because Kennikin was likely to stop it and ask the driver if he had seen a long wheelbase Land-Rover lately. It was one thing to chase me through the wilderness without knowing where I was, and quite another to know that I was actually within spitting distance. The psychological spur would stimulate his adrenal gland just that much more.

On the other hand, seeing the car cheered me because it meant that the car transporter over the Tungnaá would be on our side of the river and there would be no waiting. I have travelled a lot in places where water crossings are done by ferry – there are quite a few in Scotland – and it's a law of nature that the ferry is always on the other side when you arrive at the water's edge. But that wouldn't be so this time.

Not that this was a ferry. You cross the Tungnaá by means of a contraption – a platform slung on an overhead cable. You drive your car on to the platform and winch yourself across, averting your eyes from the white water streaming below. According to the *Ferdahanbokin*, which every traveller in the *Obyggdir* ought to consult, extreme care is necessary for people not acquainted with the system. Personally, I don't recommend it for those with queasy stomachs who have to cross in a high wind.

We arrived at the Tungnaá and the contraption was, indeed, on our side. I checked that it was secured and safe, and then drove on carefully. 'Stay in the cab,' I said to Elin. 'You can't winch with that broken wing.'

I got out and began to operate the winch, keeping an eye open for Kennikin's imminent arrival. I felt very exposed and naked and I hoped I had kept my fifteen-minute lead because crossing the Tungnaá is a slow job. But we made it without incident and I drove off the platform with a great sense of relief.

'Now we can stop the bastard,' I said as we drove away.

Elin sat up straight. 'You're not going to break the cable!' There was a note of indignation in her voice. Being shot at was all right but the wanton destruction of public property was unethical.

I grinned at her. 'I'd do it if I could, but it would take a stronger man than me.' I pulled the car off the road and looked back; the river was out of sight. 'No, I'm going to chain up the platform so Kennikin can't pull it across. He'll be stuck on the other side until someone going the other way can release it, and God knows when that will be – there's not much traffic. Stay here.'

I got out, rummaged in the tool kit, and found the snow chains. It wasn't at all likely we'd need them in the summer and they could do a better job of keeping Kennikin off my neck than lying where they were. I lifted them out and ran back down the track.

You can't really tie a chain into a knot but I tethered that platform with such a tangle of iron that would take anyone at least half an hour to free unless he happened to have an oxy-acetylene cutting torch handy. I had nearly completed the job when Kennikin arrived on the other side and the fun started.

The jeep came to a halt and four men got out, Kennikin in the lead. I was hidden behind the platform and no one saw me at first. Kennikin studied the cable and then read the instructions that are posted in Icelandic and English. He got the hang of it and ordered his men to haul the platform back across the river.

They duly hauled and nothing happened.

I was working like hell to finish the job and just got it done in time. The platform lurched away and then stopped, tethered by the chain. There was a shout from the other side and someone went running along the bank so as to get into a position to see what was stopping the platform. He saw it all right – he saw me. The next moment he had whipped out a gun and started to shoot.

The pistol is a much over-rated weapon. It has its place, which is about ten yards from its target or, better still, ten feet. The popgun that was shooting at me was a short-barrelled .38 revolver – a belly gun – with which I wouldn't trust to hit anything I couldn't reach out and touch. I was pretty safe as long as he aimed at me; if he started to shoot anywhere else I might get hit by accident, but that was a slim chance.

The others opened up as I snagged the last bit of chain into place. A bullet raised dust two yards away and that was as close as they came. Yet it's no fun being shot at so I turned and belted away up the track at a dead run. Elin was standing by the Land-Rover, her face full of concern, having heard the barrage of shots. 'It's all right,' I said. 'The war hasn't broken out.' I reached inside and took out Fleet's rifle. 'Let's see if we can discourage them.'

She looked at the rifle with abhorrence. 'Oh, God! Must you kill them? Haven't you done enough?'

I stared at her and then the penny dropped. She thought I'd got hold of that rifle by killing Fleet; she seemed to think that you couldn't take that much gun away from a man without killing him. I said, 'Elin; those men across the river were trying to kill me. The fact they didn't succeed doesn't alter their intention. Now, I'm not going to kill anyone – I said I'll discourage them.' I held up the rifle. 'And I didn't kill the man I took this from, either.'

I walked away down the track but veered away from it before I reached the river. I hunted around until I found suitable cover and then lay and watched Kennikin and his crew unsuccessfully trying to get at the platform. A 30-power scope was a bit too much optical glass for a range of a hundred yards but it had variable power so I dropped it to a magnification of six which was as low as it would go. A rock in front of me formed a convenient rest and I settled the butt against my shoulder and looked into the eye-piece.

I wasn't going to kill anyone. Not that I didn't want to, but bodies you can't get rid of are inconvenient and lead to the asking of awkward questions by the appropriate authorities. A wounded Russian, on the other hand, would be eliminated just as much as a dead one. He would be smuggled by his friends on to the trawler which was undoubtedly to hand, probably already in Reykjavik harbour. The Russians have more non-fishing trawlers than any other nation on earth.

No, I wasn't going to kill anyone, but someone would soon wish to God he were dead.

Kennikin had disappeared and the three other men were engaged in a heated discussion about how to solve their little problem. I broke it up by firing five spaced shots in thirty seconds. The first hit the man standing next to the jeep in the kneecap, and suddenly there wasn't anyone else around to shoot at. He lay on the ground, writhing and shouting, and he'd have one leg shorter than the other for the rest of his life – if he got into hospital quickly. If not, he'd be lucky to have a leg at all.

I re-sighted and squeezed the trigger again, this time shooting at the off-side front tyre of the jeep. The rifle was one of the best I've ever handled and, at a hundred yards, the trajectory was so flat that I could put a bullet exactly where I wanted it. The tyre wasn't just punctured; under the close-range hammer blow of that big .375 bullet it exploded into bits, as did the other front tyre when I let fly again.

Someone popped off with a pistol. I ignored that and fed another round into the breech. I centred the cross hairs on the front of the radiator and fired again, and the jeep rocked back on its springs under the impact. This rifle was chambered to shoot big game and anything that can crack open the frontal skull bone of a buffalo wouldn't do an engine block much good. I put the last bullet in the same place in the hope of putting the jeep permanently out of action and then withdrew, keeping my head down.

I walked up to the Land-Rover, and said to Elin, 'It's a good rifle.'

She looked at me nervously. 'I thought I heard someone scream.'

'I didn't kill anyone,' I said. 'But they won't be driving that jeep very far. Let's go on. You can drive for a bit.' I was suddenly very tired.

Chapter Six

I

We drove out of the *Obyggdir* and hit the main road system. Even if Kennikin was able to follow us we would have a good chance of losing him because this was one of the main areas of population and there was a network of roads harder to police than the simple choices of the *Obyggdir*. Elin drove while I relaxed in the passenger seat, and once we were on the good roads were able to pick up speed.

'Where to?' she asked.

'I'd like to get this vehicle out of sight,' I said. 'It's too damned conspicuous. Any suggestions?'

'You have to be at Geysir tomorrow night,' she said. 'I have friends at Laugarvatn – you must remember Gunnar.'

'Weren't you running around with him before you met me?'

She smiled. 'It wasn't serious – and we're still friends. Besides, he's married now.'

Marriage, to a lot of men, doesn't mean an automatic cancellation of their hunting licence, but I let it lie; a more-or less civilized butting match with Elin's old boy-friend was preferable to a more deadly encounter with Kennikin. 'All right,' I said. 'Head for Laugarvatn.'

We were silent for a while, then I said, 'Thank you for what you did back there when I was on Búdarháls. It was a damned silly thing to do, but it helped.'

'I thought it might distract their attention,' she said.

'It sure as hell distracted mine for a minute. Did you know you were in the sights of a rifle all the way – and there was a finger on the trigger?'

'I did feel uneasy,' she admitted, and shivered involuntarily. 'What happened up there?'

'I gave headaches to a couple of men. One of them will probably wind up in hospital at Keflavik.'

She looked at me sharply. 'Keflavik!'

'Yes,' I said. 'They were Americans.' I told her about Fleet, McCarthy and the waiting helicopter. 'I've been trying to make sense out of it ever since – without much success.'

She thought about it too, and said. 'But it *doesn't* make sense. Why would the Americans co-operate with the Russians? Are you sure they were Americans?'

'They were as American as Mom's apple-pie – at least Fleet was. I didn't get to talk to McCarthy.'

'They could be sympathizers,' said Elin. 'Fellow-travellers.'

'Then they're travelling closer than a flea to a dog.' I took out Fleet's pass to the remoter recesses of Keflavik Air Base. 'If they're fellow-travellers then the Yanks had better watch it – their furniture is riddled with woodworm.' I examined the pass and thought about the helicopter. 'It's just about the most ridiculous thing I've heard of.'

'Then what other explanation is there?'

The idea of a nest of communist sympathizers being conveniently to hand at Keflavik and able to lay their hands on a navy helicopter at a moment's notice was untenable. I said, 'I doubt if Kennikin rang up Keflavik and said, "Look boys; I'm chasing a British spy and I need your help. Can you lay on a chopper and a sharpshooter and stop him for me?" But there's someone else who could do it.'

'Who?'

'There's a man called Helms in Washington who could pick up a telephone and say, "Admiral, there'll be a couple of guys dropping in at Keflavik pretty soon. Let them have a helicopter and a crew – and don't ask too many questions about what they want it for." And the Admiral would say, "Yes, sir; yes, sir; three bags full, sir," because Helms is the boss of the CIA.'

'But why?'

'I'm damned if I know,' I said. 'But it's a bloody sight more likely than Keflavik being white-anted by Russian agents.' I thought of my brief and unsatisfactory conversation with Fleet. 'Fleet said that his orders were to pin us down until someone – presumably Kennikin – arrived. He said he'd never heard of Kennikin. He also said that when Kennikin arrived his job was over and he could go home. There's one more question I should have asked him.'

'What's that?'

'Whether his instructions called for him to show himself to Kennikin or whether they specifically forbade it. I'd give a lot to know the answer to that one.'

'You're sure we were chased by Russians? I mean, you're sure it *was* Kennikin?'

'That's a face I'll never forget,' I said. 'And there was a lot of swearing in Russian back at the Tungnaá River.'

I could almost see the wheels whizzing round as Elin thought about it. 'Try this,' she said. 'Supposing Slade is also chasing us, and suppose he asked the Americans to co-operate – but what he didn't know was that Kennikin was closer to us. The Americans were supposed to hold us up until Slade arrived – not Kennikin.'

'It's barely possible,' I conceded. 'But it shows lousy liaison. And why go to all the trouble of a sniper hidden on a hill? Why not have the Americans just make a simple pinch?' I shook my head. 'Besides, the Department isn't all that chummy with the CIA – the special relationship has its limits.'

'My explanation is the more reasonable,' said Elin.

'I'm not sure there *is* any reason involved – it's turning into a thoroughly unreasonable situation. It reminds me of what a physicist once said about his job: "The universe is not only queerer than we imagine but, perhaps, queerer than we can imagine." I can see his point now.'

Elin laughed, and I said, 'What the hell's so funny? Slade has already taken a crack at us, and may do again if Taggart hasn't pulled him off. Kennikin is sweating blood trying to get at me – and now the Americans have put in their oar. Any minute from now I'm expecting the West Germans to pitch up, or maybe the Chilean Secret Service. I wouldn't be surprised at anything. But there's one thing that really worries me.'

'What?'

I said, 'Suppose I give this gadget to Case tomorrow night. Kennikin won't know that, will he? I can't see Jack Case writing him a letter – "Dear Vaslav, Stewart doesn't have the football any more; I've got it – come and chase *me*." I'll be just as much up the creek as before. Farther, in fact, because if Kennikin catches me and I *haven't* got the damned thing then he'll be even madder than he is now, if that's possible.'

I wasn't so sure I was going to give the gadget to Case, after all. If I was going to be up the creek, I'd better retain the paddle.

II

Laugarvatn is a district educational centre which takes in children from a wide rural area. The country is so big relative to the population, and the population is so scattered, that the educational system is rather peculiar. Most of the rural schools are boarding schools and in some of them the pupils spend a fortnight at school and a fortnight at home, turn and turn about, during the winter teaching terms. The children from farther away spend all winter at school. In the summer the schools are turned into hotels for four months.

Because Laugarvatn is conveniently close to Thingvellir, Geysir, Gullfoss and other tourist attractions its two large schools come in very useful as summer hotels, and Laugarvatn has become a pony-trekking centre very popular with visitors. Personally, I've never cared much for horses, not even the multi-coloured Icelandic variety which is better-looking than most. I think the horse is a stupid animal – any animal which allows another to ride it must be stupid – and I prefer to be bounced by a Land-Rover rather than by a stubborn pony who would rather go home.

Gunnar Arnarsson was a schoolteacher in the winter and in summer ran a pony-trekking operation. Very versatile people, these Icelanders. He was away when we arrived, but his wife, Sigurlin Asgeirsdottir, made us welcome with much clucking at the sight of Elin's arm in an improvised sling.

One of the problems in Iceland is sorting out the single from the married people, because the woman does not change her name when she gets married. In fact, the whole problem of names is a trap into which foreigners usually fall with a loud thump. The surname just tells everyone who your father was; Sigurlin was the daughter of Asgeir, just as Gunnar was the son of Arnar. If Gunnar had a son and decided to name the boy after his grandfather he'd be called Arnar Gunnarsson. All very difficult and the reason why the Icelandic telephone directory is listed alphabetically under given names. Elin Ragnarsdottir was listed under 'E'.

Gunnar appeared to have done well for himself because Sigurlin was one of those tall, leggy, svelte, Scandinavian types who go over big when they get to Hollywood, and what the hell has acting got to do with it anyway? The widespread belief that the Nordic nations are populated exclusively on the distaff side by these tow-headed goddesses is, however, a regrettable illusion.

From the way she welcomed us Sigurlin knew about me, but not all, I hoped. At any rate she knew a lot – enough to hear the distant chime of wedding bells. It's funny, but as soon as a girl gets married she wants to get all her old girl-friends caught in the same trap. Because of Kennikin there weren't going to be any immediate wedding bells – the tolling of a single funeral note was more likely – but, disregarding Kennikin, I wasn't going to be pressured by any busty blonde with a match-making glint in her eye.

324

I put the Land-Rover into Gunnar's empty garage with some relief. Now it was safely off the road and under cover I felt much better. I saw that the collection of small arms was decently concealed and then went into the house to find Sigurlin coming downstairs. She gave me a peculiar look and said abruptly, 'What did Elin do to her shoulder?'

I said cautiously, 'Didn't she tell you?'

'She said she was climbing and fell against a sharp rock.'

I made an indeterminate noise expressive of agreement, but I could see that Sigurlin was suspicious. A gunshot wound tends to look like nothing else but, even to someone who has never seen one before. I said hastily, 'It's very good of you to offer us a bed for the night.'

'It's nothing,' she said. 'Would you like some coffee?'

'Thank you, I would.' I followed her into the kitchen. 'Have you known Elin long?'

'Since we were children.' Sigurlin dumped a handful of beans into a coffee grinder. 'And you?'

'Three years.'

She filled an electric kettle and plugged it in, then swung around to face me. 'Elin looks very tired.'

'We pushed it a bit in the *Obyggdir*.'

That can't have sounded convincing because Sigurlin said, 'I wouldn't want her to come to any harm. That wound . . .'

'Well?'

'She didn't fall against a rock, did she?'

There was a brain behind those beautiful eyes. 'No,' I said. 'She didn't.'

'I thought not,' she said. 'I've seen wounds like that. Before I married I was a nurse at Keflavik. An American sailor was brought into hospital once – he'd been cleaning his gun and shot himself accidentally. Whose gun was Elin cleaning?'

I sat down at the kitchen table. 'There's a certain amount of trouble,' I said carefully. 'And it's best you're not involved, so I'm not going to tell you anything about it – for your own good. I tried to keep Elin out of it from the beginning, but she's headstrong.'

Sigurlin nodded. 'Her family always were stubborn.'

I said, 'I'm going to Geysir tomorrow evening and I'd like Elin to stay here. I'll want your co-operation on that.'

Sigurlin regarded me seriously. 'I don't like trouble with guns.'

'Neither do I. I'm not exactly shouting for joy. That's why I want Elin out of it. Can she stay here for a while?'

'A gunshot wound should be reported to the police.'

'I know,' I said wearily. 'But I don't think your police are equipped to cope with this particular situation. It has international ramifications and there is more than one gun involved. Innocent people could get killed if it's not carefully handled, and with no disrespect to your police, I think they'd be likely to blunder.'

'This trouble, as you call it – is it criminal?'

'Not in the normal sense. You might call it an extreme form of political action.'

Sigurlin turned down the corners of her mouth. 'The only good thing I've heard about this is that you want to keep Elin out of it,' she said waspishly. 'Tell me, Alan Stewart; are you in love with her?'

'Yes.'

'Are you going to marry her?'

'If she'll have me after all this.'

She offered me a superior smile. 'Oh, she'll have you. You're hooked like a salmon and you won't get away now.'

'I'm not so sure of that,' I said. 'There are certain things that have come up lately that don't add to my charms in Elin's eyes.'

'Such as guns?' Sigurlin poured coffee. 'You don't need to answer that. I won't probe.' She put the cup before me. 'All right; I'll keep Elin here.'

'I don't know how you're going to do it,' I said. 'I've never been able to make her do anything she didn't want to do.'

'I'll put her to bed,' said Sigurlin. 'Strict medical supervision. She'll argue, but she'll do it. You do what you have to do and Elin will stay here. But I won't be able to keep her long. What happens if you don't come back from Geysir?'

'I don't know,' I said. 'But don't let her go back to Reykjavik. To go to the apartment would be extremely unwise.'

Sigurlin took a deep breath. 'I'll see what I can do.' She poured herself a cup of coffee and sat down. 'If it weren't for the concern you show for Elin I'd be inclined to . . .' She shook her head irritably. 'I don't like any of this, Alan. For God's sake get it cleared up as quickly as you can.'

'I'll do my best.'

III

The next day seemed very long.

At breakfast Sigurlin read the paper and suddenly said, 'Well,

well! Someone tied up the cable transport on the Tungnaá just the other side of Hald. A party of tourists was stranded on the farther side for several hours. I wonder who could have done that?'

'It was all right when we came across,' I said blandly. 'What does it say about the tourists? Anyone hurt?'

She looked at me speculatively across the breakfast table. 'Why should anyone be hurt? No, it says nothing about that.'

I changed the subject quickly. 'I'm surprised that Elin is still asleep.'

Sigurlin smiled. 'I'm not. She didn't know it, but she had a sleeping draught last night. She'll be drowsy when she wakes and she won't want to jump out of bed.'

That was one way of making sure of Elin. I said, 'I noticed your garage was empty – don't you have a car?'

'Yes. Gunnar left it at the stables.'

'When will he be back?'

'In two days – providing the party doesn't get saddle-sore.'

'When I go to Geysir I'd just as soon not use the Land-Rover,' I said.

'You want the car? All right – but I want it back in one piece.' She told me where to find it. 'You'll find the key in the glove locker.'

After breakfast I regarded the telephone seriously and wondered whether to ring Taggart. I had a lot to tell him but I thought it would be better to let it go until I heard what Jack Case had to say. Instead I went out to the Land-Rover and cleaned Fleet's rifle.

It really was a good tool. With its fancy hand-grip and free-style stock it had obviously been tailor-made to suit Fleet, whom I suspected of being an enthusiast. In every field of human endeavour there are those who push perfection to its ultimate and absurd end. In hi-fi, for example, there is the maniac who has seventeen loudspeakers and one test record. In shooting there is the gun nut.

The gun nut believes that there is no standard, off-the-shelf weapon that could be possibly good enough for him and so he adapts and chisels until he finally achieves something that looks like one of the more far-out works of modern sculpture. He also believes that the ammunition manufacturers know damn-all about their job and so he loads his own cases, carefully weighing each bullet and matching it with an amount of powder calculated to one-tenth of a grain. Sometimes he shoots very well.

I checked the ammunition from the opened box and, sure

enough, found the telltale scratches from a crimping tool. Fleet was in the habit of rolling his own, something I have never found necessary, but then my own shooting has not been of the type necessary to get a perfect grouping at x-hundred yards. It also explained why the box was unlabelled.

I wondered why Fleet should have carried as many as fifty rounds; after all, he was a good shot and had brought us to a standstill with one squeeze of the trigger. He had loaded the rifle with ordinary hunting ammunition, soft-nosed and designed to spread on impact. The closed box contained twenty-five rounds of jacketed ammunition – the military load.

It's always seemed odd to me that the bullet one shoots at an animal is designed to kill as quickly and as mercilessly as possible, whereas the same bullet shot at a man is illegal under the Geneva Convention. Shoot a hunting load at a man and you're accused of using dum-dum bullets and that's against the rules. You can roast him to death with napalm, disembowel him with a jump mine, but you can't shoot him with the same bullet you would use to kill a deer cleanly.

I looked at the cartridge in the palm of my hand and wished I had known about it earlier. One of those going into the engine of Kennikin's jeep was likely to do a lot more damage than the soft-nosed bullet I had used. While a .375 jacketed bullet with a magnum charge behind it probably wouldn't drill through a jeep from end to end at a range of a hundred yards, I wouldn't like to bet on it by standing behind the jeep.

I filled the magazine of the rifle with a mixed load, three soft-nosed and two jacketed, laid alternately. Then I examined McCarthy's Smith & Wesson automatic pistol, a more prosaic piece of iron than Fleet's jazzed-up rifle. After checking that it was in order I put it into my pocket, together with the spare clips. The electronic gadget I left where it was under the front seat. I wasn't taking it with me when I went to see Jack Case, but I wasn't going empty-handed either.

When I got back to the house Elin was awake. She looked at me drowsily, and said, 'I don't know why I'm so tired.'

'Well,' I said judiciously. 'You've been shot and you've been racketing around the *Obyggdir* for two days with not much sleep. I'm not surprised you're tired. I haven't been too wide awake myself.'

Elin opened her eyes wide in alarm and glanced at Sigurlin who was arranging flowers in a vase. I said, 'Sigurlin knows you didn't fall on any rock. She knows you were shot, but not how or why –

and I don't want you to tell her. I don't want you to discuss it with Sigurlin or anyone else.' I turned to Sigurlin. 'You'll get the full story at the right time, but at the moment the knowledge would be dangerous.'

Sigurlin nodded in acceptance. Elin said, 'I think I'll sleep all day. I'm tired now, but I'll be ready by the time we have to leave for Geysir.'

Sigurlin crossed the room and began to plump up the pillows behind Elin's head. The heartless professionalism spoke of the trained nurse. 'You're not leaving for anywhere,' she said sharply. 'Not for the next two days at least.'

'But I must,' protested Elin.

'But you must not. Your shoulder is bad enough.' Her lips compressed tightly as she looked down at Elin. 'You should really see a doctor.'

'Oh, no !' said Elin.

'Well, then, you'll do as I say.'

Elin looked at me appealingly. I said, 'I'm only going to see a man. As a matter of fact, Jack Case wouldn't say a word in your presence, anyway – you're not a member of the club. I'm just going to Geysir, have a chat with the man, and then come back here – and you might as well keep your turned-up nose out of it for once.'

Elin looked flinty, and Sigurlin said, 'I'll leave you to whisper sweet nothings into each other's ear.' She smiled. 'You two are going to lead interesting lives.'

She left the room, and I said gloomily, 'That sounds like the Chinese curse – "May you live in interesting times." '

'All right,' said Elin in a tired voice. 'I won't give you any trouble. You can go to Geysir alone.'

I sat on the edge of the bed. 'It's not a matter of you giving trouble; I just want you out of this. You disturb my concentration, and if I run into difficulties I don't want to have to watch out for you as well as myself.'

'Have I been a drag ?'

I shook my head. 'No, Elin; you haven't. But the nature of the game may change. I've been chased across Iceland and I'm pretty damned tired of it. If the opportunity offers I'll turn around and do a bit of chasing myself.'

'And I'd get in the way,' she said flatly.

'You're a civilized person,' I said. 'Very law-abiding and full of scruples. I doubt if you've had as much as a parking ticket in your life. I might manage to retain a few scruples while I'm being hunted; not many, but some. But when I'm the hunter I can't afford them. I think you might be horrified at what I'd do.'

'You'd kill,' she said. It was a statement.

'I might do worse,' I said grimly, and she shivered. 'It's not that I want to – I'm no casual murderer; I didn't want to have any part of this but I've been conscripted against my will.'

'You dress it in fine words,' she said. 'You don't have to kill.'

'No fine words,' I said. 'Just one – survival. A drafted American college boy may be a pacifist, but when the Viet Cong shoot at him with those Russian 7.62 millimetre rifles he'll shoot right back, you may depend on it. And when Kennikin comes after me he'll deserve all he runs into. I didn't ask him to shoot at me on the Tungnaá River – he didn't need my permission – but he can't have been very surprised when I shot back. Hell, he would expect it!'

'I can see the logic,' said Elin. 'But don't expect me to like it.'

'Christ!' I said. 'Do you think I like it?'

'I'm sorry, Alan,' she said, and smiled wanly.

'So am I.' I stood up. 'After that bit of deep philosophy you'd better have breakfast. I'll see what Sigurlin can offer.'

IV

I left Laugarvatn at eight that night. Punctuality may be a virtue but it has been my experience that the virtuous often die young while the ungodly live to a ripe age. I had arranged to meet Jack Case at five o'clock but it would do him no great harm to stew for a few hours, and I had it in mind that the arrangement to meet him had been made on an open radio circuit.

I arrived at Geysir in Gunnar's Volkswagen beetle and parked inconspicuously quite a long way from the summer hotel. A few people, not many, were picking their way among the pools of boiling water, cameras at the ready. Geysir itself – the Gusher – which has given its name to all the other spouters in the world, was quiescent. It has been a long time since Geysir spouted. The habit of prodding it into action by tossing rocks into the pool finally proved too much as the pressure chamber was blocked. However, Stokkur – the Churn – was blasting off with commendable efficiency and sending up its feathery plume of boiling water at seven-minute intervals.

I stayed in the car for a long time and used the field-glasses assiduously. There were no familiar faces to be seen in the next hour, a fact that didn't impress me much, however. Finally I got out of the car and walked towards the Hotel Geysir, one hand in my pocket resting on the butt of the pistol.

Case was in the lounge, sitting in a corner and reading a paper-back. I walked up to him and said, 'Hello, Jack; that's a nice tan – you must have been in the sun.'

He looked up. 'I was in Spain. What kept you?'

'This and that.'

I prepared to sit down, but he said, 'This is too public – let's go up to my room. Besides, I have a bottle.'

'That's nice.'

I followed him to his room. He locked the door and turned to survey me. 'That gun in your pocket spoils the set of your coat. Why don't you use a shoulder holster?'

I grinned at him. 'The man I took the gun from didn't have one. How are you, Jack? It's good to see you.'

He grunted sourly. 'You might change your mind about that.' With a flip of his hand he opened a suitcase lying on a chair and took out a bottle. He poured a heavy slug into a tooth glass and handed it to me. 'What the devil have you been doing? You've got Taggart really worked up.'

'He sounded pretty steamy when I spoke to him,' I said, and sipped the whisky. 'Most of the time I've been chased from hell-and-gone to here.'

'You weren't followed here?' he asked quickly.

'No.'

'Taggart tells me you killed Philips. Is that true?'

'If Philips was a man who called himself Buchner and Graham it's true.'

He stared at me. 'You admit it!'

I relaxed in the chair. 'Why not, since I did it? I didn't know it was Philips, though. He came at me in the dark with a gun.'

'That's not how Slade described it. He says you took a crack at him too.'

'I did – but that was after I'd disposed of Philips. He and Slade came together.'

'Slade says differently. He says that he was in a car with Philips when you ambushed it.'

I laughed. 'With what?' I drew the *sgian dubh* from my stocking and flipped it across the room, where it stuck in the top of the dressing-table, quivering. 'With that?'

'He says you had a rifle.'

'Where would I get a rifle?' I demanded. 'He's right, though;

I took the rifle from Philips after I disposed of him with that little pig-sticker. I put three shots into Slade's car and missed the bastard.'

'Christ!' said Case. 'No wonder Taggart is doing his nut. Have you gone off your little rocker?'

I sighed. 'Jack, did Taggart say anything about a girl?'

'He said you'd referred to a girl. He didn't know whether to believe you.'

'He'd better believe me.' I said. 'That girl isn't far from here, and she has a bullet wound in her shoulder that was given to her by Philips. He was within an ace of killing her. Now, there's no two ways about that, and I can take you to her and show you the wound. Slade says I ambushed him. Is it likely I'd do it with my fiancée watching? And why in hell would I want to ambush him?' I slid in a trick question. 'What did he say he'd done with Philips's body?'

Case frowned. 'I don't think the question came up.'

'It wouldn't,' I said. 'The last I saw of Slade he was driving away like a maniac — and there was no body in his car. I disposed of it later.'

'This is all very well,' said Case. 'But it happened after Akureyri, and in Akureyri you were supposed to deliver a package to Philips. You didn't, and you didn't give it to Slade either. Why not?'

'The operation stank,' I said, and went into it in detail.

I talked for twenty minutes and by the time I had finished Case was pop-eyed. He swallowed and his Adam's apple jumped convulsively. 'Do you really believe that Slade is a Russian agent? How do you expect Taggart to swallow that? I've never heard such a cock-and-bull story in my life.'

I said patiently, 'I followed Slade's instructions at Keflavik and nearly got knocked off by Lindholm; Slade sent Philips after me into Asbyrgi — how *did* he know the Russians were holding a fake? There's the Calvados; there's . . .'

Case held up his hands. 'There's no need to go through it all again. Lindholm might have been lucky in catching you — there's nothing to say all the roads around Keflavik weren't staked out. Slade says he didn't go after you in the Asbyrgi. As for the Calvados . . .' He threw up his hands. 'There's only your word for that.'

'What the hell are you, Jack? Prosecutor, judge and jury, too? Or have I already been judged and you're the executioner?'

'Don't fly off the handle,' he said wearily. 'I'm just trying to find out how complicated a cock-up you've made, that's all. What did you do after you left Asbyrgi?'

'We went south in the wilderness,' I said. 'And then Kennikin pitched up.'

'The one who drinks Calvados? The one you had the hassle with in Sweden?'

'The same. My old pal, Vaslav. Don't you think that was bloody coincidental, Jack? How would Kennikin know which track to chase along? But Slade knew, of course; he knew which way we went after we left Asbyrgi.'

Case regarded me thoughtfully. 'You know you're very convincing sometimes. I'm getting so I might believe this silly story if I'm not careful. But Kennikin didn't catch you.'

'It was nip and tuck,' I said. 'And the bloody Yanks didn't help.'

Case sat up. 'How do they come into this?'

I pulled out Fleet's pass and skimmed it across the room into Case's lap. 'That chap shot a hole in my tyre at very long range. I got out of there with Kennikin ten minutes behind.' I told Case all about it.

His mouth was grim. 'Now you really have gone overboard. I suppose you'll now claim Slade is a member of the CIA,' he said sarcastically. 'Why should the Americans hold you up just so Kennikin could grab you?'

'I don't know,' I said feelingly. 'I wish I did.'

Case examined the card. 'Fleet – I know that name; it came up when I was in Turkey last year. He's a CIA hatchetman and he's dangerous.'

'Not for the next month,' I said. 'I cracked his skull.'

'So what happened next?'

I shrugged. 'I went hell-for-leather with Kennikin and his boys trying to climb up my exhaust pipe – there was a bit of an affray at a river, and then I lost him. I suppose he's around here somewhere.'

'And you've still got the package?'

'Not on me, Jack,' I said softly. 'Not on me – but quite close.'

'I don't want it,' he said, and crossed the room to take my empty glass. 'The plan's changed. You're to take the package to Reykjavik.'

'Just like that,' I said. 'What if I don't want to?'

'Don't be a fool. Taggart wants it that way, and you'd better not annoy him any more. Not only have you loused up his operation but you've killed Philips, and for that he can have your hide. I have a message from him – take the package to Reykjavik and all is forgiven.'

'It must be really important,' I said, and checked my fingers. 'Let's see – I've killed two men, damn near shot the leg off another, and maybe fractured a couple of skulls – and Taggart says he can sweep all that under the carpet?'

'The Russkies and the Americans can take care of their own – they bury their own dead, if any,' said Case brutally. 'But Taggart – and only Taggart – can clear you on our side. By killing Philips you set yourself up as a legitimate target. Do as he says or he'll set the dogs on you.'

I remembered I had used a phrase like that when speaking to Taggart. I said, 'Where is Slade now?'

Case turned away from me and I heard the clink of glass against bottle. 'I don't know. When I left London Taggart was trying to contact him.'

'So he could still be in Iceland,' I said slowly. 'I don't know that I like that.'

Case whirled around. 'What you like has ceased to matter. For God's sake, what's got into you, Alan? Look, it's only a hundred kilometres to Reykjavik; you can be there in two hours. Take the bloody package and go.'

'I have a better idea,' I said. 'You take it.'

He shook his head. 'That's not on. Taggart wants me back in Spain.'

I laughed. 'Jack, the easiest way to get to the International Airport at Keflavik is through Reykjavik. You could drop off the package on the way. What's so important about me and the package together?'

He shrugged. 'My instructions are that you take it. Don't ask me why because I don't know.'

'What's in the package?'

'I don't know that either; and the way this operation is shaping I don't want to know.'

I said, 'Jack, at one time I'd have called you a friend. But you've tried to con me with this nonsense about being pulled back to Spain, and I don't believe a bloody word of it. But I do believe you when you say you don't know what's going on. I don't think anyone in this operation knows what's going on except, maybe, one man.'

Case nodded. 'Taggart has his hands on the strings,' he said. 'Neither you nor I need to know much in order to do the job.'

'I wasn't thinking of Taggart,' I said. 'I don't think he knows what's going on either. He might think he does, but he doesn't.' I looked up. 'I was thinking of Slade. This whole operation is warped to the pattern of his mind. I've worked with him before and I know how he thinks.'

'So we get back to Slade,' said Case grimly. 'You're obsessed, Alan.'

'Maybe,' I said. 'But you can make Taggart happy by telling him I'll take his damned package to Reykjavik. Where do I deliver it?'

'That's better.' Case looked down at my glass which had been held, forgotten, in his hand. He gave it to me. 'You know the Nordri Travel Agency?'

'I know it.' It was the firm for which Elin had once worked.

'I don't, but I'm told that as well as running the agency they have a big souvenir shop.'

'You were told correctly.'

'I have here a piece of wrapping paper from the souvenir shop; it's the standard stuff they gift-wrap with. You have the package neatly wrapped up. You walk in and go to the back of the shop where they sell the woollen goods. A man will be standing there carrying a copy of the *New York Times*, and under his arm there will be an identical package. You make light conversation by saying, "It's colder here than in the States," to which he will reply . . .'

' "It's even colder than Birmingham." I've been through the routine before.'

'All right; once there's a mutual identification you put your package on the counter, and so will he. From then on it's a simple exchange job.'

'And when is this simple exchange job to take place?'

'At midday tomorrow.'

'Supposing I'm not there at midday tomorrow? For all I know there may be a hundred Russians spaced out along that road at one kilometre intervals.'

'There'll be a man in the shop every midday until you turn up,' said Case.

'Taggart has touching faith in me,' I said. 'According to Slade the Department is afflicted with a manpower shortage, and here is Taggart being a spendthrift. What happens if I don't turn up for a year?'

Case didn't smile. 'Taggart brought up that problem. If you're not there within a week then someone will come looking for you, and I'd regret that because, in spite of that snide crack you made about friendship, I still love you, you silly bastard.'

'Smile when you say that, stranger.'

He grinned and sat down again. 'Now let's go through all this again, right from the beginning – right from the time Slade came to see you in Scotland.'

So I repeated my tale of woe again in great detail, with all the pros and cons, and we talked for a long time. At the end of it Case said seriously, 'If you're right and Slade has been got at then this is big trouble.'

'I don't think he's been got at,' I said. 'I think he's been a Russian agent all along. But there's something else worrying me just as much as Slade – where do the Americans fit in? It's not like them to be cosy with people like Kennikin.'

Case dismissed the Americans. 'They're just a problem of this particular operation. Slade is different. He's a big boy now and has a hand in planning and policy. If he's gone sour the whole department will have to be reorganized.'

He made a sudden sweeping motion with his hand. 'Jesus, you've got me going now! I'm actually beginning to believe you. This is nonsense, Alan.'

I held out my empty glass. 'I could do with a refill – this is thirsty work.' As Case picked up the depleted bottle, I said, 'Let me put it this way. The question has been asked and, once asked, it can't be unasked. If you put my case against Slade to Taggart, just as I've put it to you, then he'll be forced to take action. He can't afford not to. He'll have Slade under a microscope and I don't think Slade can stand close inspection.'

Case nodded. 'There's just one thing, Alan. Be sure – be very, very sure – that your prejudices aren't shouting too loud. I know why you left the Department and I know why you hate Slade's guts. You're biased. This is a serious accusation you're making, and if Slade comes out of it cleaner than the driven snow then you're in big trouble. He'll demand your head on a platter – and he'll get it.'

'He'll deserve it,' I said. 'But the problem won't arise. He's as guilty as hell.' I may have sounded confident but there was the nagging fear that perhaps I was wrong. Case's warning about bias and prejudice was sound, and I hastily re-examined the indictment against Slade. I found no flaw.

Case looked at his watch. 'Eleven-thirty.'

I put down the whisky untasted. 'It's late – I'd better be going.'

'I'll tell Taggart all about it,' said Case. 'And I'll also tell him about Fleet and McCarthy. Maybe he can get a line on that angle through Washington.'

I retrieved the *sgian dubh* from the dressing-table and slipped it into my stocking-top. 'Jack, you really haven't any idea of what this operation is all about?'

'Not the faintest clue,' he said. 'I didn't know anything about it until I was pulled out of Spain. Taggart was angry, and justifiably so, in my opinion. He said you refused to have anything to do with Slade, and you wouldn't even tell him where you were. He said you'd agreed to meet me here. All I am is a messenger boy, Alan.'

'That's what Slade told me I was,' I said morosely. 'I'm getting tired of running blind; I'm getting tired of *running*. Maybe if I stood my ground for once in a while I'd be better off.'

'I wouldn't advise it,' said Case. 'Just follow orders and get the package to Reykjavik.' He put on his jacket. 'I'll walk with you to your car. Where is it?'

'Up the road.'

He was about to unlock the door when I said, 'Jack, I don't think you've been entirely frank with me. You've dodged a couple of issues in this conversation. Now there have been some bloody funny things going on lately, such as a member of the Department coming after me with a gun – so I just want to tell you one thing. It's likely that I'll be stopped on the way to Reykjavik, and if you have any part in that I'll go right through you, friendship or no friendship. I hope you understand that.'

He smiled and said, 'For God's sake, you're imagining things.'

But the smile was strained and there was something about his expression I couldn't place, and it worried me. It was only a long time afterwards that I identified the emotion. It was pity, but by then the identification had come too late.

Chapter Seven

I

We went outside to find it was as dark as it ever gets in the Icelandic summer. There was no moon but there was visibility of sorts in a kind of ghostly twilight. There was a soft explosion among the hot pools and the eerie spectre of Strokkur rose in the air, a fading apparition which dissipated into wind-blown shreds. There was a stink of sulphur in the air.

I shivered suddenly. It's no wonder that the map of Iceland is littered with place names which tell of the giant trolls who dwell in the roots of the mountains, or that the old men still hand down the legends of man in conflict with spirits. The young Icelanders, geared to the twentieth century with their transistor radios and casual use of aircraft, laugh and call it superstition. Maybe they're right, but I've noticed that they tend to force their laughter sometimes and it has a quality of unease about it. All I know is that if I had been one of the old Vikings and had come upon Strokkur unexpectedly one dark night I'd have been scared witless.

I think Case caught something of the atmosphere because he looked across at the thinning curtain of mist as Strokkur disappeared, and said softly, 'It's really something, isn't it?'

'Yes,' I said shortly. 'The car's over there. It's quite a way.'

We crunched on the crushed lava of the road and walked past the long row of white-painted pillars which separate the road from the pools. I could hear the bubbling of hot water and the stench of sulphur was stronger. If you looked at the pools in daylight you would find them all colours, some as white and clear as gin, others a limpid blue or green, and all close to boiling point. Even in the darkness I could see the white vapour rising in the air.

Case said, 'About Slade. What was the . . . ?'

I never heard the end of that question because three heavier patches of darkness rose up about us suddenly. Someone grabbed me and said, '*Stewartsen, stanna! Förstar Ni?*' Something hard jabbed into my side.

I stopped all right, but not in the way that was expected. I let myself go limp, just as McCarthy had done when I hit him with the cosh. My knees buckled and I went down to the ground. There was a muffled exclamation of surprise and momentarily the grip on my arm relaxed and the movement in a totally unexpected direction dislodged the gun from my ribs.

As soon as I was down I spun around fast with one leg bent and the other extended rigidly. The outstretched leg caught my Swedish-speaking friend behind the knees with a great deal of force and he fell to the ground. His pistol was ready for use because there was a bang as he fell and I heard the whine of a ricocheting bullet.

I rolled over until I was prone against one of the pillars. I would be too conspicuous against that painted whiteness so I wormed off the road and into the darkness, pulling the pistol from my pocket as I went. Behind me there was a shout of '*Spheshíte!*' and another voice in a lower tone said, *'Net! Slúshayte!'* I kept very still and heard the thudding of boots as someone ran towards the hotel.

Only Kennikin's mob would have addressed me as Stewartsen and in Swedish, and now they were bellowing in Russian. I kept my head close to the ground and looked back towards the road so I could see anyone there silhouetted against the paler sky. There was a flicker of movement quite close and a crunch of footsteps, so I put a bullet in that direction, picked myself up, and ran for it.

And that was damned dangerous because, in the darkness, I could very well run headlong into a bottomless pool of boiling water. I counted my paces and tried to visualize the hot pools area as I had often seen it in daylight under less unnerving conditions. The pools vary in size from a piddling little six inches in diameter to the fifty-foot giant economy size. Heated by the subterranean volcanic activity, the water continually wells out of the pools to form a network of hot streams which covers the whole area.

After I had covered a hundred yards I stopped and dropped on one knee. Ahead of me steam rose and lay in a level blanket and I thought that was Geysir itself. That means that Strokkur was somewhere to my left and a little behind. I wanted to keep clear of Strokkur – getting too close would be dicey in the extreme.

I looked back and saw nothing, but I heard footsteps following in the line I had come, and others away to the right and getting closer. I didn't know if my pursuers knew the lie of the ground or not but, intentionally or accidentally, I was being herded right into the pools. The man on the right switched on a flash lamp, a big thing like a miniature searchlight. He directed it at the ground which was lucky for me, but he was more troubled about turning himself into goulash.

I lifted my pistol and banged off three shots in that direction and the light went out suddenly. I don't think I hit him but he had come to the acute realization that his light made him a good target. I wasn't worried about making a noise; the more noise the better as far as I was concerned. Five shots had been fired, five too many in the quiet Icelandic night, and already lights were popping on in the hotel and I heard someone call from that direction.

The man behind me let fly with two shots and I saw the muzzle flare of his bullets very close, not more than ten yards away. The bullets went wide; one I don't know where, but the other raised a fountain in the pool of Geysir. I didn't return the fire but ran to the left, skirting the pool. I stumbled through a stream of hot water, but it was barely two inches deep and I went through fast enough not to do any damage to myself and being more concerned that the splashing noise would give away my position.

There were more cries from the hotel and the slam of windows opening. Someone started up a car with a rasping noise and headlights were switched on. I paid little attention to that, but carried on, angling back towards the road. Whoever started that car had a bright idea – and no pun intended. He swung around and drove towards the pools, his headlamps illuminating the whole area.

It was fortunate for me that he did because it prevented me from running headlong into one of the pools. I saw the reflections strike from the water just in time to skid to a halt, and I teetered for a moment right on the edge. My balancing act wasn't improved much when someone took a shot at me from an unexpected direction – the other side of the pool – and something tugged briefly at the sleeve of my jacket.

Although I was illuminated by the lights of that damned car my attacker was in an even worse position because he was between me and the light and marvellously silhouetted. I slung a shot at him and he flinched with his whole body and retreated. Briefly the headlights of the car swung away and I hastily ran around the pool while he put a bullet in roughly the place I had been.

Then the lights came back and steadied and I saw him retreating backwards, his head moving from side to side nervously. He didn't see me because by this time I was flat on my belly. Slowly he went backwards until he put a foot into six inches of boiling water and jerked apprehensively. He moved fast but not fast enough, because the big gas bubble which heralds the blasting of Strokkur was already rising in the pool behind him like a monster coming to the surface.

Strokkur exploded violently. Steam, superheated by the molten magma far below, drove a column of boiling water up the shaft so that it fountained sixty feet above the pool and descended in a downpour of deadly rain. The man screamed horribly, but his shrill piping was lost in the roar of Strokkur. He flung his arms wide and toppled into the pool.

I moved fast, casting a wide circle away from the revealing lights and heading eventually towards the road. There was a confused babble of shouting and more cars were started up to add their lights to the scene, and I saw a crowd of people running towards Strokkur. I came to a pool and tossed the pistol into it, together with the spare clips of ammunition. Anyone found carrying a gun that night would be likely to spend the rest of his life in jail.

At last I got to the road and joined the crowd. Someone said, 'What happened?'

'I don't know,' I flung my hand towards the pool. 'I heard shooting.'

He dashed past me, avid for vicarious excitement – he would have run just as fast to see a bloody motor smash – and I discreetly melted into the darkness behind the line of parked cars drawn up with headlamps blazing.

After I had gone a hundred yards up the road in the direction of the Volkswagen I turned and looked back. There was a lot of excitement and waving of arms, and long shadows were cast on the shifting vapour above the hot pools, and there was a small crowd about Strokkur, edging closer but not too close because Strokkur has a short, seven-minute cycle. I realized, with some astonishment, that from the time Case and I had seen Strokkur blow when we left the hotel until the man had fallen into the pool had been only seven minutes.

Then I saw Slade.

He was standing clearly visible in the lights of a car and looking out towards Strokkur. I regretted throwing away the pistol because I would have shot him there and then had I been able, regardless of the consequences. His companion raised his arm and pointed and Slade laughed. Then his friend turned around and I saw it was Jack Case.

I found myself trembling all over, and it was with an effort that I dragged myself away up the road and looked for the Volkswagen. It was still where I had left it and I got behind the driving wheel, switched on the engine, and then sat there for a moment, letting the tension drain away. No one I know has ever been shot at from close range and retained his equanimity – his autonomic nervous system sees to that. The glands work overtime and the chemicals stir in the blood, the muscles tune up and the belly goes loose, and it's even worse when the danger has gone.

I found that my hands were trembling violently and rested them on the wheel, and presently they grew still and I felt better. I had just put the car into gear when I felt a ring of cold metal applied to the back of my neck, and a harsh, well-remembered voice said, '*God dag, Herr Stewartsen. Var forsiktig.*'

I sighed, and switched off the engine. 'Hello, Vaslav,' I said.

II

'I am surrounded by a pack of idiots of an incomparable stupidity,' said Kennikin. 'Their brains are in their trigger fingers. It was different in our day; eh, Stewartsen?'

'My name is Stewart now,' I said.

'So? Well, Herr Stewart; you may switch on your engine and proceed. I will direct you. We will let my incompetent assistants find their own way.'

The muzzle of the gun nudged me. I switched on, and said, 'Which way?'

'Head towards Laugarvatn.'

I drove out of Geysir slowly and carefully. The gun no longer pressed into the back of my neck but I knew it wasn't far away, and I knew Kennikin well enough not to go in for any damn-fool heroics. He was disposed to make light conversation. 'You've caused a lot of trouble, Alan – and you can solve a problem that's been puzzling me. Whatever happened to Tadeusz?'

'Who the hell is Tadeusz?'

'The day you landed at Keflavik he was supposed to stop you.'

'So that was Tadeusz – he called himself Lindholm. Tadeusz – that sounds Polish.'

'He's Russian; his mother is Polish, I believe.'

'She'll miss him,' I said.

'So!' He was silent for a while, then he said, 'Poor Yuri had his leg amputated this morning.'

'Poor Yuri ought to have known better than to wave a belly gun at a man armed with a rifle,' I said.

'But Yuri didn't know you had a rifle,' said Kennikin. 'Not that rifle anyway. It came as quite a surprise.' He clicked his tongue. 'You really shouldn't have wrecked my jeep like that. It wasn't nice.'

Not *that* rifle. He expected a rifle, but not the blockbuster I'd taken from Fleet. That was interesting because the only other rifle was the one I'd taken from Philips and how could he know about that? Only from Slade – another piece of evidence.

I said, 'Was the engine wrecked?'

'There was a hole shot through the battery,' he said. 'And the cooling system was wrecked. We lost all the water. That must be quite a gun.'

'It is,' I said. 'I hope to use it again.'

He chuckled. 'I doubt if you will. That little episode was most embarrassing; I had to talk fast to get out of it. A couple of inquisitive Icelanders asked a lot of questions which I didn't really feel like answering. Such as why the cable car was tied up, and what had happened to the jeep. And there was the problem of keeping Yuri quiet.'

'It must have been most uncomfortable,' I said.

'And now you've done it again,' said Kennikin. 'And in public this time. What really happened back there?'

'One of your boys got himself parboiled,' I said. 'He got too close to a spouter.'

'You can see what I mean,' said Kennikin. 'Incompetents, the lot of them. You'd think three to one would be good odds, wouldn't you? But no; they bungled it.'

The odds had been three to two, but what had happened to Jack Case? He hadn't lifted a finger to help. The image of him standing and talking to Slade still burned brightly in my mind and I felt the rage boil up within me. Every time I had turned to those I thought I could trust I had been betrayed, and the knowledge burned like acid.

Buchner/Graham/Philips I could understand; he was a member of the Department fooled by Slade. But Case knew the score – he knew of my suspicions of Slade – and he had not done one damned thing to help when I had been jumped by Kennikin's men. And ten minutes later he was hobnobbing with Slade. It seemed as though the whole Department was infiltrated although, Taggart excepted, Case was the last man I would have thought to have gone over. I thought sourly that even Taggart might be on the Moscow pay-roll – that would wrap the whole bundle into one neat package.

Kennikin said, 'I'm glad I didn't underestimate you. I rather thought you'd get away from the morons I've had wished on me, so I staked out this car. A little forethought always pays, don't you think?'

I said, 'Where are we going?'

'You don't need to know in detail,' he said. 'Just concentrate on the driving. And you will go through Laugarvatn very carefully, observing all the speed limits and refraining from drawing attention. No sudden blasts on the horn, for example.' The cold steel momentarily touched my neck. 'Understand?'

'I understand.' I felt a sudden relief. I had thought that perhaps he knew where I had spent the last twenty-four hours and that we were driving to Gunnar's house. It wouldn't have surprised me overmuch; Kennikin seemed to know everything else. He had been lying in wait at Geysir, and that had been a neat trick. The thought of Elin being taken and what might have happened to Sigurlin had made my blood freeze.

We went through Laugarvatn and on to Thingvellir, and took the Reykjavik road, but eight kilometres out of Thingvellir Kennikin directed me to turn left on a secondary road. It was a road I knew well, and it led around the lake of Thingvallavatn. I wondered where the hell we were going.

I didn't have to wonder long because at a word from Kennikin I turned off the road again and we went down a bumpy track towards the lake and the lights of a small house. One of the status symbols in Reykjavik is to have a summer chalet on the shores of Thingvallavatn, even more prized because the building restrictions have forbidden new construction and so the price has shot up. Owning a chalet on Thingvallavatn is the Icelandic equivalent of having a Rembrandt on the wall.

I pulled up outside the house, and Kennikin said, 'Blow the horn.'

I tooted and someone came out. Kennikin put the pistol to my head. 'Careful, Alan,' he said. 'Be very careful.'

He also was very careful. I was taken inside without the faintest possibility of making a break. The room was decorated in that generalized style known as Swedish Modern; when done in England it looks bleak and a little phoney, but when done by the Scandinavians it looks natural and good. There was an open fire burning which was something of a surprise. Iceland has no coal and no trees to make log fires, and an open blaze is something of a rarity; a lot of houses are heated by natural hot water, and those that aren't have oil-fired central heating. This fire was of peat which glowed redly with small flickering blue flames.

Kennikin jerked his gun. 'Sit by the fire, Alan; make yourself warm. But first Ilyich will search you.'

Ilyich was a squarely-built man with a broad, flat face. There was something Asiatic about his eyes which made me think that at least one of his parents hailed from the farther side of the Urals. He patted me thoroughly, then turned to Kennikin and shook his head.

'No gun?' said Kennikin. 'That was wise of you.' He smiled pleasantly at Ilyich, then turned to me and said, 'You see what I mean, Alan? I am surrounded by idiots. Draw up the left leg of your trousers and show Ilyich your pretty little knife.'

I obeyed, and Ilyich blinked at it in astonishment while Kennikin bawled him out. Russian is even richer than English in cutting invective. The *sgian dubh* was confiscated and Kennikin waved me to the seat while Ilyich, red-faced, moved behind me.

Kennikin put away his gun. 'Now, what will you have to drink, Alan Stewart?'

'Scotch – if you have it.'

'We have it.' He opened a cupboard near the fireplace and poured a drink. 'Will you have it neat or with water? I regret we have no soda.'

'Water will do,' I said. 'Make it a weak one.'

He smiled. 'Oh, yes; you have to keep a clear head,' he said sardonically. 'Section four, Rule thirty-five : when offered a drink by the opposition request a weak one.' He splashed water into the glass then brought it to me. 'I hope that is to your satisfaction.'

I sipped it cautiously, then nodded. If it had been any weaker it wouldn't have been able to crawl out of the glass and past my lips. He returned to the cupboard and poured himself a tumbler-full of Icelandic *brennivin* and knocked back half the contents with one gulp. I watched with some astonishment as he swallowed the raw spirit without twitching a hair. Kennikin was going downhill fast if he now did his drinking openly. I was surprised the Department hadn't caught on to it.

I said, 'Can't you get Calvados here in Iceland, Vaslav?'

He grinned and held up the glass. 'This is my first drink in four years, Alan. I'm celebrating.' He sat in the chair opposite me. 'I have reason to celebrate – it's not often that old friends meet in our profession. Is the Department treating you well?'

I sipped the watery scotch and set the glass on the low table next to my chair. 'I haven't been with the Department for four years.'

He raised his eyebrows. 'My information is different.'

'Maybe,' I said. 'But it's wrong. I quit when I left Sweden.'

'I also quit,' said Kennikin. 'This is my first assignment in four years. I have you to thank for that. I have you to thank for many things.' His voice was slow and even. 'I didn't quit of my own volition, Alan; I was sent to sort papers in Ashkhabad. Do you know where that is?'

'Turkmenistan.'

'Yes.' He thumped his chest. 'Me – Vaslav Viktorovich Kennikin – sent to comb the borders for narcotic smugglers and to shuffle papers at a desk.'

'Thus are the mighty fallen,' I said. 'So they dug you up for

345

this operation. That must have pleased you.'

He stretched out his legs. 'Oh, it did. I was very pleased when I discovered you were here. You see, at one time I thought you were my friend.' His voice rose slightly. 'You were as close to me as my own brother.'

'Don't be silly,' I said. 'Don't you know intelligence agents have no friends?' I remembered Jack Case and thought bitterly that I was learning the lesson the hard way, just as Kennikin had.

He went on as though I had not spoken. 'Closer to me than my brother. I would have put my life in your hands – I *did* put my life in your hands.' He stared into the colourless liquid in his glass. 'And you sold me out.' Abruptly he lifted the glass and drained it.

I said derisively, 'Come off it, Vaslav; you'd have done the same in my position.'

He stared at me. 'But I trusted you,' he said almost plaintively. 'That is what hurt most.' He stood up and walked to the cupboard. Over his shoulder he said, 'You know what my people are like. Mistakes aren't condoned. And so . . .' He shrugged '. . . the desk in Ashkhabad. They wasted me.' His voice was harsh.

'It could have been worse,' I said. 'It could have been Siberia. Khatanga, for instance.'

When he returned to his chair the tumbler was full again. 'It very nearly was,' he said in a low voice. 'But my friends helped – my true Russian friends.' With an effort he pulled himself back to the present. 'But we waste time. You have a certain piece of electronic equipment which is wrongfully in your possession. Where is it?'

'I don't know what you're talking about.'

He nodded. 'Of course, you would have to say that; I expected nothing else. But you must realize that you will give it to me eventually.' He took a cigarette case from his pocket. 'Well?'

'All right,' I said. 'I know I've got it, and you know I've got it; there's no point in beating around the bush. We know each other too well for that, Vaslav. But you're not going to get it.'

He took a long Russian cigarette from the case. 'I think I will, Alan; I *know* I will.' He put the case away and searched his pockets for a lighter. 'You see, this is not just an ordinary operation for me. I have many reasons for wanting to hurt you that are quite unconnected with this electronic gear. I am quite certain I shall get it. Quite certain.'

His voice was cold as ice and I felt an answering shudder run down my spine. *Kennikin will want to operate on you with a sharp knife.* Slade had said that, and Slade had delivered me into his hands.

He made a sound of annoyance as he discovered he had no means of lighting his cigarette, and Ilyich stepped from behind me, a cigarette lighter in his hand. Kennikin inclined his head to accept a light as the flint sparked. It sparked again but no flame appeared, and he said irritably, 'Oh, never mind!'

He leaned forward and picked up a spill of paper from the hearth, ignited it at the fire, and lit his cigarette. I was interested in what Ilyich was doing. He had not returned to his post behind my chair but had gone to the cupboard where the liquor was kept — behind Kennikin.

Kennikin drew on the cigarette and blew a plume of smoke, and then looked up. As soon as he saw that Ilyich was not in sight the pistol appeared in his hand. 'Ilyich, what are you doing?' The gun pointed steadily at me.

Ilyich turned with the refill cylinder of butane gas in his hand. 'Filling the lighter.'

Kennikin blew out his cheeks and rolled his eyes upwards. 'Never mind that,' he said curtly. 'Go outside and search the Volkswagen. You know what to look for.'

'It's not there, Vaslav,' I said.

'Ilyich will make sure of it,' said Kennikin.

Ilyich put the butane cylinder back into the liquor cupboard and left the room. Kennikin did not put away the pistol again but held it casually. 'Didn't I tell you? The team they have given me has been scraped from the bottom of the barrel. I'm surprised you didn't try to take advantage.'

I said, 'I might have done if you hadn't been around.'

'Ah, yes,' he said. 'We know each other very well. Perhaps too well.' He balanced the cigarette in an ashtray and picked up his glass. 'I don't really know if I will get any pleasure working on you. Don't you English have a proverb — "It hurts me as much as it hurts you." ' He waved his hand. 'But perhaps I've got it wrong.'

'I'm not English,' I said. 'I'm a Scot.'

'A difference that makes no difference is no difference. But I'll tell you something — you made a great difference to me and to my life.' He took a gulp of *brennivin.* 'Tell me — that girl you've been running around with — Elin Ragnarsdottir; are you in love with her?'

I felt myself tighten. 'She's got nothing to do with this.'

He laughed. 'Do not trouble yourself. I have no intention of harming her. Not a hair of her head shall be touched. I don't believe in

347

the Bible, but I'm willing to swear on it.' His voice turned sardonic. 'I'll even swear on the Works of Lenin, if that's an acceptable substitute. Do you believe me?'

'I believe you,' I said. I did, too. There was no comparison between Kennikin and Slade. I wouldn't have taken Slade's word had he sworn on a thousand bibles, but in this I would accept Kennikin's lightest word and trust him as he had once trusted me. I knew and understood Kennikin and I liked his style; he was a gentleman – savage, but still a gentleman.

'Well, then; answer my question. Are you in love with her?'

'We're going to be married.'

He laughed. 'That's not exactly a straight answer, but it will do.' He leaned forward. 'Do you sleep with her, Alan? When you come to Iceland do you lie under the stars together and clasp each other's bodies, and work at each other until your sweat mingles? Do you call each other by names that are sweet and soft and handle each other until the last gust of passion, that flare of ecstasy in each of you, mutually quenches the other and ebbs away into languor? Is that how it is, Alan?'

His voice was purring and cruel. 'Do you remember our last encounter in the pine woods when you tried to kill me? I wish you had been a better shot. I was in hospital in Moscow for a long time while they patched me up, but there was one patch they couldn't put back, Alan. And that is why, if you come out of this alive – and that is something I haven't decided yet – you will be no good to Elin Ragnarsdottir or to any other woman.'

I said, 'I'd like another drink.'

'I'll make it stronger this time,' he said. 'You look as though you need it.' He came across and took my glass, and backed towards the liquor cupboard. Still holding the pistol he poured whisky into the glass and added a little water. He brought it back. 'You need some colour in your cheeks,' he said.

I took the whisky from him. 'I understand your bitterness – but any soldier can expect to be wounded; it's an occupational hazard. What really hurts is that you were sold out. That's it, Vaslav, isn't it?'

'That among other things,' he agreed.

I sampled the whisky; it was strong this time. 'Where you go wrong is in your identification of who did it. Who was your boss at that time?'

'Bakayev – in Moscow.'

'And who was my boss?'

He smiled. 'That eminent British nobleman, Sir David Taggart.'

I shook my head. 'No. Taggart wasn't interested; there were bigger fish to occupy his attention at the time. You were sold out by Bakayev, your own boss, in collaboration with my boss, and I was just the instrument.'

Kennikin roared with laughter. 'My dear Alan; you've been reading too much Fleming.'

I said, 'You haven't asked who my boss was.'

He was still shaking with chuckles as he said, 'All right; who was he?'

'Slade,' I said.

The laughter suddenly stopped. I said, 'It was very carefully planned. You were sacrificed to give Slade a good reputation. It had to look good – it had to look very authentic. That's why you weren't told. All things considered, you put up a good fight, but all the time your foundations were being nibbled away by Bakayev who was passing information to Slade.'

'This is nonsense, Stewartsen,' he said; but his face had gone pale and the livid cicatrice stood out on his cheek.

'So you failed,' I said. 'And, naturally, you had to be punished, or it still wouldn't look right. Yes, we know how your people do things, and if you hadn't been sent to Ashkhabad or somewhere like it we'd have been suspicious. So you spent four years in exile to make it look right; four years of paper shuffling for doing your duty. You've been had, Vaslav.'

His eyes were stony. 'This Slade I don't know,' he said shortly.

'You ought to. He's the man you take orders from in Iceland. You thought it natural, perhaps, that you shouldn't be in command on this operation. Your people wouldn't want to give sole responsibility to a man like yourself who failed once. A reasonable attitude, you would think; and maybe you could retrieve your reputation and your honour and aspire to your former dizzy heights by a successful completion of this mission.' I laughed. 'And who do they give you for a boss? None other than the man who torpedoed you in Sweden.'

Kennikin stood up. The pistol pointed unwaveringly at my chest. 'I know who ruined the Swedish operation,' he said. 'And I can touch him from here.'

'I just took orders,' I said. 'Slade did the brainwork. Do you remember Jimmy Birkby?'

'I've never heard of the man,' said Kennikin stonily.

349

'Of course not. You'd know him better as Sven Hornlund – the man I killed.'

'The British agent,' said Kennikin. 'I remember. It was that one act of yours that made me sure of you.'

'Slade's idea,' I said. 'I didn't know who I killed. That's why I left the Department – I had a flaming row.' I leaned forward. 'Vaslav, it fits the pattern, don't you see that? Slade sacrificed one good man to make you trust me. It meant nothing to him how many of our agents were killed. But he and Bakayev sacrificed you to make Taggart trust Slade the more.'

Kennikin's grey eyes were like stones. His face was quite still except for one corner of his mouth where the scar ran down which twitched with a slight tic.

I leaned back in the chair and picked up the glass. 'Slade's sitting pretty now. He's here in Iceland running both sides of an operation. My God, what a position to be in! But it went wrong when one of the puppets refused to jump when he pulled the strings. That must have worried the hell out of him.'

'I don't know this man Slade,' repeated Kennikin woodenly.

'No? Then why are you all worked up?' I grinned at him. 'I'll tell you what to do. Next time you speak to him why don't you ask him for the truth. Not that he'll tell you; Slade never told anyone the truth in his life. But he might give himself away to such a perceptive person as yourself.'

Lights flickered through the drawn curtains and there was the sound of a car pulling up outside. I said, 'Think of the past, Vaslav; think of the wasted years in Ashkhabad. Put yourself in the position of Bakayev and ask yourself which is the more important – an operation in Sweden which can be reconstituted at any times, or the chance to put a man high in the hierarchy of British Intelligence – so high that he lunches with the British Prime Minister?'

Kennikin moved uneasily and I knew I had got to him. He was deep in thought and the pistol no longer pointed directly at me. I said, 'As a matter of interest, how long did it take to build up another Swedish outfit? Not long, I'll bet. I daresay Bakayev had an organization already working in parallel ready to go into action when you dropped out.'

It was a shot at random but it went home. It was like watching a one-armed bandit come up with the jackpot; the wheels went round and whirred and clicked and a mental bell rang loud and clear. Kennikin snorted and turned away. He looked down into the fire and the hand holding the pistol was down at his side.

I tensed myself, ready to jump him, and said softly, 'They didn't trust you, Vaslav. Bakayev didn't trust you to wreck your own organization and make it look good. I wasn't trusted either; but I was sold out by Slade who is one of your mob. You're different; you've been kicked in the teeth by your own people. How does it feel?'

Vaslav Kennikin was a good man – a good agent – and he gave nothing away. He turned his head and looked at me. 'I've listened to this fairy-story with great interest,' he said colourlessly. 'The man, Slade, I don't know. You tell a fine tale, Alan, but it won't get you out of trouble. You're not . . .'

The door opened and two men came in. Kennikin turned impatiently, and said, 'Well?'

The bigger of the men said in Russian, 'We've just got back.'

'So I see,' said Kennikin emotionlessly. He waved at me. 'Let me introduce Alan Stewartsen, the man you were supposed to bring here. What went wrong? Where's Igor?'

They looked at each other, and the big man said, 'He was taken to hospital. He was badly scalded when . . .'

'That's fine!' said Kennikin caustically. 'That's marvellous!' He turned and appealed to me. 'What do you think of this, Alan? We get Yuri safely and secretly to the trawler but Igor must go to a hospital where questions are asked. What would you do with an idiot like this?'

I grinned, and said hopefully, 'Shoot him.'

'It's doubtful if a bullet would penetrate his thick skull,' said Kennikin acidly. He looked balefully at the big Russian. 'And why, in God's name, did you start shooting? It sounded like the outbreak of revolution.'

The man gestured towards me helplessly. 'He started it.'

'He should never have been given the opportunity. If three men can't take another one quietly, then . . .'

'There were two of them.'

'Oh!' Kennikin glanced at me. 'What happened to him?'

'I don't know – he ran away,' said the big man.

I said casually, 'It's hardly surprising. He was just a guest from the hotel.' I seethed internally. So Case had just run away and left me to it. I wouldn't sell him out to Kennikin but there'd be an account to settle if I got out of this mess.

'He probably raised the alarm at the hotel,' said Kennikin.

'Can't you do anything right?'

The big man started to expostulate, but Kennikin cut him short. 'What's Ilyich doing?'

'Taking a car to pieces.' His voice was sullen.

'Go and help him.' They both turned, but Kennikin said sharply, 'Not you, Gregor. Stay here and watch Stewartsen.' He handed his pistol to the smaller man.

I said, 'Can I have another drink, Vaslav?'

'Why not?' said Kennikin. 'There's no danger of you turning into an alcoholic. You won't live that long. Watch him, Gregor.'

He left the room, closing the door behind him, and Gregor planted himself in front of it and looked at me expressionlessly. I drew up my legs very slowly and got to my feet. Gregor lifted the pistol and I grinned at him, holding up my empty glass. 'You heard what the boss said; I'm allowed a last drink.'

The muzzle of the pistol dropped. 'I'll be right behind you,' he said.

I walked across to the liquor cupboard, talking all the time. 'I'll bet you're from the Crimea, Gregor. That accent is unmistakable. Am I right?'

He was silent, but I persevered with my patter. 'There doesn't seem to be any vodka here, Gregor. The nearest to it is *brennivin*, but that comes a bad second – I don't go for it myself. Come to that, I don't like vodka very much either. Scotch is my tipple, and why not, since I'm a Scot?'

I clattered bottles and heard Gregor breathing down my neck. The Scotch went into the glass to be followed by water, and I turned with it raised in my hand to find Gregor a yard away with the pistol trained on my navel. As I have said, there *is* a place for the pistol, and this was it. It's a dandy indoor weapon. If I had done anything so foolish as to throw the drink into his face he would have drilled me clear through the spine.

I held up the glass at mouth level. '*Skal* – as we say in Iceland.' I had to keep my hand up otherwise the cylinder of butane gas would have dropped out of my sleeve, so I walked across the room in a pansified manner and sat in my chair again. Gregor looked at me with something like contempt in his eyes.

I sipped from the glass and then transferred it from one hand to the other. When I had finished wriggling about the butane cylinder was tucked in between the cushion and the arm of the chair. I toasted Gregor again and then looked at the hot-burning peat fire with interest.

On each refill cylinder of butane there is a solemn warning:

EXTREMELY INFLAMMABLE MIXTURE. DO NOT USE NEAR FIRE OR FLAME. KEEP OUT OF THE REACH OF CHILDREN. DO NOT PUNCTURE OR INCINERATE. Commercial firms do not like to put such horrendous notices on their products and usually do so only under pressure of legislation, so that in all cases the warnings are thoroughly justified.

The peat fire was glowing hot with a nice thick bed of red embers. I thought that if I put the cylinder into the fire one of two things would happen – it would either explode like a bomb or take off like a rocket – and either of these would suit me. My only difficulty was that I didn't know how long it would take to blow up. Putting it into the fire might be easy, but anyone quick enough could pull it out – Gregor, for instance. Kennikin's boys couldn't possibly be as incompetent as he made them out to be.

Kennikin came back. 'You were telling the truth,' he said.

'I always do; the trouble is most people don't recognize it when they hear it. So you agree with me about Slade.'

He frowned. 'I don't mean that stupid story. What I am looking for is not in your car. Where is it?'

'I'm not telling you, Vaslav.'

'You will.'

A telephone bell rang somewhere. I said, 'Let's have a bet on it.'

'I don't want to get blood on the carpet in here,' he said. 'Stand up.' Someone took the telephone receiver off the hook.

'Can't I finish my drink first?'

Ilyich opened the door and beckoned to Kennikin, who said, 'You'd better have finished that drink by the time I get back.'

He left the room and Gregor moved over to stand in front of me. That wasn't very good because as long as he stood there I wouldn't have a chance of jamming the butane cylinder into the fire. I touched my forehead and found a thin film of sweat.

Presently Kennikin came back and regarded me thoughtfully. 'The man you were with at Geysir – a guest at the hotel, I think you said.'

'That's right.'

'Does the name – John Case – mean anything to you?'

I looked at him blankly. 'Not a thing.'

He smiled sadly. 'And you are the man who said he always told the truth.' He sat down. 'It seems that what I am looking for has ceased to have any importance. More accurately, its importance has diminished relative to yourself. Do you know what that means?'

'You've lost me,' I said, and I really meant it. This was a new twist.

Kennikin said, 'I would have gone to any length necessary to get the information from you. However, my instructions have changed. You will not be tortured, Stewartsen, so put your mind at ease.'

I let out my breath. 'Thanks!' I said wholeheartedly.

He shook his head pityingly. 'I don't want your thanks. My instructions are to kill you immediately.'

The telephone bell rang again.

My voice came out in a croak. 'Why?'

He shrugged. 'You are getting in the way.'

I swallowed. 'Hadn't you better answer that telephone? It might be a change of instruction.'

He smiled crookedly. 'A last minute reprieve, Alan? I don't think so. Do you know why I told you of these instructions? It's not normally done, as you know.'

I knew all right, but I wouldn't give him the satisfaction of telling him. The telephone stopped ringing.

'There are some good things in the Bible,' he said. 'For instance – "An eye for an eye, and a tooth for a tooth." I had everything planned for you, and I regret my plans cannot now be implemented. But at least I can watch you sweat as you're sweating now.'

Ilyich stuck his head around the door. 'Reykjavik,' he said.

Kennikin made a gesture of annoyance. 'I'm coming.' He rose. 'Think about it – and sweat some more.'

I put out my hand. 'Have you a cigarette?'

He stopped in mid-stride and laughed aloud. 'Oh, very good, Alan. You British are strong on tradition. Certainly you may have the traditional last cigarette.' He tossed me his cigarette case. 'Is there anything else you would like?'

'Yes,' I said. 'I would like to be in Trafalgar Square on New Year's Eve in the year 2000.'

'My regrets,' he said, and left the room.

I opened the case, stuck a cigarette in my mouth, and patted my pockets helplessly; then I stooped very slowly to pick up one of the paper spills from the hearth. I said to Gregor, 'I'm just going to light my cigarette,' and bent forward to the fire, hoping to God he wouldn't move from the door.

I held the spill in my left hand and leaned forward so that my right hand was screened by my body, and thrust the cylinder into the embers at the same time as I lifted the flaming spill and returned to my seat. Waving it in a circle to attract Gregor's eyes

354

from the fire, I applied it to the tip of the cigarette, drew in smoke and blew a plume in his direction. I deliberately allowed the flame to burn down so that it touched my fingers.

'Ouch!' I exclaimed, and shook my hand vigorously. Anything to keep him from looking directly at the fire. It took all the will-power I had to refrain from glancing at it myself.

The telephone was slammed down and Kennikin came stalking back. 'Diplomats!' he said in a scathing voice. 'As though I don't have enough troubles.' He jerked his thumb at me. 'All right; on your feet.'

I held up the cigarette. 'What about this?'

'You can finish it outside. There'll be just enough . . .'

The blast of the exploding cylinder was deafening in that enclosed area, and it blew the peat fire all over the room. Because I was expecting it I was quicker off the mark than anyone else. I ignored the red-hot ember which stung my neck, but Gregor found he couldn't do the same with the ember which alighted on the back of his hand. He gave a yell and dropped the gun.

I dived across the room, seized the pistol and shot him twice through the chest. Then I turned to nail Kennikin before he could recover. He had been beating red-hot bits of peat from his jacket but now he was turning at the sound of the shots. I lifted the pistol and he grabbed a table-lamp and threw it at me. I ducked, my shot went wild, and the table-lamp sailed over my head to hit Ilyich straight in the face as he opened the door to find out what the hell was going on.

That saved me the trouble of opening it. I shouldered him aside and stumbled into the hall to find that the front door was open. Kennikin had given me a bad time, and much as I would have liked to have fought it out with him this was not the time for it. I ran out of the house and past the Volkswagen which was minus all four wheels, and on the way took a snap shot at the big Russian to encourage him to keep his head down. Then I ran into the darkness which, by now, was not as dark as I would have liked, and took to the countryside fast.

The countryside thereabouts consisted of humpy lava covered by a thick layer of moss and occasional patches of dwarf birch. At full speed and in broad daylight a man might make one mile an hour without breaking an ankle. I sweated over it, knowing that if I broke my ankle, or as much as sprained it, I would be picked up easily and probably shot on the spot.

I went about four hundred yards, angling away from the lake shore and up towards the road, before I stopped. Looking back I saw the windows of the room in which I had been held; there was a curious flickering and I saw that the curtains were going up in flames. There were distant shouts and someone ran in front of the window, but it seemed that no one was coming after me. I don't think any of them knew which direction I'd taken.

The view ahead was blocked by the bulk of an old lava flow and I reckoned the road was on the other side of that. I moved forward again and began to climb over it. It would be dawn soon and I wanted to get out of sight of the house.

I went over the top of the lava flow on my belly and once safely screened on the other side I got to my feet. Dimly, in the distance, I could see a straight dark line which could only be the road, and I was just about to make for it when someone put a stranglehold on my neck and a hand clamped on my wrist with bone-crushing pressure. 'Drop the gun!' came a hoarse whisper in Russian.

I dropped the pistol and was immediately flung away so that I stumbled and fell. I looked up into the glare of a flashlight which illumined a pistol held on me. 'Christ, it's you!' said Jack Case.

'Put that bloody light out,' I said, and massaged my neck. 'Where the hell were you when the whistle blew at Geysir?'

'I'm sorry about that,' said Case. 'He was at the hotel when I arrived.'

'But you said . . .'

There was a note of exasperation in Case's voice. 'Jesus, I couldn't tell you he was there. In the mood you were in you'd have slaughtered him.'

'A fine friend you turned out to be,' I said bitterly. 'But this is no time to go into it. Where's your car – we can talk later.'

'Just off the road down there.' He put away his gun.

I came to a snap decision; this was no time to trust Case or anyone else. I said, 'Jack, you can tell Taggart I'll deliver his package to Reykjavik.'

'All right, but let's get out of here.'

I moved close to him. 'I don't trust you, Jack,' I said, and sank three rigid fingers into his midriff. The air exploded violently from his lungs and he doubled up. I chopped at the back of his neck and he collapsed at my feet. Jack and I had always been level on the unarmed combat mat and I don't think I could have taken him so easily had he known what was coming.

In the distance a car started and its engine throbbed. I saw the glow of headlights to my right and dropped flat. I could hear the car coming up the spur track towards the road, but it turned away and moved in the opposite direction – the way I had driven in from Thingvellir.

When it was out of earshot I reached out and began to search Case's pockets. I took his keys and stripped him of his shoulder holster and pistol. Gregor's pistol I wiped clean and threw away. Then I went to look for Case's car.

It was a Volvo and I found it parked just off the road. The engine turned over easily at the touch of a button and I moved away without lights. I would be going all the way around Thing-vallavatn and it would be a long way to Laugarvatn, but I certainly didn't feel like going back.

Chapter Eight

I

I got into Laugarvatn just before five in the morning and parked the car in the drive. As I got out I saw the curtains twitch and Elin ran out and into my arms before I got to the front door. 'Alan!' she said. 'There's blood on your face.'

I touched my cheek and felt the caked blood which had oozed from a cut. It must have happened when the butane cylinder went up. I said, 'Let's get inside.'

In the hall we met Sigurlin. She looked me up and down, then said, 'Your jacket's burnt.'

I glanced at the holes in the fabric. 'Yes,' I said. 'I was careless, wasn't I?'

'What happened?' asked Elin urgently.

'I had . . . I had a talk with Kennikin,' I said shortly. The reaction was hitting me and I felt very weary. I had to do something about it because there was no time to rest. 'Do you have any coffee?' I asked Sigurlin.

Elin gripped my arm. 'What happened? What did Kenni . . .?'

'I'll tell you later.'

Sigurlin said, 'You look as though you haven't slept for a week. There's a bed upstairs.'

I shook my head. 'No. I . . . we . . . are moving out.'

She and Elin exchanged glances, and then Sigurlin said practically, 'You can have your coffee, anyway. It's all ready – we've been drinking the stuff all night. Come into the kitchen.'

I sat down at the kitchen table and spooned a lot of sugar into a steaming cup of black coffee. It was the most wonderful thing I've ever tasted. Sigurlin went to the window and looked at the Volvo in the drive. 'Where's the Volkswagen?'

I grimaced. 'It's a write-off.' The big Russian had said that Ilyich was taking it to pieces, and from the fleeting glimpse I had of it he had been right. I said, 'What's it worth, Sigurlin?' and put my hand in my pocket for my cheque-book.

She made an impatient gesture. 'That can wait.' There was an edge to her voice. 'Elin told me everything. About Slade – about Kennikin – everything.'

'You shouldn't have done that, Elin,' I said quietly.

'I had to talk about it to someone,' she burst out.

'You must go to the police,' said Sigurlin.

I shook my head. 'So far this has been a private fight. The only casualties have been among the professionals – the men who know the risks and accept them. No innocent bystanders have been hurt. I want to keep it that way. Anyone who monkeys around with this without knowing the score is in for trouble – whether he's wearing a police uniform or not.'

'But it needn't be handled at that level,' she said. 'Let the politicians handle it – the diplomats.'

I sighed and leaned back in my chair. 'When I first came to this country someone told me that there are three things which an Icelander can't explain – not even to another Icelander: the Icelandic political system, the Icelandic economic system, and the Icelandic drinking laws. We're not worried about alcohol right now, but politics and economics are right at the top of my list of worries.'

Elin said, 'I don't really know what you're talking about.'

'I'm talking about that refrigerator,' I said. 'And that electric coffee-grinder.' My finger stabbed out again. 'And the electric kettle and the transistor radio. They're all imported and to afford imports you have to export – fish, mutton, wool. The herring shoals have moved a thousand miles away, leaving your inshore herring fleet high and dry. Aren't things bad enough without making them worse?'

Sigurlin wrinkled her brow. 'What do you mean?'

'There are three nations involved – Britain, America and Russia. Supposing a thing like this is handled at diplomatic level with an exchange of Notes saying: "Stop fighting your battles on Icelandic territory." Do you really think a thing like that could be kept secret? Every country has political wild men – and I'm sure Ice-

358

land is no exception – and they'd all jump on the bandwagon.'

I stood up. 'The anti-Americans would shout about the Base at Keflavik; the anti-communists would have a good handle to grab hold of; and you'd probably restart the Fishing War with Britain because I know a lot of Icelanders who aren't satisfied with the settlement of 1961.'

I swung around to face Sigurlin. 'During the Fishing War your trawlers were denied entry to British ports, so you have built up a fair trade with Russia, which you still have. What do you think of Russia as a trading partner?'

'I think they're very good,' she said instantly. 'They've done a lot for us.'

I said deliberately, 'If your government is placed in the position of having to take official notice of what's going on then that good relationship might be endangered. Do you want that to happen?'

Her face was a study in consternation. I said grimly, 'If this lark ever comes into the open it'll be the biggest *cause célèbre* to hit Iceland since Sam Phelps tried to set up Jorgen Jorgensen as king back in 1809.'

Elin and Sigurlin looked at each other helplessly. 'He's right,' said Sigurlin.

I knew I was right. Under the placid level of Icelandic society were forces not safe to tamper with. Old animosities still linger among the longer-memoried and it wouldn't take much to stir them up. I said, 'The less the politicians know, the better it will be for everybody. I like this country, damn it; and I don't want the mud stirred up.' I took Elin's hand. 'I'll try to get this thing cleaned up soon. I think I know a way.'

'Let them have the package,' she said urgently. 'Please, Alan; let them have it.'

'I'm going to,' I said. 'But in my own way.'

There was a lot to think about. The Volkswagen, for instance. It wouldn't take Kennikin long to check the registration and find out where it came from. That meant he'd probably be dropping in before the day was over. 'Sigurlin,' I said. 'Can you take a pony and join Gunnar?'

She was startled. 'But why . . .?' She took the point. 'The Volkswagen?'

'Yes; you might have unwelcome visitors. You'd be better out of the way.'

'I had a message from Gunnar last night, just after you left. He's staying out another three days.'

'That's good,' I said. 'In three days everything should be over.'

'Where are you going?'

'Don't ask,' I warned. 'You know too much already. Just get yourself in a place where there's no one to ask questions.' I snapped my fingers. 'I'll shift the Land-Rover too. I'm abandoning it, but it had better not be found here.'

'You can park it in the stables.'

'That's a thought. I'm going to move some things from the Land-Rover into the Volvo. I'll be back in a few minutes.'

I went into the garage and took out the electronic gadget, the two rifles and all the ammunition. The guns I wrapped in a big piece of sacking which I found and they went into the boot. Elin came out, and said, 'Where *are* we going?'

'Not we,' I said. 'Me.'

'I'm coming with you.'

'You're going with Sigurlin.'

That familiar stubborn, mulish look came on to her face. 'I liked what you said in there,' she said. 'About not wanting to cause trouble for my country. But it is my country and I can fight for it as well as anyone else.'

I nearly laughed aloud. 'Elin,' I said. 'What do you know about fighting?'

'As much as any other Icelander,' she said evenly.

She had something there. 'You don't know what's going on,' I said.

'Do you?'

'I'm beginning to catch on. I've just about proved that Slade is a Russian agent – and I loaded Kennikin just like a gun and pointed him at Slade. When they meet he's likely to go off, and I wouldn't like to be in Slade's position when it happens. Kennikin believes in direct action.'

'What happened last night? Was it bad?'

I slammed the boot closed. 'It wasn't the happiest night of my life,' I said shortly. 'You'd better get some things together. I want this house unoccupied within the hour.' I took out a map and spread it out.

'Where are you going?' Elin was very persistent.

'Reykjavik,' I said. 'But I want to go to Keflavik first.'

'That's the wrong way round,' she pointed out. 'You'll get to Reykjavik first – unless you go south through Hveragerdi.'

'That's the problem,' I said slowly, and frowned as I looked at the map. The web of roads I had visualized existed all right but not as extensively as I had imagined. I didn't know about the

Department's supposed manpower shortage, but Kennikin certainly wasn't suffering that way; I had counted ten different men with Kennikin at one time or another.

And the map showed that the whole of the Reykjanes Peninsula could be sealed off from the east by placing men at two points – Thingvellir and Hveragerdi. If I went through either of those towns at a normal slow speed I'd be spotted; if I went through hell-for-leather I'd attract an equivalent amount of attention. And the radio-telephone which had worked for me once would now work against me, and I'd have the whole lot of them down on me.

'Christ!' I said. 'This is bloody impossible.'

Elin grinned at me cheerfully. 'I know an easy way,' she said too casually. 'One that Kennikin won't think of.'

I looked at her suspiciously. 'How?'

'By sea.' She laid her finger on the map. 'If we go to Vik I know an old friend who will take us to Keflavik in his boat.'

I regarded the map dubiously. 'It's a long way to Vik, and it's in the wrong direction.'

'All the better,' she said. 'Kennikin won't expect you to go there.'

The more I studied the map, the better it looked. 'Not bad,' I said.

Elin said innocently, 'Of course, I'll have to come with you to introduce you to my friend.'

She'd done it again.

II

It was an odd way to get to Reykjavik because I pointed the Volvo in the opposite direction and put my foot down. It was with relief that I crossed the bridge over the Thjòrsá River because that was a bottleneck I was sure Kennikin would cover, but we got across without incident and I breathed again.

Even so, after we passed Hella I had a belated attack of nerves and left the main road to join the network of bumpy tracks in Landeyjasandur, feeling that anyone who could find me in that maze would have to have extrasensory perception.

At midday Elin said decisively, 'Coffee.'

'What have you got? A magic wand?'

'I've got a vacuum flask – and bread – and pickled herring. I raided Sigurlin's kitchen.'

'Now I'm glad you came,' I said. 'I never thought of that.' I pulled the car to a halt.

'Men aren't as practical as women,' said Elin.

As we ate I examined the map to check where we were. We had just crossed a small river and the farmstead we had passed was called Bergthórshvoll. It was with wonder that I realized we were in the land of Njal's Saga. Not far away was Hlidarendi, where Gunnar Hamundarsson was betrayed by Hallgerd, his wife, and had gone down fighting to the end. Skarp-Hedin had stalked over this land with death on his face and his war-axe raised high, tormented by the devils of revenge. And here, at Bergthórshvoll, Njal and his wife, Bergthóra, had been burned to death with their entire family.

All that had happened a thousand years ago and I reflected, with some gloom, that the essential nature of man had not changed much since. Like Gunnar and Skarp-Hedin I travelled the land in imminent danger of ambush by my enemies and, like them, I was equally prepared to lay an ambush if the opportunity arose. There was another similarity; I am a Celt and Njal had a Celtic name, nordicized from Neil. I hoped the Saga of Burnt Njal would not be echoed by the Saga of Burnt Stewart.

I aroused myself from these depressing thoughts, and said, 'Who is your friend in Vik?'

'Valtyr Baldvinsson, one of Bjarni's old school friends. He's a marine biologist studying the coastal ecology. He wants to find out the extent of the changes when Katla erupts.'

I knew about Katla. 'Hence the boat,' I said. 'And what makes you think he'll run us to Keflavik?'

Elin tossed her head. 'He will if I ask him to.'

I grinned. 'Who is this fascinating woman with a fatal power over men? Can it be other than Mata Hari, girl spy?'

She turned pink but her voice was equable as she said, 'You'll like Valtyr.'

And I did. He was a square man who, but for his colouring, looked as though he had been rough-hewn from a pillar of Icelandic basalt. His torso was square and so was his head, and his hands had stubby, spatulate fingers which appeared to be too clumsy for the delicate work he was doing when we found him in his laboratory. He looked up from the slide he was mounting and gave a great shout. 'Elin! What are you doing here?'

'Just passing by. This is Alan Stewart from Scotland.'

My hand was enveloped in a big paw. 'Good to meet you,' he said, and I had the instant feeling he meant it.

He turned to Elin. 'You're lucky to have caught me here. I'm leaving tomorrow.'

Elin raised her eyebrows. 'Oh! Where for?'

'At last they've decided to put a new engine into that relic of a longship they've given me instead of a boat. I'm taking her round to Reykjavik.'

Elin glanced at me and I nodded. In the course of events you have to be lucky sometimes. I had been wondering how Elin was going to cajole him into taking us to Keflavik without arousing too many suspicions, but now the chance had fallen right into our laps.

She smiled brilliantly. 'Would you like a couple of passengers? I told Alan I hoped you could take us to have a look at Surtsey, but we wouldn't mind going on to Keflavik. Alan has to meet someone there in a couple of days.'

'I'd be glad to have company,' Valtyr said jovially. 'It's a fair distance and I'd like someone to spell me at the wheel. How's your father?'

'He's well,' said Elin.

'And Bjarni? Has Kristin given him that son yet?'

Elin laughed. 'Not yet – but soon. And how do you know it won't be a daughter?'

'It will be a boy!' he said with certainty. 'Are you on holiday, Alan?' he asked in English.

I replied in Icelandic, 'In a manner of speaking. I come here every year.'

He looked startled, and then grinned. 'We don't have many enthusiasts like you,' he said.

I looked around the laboratory; it appeared to be a conventional biological set-up with the usual rows of bottles containing chemicals, the balance, the two microscopes and the array of specimens behind glass. An odour of formalin was prevalent. 'What are you doing here?' I asked.

He took me by the arm and led me to the window. With a large gesture he said, 'Out there is the sea with a lot of fish in it. It's hazy now but in good weather you can see Vestmannaeyjar where there is a big fishing fleet. Now come over here.'

He led me to a window on the other side of the room and pointed up towards Myrdalsjökull. 'Up there is the ice and, under the ice, a big bastard called Katla. You know Katla?'

'Everybody in Iceland knows of Katla,' I said.

He nodded. 'Good! I've been studying the sea off this coast and all the animals in it, big and small – and the plants too. When

363

Katla erupts sixty cubic kilometres of ice will be melted into fresh water and it will come into the sea here; as much fresh water as comes out of all the rivers of Iceland in a year will come into the sea in one week and in this one place. It will be bad for the fish and the animals and the plants because they aren't accustomed to so much fresh water all at once. I want to find out how badly they will be hit and how long they take to recover.'

I said, 'But you have to wait until Katla erupts. You might wait a long time.'

He laughed hugely. 'I've been here five years – I might be here another ten, but I don't think so. The big bastard is overdue already.' He thumped me on the arm. 'Could blow up tomorrow – then we don't go to Keflavik.'

'I won't lose any sleep over it,' I said drily.

He called across the laboratory, 'Elin, in your honour I'll take the day off.' He took three big strides, picked her up and hugged her until she squealed for mercy.

I didn't pay much attention to that because my eyes were attracted to the headline of a newspaper which lay on the bench. It was the morning newspaper from Reykjavik and the headline on the front page blared : GUN BATTLE AT GEYSIR.

I read the story rapidly. Apparently a war had broken out at Geysir to judge from this account, and everything short of light artillery had been brought into play by persons unknown. There were a few eye-witness reports, all highly inaccurate, and it seemed that a Russian tourist, one Igor Volkov, was now in hospital after having come too close to Strokkur. Mr Volkov had no bullet wounds. The Soviet Ambassador had complained to the Icelandic Minister of Foreign Affairs about this unprovoked assault on a Soviet citizen.

I opened the paper to see if there was a leading article on the subject and, of course, there was. In frigid and austere tones the leader writer enquired of the Soviet Ambassador the reason why the aforesaid Soviet citizen, Igor Volkov, was armed to the teeth at the time, since there was no record of his having declared any weapons to the Customs authorities when he entered the country.

I grimaced. Between us, Kennikin and I were in a fair way to putting a crimp into Icelandic-Soviet relations.

III

We left rather late the next morning and I wasn't in a good mood because I had a thick head. Valtyr had proved to be a giant among drinkers and, since I was suffering from lack of sleep, my efforts to keep up with him had been disastrous. He put me to bed, laughing boisterously, and woke up himself as fresh as a daisy while I had a taste in my mouth as though I had been drinking the formalin from his specimen jars.

My mood wasn't improved when I telephoned London to speak to Taggart only to find he was absent from his office. The bland official voice declined to tell me where he was but offered to pass on a message, an invitation which I, in my turn, declined to accept. The curious actions of Case had led me to wonder who in the Department was trustworthy, and I wouldn't speak to anyone but Taggart.

Valtyr's boat was anchored in a creek, a short distance from the open beach, and we went out to it in a dinghy. He looked curiously at the two long, sackcloth-covered parcels I took aboard but made no comment, while I hoped they did not look too much like what they actually were. I wasn't going to leave the rifles behind because I had an idea I might need them.

The boat was about twenty-five feet overall, with a tiny cabin which had sitting headroom and a skimpy wooden canopy to protect the man at the wheel from the elements. I had checked the map to find the sea distance from Vik to Keflavik and the boat seemed none too large. I said, 'How long will it take?'

'About twenty hours,' said Valtyr, and added cheerfully, 'If the bastard engine keeps going. If not, it takes forever. You get seasick?'

'I don't know,' I said. 'I've never had the chance to find out.'

'You have the chance now.' He bellowed with laughter.

We left the creek and the boat lifted alarmingly to the ocean swells and a fresh breeze streamed Elin's hair. 'It's clearer today,' said Valtyr. He pointed over the bows. 'You can see Vestmannaeyjar.'

I looked towards the group of islands and played the part which Elin had assigned me. 'Where is Surtsey from here?'

'About twenty kilometres to the south-west of Heimaey – the big island. You won't see much of it yet.'

We plunged on, the little boat dipping into the deep swells and

occasionally burying her bows in the water and shaking free a
shower of spray when she came up. I'm not any kind of a seaman
and it didn't look too safe to me, but Valtyr took it calmly enough,
and so did Elin. The engine, which appeared to be a toy diesel about
big enough to go with a Meccano set, chugged away, aided by a
crack from Valtyr's boot when it faltered, which it did too often
for my liking. I could see why he was pleased at the prospect of
having a new one.

It took six hours to get to Surtsey, and Valtyr circled the island,
staying close to shore, while I asked the appropriate questions. He
said, 'I can't land you, you know.'

Surtsey, which came up thunderously and in flames from the
bottom of the sea, is strictly for scientists interested in finding out
how life gains hold in a sterile environment. Naturally they don't
want tourists clumping about and bringing in seeds on their boots.
'That's all right,' I said. 'I didn't expect to go ashore.'

Suddenly he chuckled. 'Remember the Fishing War?'

I nodded. The so-called Fishing War was a dispute between
Iceland and Britain about off-shore fishing limits, and there was
a lot of bad blood between the two fishing fleets. Eventually it had
been settled, with the Icelanders making their point of a twelve-
mile limit.

Valtyr laughed, and said, 'Surtsey came up and pushed our
fishing limit thirty kilometres farther south. An English skipper I
met told me it was a dirty trick – as though we'd done it deliberately.
So I told him what a geologist told me; in a million years our
fishing limit will be pushed as far south as Scotland.' He laughed
uproariously.

When we left Surtsey I abandoned my pretended interest and
went below to lie down. I was in need of sleep and my stomach had
started to do flip-flops so that I was thankful to stretch out, and I
fell asleep as though someone had hit me on the head.

IV

My sleep was long and deep because when I was awakened by
Elin she said, 'We're nearly there.'

I yawned. 'Where?'

'Valtyr is putting us ashore at Keflavik.'

I sat up and nearly cracked my head on a beam. Overhead a jet
plane whined and when I went aft into the open I saw that the
shore was quite close and a plane was just dipping in to land. I

stretched, and said, 'What time is it?'

'Eight o'clock,' said Valtyr. 'You slept well.'

'I needed it after a session with you,' I said, and he grinned.

We tied up at eight-thirty, Elin jumped ashore and I handed her the wrapped rifles. 'Thanks for the ride, Valtyr.'

He waved away my thanks. 'Any time. Maybe I can arrange to take you ashore on Surtsey – it's interesting. How long are you staying?'

'For the rest of the summer,' I said. 'But I don't know where I'll be.'

'Keep in touch,' he said.

We stood on the dockside and watched him leave, and then Elin said, 'What are we doing here?'

'I want to see Lee Nordlinger. It's a bit chancy, but I want to know what this gadget is. Will Bjarni be here, do you think?'

'I doubt it,' said Elin. 'He usually flies out of Reykjavik Airport.'

'After breakfast I want you to go to the Icelandair office at the airport here,' I said. 'Find out where Bjarni is, and stay there until I come.' I rubbed my cheek and felt unshaven bristles. 'And stay off the public concourse. Kennikin is sure to have Keflavik Airport staked out and I don't want you seen.'

'Breakfast first,' she said. 'I know a good café here.'

When I walked into Nordlinger's office and dumped the rifles in a corner he looked at me with some astonishment, noting the sagging of my pockets under the weight of the rifle ammunition, my bristly chin and general uncouthness. His eyes flicked towards the corner. 'Pretty heavy for fishing tackle,' he commented. 'You look beat, Alan.'

'I've been travelling in rough country,' I said, and sat down. 'I'd like to borrow a razor, and I'd like you to look at something.'

He slid open a drawer of his desk and drew out a battery-powered shaver which he pushed across to me. 'The washroom's two doors along the corridor,' he said. 'What do you want me to look at?'

I hesitated. I couldn't very well ask Nordlinger to keep his mouth shut no matter what he found. That would be asking him to betray the basic tenets of his profession, which he certainly wouldn't do. I decided to plunge and take a chance, so I dug the metal box from my pocket, took off the tape which held the lid on, and shook out the gadget. I laid it before him. 'What's that, Lee?'

He looked at it for a long time without touching it, then he said, 'What do you want to know about it?'

'Practically everything,' I said. 'But to begin with – what nationality is it?'

He picked it up and turned it around. If anyone could tell me anything about it, it was Commander Lee Nordlinger. He was an electronics officer at Keflavik Base and ran the radar and radio systems, both ground-based and airborne. From what I'd heard he was damned good at his job.

'It's almost certainly American,' he said. He poked his finger at it. 'I recognize some of the components – these resistors, for instance, are standard and are of American manufacture.' He turned it around again. 'And the input is standard American voltage and at sixty cycles.'

'All right,' I said. 'Now – what is it?'

'That I can't tell you right now. For God's sake, you bring in a lump of miscellaneous circuitry and expect me to identify it at first crack of the whip. I may be good but I'm not that good.'

'Then can you tell me what it's not?' I asked patiently.

'It's no teenager's transistor radio, that's for sure,' he said, and frowned. 'Come to that, it's like nothing I've ever seen before.' He tapped the odd-shaped piece of metal in the middle of the assembly. 'I've never seen one of these, for example.'

'Can you run a test on it?'

'Sure.' He uncoiled his lean length from behind the desk. 'Let's run a current through it and see if it plays "The Star-Spangled Banner".'

'Can I come along?'

'Why not?' said Nordlinger lightly. 'Let's go to the shop.' As we walked along the corridor he said, 'Where did you get it?'

'It was given to me,' I said uncommunicatively.

He gave me a speculative glance but said no more. We went through swing doors at the end of a corridor and into a large room which had long benches loaded with electronic gear. Lee signalled to a petty officer who came over. 'Hi, Chief; I have something here I want to run a few tests on. Have you a test bench free?'

'Sure, Commander.' The petty officer looked about the room. 'Take number five; I guess we won't be using that for a while.'

I looked at the test bench; it was full of knobs and dials and screens which meant less than nothing. Nordlinger sat down. 'Pull up a chair and we'll see what happens.' He attached clips to the terminals on the gadget, then paused. 'We already know certain things about it. It isn't part of an airplane; they don't use such a heavy voltage. And it probably isn't from a ship for roughly the same reason. So that leaves ground-based equipment. It's designed to plug into the normal electricity system of the North American continent – it could have been built in Canada. A lot of Canadian firms use American manufactured components.'

I jogged him along. 'Could it come from a TV set?'

'Not from any TV I've seen.' He snapped switches. 'A hundred ten volts – sixty cycles. Now, there's no amperage given so we have to be careful. We'll start real low.' He twisted a knob delicately and a fine needle on a dial barely quivered against the pin.

He looked down at the gadget. 'There's current going through now but not enough to give a fly a heart attack.' He paused, and looked up. 'To begin with, this thing is crazy; an alternating current with these components isn't standard. Now, let's see – first we have what seems to be three amplification stages, and that makes very little sense.'

He took a probe attached to a lead. 'If we touch the probe here we should get a sine wave on the oscilloscope . . .' He looked up. '. . . which we do. Now we see what happens at this lead going into this funny-shaped metal ginkus.'

He gently jabbed the probe and the green trace on the oscilloscope jumped and settled into a new configuration. 'A square wave,' said Nordlinger. 'This circuit up to here is functioning as a chopper – which is pretty damn funny in itself for reasons I won't go into right now. Now let's see what happens at the lead going *out* of the ginkus and into this mess of boards.'

He touched down the probe and the oscilloscope trace jumped again before it settled down. Nordlinger whistled. 'Just look at that spaghetti, will you?' The green line was twisted into a fantastic waveform which jumped rhythmically and changed form with each jump. 'You'd need a hell of a lot of Fournier analysis to sort that out,' said Nordlinger. 'But whatever else it is, it's pulsed by this metal dohickey.'

'What do you make of it?'

'Not a damn thing,' he said. 'Now I'm going to try the output stage; on past form this should fairly tie knots into that oscilloscope – maybe blow it up.' He lowered the probe and we looked expectantly at the screen.

I said, 'What are you waiting for?'

'I'm waiting for nothing.' Nordlinger looked at the screen blankly. 'There's no output.'

'Is that bad?'

He looked at me oddly. In a gentle voice he said, 'It's impossible.'

I said, 'Maybe there's something broken in there.'

'You don't get it,' said Nordlinger. 'A circuit is just what it says —
a circle. You break the circle anywhere you get no current flow anywhere.' He applied the probe again. 'Here there's a current of a
pulsed and extremely complex form.' Again the screen jumped into
life. 'And here, in the same circuit, what do we get?'

I looked at the blank screen. 'Nothing?'

'Nothing, he said firmly. He hesitated. 'Or, to put it more precisely, nothing that can show on this test rig.' He tapped the gadget.
'Mind if I take this thing away for a while?'

'Why?'

'I'd like to put it through some rather more rigorous tests. We
have another shop.' He cleared his throat and appeared to be a
little embarrassed. 'Uh . . . you won't be allowed in there.'

'Oh — secret stuff.' That would be in one of the areas to which
Fleet's pass would give access. 'All right, Lee; you put the gadget
through its paces and I'll go and shave. I'll wait for you in your
office.'

'Wait a minute,' he said. 'Where did you get it, Alan?'

I said, 'You tell me what it does and I'll tell you where it came
from.'

He grinned. 'It's a deal.'

I left him disconnecting the gadget from the test rig and went
back to his office where I picked up the electric shaver. Fifteen
minutes later I felt a lot better after having got rid of the hair. I
waited in Nordlinger's office for a long time — over an hour and a
half — before he came back.

He came in carrying the gadget as though it was a stick of dynamite and laid it gently on his desk. 'I'll have to ask you where you
got this,' he said briefly.

'Not until you tell me what it does,' I said.

He sat behind his desk and looked at the complex of metal and
plastic with something like loathing in his eyes. 'It does nothing,'
he said flatly. 'Absolutely nothing.'

'Come off it,' I said. 'It must do *something*.'

'Nothing!' he repeated. 'There is no measurable output.' He
leaned forward and said softly, 'Alan, out there I have instruments
that can measure any damn part of the electromagnetic spectrum
from radio waves of such low frequency you wouldn't believe possible right up to cosmic radiation — and there's nothing coming out
of this contraption.'

'As I said before — maybe something has broken.'

'That cat won't jump; I tested everything.' He pushed at it and
it moved sideways on the desk. 'There are three things I don't like

about this. Firstly, there are components in here that are not re-
motely like anything I've seen before, components of which I don't
even understand the function. I'm supposed to be pretty good at
my job, and that, in itself, is enough to disturb me. Secondly, it's
obviously incomplete – it's just part of a bigger complex – and yet
I doubt if I would understand it even if I had everything. Thirdly
– and this is the serious one – it shouldn't work.'

'But it isn't working,' I said.

He waved his hand distractedly. 'Perhaps I put it wrong. There
should be an output of some kind. Good Christ, you can't keep
pushing electricity into a machine – juice that gets used up – without
getting something out. That's impossible.'

I said, 'Maybe it's coming out in the form of heat.'

He shook his head sadly. 'I got mad and went to extreme
measures. I pushed a thousand watts of current through it in the
end. If the energy output was in heat then the goddamn thing would
have glowed like an electric heater. But no – it stayed as cool as
ever.'

'A bloody sight cooler than you're behaving,' I said.

He threw up his hands in exasperation. 'Alan, if you were a
mathematician and one day you came across an equation in which
two and two made five without giving a nonsensical result then
you'd feel exactly as I do. It's as though a physicist were con-
fronted by a perpetual motion machine which works.'

'Hold on,' I said. 'A perpetual motion machine gets something
for nothing – energy usually. This is the other way round.'

'It makes no difference,' he said. 'Energy can neither be created
nor destroyed.' As I opened my mouth he said quickly, 'And don't
start talking about atomic energy. Matter can be regarded as
frozen, concentrated energy.' He looked at the gadget with grim
eyes. 'This thing is destroying energy.'

Destroying energy! I rolled the concept around my cerebrum
to see what I could make of it. The answer came up fast – nothing
much. I said, 'Let's not go overboard. Let's see what we have. You
put an input into it and you get out . . .'

'Nothing,' said Nordlinger.

'Nothing you can measure,' I corrected. 'You may have some
good instrumentation here, Lee, but I don't think you've got the
whole works. I'll bet that there's some genius somewhere who not
only knows what's coming out of there but has an equally involved
gadget that can measure it.'

'Then I'd like to know what it is,' he said. 'Because it's right outside my experience.'

371

I said, 'Lee, you're a technician, not a scientist. You'll admit that?'

'Sure; I'm an engineer from way back.'

'That's why you have a crew-cut – but this was designed by a long-hair.' I grinned. 'Or an egghead.'

'I'd still like to know where you got it.'

'You'd better be more interested in where it's going. Have you got a safe – a really secure one?'

'Sure.' He did a double-take. 'You want *me* to keep *this*?'

'For forty-eight hours,' I said. 'If I don't claim it in that time you'd better give it to your superior officer together with all your forebodings, and let him take care of it.'

Nordlinger looked at me with a cold eye. 'I don't know but what I shouldn't give it to him right now. Forty-eight hours might mean my neck.'

'You part with it now and it will be my neck,' I said grimly.

He picked up the gadget. 'This is American and it doesn't belong here at Keflavik. I'd like to know where it does belong.'

'You're right about it not belonging here,' I said. 'But I'm betting it's Russian – and they want it back.'

'For God's sake!' he said. 'It's full of American components.'

'Maybe the Russians learned a lesson from Macnamara on cost-effectiveness. Maybe they're shopping in the best market. I don't give two bloody hoots if the components were made in the Congo – I still want you to hold on to it.'

He laid the gadget on his desk again very carefully. 'Okay – but I'll split the difference; I'll give you twenty-four hours. And even then you don't get it back without a full explanation.'

'Then I'll have to be satisfied with that,' I said. 'Providing you lend me your car. I left the Land-Rover in Laugarvatn.'

'You've got a goddamn nerve.' Nordlinger put his hand in his pocket and tossed the car key on the desk. 'You'll find it in the car park near the gate – the blue Chevrolet.'

'I know it.' I put on my jacket and went to the corner to pick up the rifles. 'Lee, do you know a man called Fleet?'

He thought for a moment. 'No.'

'Or McCarthy?'

'The CPO you met in the shop is McCarthy.'

'Not the same one,' I said. 'I'll be seeing you, Lee. We'll go fishing some time.'

'Stay out of jail.'

I paused at the door. 'What makes you say a thing like that?'

His hand closed over the gadget. 'Anyone who walks around with a thing like this ought to be in jail,' he said feelingly.

I laughed, and left him staring at it. Nordlinger's sense of what was right had been offended. He was an engineer, not a scientist, and an engineer usually works to the rule book – that long list of verities tested through the centuries. He tends to forget that the rule book was originally compiled by scientists, men who see nothing strange in broken rules other than an opportunity to probe a little deeper into the inexplicable universe. Any man who can make the successful transition from Newtonian to quantum physics without breaking his stride can believe anything any day of the week and twice as much on Sundays. Lee Nordlinger was not one of these men, but I'd bet the man who designed the gadget was.

I found the car and put the rifles and the ammunition into the boot. I was still wearing Jack Case's pistol in the shoulder holster and so now there was nothing to spoil the set of my coat. Not that I was any more presentable; there were scorch marks on the front from the burning peat of Kennikin's fire, and a torn sleeve from where a bullet had come a shade too close at Geysir. It was stained with mud and so were my trousers, and I was looking more and more like a tramp – but a clean-shaven tramp.

I climbed into the car and trickled in the direction of the International Airport, thinking of what Nordlinger hadn't been able to tell me about the gadget. According to Lee it was an impossible object and that made it scientifically important – so important that men had died and had their legs blown off and had been cooked in boiling water because of it.

And one thing made me shiver. By Kennikin's last words just before I made my escape from the house at Thingvallavatn he had made it quite clear that I was now more important than the gadget. He had been prepared to kill me without first laying his hands on it and, for all he knew, once I was dead the gadget would have been gone forever with me.

I had Nordlinger's evidence that the gadget was of outstanding scientific importance, so what was it about me that made me even more important than that? It's not often in this drear technological world that a single man becomes of more importance than a scientific breakthrough. Maybe we were returning to sanity at last, but I didn't think so.

There was a side entrance to the Icelandair office which one could use without going through the public concourse, so I parked and went in. I bumped pleasantly into a hostess, and asked, 'Is Elin Ragnarsdottir around?'

'Elin? She's in the waiting-room.'

I walked into the waiting-room and found her alone. She jumped up quickly. 'Alan, you've been so long!'

'It took longer than expected.' Her face was strained and there seemed to be a sense of urgency about her. 'You didn't have trouble?'

'No trouble – not for me. Here's the newspaper.'

I took it from her. 'Then what's the matter?'

'I think you'd better . . . you'd better read the paper.' She turned away.

I shook it open and saw a photograph on the front page, a life-size reproduction of my *sgian dubh*. Underneath, the black headline screamed: HAVE YOU SEEN THIS KNIFE?

The knife had been found embedded in the heart of a man sitting in a car parked in the driveway of a house in Laugarvatn. The man had been identified as a British tourist called John Case. The house and the Volkswagen in which Case had been found belonged to Gunnar Arnarsson who was absent, being in charge of a pony-trekking expedition. The house had been broken into and apparently searched. In the absence of Gunnar Arnarsson and his wife, Sigurlin Asgeirsdottir, it was impossible to tell if anything had been stolen. Both were expected to be contacted by the police.

The knife was so unusual in form that the police had requested the newspaper to publish a photograph of it. Anyone who had seen this knife or a similar knife was requested to call at his nearest police station. There was a boxed paragraph in which the knife was correctly identified as a Scottish *sgian dubh*, and after that the paragraph degenerated into pseudo-historical blather.

The police were also trying to find a grey Volvo registered in Reykjavik; anyone having seen it was requested to communicate with the police at once. The registration number was given.

I looked at Elin. 'It's a mess, isn't it?' I said quietly.

'It *is* the man you went to see at Geysir?'

'Yes.' I thought of how I had mistrusted Jack Case and left him unconscious near Kennikin's house. Perhaps he had not been untrustworthy at all because I had no illusions about who had killed him. Kennikin had the *sgian dubh* and Kennikin had the Volkswagen – and probably Kennikin had stumbled across Case in his search for me.

But why had Case been killed?

'This is dreadful,' said Elin. 'Another man killed.' Her voice was filled with despair.

'I didn't kill him,' I said baldly.

She picked up the paper. 'How did the police know about the Volvo?'

'Standard procedure,' I said. 'As soon as Case was identified the police would dig into whatever he'd been doing since he entered the country. They'd soon find he hired a car – and it wasn't the Volkswagen he was found in.'

I was glad the Volvo was tucked away out of sight in Valtyr's garage in Vik. 'When is Valtyr going back to Vik?' I asked.

'Tomorrow,' said Elin.

It seemed as though everything was closing in on me. Lee Nordlinger had given me a twenty-four hour ultimatum; it was too much to hope that Valtyr wouldn't check on the Volvo as soon as he got back to Vik – he might even go to the Reykjavik police if he felt certain it was the car they were searching for. And when the police laid hands on Sigurlin then the balloon would certainly go up – I couldn't see her keeping silent in the face of a corpse parked in her home.

Elin touched my arm. 'What are you going to do?'

'I don't know,' I said. 'Right now I just want to sit and think.'

I began to piece the fragments together and gradually they made some kind of sense which hinged around Kennikin's sudden switch of attitude after he had captured me. At first he had been all for extracting the gadget from me and he was looking forward with unwholesome delight to the operation. But then he lost interest in the gadget and announced that my death was the more important, and that was just after he had received a telephone call.

I ticked off the sequence of events. At Geysir I had told Case of my suspicions of Slade, and Case had agreed to pass them on to Taggart. No matter what happened Slade would then be thoroughly investigated. But I had seen Slade talking to Case just before Kennikin took me. Suppose that Case had aroused Slade's suspicions in some way? Slade was a clever man – a handler of men – and maybe Case had shown his hand.

What would Slade do? He would contact Kennikin to find if I had been captured. He would insist that his cover next to Taggart should remain unbroken at all costs and that this was more important than the gadget. He would say, 'Kill the bastard!' That was why Kennikin had switched.

And it would be just as important to kill Jack Case before he talked to Taggart.

I had played right into Slade's hands and left Case for Kennikin to find, and Kennikin had stabbed him with my knife. Kennikin had traced where the Volkswagen had come from and gone looking for me, and he had left the body of Case. Terrorist tactics.

It all tied together except for one loose end which worried me. Why, when I had been jumped at Geysir by Kennikin's mob, had Jack Case run out on me? He hadn't lifted a finger to help; he hadn't fired a shot in my defence even though he was armed. I knew Jack Case and that was very unlike him, and that, together with his apparent chumminess with Slade, had been the basis of my mistrust of him. It worried me very much.

But it was all past history and I had the future to face and decisions to make. I said, 'Did you check on Bjarni?'

Elin nodded listlessly. 'He's on the Reykjavik-Höfn run. He'll be in Reykjavik this afternoon.'

'I want him over here,' I said. 'And you're to stick in this office until he comes. You're not to move out of it even for meals. You can have those sent up. And most emphatically you're not to go out into the concourse of the airport; there are too many eyes down there looking for you and me.'

'But I can't stay here forever,' she protested.

'Only until Bjarni comes. Then you can tell him anything you think fit – you can even tell him the truth. Then you're to tell him what he must do.'

She frowned. 'And that is?'

'He's got to get you on a plane and out of here, and he has to do it discreetly without going through normal channels. I don't care if he has to dress you up as a hostess and smuggle you aboard as one of the crew, but you mustn't go down into the concourse as an ordinary passenger.'

'But I don't think he could do that.'

'Christ!' I said. 'If he can smuggle in crates of Carlsberg from Greenland he can smuggle you out. Come to think of it, going to Greenland might not be such a bad idea; you could stay in Narsassuaq until all this blows over. Not even Slade, clever though he is, would think of looking there.'

'I don't want to go.'

'You're going,' I said. 'I want you from underfoot. If you think things have been rough for the last few days then compared to the next twenty-four hours they'll seem like an idyllic holiday. I want you out of it, Elin, and, by God, you'll obey me.'

'So you think I'm useless,' she said bitterly.

'No, I don't; and you've proved it during the last few days. Everything you've done in that time has been against your better judgement, but you've stuck by me. You've been shot and you've been shot at, but you still helped out.'

'Because I love you,' she said.

'I know – and I love you. That's why I want you out of here. I don't want you killed.'

'And what about you?' she demanded.

'I'm different,' I said. 'I'm a professional. I know what to do and how to do it; you don't.'

'Case was a professional too – and he's dead. So was Graham, or whatever his name really was. And that man, Volkov, was hurt at Geysir – and he was a professional. You said yourself that the only people hurt so far have been the professionals. I don't want you hurt, Alan.'

'I also said that no innocent bystanders have been hurt,' I said. 'You're an innocent bystander – and I want to keep it that way.'

I had to do something to impress the gravity of the situation upon her. I looked around the room to check its emptiness, then quickly took off my jacket and unslung Case's shoulder holster complete with gun. I held it in my hand and said, 'Do you know how to use this?'

Her eyes dilated. 'No!'

I pointed to the slide. 'If you pull this back a bullet is injected into the breech. You push over this lever, the safety catch, then you point it and pull the trigger. Every time you pull a bullet comes out, up to a maximum of eight. Got that?'

'I think so.'

'Repeat it.'

'I pull back the top of the gun, push over the safety catch and pull the trigger.'

'That's it. It would be better if you squeezed the trigger but this is no time for finesse.' I put the pistol back into the holster and pressed it into her reluctant hands. 'If anyone tries to make you do anything you don't want to do just point the gun and start shooting. You might not hit anyone but you'll cause some grey hairs.'

The one thing that scares a professional is a gun in the hands of an amateur. If another professional is shooting at you at least you know he's accurate and you have a chance of out-manoeuvring him. An amateur can kill you by accident.

I said, 'Go into the loo and put on the holster under your jacket. When you come back I'll be gone.'

She accepted the finality of the situation along with the pistol. 'Where are you going?'

'The worm is turning,' I said. 'I'm tired of running, so I'm going hunting. Wish me luck.'

She came close to me and kissed me gently and there were unshed tears in her eyes and the gun in its holster was iron-hard between us. I patted her bottom and said, 'Get along with you,' and watched as she turned and walked away. When the door closed behind her I also left.

Chapter Nine

I

Nordlinger's Chevrolet was too long, too wide and too soft-sprung and I wouldn't have given a thank you for it in the *Obyggdir*, but it was just what I needed to get into Reykjavik fast along the International Highway which is the only good bit of paved road in Iceland. I did the twenty-five miles to Hafnarfjördur at 80 mph and cursed when I was slowed down by the heavy traffic building up around Kopavogur. I had an appointment at midday in the souvenir shop of the Nordri Travel Agency and I didn't want to miss it.

The Nordri Travel Agency was in Hafnarstraeti. I parked the car in a side street near Naust and walked down the hill towards the centre of the town. I had no intention at all of going into Nordri; why would I when Nordlinger had the gadget tucked away in his safe? I came into Hafnarstraeti and ducked into a bookshop opposite Nordri. There was a café above the shop with a flight of stairs leading directly to it so that one could read over a cup of coffee. I bought a newspaper as cover and went upstairs.

It was still before the midday rush so I got a seat at the window and ordered pancakes and coffee. I spread open the paper and then glanced through the window at the crowded street below and found that, as I had planned, I had a good view of the travel agency which was on the other side of the street. The thin gauze curtains didn't obstruct my view but made it impossible for anyone to recognize me from the street.

The street was fairly busy. The tourist season had begun and the first hardy travellers had already started to ransack the souvenir shops and carry home their loot. Camera-hung and map in hand they were easy to spot, yet I inspected every one of them because the man I was looking for would probably find it convenient to be mistaken for a tourist.

This was a long shot based on the fact that everywhere I had gone in Iceland the opposition had shown up. I had followed instructions on arrival and gone the long way around to Reykjavik and Lindholm had been there. I had gone to earth in Asbyrgi and Graham had pitched up out of the blue. True, that was because of the radio bug planted on the Land-Rover, but it had happened. Fleet had lain in wait and had shot up the Land-Rover in a deliberate ambush, the purpose of which was still a mystery. Yet he, like Lindholm, had known *where* to wait. Kennikin had jumped me at Geysir and I'd got away from that awkward situation by the thickness of a gnat's whisker.

And now I was expected to call at the Nordri Travel Agency. It was a thin chance but it seemed logical to suppose that if past form was anything to go on then the place would be staked out. So I took a more than ordinary interest in those below who window-shopped assiduously, and I hoped that if Kennikin was laying for me I'd be able to recognize his man. He couldn't have brought a whole army to Iceland and, one way or another, I'd already laid eyes on a lot of his men.

Even so, it was a full half-hour before I spotted him, and that was because I was looking at him from an unfamiliar angle – from above. It is very hard to forget a face first seen past the cross hairs of a telescopic sight, yet it was only when he lifted his head that I recognized one of the men who had been with Kennikin on the other side of the Tungnaá River.

He was pottering about and looking into the window of the shop next to Nordri and appeared to be the perfect tourist complete with camera, street map and sheaf of picture postcards. I whistled up the waitress and paid my bill so that I could make a quick getaway, but reserved the table for a little longer by ordering another coffee.

He wouldn't be alone on a job like this and so I was interested in his relationship with the passers-by. As the minutes ticked on he appeared to become increasingly restless and consulted his watch frequently and, at one o'clock exactly, he made a decisive move. He lifted his hand and beckoned, and another man came into my line of sight and crossed the street towards him.

I gulped my coffee and went downstairs to lurk at the newspaper counter while observing my friends through the glass doors of the bookshop. They had been joined by a third man whom I recognized immediately – none other than Ilyich who had unwittingly provided me with the butane bomb. They nattered for a while and then Ilyich stuck out his arm and tapped his wrist-watch, shrugging expressively. They all set off up the street towards Posthusstraeti and I followed.

From the bit of action with the watch it seemed that they not only knew the rendezvous I was supposed to keep but the time I was to keep it. They had pulled off duty at one o'clock like workmen clocking off the job. It wouldn't have surprised me overmuch if they knew the passwords as well.

At the corner of Posthusstraeti two of them got into a parked car and drove away, but Ilyich turned smartly to the right across the street and headed at a quick clip towards the Hotel Borg, into which he disappeared like a rabbit diving into its hole. I hesitated for a moment and then drifted in after him.

He didn't stop to collect a key at the desk but went immediately upstairs to the second floor, with me on his heels. He walked along a corridor and knocked at a door, so I did a smart about-turn and went downstairs again where I had a good view of the foyer. This meant another obligatory cup of coffee with which I was already awash, but that's the penalty of a trailing job. I spread my newspaper at arm's length and waited for Ilyich to appear again.

He wasn't away long – a matter of ten minutes – and when he came back I knew triumphantly that all my suspicions had been correct and that everything I had done in Iceland was justified. He came downstairs talking to someone – and that someone was Slade!

They came through the lounge on their way to the dining-room and Slade passed my table no farther away than six feet. It was to be expected that he would wait in his room for a report, positive or negative, and then head for the fleshpots. I shifted in my chair and watched where they would sit and, during the brouhaha of the seating ceremony I left quickly and walked into the foyer and out of sight.

Two minutes later I was on the second floor and tapping at the same door Ilyich had knocked on, hoping that no one would answer. No one did and so, by a bit of trickery involving a plastic sheet from my wallet, I went inside. That was something I had learned at school – the Department had trained me well.

I wasn't stupid enough to search Slade's luggage. If he was as smart as I thought he would have gimmicked it so that he could tell at a glance whether a suitcase had been opened. Standard procedure when on a job, and Slade had a double advantage – he'd been trained by both sides. But I did inspect the door of his wardrobe, checking to see if there were any fine hairs stuck down with dabs of saliva which would come free if the door was opened. There was nothing, so I opened the door, stepped inside, and settled down to wait in the darkness.

I waited a long time. That I expected, having seen the way Slade gourmandized, yet I wondered how he would take to the Icelandic cuisine which is idiosyncratic, to say the least. It takes an Icelander to appreciate *hakarl* – raw shark meat buried in sand for several months – or pickled whale blubber.

It was quarter to three when he came back and by that time my own stomach was protesting at the lack of attention; it had had plenty of coffee but very little solid food. Ilyich was with him and it came as no surprise that Slade spoke Russian like a native. Hell, he probably *was* a Russian, as had been Gordon Lonsdale, another of his stripe.

Ilyich said, 'Then there's nothing until tomorrow?'

'Not unless Vaslav comes up with something,' said Slade.

'I think it's a mistake,' said Ilyich. 'I don't think Stewartsen will go near the travel agency. Anyway, are we sure of the information?'

'We're sure,' said Slade shortly. 'And he'll be there within the next four days. We've all underestimated Stewart.'

I smiled in the darkness. It was nice to have an unsolicited testimonial. I missed what he said next, but Ilyich said, 'Of course, we don't do anything about the package he will carry. We let him get rid of it in the agency and then we follow him until we get him alone.'

'And then?'

'We kill him,' said Ilyich unemotionally.

'Yes,' said Slade. 'But there must be no body found. There has been too much publicity already; Kennikin was mad to have left the body of Case where he did.' There was a short silence and then he said musingly, 'I wonder what Stewartsen did with Philips?'

To this rhetorical question Ilyich made no answer, and Slade said, 'All right; you and the others are to be at the Nordri Agency at eleven tomorrow. As soon as you spot Stewart I must be notified by telephone immediately. Is that understood?'

'You will be informed,' said Ilyich. I heard the door open. 'Where is Kennikin?' he asked.

'What Kennikin does is no concern of yours,' said Slade sharply. 'You may go.'

The door slammed.

I waited and heard a rustle of paper and a creak followed by a metallic click. I eased open the wardrobe door a crack and looked into the room with one eye. Slade was seated in an armchair with a newspaper on his knee and was applying a light to a fat cigar. He got the end glowing to his satisfaction and looked about for an ash-tray. There was one on the dressing-table so he got up and moved his chair so that the ash-tray would be conveniently to hand.

It was convenient for me too, because the action of moving the chair had turned his back to me. I took my pen from my pocket and opened the wardrobe door very slowly. The room was small and it only needed two steps to get behind him. I made no sound and it must have been the fractional change of the quality of the light in the room that made him begin to turn his head. I rammed the end of the pen in the roll of fat at the back of his neck and said, 'Stop right there or you'll be minus a head.'

Slade froze, and I snaked my other hand over his shoulder to the inside of his jacket where I found a pistol in a shoulder holster. Everyone seemed to be wearing guns these days and I was becoming exceptionally competent at disarming people.

'I don't want a move from you,' I said, and stepped back. I worked the action of the pistol to make sure it was loaded, and threw off the safety catch. 'Stand up.'

Obediently he stood, still clutching the newspaper. I said, 'Walk straight forward to the wall in front of you, lean against it with your hands high and your arms held wide.'

I stepped back and watched him critically as he went through the evolution. He knew what I was going to do; this was the safest way of searching a man. Being Slade, he tried to pull a fast one, so I said, 'Pull your feet out from the wall and lean harder.' That meant he would be off-balance to begin with if he tried anything – just enough to give me that extra fraction of a second that is all important.

He shuffled his feet backwards and I saw the tell-tale quiver of his wrists as they took up the weight of his body. Then I searched him swiftly, tossing the contents of his pockets on to the bed. He carried no other weapon, unless you consider a hypodermic syringe a weapon, which I was inclined to do when I saw the wallet of ampoules that went with it. Green on the left for a six-hour certain knock-out; red on the right for death in thirty seconds equally certainly.

'Now bend your knees and come down that wall very slowly.' His knees sagged and I brought him into the position in which I had had Fleet – belly down and arms wide stretched. It would take a better man than Slade to jump me from that position; Fleet

382

might have done it had I not rammed his rifle in the small of his back, but Slade was not as young and he had a bigger paunch.

He lay with his head on one side, his right cheek pressed to the carpet and his left eye glaring at me malevolently. He spoke for the first time. 'How do you know I won't have visitors this afternoon?'

'You're right to worry about that,' I said. 'If anyone comes through that door you're dead.' I smiled at him. 'It would be a pity if it was a chamber-maid, then you'd be dead for nothing.'

He said, 'What the devil do you think you're doing, Stewart? Have you gone out of your mind? I think you must have – I told Taggart so and he agrees with me. Now, put away that gun and let me stand up.'

'I must say you try,' I said admiringly. 'Nevertheless, if you move a muscle towards getting up I'll shoot you dead.' His only reaction to that was a rapid blinking of the one eye I could see.

Presently he said, 'You'll hang for this, Stewart. Treason is still a capital crime.'

'A pity,' I said. 'At least *you* won't hang, because what you are doing isn't treason – merely espionage. I don't think spies are hanged – not in peacetime, anyway. It would be treason if you were English, but you're not; you're a Russian.'

'You're out of your mind,' he said disgustedly. 'Me – a Russian!'

'You're as English as Gordon Lonsdale was Canadian.'

'Oh, wait until Taggart gets hold of you,' he said. 'He'll put you through the wringer.'

I said, 'What are you doing consorting with the opposition, Slade?'

He actually managed to summon up enough synthetic indignation to splutter. 'Dammit!' he said. 'It's my job. You did the same; you were Kennikin's right-hand man at one time. I'm following orders – which is more than you are doing.'

'That's interesting,' I said. 'Your orders are very curious. Tell me more.'

'I'll tell nothing to a traitor,' he said virtuously.

I must say that at that moment I admired Slade for the first time. Lying in a most undignified position and with a gun at his head he wasn't giving an inch and was prepared to fight to the end. I had been in his position myself when I had got next to Kennikin in Sweden and I knew how nerve-abrading a life it was – never knowing from one day to another whether one's cover had been blown. Here he was, still trying to convince me that he was as pure as the latest brand of detergent, and I knew that if I let up on him for a fraction of a second so that he could get the upper hand I would be a dead man in that very second.

I said, 'Come off it, Slade. I heard you tell Ilyich to kill me. Don't tell me that was an order passed on from Taggart.'

'Yes,' he said, without a flicker of an eyelash. 'He thinks you've gone over. I can't say I blame him, either, considering the way you've been behaving.'

I almost burst out laughing at his effrontery. 'By God, but you're good!' I said. 'You lie there with your face hanging out and tell me that. I suppose Taggart also told you to ask the Russkies to do the job for him.'

Slade's exposed cheek wrinkled up into the rictus of a half smile. 'It's been done before,' he said. 'You killed Jimmy Birkby.'

Involuntarily my finger tightened on the trigger, and I had to take a deep breath before I relaxed. I tried to keep my voice even as I said, 'You've never been nearer death than now, Slade. You shouldn't have mentioned Birkby – that's a sore point. Let's not have any more comedy. You're finished and you know it quite well. You're going to tell me a lot of things I'm interested in, and you're going to tell it fast, so speak up.'

'You can go to hell,' he said sullenly.

'You're a great deal nearer hell right now,' I said. 'Let me put it this way. Personally, I don't give a damn if you're English or Russian, a spy or a traitor. I don't give a damn for patriotism either; I've got past that. With me this is purely personal – on a man-to-man basis, if you like. The foundation for most murders. Elin was nearly killed in Asbyrgi on your instructions, and I've just heard you tell a man to kill me. If I kill you right now it will be self-defence.'

Slade lifted his head a little and turned it so that he could look at me straight. 'But you won't do it,' he said.

'No?'

'No,' he said with certainty. 'I told you before – you're too soft-centred. You might kill me under different circumstances; if I were running away, for instance, or if we were shooting at each other. But you won't kill me while I'm lying here. You're an English gentleman.' He made it sound like a swearword.

'I wouldn't bet on it,' I said. 'Maybe Scots are different.'

'Not enough to matter,' he said indifferently.

I watched him look into the muzzle of the pistol without a quiver and I had to give the devil his due. Slade knew men and he had my measure as far as killing was concerned. He also knew that if he came for me I would shoot to kill. He was safe enough while lying defenceless, but action was another thing.

He smiled, 'You've already proved it. You shot Yuri in the leg – why not in the heart? By Kennikin's account you were shooting accurately enough across that river to have given every man a free shave without benefit of barber. You could have killed Yuri – but you didn't!'

'Maybe I wasn't feeling in the mood at the time. I killed Gregor.'

'In the heat of action. Your death or his. Any man can make that kind of decision.'

I had the uneasy feeling that the initiative was passing from me and I had to get it back. I said, 'You can't talk if you're dead – and you're going to talk. Let's begin by you telling me about the electronic gadget – what is it?'

He looked at me contemptuously and tightened his lips.

I glanced at the pistol I held. God knows why Slade carried it because it was a .32 – a popgun just as heavy to lug about as a modern .38 but without the stopping power. But maybe he was a crack shot and could hit his target every time so that wouldn't matter much. What would matter when shooting in a populous place was that the muzzle blast was much less and so were the decibels. You could probably fire it in a busy street and no one would take much notice.

I looked him in the eye and then put a bullet into the back of his right hand. He jerked his hand convulsively and a strangled cry broke from his lips as the muzzle of the pistol centred on his head again. The noise of the shot hadn't even rattled the windows.

I said, 'I may not shoot to kill you but I'll cut you to pieces bit by bit if you don't behave yourself. I hear from Kennikin that I'm a fair hand at surgical operations too. There are worse things than getting yourself shot dead. Ask Kennikin sometime.'

Blood oozed from the back of his hand and stained the carpet, but he lay still, staring at the gun in my hand. His tongue came out and licked dry lips. 'You bloody bastard!' he whispered.

The telephone rang.

We stared at each other for the time it took to ring four times. I walked around him, keeping clear of his legs, and I picked up the telephone whole and entire complete with base. I dumped it next to him, and said, 'You'll answer that, and you'll remember two things – I want to hear *both* ends of the conversation and that there are plenty of other parts of your fat anatomy I can work on.' I jerked the gun. 'Pick it up.'

Awkwardly he picked up the handset with his left hand. 'Yes?'

I jerked the gun again and he held up the telephone so that I could hear the scratchy voice. 'This is Kennikin.'

'Be natural,' I whispered.

Slade licked his lips. 'What is it?' he asked hoarsely.

'What's the matter with your voice?' said Kennikin.

Slade grunted, his eye on the gun I held. 'I have a cold. What do you want?'

'I've got the girl.'

There was a silence and I could feel my heart thumping in my chest. Slade went pale as he watched my finger curl around the trigger and slowly take up the pressure. I breathed, 'Where from?'

Slade coughed nervously. 'Where did you find her?'

'At Keflavik Airport – hiding in the Icelandair office. We know her brother is a pilot, and I had the idea of looking for her there. We took her out without any trouble.'

That made it true. 'Where now?' I whispered into Slade's ear and put the gun to the nape of his neck.

He asked the question, and Kennikin said, 'In the usual place. When can I expect you?'

'You'll be right out.' I pressed the muzzle harder into his fat and felt him shiver.

'I'll leave straight away,' said Slade, and I quickly cut the contact by depressing the telephone bar.

I jumped back fast in case he tried to start something, but he just lay there gazing at the telephone. I felt like screaming, but there was no time for that. I said, 'Slade, you were wrong – I *can* kill. You know that now, don't you?'

For the first time I detected fear in him. His fat jowl developed a tremor and his lower lip shook so that he looked like a fat boy about to burst into tears. I said, 'Where's the usual place?'

He looked at me with hatred and said nothing. I was in a quandary; if I killed him I would have got nothing out of him, yet I didn't want to damage him too much because I wanted him fit to walk the streets of Reykjavik without occasioning undue attention. Still, he didn't know my problem, so I said, 'You'll still be alive when I've finished with you, but you'll wish you weren't.'

I put a bullet just by his ear and he jerked violently. Again the noise of the shot was very small and I think he must have doctored the cartridges by taking out some of the powder to reduce the bang. It's an old trick when you want to shoot without drawing notice to yourself and, if done carefully and the gun is fired at not too great a range, the bullet is still lethal. It's much better than using a silencer which is a much overrated contraption and danger-

ous to the user. A silencer is good for one quiet shot – after that the
steel wool packing becomes compressed and the back pressure
builds up so high that the user is in danger of blowing off his own
hand.

I said, 'I'm a good shot, but not all that good. I intended to
put that bullet exactly where I did, but only you know the accuracy
of this popgun. I'm inclined to think it throws to the left a bit, so
if I try to clip your right ear you stand a fair chance of stopping
one in the skull.'

I shifted the gun a little and took aim. He broke – his nerve gone
completely. 'For God's sake, stop!' This sort of Russian roulette
wasn't to his taste.

I sighted on his right ear. 'Where's the usual place?'

There was a sheen of sweat on his face. 'At Thingvallavatn.'

'The house to which I was taken after Geysir?'

'That's it.'

'You'd better be right,' I said. 'Because I have no time to waste
in chasing about Southern Iceland.' I lowered the gun and Slade's
expression changed to one of relief. 'Don't start cheering yet,'
I advised. 'I hope you don't think I'm going to leave you here.'

I went to the stand at the bottom of the bed and flipped open
the lid of his suitcase. I took out a clean shirt and tossed it to him.
'Rip some strips off that and bind up your hand. Stay on the floor
and don't get any smart ideas such as throwing it at me.'

While he tore up the shirt awkwardly I rummaged about in the
suitcase and came up with two clips of .32 ammunition. I dropped
them into my pocket then went to the wardrobe and took out
Slade's topcoat, the pockets of which I had already searched. 'Stand
up facing the wall and put that on.'

I watched him carefully, alert for any trickery. I knew that if I
made one false step he would take full advantage of it. A man who
could worm his way into the heart of British Intelligence hadn't
done it by being stupid. The mistakes he had made weren't such as
would normally have discommoded him and he had done his
damndest to rectify them by eliminating me. If I weren't careful he
could still pull it off.

I picked up his passport and his wallet from the bed and pocketed
them, then threw his hat across the room so that it landed at his
feet. 'We're going for a walk. You'll keep that bandaged hand in
your coat pocket and you'll behave like the English gentleman
you're not. One wrong move from you and I'll shoot you dead and
take my chances, and I don't care if it has to be in the middle of
Hafnarstraeti. I hope you realize that Kennikin did exactly the

wrong thing in taking Elin.'

He spoke to the wall. 'Back in Scotland I warned you about that. I told you not to let her get involved.'

'Very thoughtful of you,' I said. 'But if anything happens to her you're a dead man. You may have been right about my inability to kill before, but I hope you're not counting on it now because one of Elin's nail parings is of more importance to me than the whole of your lousy body. You'd better believe that, Slade. I protect my own.'

I saw him shudder. 'I believe you,' he said quietly.

I really think he did. He knew he had encountered something more primitive than patriotism or the loyalty of a man to his group. This was much more fundamental, and while I might not have killed him because he was a spy I would kill without mercy any man who got between me and Elin.

'All right,' I said. 'Pick up your hat and let's go.'

I escorted him into the corridor, made him lock the door, and then took the key. I had one of his jackets draped over my arm to hide the gun, and I walked one pace behind him and to the right. We left the hotel and walked the streets of Reykjavik to where I had left Nordlinger's car. 'You'll get behind the wheel,' I said.

We performed an intricate ballet in getting into the car. While unlocking it and getting him settled I had to make sure that never for one moment could he take advantage and, at the same time, our antics had to look reasonably normal to the passers-by. At last I managed to get him seated and myself behind him in the rear.

'Now you'll drive,' I said.

'But my hand,' he protested. 'I don't think I can.'

'You'll do it. I don't care how much it hurts – but you'll do it. And never for one moment will you exceed thirty miles an hour. You won't even think of putting the car into a ditch or crashing it in any other way. And the reason you won't think of such things is because of this.' I touched his neck with the cold metal of the pistol.

'This will be behind you all the way. Just imagine that you're a prisoner and I'm one of Stalin's boys back in the bad old days. The approved method of execution was an unexpected bullet in the back of the head, wasn't it? But if you do anything naughty this is one bullet you can expect for sure. Now, take off, and do it carefully – my trigger finger is allergic to sudden jerks.'

I didn't have to tell him where to drive. He drove along the Tjarnargata with the duck-strewn waters of the Tjörnin lake on our left, past the University of Iceland, and so into Miklabraut and out of town. He drove in silence and once on the open road he obeyed orders and never let the speed drift above thirty miles an hour. I think this was less out of sheer obedience and more because changing gears hurt his hand.

After a while he said, 'What do you think you're going to gain by this, Stewart?'

I didn't answer him: I was busy turning out the contents of his wallet. There wasn't anything in it of interest – no plans for the latest guided missile or laser death ray that a master spy and double agent might have been expected to carry. I transferred the thick sheaf of currency and the credit cards to my own wallet; I could use the money – I was out of pocket on this operation – and should he escape death he would find the shortage of funds a serious disability.

He tried again. 'Kennikin won't believe anything you say, you know. He won't be bluffed.'

'He'd better be,' I said. 'For your sake. But there'll be no bluff.'

'Your work will be cut out convincing Kennikin of that,' said Slade.

'You'd better not push that one too hard,' I said coldly. 'I might convince him by taking your right hand – the one with the ring on the middle finger.'

That shut him up for a while and he concentrated on his driving. The Chevrolet bounced and rolled on its soft springing as the wheels went over the corrugated dips and rises of the road. We would have got a smoother ride had we travelled faster but, as it was, we climbed up and down every minuscule hill and valley. I dared not order him to speed up, much as I wanted to get to Elin; 30 mph gave me the leeway both to shoot Slade and get out safely should he deliberately run the car off the road.

Presently I said, 'I notice you've given up your protestations of innocence.'

'You wouldn't believe me no matter what I told you – so why should I try?'

He had a point there. 'I'd just like to clear up a few things, though. How did you know I was going to meet Jack Case at Geysir?'

'When you make a call on open radio to London you can expect people to listen,' he said.

'You listened and you told Kennikin.'

He half-turned his head. 'How do you know it wasn't Kennikin who listened?'

'Keep your eyes on the road,' I said sharply.

'All right, Stewart,' he said. 'There's no point in fencing. I admit it all. You've been right all along the line. Not that it will do you much good; you'll never get out of Iceland.' He coughed. 'What gave me away?'

'Calvados,' I said.

'Calvados!' he repeated. He was at a loss. 'What the hell is that supposed to mean?'

'You knew that Kennikin drinks Calvados. No one else did, except me.'

'I see! That's why you asked Taggart about Kennikin's drinking habits. I was wondering about that.' His shoulders seemed to sag and he said musingly, 'It's the little things. You cover every possibility; you train for years, you get yourself a new identity – a new personality – and you think you're safe.' He shook his head slowly. 'And then it's a little thing like a bottle of Calvados that you saw a man drink years before. But surely that wasn't enough?'

'It started me thinking. There was something else, of course. Lindhom – who was conveniently in the right place at the right time – but that could have been coincidence. I didn't get around to suspecting you until you sent in Philips at Asbyrgi – that was a bad mistake. You ought to have sent Kennikin.'

'He wasn't immediately available.' Slade clicked his tongue. 'I ought to have gone in myself.'

I laughed gently. 'Then you'd be where Philips is now. Count your blessings, Slade.' I looked ahead through the windscreen and then leaned forward to check the position of his hands and feet to make sure he wasn't conning me – lulling me with conversation. 'I suppose there was a man called Slade once.'

'A boy,' said Slade. 'We found him in Finland during the war. He was fifteen then. His parents were British and had been killed in a bombing raid by our Stormoviks. We took him into our care, and later there was a substitution – me.'

'Something like Gordon Lonsdale,' I said. 'I'm surprised you survived inspection in the turmoil after the Lonsdale case.'

'So am I,' he said bleakly.

'What happened to young Slade?'

'Siberia perhaps. But I don't think so.'

I didn't think so either. Young Master Slade would have been interrogated to a fare-thee-well and then dispatched to some anonymous hole in the ground.

I said, 'What's your name – the real Russian one, I mean?'

He laughed. 'You know, I've quite forgotten. I've been Slade for the better part of my life, for so long that my early life in Russia seems like something I once dreamed.'

'Come off it ! No one forgets his name.'

'I think of myself as Slade,' he said. 'I think we'll stick to it.'

I watched his hand hovering over the button of the glove compartment. 'You'd better stick to driving,' I said drily. 'There's only one thing you'll find in the glove compartment and that's a quick, sweet death.'

Without hurrying too much he withdrew his hand and put it back where it belonged – on the wheel. I could see that his first fright was over and he was regaining confidence. More than ever I would have to watch him.

An hour after leaving Reykjavik we arrived at the turn-off to Lake Thingvallavatn and Kennikin's house. Watching Slade, I saw that he was about to ignore it, so I said, 'No funny business – you know the way.'

He hastily applied the brakes and swung off to the right and we bumped over a road that was even worse. As near as I could remember from the night drive I had taken with Kennikin along this same road the house was about five miles from the turn-off. I leaned forward and kept one eye on the odometer, one eye on the countryside to see if I could recognize anything, and the other on Slade. Having three eyes would be useful to a man in my position, but I had to make do with two.

I spotted the house in the distance or, at least, what I thought was the house, although I could not be entirely sure since I had previously only seen it in darkness. I laid the gun against Slade's neck. 'You drive past it,' I said. 'You don't speed up and you don't slow down – you just keep the same pace until I tell you to stop.'

As we went past the drive that led to the house I glanced sideways at it. It was about four hundred yards off the road and I was certain this was the place. I was absolutely sure when I spotted the lava flow ahead and to the left where I had encountered Jack Case. I tapped Slade's shoulder. 'In a little while you'll see a level place to the left where they've been scooping out lava for road-making. Pull in there.'

I kicked the side of the door and swore loudly as though I had hurt myself. All I wanted to do was to make noise enough to cover the sound of my taking the clip out of the pistol and working the slide to eject the round in the breech. That would leave me unarmed and it wouldn't do for Slade to know it. I was going to hit him very hard with the butt of the pistol and to do that with a loaded gun was to ask for a self-inflicted gun shot.

He pulled off the road and even before the car rolled to a halt I let him have it, striking sideways in a chopping motion at the base of his neck. He moaned and fell forward and his feet slipped on the foot pedals. For one alarming moment the car bucked and lurched but then the engine stalled and it came to a standstill.

I dipped into my pocket and put a full clip into the pistol and jacked a round into the breech before I examined Slade at close quarters. What I had done to him was in a fair way towards breaking his neck, but I found that his head lolled forward because I had merely knocked him cold. I made sure of that by taking the hand which had a bullet hole through the palm and squeezing it hard. He didn't move a muscle.

I suppose I should have killed him. The knowledge in his head culled from his years in the Department was a deadly danger, and my duty as a member of the Department was to see that the knowledge was permanently erased. I didn't even think of it. I needed Slade as one hostage to set against another and I had no intention of exchanging dead hostages.

E. M. Forster once said that if he had to choose between betraying his country and betraying his friend then he hoped he would have the guts to betray his country. Elin was more than my friend – she was my life – and if the only way I could get her was to give up Slade then I would do so.

I got out of the car and opened the boot. The sacking which was wrapped around the rifles came in handy for tearing into strips and binding Slade hand and foot. I then put him in the boot and slammed the lid on him.

The Remington carbine I had taken from Philips I hid in a crevice of lava close to the car, together with its ammunition, but Fleet's piece of light artillery I slung over my shoulder as I walked towards the house. It was very likely that I would need it.

II

The last time I had been anywhere near this house it had been dark and I had plunged away not knowing the lie of the land. Now, in the daylight, I found I could get to within a hundred yards of the front door without breaking cover. The ground was broken and three big lava flows had bled across the landscape during some long-gone eruption and had hardened and solidified while in full spate to form jagged ridges full of crevices and holes. The ever-present moss grew thickly, covering the spiky lava with soft vegetable cushions. The going was slow and it took me half an hour to get as close to the house as I dared.

I lay on the moss and studied it. It was Kennikin's hideaway, all right, because a window was broken in the room where I had been kept captive and there were no curtains at that window. The last time I had seen them they had been going up in flames.

A car stood outside the front door and I noticed that the air over the bonnet shimmered a little. That meant that the engine was still hot and someone had just arrived. Although my own journey had been slow, Kennikin had farther to travel from Kefla-vik – there was a good chance that whatever he intended to do to Elin to get her to tell him where I was had not yet begun. And, possibly, he would wait for Slade before starting. For Elin's sake I hoped so.

I loosened a big slab of moss and pushed Fleet's rifle out of sight beneath it, together with the ammunition for it. I had brought it along as insurance – it was useless in the boot of the car, anyway. It would also be useless in the house too, but now it was tucked away within a fast sprint of the front door.

I withdrew and began a painful retreat across the lava beds until I reached the driveway, and the walk towards the house was the longest distance I have ever walked, psychologically if not physic-ally. I felt as a condemned man probably feels on his way to the scaffold. I was walking quite openly to the front door of the house and if anyone was keeping a watch I hoped his curiosity would get the better of him enough to ask *why* I was coming instead of shoot-ing me down ten paces from the threshold.

I crunched my way to the car and casually put out my hand. I had been right; the engine was still warm. There was a flicker of movement at one of the windows so I carried on and walked to the door. I pressed the bell-push and heard the genteel peal of chimes inside the house.

Nothing happened for a while but soon I heard boots crushing loose lava chips and I looked sideways to see a man coming around the corner of the house to my left. I looked to the right and saw another, and both were strolling towards me with intent expres-sions on their faces.

I smiled at them and jabbed the bell-push again and the chimes jingled softly just as in any house in the stockbroker belt. The door opened and Kennikin stood there. He had a gun in his hand.

'I'm the man from the Prudential,' I said pleasantly. 'How's your insurance, Vaslav?'

Chapter Ten

I

Kennikin looked at me expressionlessly and his pistol was pointing at my heart. 'Why shouldn't I kill you now?'

'That's what I've come to talk to you about,' I said. 'It really would be a bad thing if you did.' I heard footsteps behind me as the outflankers moved in for the kill. 'Aren't you interested to know why I'm here? Why I walked up and rang the bell?'

'It did cross my mind that it was strange,' said Kennikin. 'You won't object to a slight search?'

'Not at all,' I said, and felt heavy hands on me. They took Slade's gun and the clips of ammunition. 'This is most inhospitable,' I said. 'Keeping me at the door like this. Besides, what will the neighbours think?'

'We have no neighbours for some considerable distance,' said Kennikin, and looked at me with a puzzled expression. 'You're very cool, Stewartsen. I think you must have gone mad. But come in.'

'Thanks,' I said, and followed him into the familiar room where we had talked before. I glanced at the burnt patches on the carpet and said, 'Heard any good explosions lately?'

'That was very clever,' said Kennikin. He waved his pistol. 'Sit down in the same chair. You will observe there is no fire.' He sat down opposite me. 'Before you say anything I must tell you that we have the girl, Elin Ragnarsdottir.'

I stretched out my legs. 'What on earth do you want her for?'

'We were going to use her to get you,' he said. 'But it seems that is no longer necessary.'

'Then there's no need to keep her. You can let her go.'

Kennikin smiled. 'You're really funny, Stewartsen. It's a pity the English music hall has gone into eclipse; you could make quite a good living as a comedian.'

'You ought to hear me wow them in the working men's clubs,' I said. 'That should appeal to a good Marxist such as yourself. But I wasn't being funny, Vaslav. She is going to walk out of this house unharmed, and you are going to let her go.'

He narrowed his eyes. 'You'd better elaborate on that.'

394

'I walked in here on my own feet,' I said. 'You don't think I'd do that unless I could trump your ace. You see, I've got Slade. Tit for tat.' His eyes opened wide, and I said, 'But I forget – you don't know a man called Slade. You told me so yourself, and we all know that Vaslav Viktorovich Kennikin is an honourable man who doesn't stoop to fibs.'

'Even supposing I did know this Slade, what proof have you of this? Your word?'

I put my hand to my breast pocket and stopped sharply as his gun came up. 'Not to worry,' I said. 'But do you mind if I dig for a bit of evidence?' I took the jerk of the gun as assent and extracted Slade's passport from my pocket and tossed it to him.

He stooped to where it had fallen and picked it up, flicking open the pages with one hand. He studied the photograph intently and then snapped the passport closed. 'This is a passport made out in the name of Slade. It is no proof of possession of the man. To hold a passport is meaningless; I, myself, possess many passports in many names. In any case, I know of no Slade. The name means nothing to me.'

I laughed. 'It's so unlike you to talk to yourself. I know for a fact that not two hours ago you spoke to a non-existent man at the Hotel Borg in Reykjavik. This is what you said, and this is what he said.' I recited the telephone conversation verbatim. 'Of course, I could have been wrong about what Slade said, since he doesn't exist.'

Kennikin's face tightened. 'You have dangerous knowledge.'

'I have more than that – I have Slade. I had him even as he spoke to you. My gun was in his fat neck.'

'And where is he now?'

'For Christ's sake, Vaslav!' I said. 'You're talking to me, not some muscle-bound, half-witted ape like Ilyich.'

He shrugged. 'I had to try.'

I grinned. 'You'll have to do a bloody sight better than that. I can tell you this, though – if you go looking for him, by the time you find him he'll be cold meat. Those are my orders.'

Kennikin pulled at his lower lip, thinking deeply. 'Orders you have received – or orders you have given?'

I leaned forward, preparing to lie heroically. 'Let's make no mistake about this, Vaslav. Those are orders I've given. If you, or anyone who even smells like you, gets close to Slade, then Slade dies. Those are the orders I have given and they'll be followed, you may depend upon it.'

At all costs I had to drive out of his mind any suggestion that I had been given orders. The only man who could give me orders was Taggart, and if he had issued such orders then the game was blown as far as Slade was concerned. If Kennikin believed for one minute that Taggart had penetrated Slade's cover then he'd cut his losses by killing me and Elin, and get the hell back to Russia as fast as he could move.

I buttressed the argument by saying, 'I may be rapped over the knuckles when the Department catches up with me, but until then those orders stand – Slade will catch a bullet if you go near him.'

Kennikin smiled grimly. 'And who will pull the trigger? You've said you're working independently of Taggart, and I know you're alone.'

I said, 'Don't sell the Icelanders short, Vaslav. I know them very well and I have a lot of friends here – and so does Elin Ragnarsdottir. They don't like what you've been doing in their country and they don't like one of their own being put in danger.'

I leaned back in the chair. 'Look at it this way. This is a biggish country with a small population. Everyone knows everyone else. Damn it, everyone is related to everyone else if you push it back far enough – and the Icelanders do. I've never known a people, other than the Scots, who are so genealogically minded. So everyone cares what happens to Elin Ragnarsdottir. This isn't a mass society where people don't even know their next-door neighbour. By taking Elin Ragnarsdottir you've laid yourself wide open.'

Kennikin looked thoughtful. I hoped I had given him something to chew over for a long time, but I didn't have the time so I pushed him. 'I want the girl down here in this room – intact and in one piece. If any harm has come to her then you've made a big mistake.'

He regarded me keenly, and said, 'It's obvious you haven't informed the Icelandic authorities. If you had, the police would be here.'

'You're so right,' I said. 'I haven't, and for good reasons. Firstly, it would cause an international brouhaha, which would be lamentable. Secondly, and more important, all the authorities could do would be to deport Slade. My friends are tougher-minded – they'll kill him if necessary.' I leaned over and jabbed Kennikin in the knee with a hard forefinger. 'And *then* they'll blow you off to the police, and you'll be up to your neck in uniforms and diplomats.' I straightened up. 'I want to see the girl, and I want to see her now.'

'You talk straight,' he said. 'But, then, you always did . . .' His voice tailed away, and he whispered '. . . until you betrayed me.'

'I don't see you have any options,' I said. 'And just to screw it tighter I'll tell you something else. There's a time limit. If my friends don't get the word from Elin's own lips within three hours then Slade gets what's coming to him.'

I could see Kennikin visibly debating it with himself. He had to make a choice and a damned thin one it was. He said, 'Your Icelandic friends – do they know who Slade is?'

'You mean that he's in Russian Intelligence?' I said. 'Or in British Intelligence, for that matter?' I shook my head. 'All they know is that he's a hostage for Elin. I didn't tell them anything else about him. They think you're a crowd of gangsters and, by God, they're not far wrong!'

That clinched it. He thought he had me isolated, that only Elin and I knew the truth that Slade was a double agent. Given that premise which, God knows, was true enough since my Icelandic friends were pure invention, then he could do a deal. He was faced with the choice of sacrificing Slade, who had been laboriously built up over many years into a superlative Trojan Horse, for a no-account Icelandic girl. The choice was obvious. He would be no worse off than before he had taken her, and his weasel mind would already be working out ways of double-crossing me.

He sighed. 'At least you can see the girl.' He signalled to the man standing behind him who left the room.

I said, 'You've really queered this one, Vaslav. I don't think Bakayev is going to be too cheerful about it. It'll be Siberia for sure this time, if not worse – and all because of Slade. It's funny, isn't it? You spent four years in Ashkhabad because of Slade, and now what do you have to look forward to?'

There was a look almost of pain in his eyes. 'Is it true – what you said about Slade and Sweden?'

'Yes, Vaslav,' I said. 'It was Slade who cut the ground from under you there.'

He shook his head irritably. 'There's one thing I don't understand,' he said. 'You say you are willing to trade Slade for the girl. Why should a member of your Department do that?'

'I swear to God you don't listen to me. I'm not a member of the Department – I quit four years ago.'

He pondered. 'Even so – where are your loyalties?'

'My loyalties are my business,' I said curtly.

'The world well lost for a woman?' he said mockingly. 'I've been cured of that way of thinking – and you were the doctor.'

'Now, you're not still harping on that,' I said. 'If you hadn't jumped when you should have fallen flat you'd have been killed decently.'

The door opened and Elin came in under escort. I was about to get up but subsided again as Kennikin lifted his pistol warningly. 'Hello, Elin; you'll forgive me if I don't get up.'

Her face was pale and when she saw me it acquired a bleak look. 'You, too!'

'I'm here by choice,' I said. 'Are you all right? They didn't hurt you?'

'Not more than was necessary,' she said. 'Just some arm twisting.' She put her hand to her wounded shoulder.

I smiled at her. 'I've come to collect you. We'll be leaving soon.'

'That's a matter of opinion,' said Kennikin. 'How do you expect to do it?'

'In the normal way – through the front door,' I said.

'Just like that!' Kennikin smiled. 'And what about Slade?'

'He'll be returned unharmed.'

'My dear Alan! Not long ago you accused *me* of being unrealistic. You'll have to work out a better exchange mechanism than that.'

I grinned at him. 'I didn't think you'd fall for it but, as you said, one has to try. I daresay we can work out something equitable.'

'Such as?'

I rubbed my chin. 'Such as sending Elin away. She'll contact our friends and then you exchange Slade for me. The arrangements can be made by telephone.'

'That sounds logical,' said Kennikin. 'But I'm not sure it's reasonable. Two for one, Alan?'

'It's a pity you can't ask Slade if it's reasonable or not.'

'You make a point.' Kennikin moved restlessly. He was trying to find the flaws in it. 'We get Slade back unharmed?'

I smiled apologetically. 'Er . . . well – not entirely. He's been leaking blood through a hole, but it's minor and not fatal. And he might have a headache – but why should you care about that?'

'Why, indeed?' Kennikin stood up. 'I think I can go along with you on this, but I'd like to think about it a little more.'

'Not for too long,' I said warningly. 'Remember the time limit.'

Elin said, 'Have you really captured Slade?'

I stared at her, trying to pass an unspoken message and hoping to God she didn't let me down. 'Yes. Our friends are taking care of him – Valtyr is in charge.'

'Valtyr!' She nodded. 'He's big enough to handle anyone.'

I switched my eyes back to Kennikin and tried not to show too much relief at the way Elin had played that one. 'Buck it up, Vaslav,' I said. 'Time's a-wasting.'

He came to the decision quickly. 'Very well, it shall be as you say.' He looked at his watch. 'I also shall lay down a time limit. If there is no telephone call within two hours then you will die regardless of what may happen to Slade.' He swung on his heels and faced Elin. 'Remember that, Elin Ragnarsdottir.'

'There's just one thing,' I said. 'I'll have to talk to Elin before she leaves to tell her where to find Valtyr. She doesn't know, you see.'

'Then you'll do it in my hearing.'

I gave him a pained look. 'Don't be an idiot. You'd know as much as I do, and that might be unwise. You'd know where Slade is and you might be tempted to get him out. And where would that leave me?' I stood up cautiously. 'I talk to Elin privately or not at all. It's another stalemate, Vaslav, but I'm sure you understand that I have to look out for my own skin.'

'Yes, I'm sure you do,' he said contemptuously. He gestured with the gun. 'You may talk in the corner, but I remain in the room.'

'Fair enough.' I jerked my head at Elin and we walked over to the corner. I stood with my back to Kennikin because, for all I knew, lip-reading in six languages might have been one of his minor talents.

Elin whispered, 'Have you really got Slade?'

'Yes, but Valtyr doesn't know about it, nor anyone else. I've sold Kennikin a credible story but not the true one. But I *have* got Slade.'

She put her hand to my chest. 'They took me so quickly,' she said. 'I couldn't do anything. I was afraid, Alan.'

'That doesn't matter now,' I said. 'You're going to walk out of here, and this is how you do it. You . . .'

'But you are staying.' There was pain in her eyes.

'I won't be staying long if you do as I say. Listen carefully. You'll leave here, walk up to the road and turn left. About half a mile along you'll come to a big dreamboat of an American car. Whatever you do, don't open the boot. Just climb into it and go like a bat out of hell to Keflavik. Got that?'

She nodded. 'What do I do there?'

'See Lee Nordlinger. Raise a storm and demand to see a CIA agent. Lee and everyone else will deny having such an article on the premises, but if you persist long enough they'll dig one up. You can tell Lee it's about the gadget he tested; that might help. Tell the CIA man the whole story and then tell him to open the boot of the car.' I grinned wryly. 'But don't call it the boot or he won't know what the hell you're talking about. Call it the trunk.'

'So what's in there?'

'Slade,' I said.

She stared at me. 'He's *here*! Just outside this house!'

'It was all I could do at short notice,' I said. 'I had to act quickly.'

'But what about you?'

'Get the CIA man to make the telephone call. You'll have just on two hours from the time you leave here, so you'll have to be bloody persuasive. If you can't do it in time or if the CIA man won't be persuaded, then make the call yourself and spin Kennikin some kind of yarn. Set up a meeting to exchange me for Slade. It might be phoney but it will buy me time.'

'What if the Americans won't believe me?'

'Tell them you know about Fleet and McCarthy. Tell them you'll give it to the Icelandic newspapers. That should produce some kind of reaction. Oh, yes; and tell them that all your friends know exactly where you are – just as insurance.' I was trying to cover all the possibilities.

She closed her eyes briefly as she memorized her instructions. When she opened them, she asked, 'Is Slade alive?'

'Of course he is. I told Kennikin the truth about that. He's damaged but alive.'

She said, 'I was thinking the CIA might believe Slade rather than me. He might even know the CIA people at Keflavik.'

'I know,' I said. 'But we have to take that risk. That's why you must tell the whole story before producing Slade. Get your oar in first. If you pitch it really hot they won't just let him walk out.'

She didn't seem too happy about that, and neither was I, but it was the best we could do. I said, 'Make it fast, but not so fast that you have an accident in that car.' I put my hand under her chin and tipped her head up. 'Everything will be all right. You'll see.'

She blinked rapidly. 'There's something you must know. That gun you gave me – I've still got it.'

It was my turn to blink. '*What!*'

'They didn't search me. I have it on me – in the holster under this anorak.'

I looked at her. Her anorak was admittedly very loose and no sign of the gun was visible. Someone had slipped. It was unlikely that an Icelandic girl would be armed, but even so it was bad workmanship. No wonder Kennikin went off pop periodically about the quality of his team. Elin said, 'Can I pass it to you safely?'

'Not a chance,' I said regretfully, aware of Kennikin at my back. He would be watching like a hawk, and a Smith & Wesson .38 pistol isn't something you can palm in your hand like a playing-card. 'You'd better keep it. Who knows, you might need it.'

I put my hand on her good shoulder and drew her towards me. Her lips were cold and hard under mine, and she trembled slightly. I drew back my head, and said, 'You'd better go,' and turned to face Kennikin.

'Very touching,' he said.

'There's one thing,' I said. 'Your time limit is too short. Two hours isn't enough.'

'It will have to do,' he said uncompromisingly.

'Be reasonable, Vaslav. She has to drive through Reykjavik. The day is getting on and by the time she reaches town it will be just after five o'clock – right in the middle of the rush hour when people are going home. You wouldn't want to lose Slade because of a traffic jam, would you?'

'You're not thinking of Slade,' he said. 'You're thinking of yourself. You're thinking of the bullet in your head.'

'Maybe I am, but you'd better think of Slade because if I'm dead then so is he.'

He nodded shortly. 'Three hours,' he said. 'Not a minute more.'

Kennikin was a logical man and susceptible to a reasoned argument. I had won Elin another hour in which to convince the top brass at Keflavik. 'She goes alone,' I said. 'No one follows her.'

'That is understood.'

'Then give her the telephone number she is to call. It would be a pity if she walked out without it.'

Kennikin took out a notebook and scribbled down a number, then ripped out the sheet and gave it to her. 'No tricks,' he said. 'Especially no police. If there is an undue number of strangers around here, then he dies. You'd better know that I mean it.'

In a colourless voice she said, 'I understand. There will be no tricks.'

She looked at me and there was something in her eyes that made my heart turn over, and then Kennikin took her by the elbow and led her to the door. A minute later I saw her through the window, walking away from the house up towards the road.

Kennikin returned. 'We'll put you somewhere safe,' he said, and jerked his head at the man who held a gun on me. I was led upstairs and into an empty room. Kennikin surveyed the bare walls and shook his head sadly. 'They did these things so much better in medieval times,' he said.

I was in no mood for light conversation but I played along with him. I had the idea that, perhaps, he wouldn't mind at all if Slade didn't show up. Then he would be able to get down to the delightful business of killing me – slowly. And I had put the idea into his mind; I had tried to antagonize him towards Slade. Maybe it hadn't been such a good idea.

I said, 'What do you mean?'

'In those days they built with stone.' He strode to the window and thumped on the exterior wall. It responded with a wooden hollowness. 'This place is built like an eggshell.'

That was true enough. The chalets around Thingvallavatn are holiday cottages, not designed for permanent occupancy. A timber frame, skinned on each side with thin planking and with a filling of foamed polystyrene for insulation, finished off with a skim of plaster maybe half an inch thick on the interior to make the place look nice. The nearest thing to a permanent tent.

Kennikin went to the opposite wall and rapped on it with his knuckles. It echoed even more hollowly. 'You could get through this partition wall in fifteen minutes, using nothing more than your hands. Therefore this man will stay in here with you.'

'You needn't worry,' I said sourly. 'I'm not Superman.'

'You don't need to be Superman to tangle the feet of the incompetents I've been given for this operation,' said Kennikin, equally sourly. 'You've proved that already. But I think the orders I give now will penetrate the thickest head.' He turned to the man with the gun. 'Stewartsen will sit in that corner. You will stand in front of the door. Do you understand?'

'Yes.'

'If he moves, shoot him. Understand?'

'Yes.'

'If he speaks, shoot him. Understand?'

'Yes.'

'If he does anything else at all, shoot him. Understand?'

'Yes,' said the man with the gun stolidly.

Kennikin's orders weren't leaving much room for manoeuvre. He said musingly, 'Now, have I forgotten anything? Oh, yes! You said that Slade had a hole in him – right?'

'Not much of one,' I said. 'Just in the hand.'

He nodded, and said to the guard, 'When you shoot him, don't kill him. Shoot him in the stomach.' He turned on his heel and left the room. The door slammed behind him.

II

I looked at the guard and the guard looked right back at me. His gun was trained on my belly and didn't deviate a hair's-breadth. With his other hand he gestured wordlessly towards the corner, so I backed into it until my shoulder-blades touched and then bent my knees until I was squatting on my heels.

He looked at me expressionlessly. 'Sit!' he said economically.

I sat. He wasn't going to be bluffed. He stood in front of the door about fifteen feet away and he was impregnable. He had the look of a man who would obey orders to the letter; if I rushed him I'd catch a bullet and I couldn't even con him into doing anything stupid. It was going to be a long three hours.

Kennikin had been right. Left alone in the room and I'd have gone through the partition wall, and it wouldn't have taken me any fifteen minutes either. True, once through the wall I would still be in the house, but I'd be in an unexpected place and surprise, as all generals know, wins battles. Now that Elin was gone I was prepared to do anything to get away, and Kennikin knew it.

I looked at the window. All I could see was a small patch of blue sky and a fleecy cloud drifting by. The time oozed on, maybe half an hour, and I heard the crunch of tyres as a car drew up outside. I didn't know how many men had been in the house when I arrived, although I knew of three, but now there were more and the odds had lengthened.

I turned my wrist slowly and drew back the cuff of my jacket to look at my watch, hoping to God that the guard would not interpret that as an unnatural action. I kept my eye on him and he looked back at me blankly, so I lowered my gaze to see what time it was. It had not been half an hour – only fifteen minutes had passed. It was going to be a longer three hours than I had thought.

Five minutes after that there was a tap on the door and I heard the raised voice of Kennikin. 'I'm coming in.'

The guard stepped to one side as the door opened. Kennikin came in and said, 'I see you've been a good boy.' There was something in the way he said it that made me uneasy. He was too damned cheerful.

'I'd like to go over what you told me again,' he said. 'According to you, Slade is being kept with friends of yours – Icelandic friends – I think you said. These friends will kill him unless they get you in exchange. Am I right?'

'Yes,' I said.

He smiled. 'Your girl-friend is waiting downstairs. Shall we join her?' He waved largely. 'You can get up – you will not be shot.'

I stood up stiffly, and wondered what the hell had gone wrong. I was escorted downstairs and found Elin standing in front of the empty fireplace flanked by Ilyich. Her face was pale and she whispered, 'I'm sorry, Alan.'

'You must think I'm stupid,' said Kennikin. 'You don't suppose I thought you had walked here? You tramped up to the front door and immediately I wondered where you had left your car. You had to have a car because this is no country for walking, so I sent a man to look for it even before you rang the bell.'

'You always were logical,' I said.

He was enjoying himself. 'And what do you suppose my man found? A large American car complete with key. He had not been there long when this young lady came up in a very great hurry, so he brought her – and the car – back here. You see, he was unaware of the agreement we had reached. We can't blame him for that, can we?'

'Of course not,' I said flatly. *But had he opened the boot?* 'I don't see that this makes any difference.'

'No, you wouldn't. But my man had standing orders. He knew we were looking for a small package containing electronic equipment, and so he searched the car. He didn't find the package.'

Kennikin stopped and looked at me expectantly. He was really relishing this. I said, 'Do you mind if I sit down? And for God's sake, give me a cigarette – I've run out.'

'My dear Alan – but of course,' he said solicitously. 'Take your usual chair.' He produced his cigarette case and carefully lit my cigarette. 'Mr Slade is very angry with you. He doesn't like you at all.'

'Where is he?'

'In the kitchen having his hand bound up. You're a very good diagnostician, Alan; he *does* have a headache.'

My stomach felt as though it had a ball of lead in it. I drew on the cigarette, and said, 'All right; where do we go from here?'

'We carry on from where we left off the night we came here

from Geysir. Nothing has changed.'

He was wrong – Elin was here. I said, 'So now you shoot me.'

'Perhaps. Slade wants to talk to you first.' He looked up. 'Ah, here he is.'

Slade looked bad. His face was grey and he staggered slightly as he walked in. When he came closer I saw that his eyes had a curiously unfocused appearance and I guessed he was still suffering from concussion. Someone had bound up his hand neatly with clean gauze bandages, but his clothes were rumpled and stained and his hair stood on end. As he was a man who usually cared very much for outward appearances, I guessed he was probably very disturbed.

I was right, and I found out how much he was disturbed pretty danmed quick.

He walked up and looked down at me and gestured with his left hand. 'Pick him up and take him over there – to the wall.'

I was grabbed before I could move. Someone put a hammer lock on me from behind and I was dragged from the chair and hustled across the room. As I was slammed against the wall, Slade said, 'Where's my gun?'

Kennikin shrugged. 'How should I know?'

'You must have taken it from Stewart.'

'Oh, that one.' Kennikin pulled it from his pocket. 'Is this it?'

Slade took the pistol and walked over to me. 'Hold his right hand against the wall,' he said, and held up his bandaged hand before my eyes. 'You did that, Stewart, so you know what's going to happen now.'

A hard hand pinned my wrist to the wall and Slade raised his gun. I had just sense enough and time enough to stop making a fist and to spread my fingers so he wouldn't shoot through them before he pulled the trigger and I took the bullet in the palm of my hand. Curiously enough, after the first stabbing shock it didn't hurt. All I felt was a dead numbness from shoulder to fingertip. It would hurt soon enough as the shock wore off, but it didn't hurt then.

My head swam and I heard Elin scream, but the cry seemed to come from a long way away. When I opened my eyes I saw Slade looking at me unsmilingly. He said curtly, 'Take him back to his chair.' It had been a purely vindictive act of revenge and now it was over and he was back to business as usual.

I was dumped back into the chair and I raised my head to see Elin leaning against the chimney piece with tears streaming down her face. Then Slade moved between us and I lost sight of her.

'You know too much, Stewart,' he said. 'So you must die – you know that.'

'I know you'll do your best,' I said dully. I now knew why Slade had cracked in the hotel room because the same thing was happening to me. I found I couldn't string two consecutive thoughts together to make sense and I had a blinding headache. The penetration of a bullet into flesh has that effect.

Slade said, 'Who knows about me – apart from the girl?'

'No one,' I said. 'What about the girl?'

He shrugged. 'You'll be buried in the same grave.' He turned to Kennikin. 'He might be telling the truth. He's been on the run and he hasn't had a chance to let anyone know.'

'He might have written a letter,' said Kennikin doubtfully.

'That's a risk I'll have to take. I don't think Taggart has any suspicions. He might be annoyed because I've dropped out of sight but that will be all. I'll be a good boy and take the next plane back to London.' He lifted his wounded hand and grinned tightly at Kennikin. 'And I'll blame this on you. I've been wounded trying to save this fool.' He reached out and kicked my leg.

'What about the electronic equipment?'

'What about it?'

Kennikin took out his cigarette case and selected a cigarette. 'It seems a pity not to complete the operation as planned. Stewartsen knows where it is, and I can get the information from him.'

'So you could,' said Slade thoughtfully. He looked down at me. 'Where is it, Stewart?'

'It's where you won't find it.'

'That car wasn't searched,' said Kennikin. 'When you were found in the boot everything else was forgotten.' He snapped out orders and his two men left the room. 'If it is in the car they'll find it.'

'I don't think it's in the car,' said Slade.

'I didn't think *you* were in the car,' said Kennikin waspishly. 'I wouldn't be at all surprised to find it there.'

'You may be right,' said Slade. His voice indicated that he didn't think so. He bent over me. 'You're going to die, Stewart – you may depend on it. But there are many ways of dying. Tell us where the package is and you'll die cleanly and quickly. If not, I'll let Kennikin work on you.'

I kept my mouth firmly shut because I knew that if I opened it he would see the tremulous lower lip that is a sign of fear.

He stood aside. 'Very well. You can have him, Kennikin.' A vindictive note entered his voice. 'The best way to do it is to shoot him to pieces slowly. He threatened to do it to me.'

Kennikin stepped in front of me, gun in hand. 'Well, Alan; we come to the end of the road, you and I. Where is the radar equipment?'

Even then when facing his gun I noted that new piece of information. *Radar equipment.* I screwed up my face and managed a smile. 'Got another cigarette, Vaslav?'

No answering smile crossed his face. His eyes were bleak and his mouth was set in grim lines. He had the face of an executioner. 'There is no time for tradition – we are done with that foolery.'

I looked past him. Elin was standing there, forgotten, and there was an expression of desperation on her face. But her hand was inside her anorak and coming out slowly, grasping something. The jolting realization came that she still had the gun!

That was enough to bring me to my senses fast. When all hope is gone and there is nothing more to look forward to than death one sinks into a morass of fatalism as I had done. But given the faintest hint that all is not lost and then a man can act – and my action now was to talk and talk fast.

I turned my head and spoke to Slade. I had to attract his attention to me so he would not even think of looking at Elin. 'Can't you stop him?' I pleaded.

'You can stop him. All you have to do is to tell him what we want to know.'

'I don't know about that,' I said. 'I'll still die, anyway.'

'But easier,' said Slade. 'Quickly and without pain.'

I looked back to Kennikin and, over his shoulder, saw that Elin had now withdrawn the pistol and it was in plain sight. She was fiddling with it and I hoped to God she remembered the sequence of actions she would have to go through before it would fire.

'Vaslav,' I said. 'You wouldn't do this to an old mate. Not you.'

His pistol centred on my belly and then dropped lower. 'You don't have to guess to know where I'm going to put the first bullet,' he said. His voice was deadly quiet. 'I'm just following Slade's orders – and my own inclination.'

'Tell us,' urged Slade, leaning forward.

I heard the snap of metal as Elin pulled back the slide of the pistol. So did Kennikin and he began to turn. Elin held the pistol in both hands and at arm's length and as Kennikin began his turn she fired and kept on firing.

I distinctly heard the impact of the first bullet in Kennikin's back. His hand tightened convulsively around his gun and it exploded in my face, the bullet burying itself in the arm of the chair next to my elbow. By then I was moving. I dived for Slade head first and rammed him in the paunch. My skull was harder than his belly and the breath came out of him in a great whoosh and he folded up and lay gasping on the floor.

I rolled over, aware that Elin was still shooting and that bullets were still whanging across the room. 'Stop!' I yelled.

I scooped up Slade's popgun and came up under Elin's elbow, grabbing her by the wrist. 'For Christ's sake, stop!'

I think she had shot off the whole magazine. The opposite wall was pock-marked and Kennikin lay in front of the chair in which I had been sitting. He lay face upwards gazing at the ceiling. Elin had hit him twice more which was hardly surprising, considering she had been shooting at a range of less than six feet. Come to think of it, I was fortunate she hadn't put a bullet into me. There was a ragged red spot dead centre in Kennikin's forehead to prove he'd had the vitality to turn around and try to shoot back. Another bullet had caught him in the angle of the jaw and had blown off the bottom half of his face.

He was very dead.

I didn't stop to ruminate about how in the midst of life we are in death. I dragged Elin behind me and headed for the door. The boys outside might be prepared for the odd shot, especially after Slade's little demonstration, but the barrage Elin had laid down would be a matter for urgent investigation and that had to be discouraged.

At the door I let go of Elin's wrist with my left hand and swapped it for the gun I held in my wounded right hand. With a hole through the palm I couldn't possibly use a gun in that hand, even one with as little recoil as Slade's gimmicked weapon. I'm a lousy pistol shot at the best of times and even worse when shooting left-handed; but one of the nice things about gun battles is that the man you're shooting at doesn't ask you for a proficiency certificate before he decides to duck.

I glanced at Elin. She was obviously in a state of shock. No one can shoot a man to death without undergoing an emotional upheaval – especially for the first time, especially when a civilian, especially when a woman. I put a snap in my voice. 'You'll do exactly as I say without question. You'll follow me and you'll run like hell without any hesitation.'

She choked back a rasping sob and nodded breathlessly, so I went out of the front door, and I went out shooting. Even as we went someone took a crack at us from the *inside* of the house and a bullet clipped the architrave of my ear. But I had no time to worry about that because the pair who had been sent to search the Chevrolet were heading right at me.

I shot at them and kept on squeezing the trigger and they vanished from view, diving to right and left, and we belted between them. There was a tinkle of glass as somebody decided it was quicker to smash a window than to open it, and then the bullets came after us. I dropped Slade's gun and again grasped Elin by the wrist and forced her to follow me in a zigzag. Behind I could hear the heavy thud of boots as someone chased us.

Then Elin was hit. The bullet pushed her forward into a stumble but, as her knees gave in, I managed to put my arm around her to hold her up. We were then ten yards from the edge of the lava flow where I had hidden the rifle, and how we managed to travel that short distance I still don't know. Elin could still use her legs and that helped, and we scrambled up towards the top of the flow, over the mossy humps, until I stopped and laid my hands on the butt of Fleet's rifle.

I was jacking a round into the breech even before I got it clear of the moss. Elin fell to the ground as I swung around holding the rifle in my left hand. Even with a hole in the palm of my right hand I could still pull the trigger, and I did so to some effect.

The magazine contained the mixed load I had carefully put into it – steel-jacketed and soft-nosed bullets. The first one that came out was jacketed; it hit the leading pursuer in the chest and went through him as though he wasn't there. He came on for four more paces before his heart realized it had a hole in it and it was time to quit beating, then he dropped on the spot, nearly at my feet, with a surprised look on his face.

By that time I had shot the man just behind him, and that was spectacular. A man hit by a soft-nosed bullet driven by a magnum charge at a range of twenty yards isn't as much killed as disintegrated, and this character came apart at the seams. The bullet hit him in the sternum and then started to expand, lifted him clear off the ground and throwing him back four feet before lifting his spine out and splattering it over the landscape.

Everything was suddenly quiet. The deep-throated bellow of Fleet's gun had told everyone concerned that something new had been added to the game and they held their fire while they figured what was going on. I saw Slade by the door of the house, his hand clutched to his belly. I lifted the rifle again and took a shot at him, too quickly and with shaking hands. I missed him but gave him a hell of a fright because he ducked back in haste and there was no one to be seen.

Then a bullet nearly parted my hair and from the sound of the report I knew someone in the house also had a rifle. I got down off the skyline and reached for Elin. She was lying on the moss, her face screwed up with pain and trying to control her laboured breathing. Her hand was at her side and, when she withdrew it, it was red with blood.

I said, 'Does it hurt much?'

'When I breathe,' she said with a gasp. 'Only then.'

That was a bad sign, yet from the apparent position of the wound she had not been hit in the lung. There wasn't anything I could do there and then. For the next few minutes I'd be busy making sure we stayed alive for the next few minutes. There's not much point in worrying about dying of septicaemia in the next week when you might have your head blown off in the next thirty seconds.

I scrabbled for the box of ammunition, took the magazine from the rifle and reloaded it. The numbness had left my hand and it was now beginning to really hurt. Even the experimental flexing of my trigger finger sent a shock up my arm as though I'd grabbed a live wire, and I didn't know if I could do much more shooting. But it's surprising what you can do when you're pushed to it.

I poked my head carefully around a slab of lava and took a look at the house. Nobody and nothing moved. Just to my front lay the bodies of the men I had shot, one lying as though peacefully asleep and the other dreadfully shattered. In front of the house were the two cars; Kennikin's car appearing to be quite normal, but Nordlinger's Chevrolet was a bit of a wreck – they had ripped the seats out in the search for the package and the two nearer doors gaped open. I'd be running up quite a bill for damage to people's cars.

Those cars were less than a hundred yards away and, dearly as I wanted one of them, I knew it was hopeless to try. I also knew we couldn't leave on foot. Apart from the fact that walking on the lava beds is a sport which even the Icelanders aren't keen on, there was Elin to consider. I couldn't leave her, and if we made a break for it we'd be picked up within fifteen minutes.

Which left only one thing – since neither the Mounties nor the US Cavalry were going to show up on the horizon in the time-honoured manner, I had to fight a pitched battle against an unknown number of men securely ensconced in that house – and win.

I studied the house. Kennikin hadn't thought much of it as a prison. 'Built like an eggshell', he had said. A couple of planks thick, a half-inch of plaster and a few inches of foamed polystyrene.

Most people would regard a house as bullet-proof, but I laugh every time I see a Western film when the hero takes refuge in a clapboard hut and the baddies carefully shoot at the windows.

Even a 9 mm bullet from a Luger will penetrate nine inches of pine board from very close range, and that's a pee-wee bullet compared to the .44 fired by the Western Colt. A few well-placed shots would whittle away the shack from around our hero.

I looked at the house and wondered how those flimsy walls would stand up against the awesome power of Fleet's rifle. The soft-nosed bullets mightn't do much – they would tend to splash on impact; but the jacketed bullets should have a hell of a lot of penetrative power. It was time to find out, but first I had to locate that rifleman.

I withdrew my head and looked at Elin. She seemed better now that she had her breathing under control. 'How are you feeling now?'

'My God!' she said. 'How do you think I feel?'

I grinned at her with some relief. That spurt of temper showed she had improved. 'Everything will get better from now on.'

'It can hardly get worse.'

'Thanks for what you did in there,' I said. 'It was very brave.' Considering the attitude she had previously shown towards killing it was much more than that.

She shivered. 'It was horrible!' she said in a low voice. 'I shall see it as long as I live.'

'You won't,' I said with certainty. 'The mind has a knack of forgetting things like that. That's why wars are so long and frequent. But just so you don't have to do it again, you can do something for me.'

'If I can.'

I pointed to a lump of lava above her head. 'Can you push that over the edge when I tell you to? But don't expose yourself or you'll get a bullet.'

She looked up at the lava fragment. 'I'll try.'

'Don't do it until I say.' I pushed the rifle ahead of me and looked at the house. Still nothing moved and I wondered what Slade was up to. 'Right,' I said. 'Shove it over.'

There was a clatter as the rock moved and rolled down the slope of the lava flow. A rifle spoke and a bullet sang overhead and then another, better aimed, struck rock splinters a little to the left. Whoever was shooting knew his work, but I had him spotted. He was in an upstairs room and, by the shadowy movement I had seen, he was kneeling at the window with his head barely showing.

I took aim, not at the window but at the wall below it and a little to the left. I squeezed the trigger and, through the scope, saw the wood of the wall planking splinter under the impact. There was a faint cry and a shift of light at the window, and then I saw the man in full sight standing with his hands to his chest. He staggered backwards and vanished.

I had been right – Fleet's rifle would shoot through walls.

I shifted sights to the downstairs rooms and methodically put a bullet into the wall alongside every window on the ground floor, just where it would be natural for a man to wait in cover. Every time I squeezed the trigger the torn sinews in my hand shrieked in protest and I relieved my feelings by bellowing at the top of my voice.

I felt Elin tug at my trouser leg. 'What's the matter?' she said worriedly.

'Don't hinder the man on the job,' I said, and dropped back. I took out the empty magazine. 'Fill that up – it's difficult for me.' These periods with an empty gun worried me and I wished Fleet had had a spare clip. To be jumped on by somebody now would be slightly disastrous.

I saw that Elin was coping with reloading the clip with the right bullets and took a look at the house again. Someone was wailing over there and there were confused shouts. I had no doubt that the house was now filled with a considerable amount of consternation; the idea that a bullet can rip through a wall and hit the man behind it is highly unsettling for the man behind the wall.

'Here,' said Elin, and passed me the full clip of five rounds. I slotted it into the gun and poked it forward again just in time to see a man break from the front door and take cover behind the Chevrolet. I could see his feet through the telescopic sight. The door nearer to me was swung wide open and, with a mental apology to Lee Nordlinger, I put a bullet through the car and through the metal of the opposite door. The feet moved and the man came into view and I saw it was Ilyich. His hand was at his neck and blood spurted from between his fingers. He tottered a few more steps then dropped, rolled over and lay still.

It was becoming very difficult for me to work the bolt action with my ruined hand. I said to Elin, 'Can you crawl over here beside me?' She came up on my right side, and I said, 'Lift up that lever, pull it back, and ram it forward again. But keep your head down while you're doing it.'

She operated the bolt while I held the rifle firm with my left hand, and she cried out as the empty brass case jumped out into her face unexpectedly. In this dot-and-carry-one manner I put another three rounds into selected points of the house where I thought they would do most damage. When Elin put the last round into the breech I took out the magazine and told her to fill it again.

I felt happier with that one round in the breech as an insurance against emergency, and I settled down to observe the house and to compile an interim report. I had killed three men for certain, wounded another – the rifleman upstairs – and possibly yet another, judging from the moaning still coming from the house. That was five – six if Kennikin was included. I doubted if there were many more, but that didn't mean that more weren't on their way – someone could have used a telephone.

I wondered if it was Slade who was doing the wailing. I knew his voice but it was difficult to tell from that inarticulate and unstructured sound. I glanced down at Elin. 'Hurry up!' I said.

She was fiddling desperately. 'One of them is stuck.'

'Do your best.' Again I peered around the rock in front of me and my eye was caught by a movement beyond the house. Someone was doing what they all ought to have done at the start of this action – getting away from the back of the house. It was only because of the sheer unexpectedness of the gun power I wielded that they hadn't done it before – and it was dangerous because I could be outflanked.

I racked up the telescopic sight to a greater magnification and looked at the distant figure. It was Slade and he was apparently unhurt except for his bandaged hand. He was leaping like a bloody chamois from hummock to hummock at a breakneck speed, his coat tails flying in the breeze and his arms outstretched to preserve his balance. I estimated that he was a little under three hundred yards away and moving farther every second.

I took a deep breath and let it out slowly to steady myself and then took aim carefully. I was in considerable pain and had difficulty in controlling the wavering sight. Three times I almost squeezed off the shot and three times I relaxed the pressure on the trigger because the sight had drifted off target.

My father bought me my first rifle when I was twelve and, wisely, he chose a .22 single-shot. When a boy hunts rabbits and hares and knows that he has only one shot at his disposal then he also knows that the first and only shot must count, and no finer training in good shooting habits is possible. Now, again, I had only one shot available and I was back in my boyhood again, but it was no rabbit I was shooting – more like a tiger.

413

It was difficult to concentrate and I felt dizzy and a wash of greyness passed momentarily in front of my eyes. I blinked and it cleared away and Slade stood out preternaturally clearly in the glass. He had begun to move away at an angle and I led him in the sight and let him run into an aiming point. There was a roaring of blood in my ears and the dizziness came again.

My finger painfully took up the final pressure and the butt of the rifle jolted my shoulder and Slade's nemesis streaked towards him at 2000 miles an hour. The distant figure jerked like a marionette with suddenly cut strings, toppled over, and disappeared from sight.

I rolled over as the roaring in my ears increased. The dizziness built up again and the recurring waves of greyness turned to black. I saw the sun glowing redly through the darkness and then I passed out, the last thing I heard being Elin's voice crying my name.

III

'It was a deception operation,' said Taggart.

I was lying in a hospital bed in Keflavik and there was a guard on the door, not so much to keep me imprisoned as to shield me from prying eyes. I was a potential *cause célèbre*, a *casus belli* and all those other foreign phrases which the leader writers of *The Times* trot out so readily in moments of crisis, and all attempts were being made to keep the situation potential and to prevent it from becoming actual. All parties concerned wanted the whole thing hushed up, and if the Icelandic government knew what had been going on they were damned careful not to say so.

Taggart was with another man, an American, whom he introduced as Arthur Ryan. I recognized Ryan; the last time I had seen him was through the sights of Fleet's rifle – he had been standing beside a helicopter on the other side of the Búdarháls ridge.

It was the second time they had come to see me. The first time I was drowsy with dope and not very coherent, but still coherent enough to ask two questions.

'How's Elin?'

'She's all right,' said Taggart soothingly. 'In better shape than you are, as a matter of fact.' He told me that the bullet had been a ricochet and had the force taken out of it; it had just penetrated the flesh and lodged between two ribs. 'She's as right as rain,' said Taggart heartily.

I looked at him with dislike but I was too wobbly to push it then. I said, 'How did I get here?'

Taggart glanced at Ryan who took a pipe from his pocket, looked at it uncertainly, and then put it away again. He said in a slow voice, 'That's quite a girl you have, Mr Stewart.'

'What happened?'

'Well, when you passed out she didn't know what to do. She thought about it a bit, then she loaded the rifle and started to put even more holes in that house.'

I thought of Elin's attitude towards killing. 'Did she hit anyone?'

'I guess not,' said Ryan. 'I think you did most of the damage. She shot off all the ammunition – and there was a hell of a lot of it – and then she waited a while to see what would happen. Nothing did, so she stood up and walked into the house. I think that was a very brave thing to do, Mr Stewart.'

I thought so too.

Ryan said, 'She found the telephone and rang the Base, here, and contacted Commander Nordlinger. She was very forceful and got him really stirred up. He got even more stirred up when the phone went dead.' He grimaced. 'It's not surprising she fainted – that place was like a slaughterhouse. Five dead and two badly wounded.'

'Three wounded,' said Taggart. 'We found Slade afterwards.'

Soon after that they went away because I was in no shape for serious conversation, but twenty-four hours later they were back and Taggart was talking about deception.

'When can I see Elin?' I said abruptly.

'This afternoon,' said Taggart. 'She's quite all right, you know.'

I looked at him stonily. 'She'd better be.'

He gave an embarrassed cough. 'Don't you want to know what it was all about?'

'Yes,' I said. 'I would. I'd certainly like to know why the Department did its damndest to get me killed.' I switched my eyes to Ryan. 'Even to the extent of getting the co-operation of the CIA.'

'As I say, it was a deception operation, a scheme cooked up by a couple of American scientists.' Taggart rubbed his chin. 'Have you ever considered *The Times* crossword puzzle?'

'For God's sake!' I said. 'No, I haven't.'

Taggart smiled. 'Let us assume it takes some maniacal genius eight hours to compile it; then it has to be set up in type, a block made, and printed in the paper. This involves quite a few people for a short time. Let us say that a total of forty man-hours is used up in this way – one working man-week.'

'So?'

'So consider the consumer end of the operation. Let's assume that ten thousand readers of *The Times* apply their brain power to working out the damned thing – and that each one takes an hour. That's ten thousand hours – five man-years. You see the implication? One man-week of labour has tied up five man-years of brain power in totally unproductive activity.' He looked at Ryan. 'I think you can take it from there.'

Ryan had a low, even voice. 'There are a lot of discoveries made in the physical sciences which have no immediate application, or any conceivable application, for that matter. One example is silly putty. Have you ever seen the stuff?'

'I've heard of it,' I said, wondering what they were getting at. 'I've never seen it.'

'It's funny stuff,' said Ryan. 'You can mould it like putty, but if you leave it alone it flows like water. Furthermore, if. you hit it with a hammer it shatters like glass. You'd think a substance with such diverse properties would be useful, but so far no one has thought of a single goddamn thing to do with it.'

'I believe they're now putting it into the middle of golf balls,' offered Taggart.

'Yeah, a real technological breakthrough,' said Ryan ironically. 'In electronics there are quite a few effects like that. The electret, for example, carries a permanent electric charge like a magnet carries a magnetic field. That idea has been around for forty years and only now has a use been found for it. When the scientists began to kick the quantum theory around they came up with any number of odd effects – the tunnel diode, the Josephson effects, and a lot more – some of them usable and some not. A fair number of these discoveries have been made in laboratories working on defence contracts and they're not generally known.'

He shifted uneasily in his chair. 'Mind if I smoke?'

'Go ahead.'

Thankfully he took out his pipe and began to fill it. 'One scientist, a guy called Davies, surveyed the field and came up with an idea. As a scientist he's not very bright – certainly not of the first rank – but his idea was bright enough even if he merely intended it as a practical joke. He figured it was possible to put together an electronic package, utilizing a number of these mysterious but unusable effects, which would baffle a really big brain. In fact, he did put together such a package, and it took five top research men at Caltech six weeks to discover they'd been fooled.[2]

I began to get the drift. 'The deception operation.'

Ryan nodded. 'One of the men who was fooled was a Dr Atholl, and he saw possibilities in it. He wrote a letter to someone important and in due course the letter was passed on to us. One of the sentences in the letter is outstanding – Dr Atholl said this was a concrete example of the aphorism: "Any fool can ask a question which the wisest of men cannot answer." Davies's original package was relatively unsophisticated, but what we finally came up with was really complex – and it was designed to do precisely nothing.'

I thought of how Lee Nordlinger had been baffled and began to smile. 'What are you laughing at?' asked Taggart.

'Nothing much. Carry on.'

Taggart said, 'You see the principle, Stewart; it's just like *The Times* crossword. The design of the package didn't take much brain power – three scientists worked on it for a year. But if we could get it into the hands of the Russians it could tie up some of their finest minds for a hell of a long time. And the joke is that the problem was fundamentally unsolvable – there was no answer.'

'But we had a problem,' said Ryan. 'How to get it into the hands of the Russians. We started by feeding them a line by a series of carefully controlled leaks. The word was that American scientists had invented a new form of radar with fascinating properties. It had over the horizon capability, it showed a detailed picture and not just a green blob on a screen, and it wasn't affected by ground-level clutter and so could detect a low-level air attack. Any nation would sell its Premier's daughter into white slavery for a gadget like that, and the Russians began to bite.'

He pointed out of the window. 'You see that funny antenna out there – that's supposed to be it. The radar is supposed to be having a field test here at Keflavik, and we've had jet fighters skimming the waves for five hundred miles around here for the last six weeks just to add to the plausibility. And that's when we brought you British in.'

Taggart said, 'We told another story to the Russians. Our American friends were keeping this radar to themselves and we were annoyed about it, so annoyed that we decided to have a look at it ourselves. In fact, one of our agents was sent to pinch a bit of it – an important bit.' He flicked a finger at me. 'You, of course.'

I swallowed. 'You mean I was intended to let the Russians have it!'

'That's right,' said Taggart blandly. 'And you were hand-picked. Slade pointed out – and I agreed – that you were probably not a good agent any more, but you had the advantage, for our purposes, of being known to the Russians as a good agent. Everything was set up and then you fooled everybody – us and the Russians. In fact, you were a devil of a lot better than anyone supposed.'

I felt the outrage beginning to build up, and said deliberately, 'You lousy, amoral son of a bitch! Why didn't you let me in on it? It would have saved a hell of a lot of trouble.'

He shook his head. 'It had to look authentic.'

'By God!' I said. 'You sold me – just as Bakayev sold Kennikin in Sweden.' I grinned tightly. 'It must have complicated things when Slade turned out to be a *Russian* agent.'

Taggart glanced sideways at Ryan and appeared to be embarrassed. 'Our American friends are a bit acid about that. It wrecked the operation.' He sighed, and said plaintively, 'Counter-espionage work is the very devil. If we don't catch any spies then everybody is happy; but when we do our job and catch a spy then there's a scream to high heaven that we *haven't* been doing our job.'

'You break my heart,' I said. '*You* didn't catch Slade.'

He changed the subject quickly. 'Well, there Slade was – in charge of the operation.'

'Yeah,' said Ryan. 'In charge of *both* sides. What a sweet position to be in. He must have thought he couldn't lose.' He leaned forward. 'You see, once the Russians knew about the operation they decided they had no objection to grabbing the package if they thought it would fool us into believing they'd been fooled. A sort of double blind thing.'

I looked at Taggart with distaste. 'What a bastard you are,' I said. 'You must have known that Kennikin would do his best to kill me.'

'Oh, no!' he said earnestly. 'I didn't know about Kennikin. I think Bakayev must have realized they were wasting a good man so they decided to rehabilitate him by sending him on this operation. Perhaps Slade had something to do with it too.'

'He would!' I said bitterly. 'And because I was supposed to be a pushover they gave Kennikin a scratch team. He was complaining about that.' I looked up. 'And what about Jack Case?' I demanded.

Taggart didn't bat an eyelid. 'He had my orders to steer you to the Russians – that's why he didn't help you at Geysir. But when he talked to Slade you had already filled him up with your suspicions. He must have tried to pump Slade, but Slade is a clever man and realized it. That was the end of Case. Slade was doing everything to make sure his cover wasn't blown and in the end you were more important to him than that damned package.'

'Write off Jack Case,' I said sourly. 'He was a good man. When did you catch on to Slade?'

'I was slow there,' said Taggart. 'When you telephoned me I thought you'd done your nut, but after I sent Case here I found I couldn't get hold of Slade. He'd made himself unobtainable. That's against all procedure so I began to look into his record. When I found he'd been in Finland as a boy and that his parents were killed during the war I remembered that you'd mentioned Lonsdale and I wondered if the same trick hadn't been played.' He grimaced. 'But when Case's body was discovered with your pet knife in it, I didn't know what the hell to think.' He nudged Ryan. 'The knife.'

'What! Oh, yes – the knife.' Ryan put his hand into his breast pocket and produced the *sgian dubh*. 'We managed to get it from the police. I guess you'd like to have it back.' He held it out. 'It's a real cute knife; I like that jewel in the hilt.'

I took it. A Polynesian would have said it had *mana*; my own distant ancestors would have named it and called it *Weazand Slitter* or *Blood Drinker*, but to me it was just my grandfather's knife and his grandfather's before him. I laid it gently on the bed-side table.

I said to Ryan. 'Your people shot at me. What was the idea of that?'

'Hell,' he said. 'You'd gone crazy and the whole operation was in danger. We were floating about in a chopper above that goddamn wilderness and we saw you, and we saw the Russians chasing you, and we reckoned you had a good chance of getting clear away. So we dropped a guy to stop you in your tracks. And we couldn't be too obvious about it because it had to look good to the Russians. We didn't know then that the whole operation was a bust, anyway.'

Neither Taggart nor Ryan had a grain of morality, but I didn't expect it. I said, 'You're lucky to be alive. The last time I saw you was through the sights of Fleet's rifle.'

'Jesus!' he said. 'I'm glad I didn't know it at the time. Talking about Fleet; you busted him up but good – but he'll survive.' He rubbed his nose. 'Fleet is sort of married to that rifle of his. He'd like to have it back.'

I shook my head. 'I've got to get something out of this deal. If Fleet is man enough let him come and get it.'

Ryan scowled. 'I'll doubt if he will. We've all had a bellyful of you.'

There was just one more thing. I said, 'So Slade is still alive.'

'Yes,' said Ryan. 'You shot him through the pelvis. 'If he ever walks again he'll need steel pins through his hips.'

'The only walking Slade will do for the next forty years is in the exercise yard of a prison,' said Taggart. He stood up. 'All this comes under the Official Secrets Act, Stewart. Everything has to be hushed. Slade is in England already; he was flown across yesterday in an American aircraft. He'll stand trial as soon as he comes out of hospital but the proceedings will be in camera. You'll keep quiet, and so will that girl-friend of yours. The sooner you turn her into a British subject the better I'll be pleased. I'd like to have some control over her.'

'Christ Almighty!' I said wearily. 'You can't even act as Cupid without an ulterior motive.'

Ryan joined Taggart at the door. He turned, and said, 'I think Sir David owes you a lot, Mr Stewart; a lot more than thanks, anyway – which I notice he hasn't proffered.' He looked at Taggart from the corner of his eye, and I thought there was no love lost between them.

Taggart was impervious; he didn't turn a hair. 'Oh, yes,' he said casually. 'I daresay something can be arranged. A medal, perhaps – if you like such trinkets.'

I found that my voice was shaking. 'All I want is your permanent absence,' I said. 'I'll keep quiet for just as long as you stay away from us, but if you, or any of the boys from the Department, come within shouting distance, I'll blow the gaff.'

'You won't be disturbed again,' he said, and they went out. A moment later he popped his head around the door. 'I'll send in some grapes.'

IV

Elin and I were flown to Scotland by courtesy of the CIA and the US Navy plane laid on by Ryan, and we were married in Glasgow by a special licence provided by Taggart. Both of us were still in bandages.

I took Elin back to the glen under Sgurr Dearg. She liked the scenery, especially the trees – the marvellous un-Icelandic trees – but she didn't think much of the cottage. It was small and it depressed her and I wasn't at all surprised; what suits a bachelor is not good for a married man.

'I'm not going to live in the big house,' I said. 'We'd rattle around in there and, anyway, I usually rent it to Americans who come for the shooting. We'll let a gillie have the cottage and we'll build our own house a little farther up the glen, by the river.'

So we did.

I still have Fleet's rifle. I don't keep it over the fireplace as a trophy but decently in the gun cabinet along with all the other working tools. I use it sometimes when the deer herd needs culling, but not too often. It doesn't give the deer much of a chance.